Wicket Maiden

Chrissie Harrison

Valericain
Press

Copyright © 2025 by Chris Towndrow
Valericain Press
Richmond, London, UK
www.valericainpress.co.uk

Wicket Maiden – 1st Edition, 2025.

Paperback ISBN : 978-1-7384470-84
eBook ISBN : 978-1-7384470-91

wicket maiden (n.)

1: an over in which no runs are scored with the bat and at least one wicket is taken by the bowler
2: a groundbreaking romantic comedy novel

To the UK's professional women cricketers, especially DWH

1st Over

B reathe. *I've got this.*

Ellie gazed around, revelling in the atmosphere.

The music pumping across the stadium dipped in volume, allowing the announcer's enthusiastic voice to carry across the crowd.

"Please welcome your opening batters for the Scorpions, Ellie Waites and Bryony Taylor."

Cheers rippled through the stands.

Ellie's neck prickled. How she'd missed this.

The opposition fanned out into their fielding positions. Ellie swung her bat in vertical loops, loosening her right shoulder, then strode out. No point in running. What's thirty seconds when you've waited eight months?

Thirty-seven weeks.

Two hundred and sixty-one days.

Not that Ellie had been counting. Much.

With every step towards the middle, she corralled her thoughts. *Focus. I've got this.*

She passed Bryony at the non-striker's end, exchanging a fist bump, then went to the crease.

'Two, please,' she called to the umpire, asking where her middle stump was.

The umpire motioned for Ellie to move the toe of her bat slightly left. Ellie scratched out her mark, adjusted the helmet's chin strap, then surveyed the field. Beneath the red shirt, her heart pounded.

"Bowling from the Pavilion End, for the Warriors, Georgia Bright."

A smatter of applause from the few hundred Away fans.

Ellie took stock of the positives, everything to alleviate any silly nerves: a home game at the Aurora Stadium, a ground she knew like the back of her hand. Weeks of intense practice and fitness training. A batting partner she had a great rapport with. Above everything, cricket was a team sport. Today wasn't about her. It never was. What did the circumstances demand? The same as ever: a strong start.

Still. Two hundred and sixty-one days.

All the prep in the world is no substitute for a match.

Don't screw it up.

She moistened dry lips, taking deep, even breaths.

The announcer counted down from 10, matching the visuals on the big screens, the pulses of music. At 0, a cheer encircled the ground.

Then the world fell silent. The eye of the storm. Ellie gripped the bat tighter.

The umpire's outstretched arm dropped. 'Play.'

Georgia ran in. Right arm, fast medium, sometimes took an over to find line and length.

Let's hope so today. Could do with a few sighters.

The white ball arced down out of the cloudy sky.

Ellie swung. Missed. The ball rapped into the knee roll of her left pad.

Georgia threw her arms aloft. 'Howzaaaat!' The wicketkeeper shouted likewise, appealing for Leg Before Wicket.

Ellie regained her balance and tapped the bat on the ground. With fake nonchalance, she stepped away, studiously avoiding eye contact with anyone. Her pulse raced. Perspiration leached into her gloves.

Not LBW first ball. Please, not first ball.

The delivery had edged to her left, down Leg side... missing the wickets?

Going down Leg, umpire? Ellie pleaded silently, a lump in her throat.

'Not out,' the umpire called.

Ellie's held breath burst from her.

The bowler's shoulders fell. She trudged back to her mark.

Ellie walked towards Bryony, meeting her halfway. A gentle grimace and a fist bump acknowledged the near miss, then Ellie returned to the crease.

Focus. Watch the ball.

The bowler ran in. Ellie picked the ball's line and length better this time. For a split-second, she considered chasing the wide delivery, helping it round to Fine Leg, but passed up the chance. No point in risking snicking it to the keeper.

Definitely not on my second ball.

The umpire's arms indicated a Wide.

Ellie tamped down the cropped grass, shook the tension from her shoulders, then reassessed the fielders, noting the gaps. Georgia ran in again, concentrating hard. Would she overcompensate for the last two deliveries, her line veering too far down the Off side?

Play the actual delivery, not what you want it to be.

The delivery was short, outside Off stump. With a slash of the bat, Ellie cracked the ball past the Point fielder, and it raced to the boundary.

A cheer from the crowd, accompanied by a burst of thumping music from the DJ, said more than the umpire's signal of 4.

Off the mark. Phew.

The next delivery was an easy single, then Ellie leant on her bat at the non-striker's end and stole a moment to absorb the surroundings, the buzz, the challenge.

This. Give me this forever.

Except she didn't have forever. Female pros seldom played beyond age 36, so at 32, Ellie had maybe three good years left. She had to make them count. There was unfinished business. Goals. Dreams.

Today was the first step back on that road.

Soon, she was in the groove. Ten overs later, things were looking promising.

"At the end of the Powerplay, the Scorpions are forty-eight without loss."

The big screens showed Bryony's current score of 16 and Ellie's 28. Despite the difference, Bryony was doubtless in better touch. She was a rising star, ten years Ellie's junior and with a grace Ellie didn't exactly *envy*... although Bryony essentially taking Ellie's spot in the England squad last year had hurt a little. But there was no room for ill-will. Bryony was the future, and Ellie enjoyed mentoring the junior players.

Ellie took guard at the batting crease, then reviewed the changed field.

Beyond the boundary rope, the stands were decorated with familiar blobs of red, spectators in their replica shirts. Couples, families, and many wide-eyed young girls. The future of women's cricket. Ellie had missed that as much as she'd missed playing. The engagement with fans, the sense of being someone to look up to. As a youngster, she had admired the greats of the game, and it was her duty—and pleasure—to pay it forward.

To Ellie's left, a flash of colour caught her eye. Someone in a yellow top.

A young woman. Paige?

The bowler ran in.

Momentarily distracted, Ellie was caught between playing forwards and staying back, attack or defence. She cut her hands down. Too late.

A familiar thwack behind. Her spirits dived. Shouts from the bowler and wicketkeeper. Ellie glanced around, knowing precisely what she'd see. All three stumps were askew.

Castled. Shit.

She whacked the bat against her right pad, exchanged a resigned fist bump with Bryony, then trudged back towards the pavilion.

Halfway there, she glanced heavenwards. It couldn't have been Paige in the crowd, wearing her favourite colour. Ellie might wish her sister was there, but she wasn't and would never be.

Ellie's heart clouded. She shook her head, downcast and disappointed.

The applause rippled and abated.

Oh well. 28. Three fours. Could have been worse.

But they're not applauding that. They're just happy to see me back.

Her spiked boots clacked up the stone steps. She pulled off her helmet. Failure was part of the job—a statistical inevitability, like picking up injuries or being left out of the XI. She only wished a loss of focus hadn't caused today's premature end. It wasn't the first time.

Still. First game back. Have to start somewhere.

As she climbed the last step, nearby in the crowd a girl was holding aloft a homemade sign: "WELCOME BACK ELLIE".

Ellie's mood immediately lifted.

Grace is a darling. You can't buy supporters like that.

Grace was one of Ellie's superfans, a poster child for the Scorpions' engagement with local schools and the community. Ellie offered a wave, then climbed the metal staircase to the pavilion's first floor.

She sank onto the changing room bench and pulled off her gloves and pads.

For five minutes, she sat with her thoughts, wishing the disappointment away. Emotional distractions were a weakness, something she desperately wanted to eliminate from her game. She was a fine player—when she focussed on cricket and didn't get sidetracked.

She tucked an index finger inside the front of her collar and caressed the small pendant.

The door swung open. One of the staff, Ops Director Sandy, entered. She was carrying what looked like mail-order flowers.

Ellie frowned. 'Whose birthday?'

Sandy proffered the bouquet. 'Not yours, Ells. Even so...'

She took the unexpected delivery and set it on the bench. 'Interesting.'

Sandy thumbed at the door. 'I'll leave you be.'

'Thanks, Sands.'

Curious, Ellie inspected the bouquet, inhaling the rich perfume, then fingered the tiny card from its cream-coloured envelope.

"Good luck today, Eleanor darling. Pleased to hear you're on the mend. Love, Mum and Dad."

'Wow,' she muttered.

Her parents were passively supportive rather than active cheerleaders. In the last fifteen years, there hadn't been *explicit* grumbles about Ellie pursuing a sporting career, instead of something sensible and long-lasting, like Medicine or Law, but the signs were there. Yes, they'd attended her first senior game for the Scorpions, many years ago, and her first England match, but nothing since.

When she'd torn her adductor tendon eight months ago, and the initial signs weren't good, Ellie sensed they were hoping it was curtains for her cricketing life. Then they could have, perhaps smugly, watched—even encouraged—a new direction. As it was, Ellie wouldn't let go of her passion that easily.

Do them proud by your deeds, not by getting sentimental or pissy.

She closed her eyes and spent a few minutes doing box breathing, centring herself. Favourite fragrances of hyacinth and winter hazel tickled her nostrils.

A smile spread across her face.

She stowed the kit in her bag, released her long, mousy brown hair from its clasp and retied it. Then she pulled on her Scorpions hoodie and headed to the pitch side to support the team.

I've got this.

I'm back.

2nd Over

The train pulled into Maidstone an hour late.

Adam had already been held up for ninety minutes before the signal failure debacle. It seemed the wealthier a client was, the more hassle they presented. Losing a sale was as frustrating for his ego as it was for his bank account. Today, it was worse because he'd been determined to be at Ellie's return game in good time.

And I took a meeting on a Bank Holiday Monday! What a waste.

As he stood outside the station, waiting for a bus to the stadium, he wondered how her innings had gone. It would be a shame if she'd returned in a blaze of glory and he'd missed it. Still, he came for the whole team, not solely her. The excitement. The atmosphere. Yet, hers was the talent and athleticism he'd been wowed by. Hers was the personality, the cheeky wit he'd connected with when he'd seen interviews or heard her on player mic during televised games.

In some ways, Adam was jealous of Ellie's linear, focused, salaried job. Perhaps he'd been naïve, when studying a Photography & Fine Art degree, that passion and endeavour would inevitably lead to a demand for his work. In reality, selling paintings was feast-or-famine... as this morning proved perfectly. Hence, he'd been forced to diversify beyond his passion for creating vibrant and engaging portraiture.

In his youth, Dad had been an amateur photographer, as well as playing cricket for their local side, and both interests had lodged in Adam's mind. Whilst Adam enjoyed landscape photography, these images weren't as lucrative as business headshots, so he'd embraced other avenues. Lately, he'd experimented with digital drawing, and his passion for cricket had catalysed an interest in sports photography. In an ideal world, he'd be the Scorpions' official photographer, but they already had a guy.

When he won corporate work—like a series of photo prints for the walls of an office—he believed that, as well as offering creative talent, he was easy to do business with... and cheaper than them hiring a big agency.

Being a jack-of-all-trades wasn't ideal, but necessary.

The local bus arrived, belching black diesel. He stepped forwards to help an elderly lady with her shopper, then he and a handful of others boarded.

To pass the journey, he exchanged messages with his best mate Jez about a possible trip to their favourite crazy golf course. Nine holes of frustrating silliness, followed by a pie and a pint, was a great way to shoot the breeze. Lately, Jez's breezes were mostly about his boss being an arsehole, digital currency, and the poor form of the local football club.

As Adam had neither a boss, a financial portfolio, nor a passion for football, chatting with Jez helped to throw his life into perspective. Whilst a steady income would be welcome, at least his chosen sporting team were one of the best in the country.

He checked the Scorpions' Instagram account. It stated the match score: 240-6 from their 50 overs. Ellie wasn't mentioned, which he assumed meant she hadn't done anything spectacular. He scrolled to her account, @EllieWaites20. Many players' usernames included their squad number. In Ellie's last post, she was clasping the Scorpions logo on her shirt, a signature move. The text read, "Busting to get out there again. #BewareTheScorpions".

He glanced at his watch, hurrying the bus driver along. His stomach grumbled; the meeting overrun, and his unwillingness to eat anything that passed for food at a station kiosk, was making for a late lunch.

With a hiss of air brakes, the bus arrived at the Aurora Stadium.

As the game had long started, the turnstiles were deserted, so Adam waved his Membership Card under the reader and passed through the gate.

The security guard nodded in recognition.

'Alright, Barry,' Adam said.

Barry looked at his watch. 'You after a half-price refund or something?' he joked.

'No rest for the wicked.'

As usual, Adam went to the East side and found a prime spot in the front row between Square Leg and Mid-Wicket. The fine May Bank Holiday weekend had drawn many families to the beach, so the crowd was small, maybe a couple of thousand. Still, those numbers used to be rare at a domestic women's game. Now, the sport was on the up.

The second innings had begun, and the Warriors were 24-1. Adam soaked up the atmosphere for a few minutes until the mouthwatering smell of fish and chips drifted down from the concourse, so he set off in pursuit of calories.

Ten minutes later, he was back in his seat. Ellie was patrolling the boundary nearby. She was picked to field there due to her excellent running pace and powerful, accurate throwing arm.

Soon, a shot careered across the grass towards Adam's position. Ellie closed it down with cheetah-like speed but missed at the last, diving in vain as the ball crossed the boundary rope.

As she picked herself up, a muttered 'Fuck' drifted across. Ellie Waites wore her heart and passion on her sleeve. The lengthy injury layoff must have been frustrating.

She collected the ball from where it nestled against the advertising hoarding six feet away. He offered a smile. Her brow arched... in recognition? Then she launched the ball towards the keeper, a laser-guided missile, and retook her position.

3rd Over

Ellie watched intently, muscles tensed, ready to chase down any ball in her area. However, she didn't need to field the next shot. Nobody did. The delivery from Scorpions' spin bowler Naira "Roddy" Rodrigues looped and gripped and turned, beating the bat of the Warriors number 3 and clattering into the bails.

Eleven girls leapt into the air. Ellie jogged to the middle, exchanged high tens with each of them, then pulled Naira into a hug. Ellie would have been jealous of a delivery like that, but it was years since she'd been asked to contribute as a spin bowler. She still practised, but with three quality spinners in the squad, she'd probably never bowl competitively again. The captain, Danica, always had to go with her best options. Today, it was working handsomely, as, for the next hour, the Scorpions had a stranglehold on the game. With only nine of the fifty overs left to bat, the Warriors were 84 short of their target.

However, when the next over went for 17 runs, Ellie began to worry. Maths, and the new batter's aggressive approach, threatened the Scorpions' victory.

Then came the moment. A mistimed shot skewed the ball high into the air. Ellie accelerated, weaving as she tracked the falling ball's trajectory.

Shit. Going to be short.

She urged on, and with three yards before the ball hit the grass, she leapt forwards. The ball smacked into her right palm. She gripped hard, clapping her left hand over it, as she crashed to the turf. Her knees, hips and elbows jarred with the impact, knocking breath from her lungs.

She came to rest, prone, panting, arms outstretched, like a downed Supergirl.

The ball must have still been in her grasp, because the crowd were cheering, and five girls were jogging over, whooping. Music pumped from the speakers. Hundreds of hands clapped in time to the beat.

Dopamine flooded her brain.

Yeah. I've still got it.

She pulled herself up, tossed the ball away, and was enveloped in hugs. Amidst the mêlée, she glanced at the replay on the big screen.

That's one for the album.

The girls retook their positions. Ellie walked back to the boundary rope, licked an index finger and chalked an imaginary line in the air. The crowd responded with whistles. Amongst them, the figure she recognised from earlier, and many previous games, applauded.

Thanks, Cricket Fan Guy.

Twenty minutes later, the last ball of the innings was knocked for a consolation single run. Ellie punched the air and jogged to the middle.

"The Scorpions win by eighteen runs," boomed the announcer. Music kicked in.

After the back pats and high fives, the squads lined up for handshakes, then Danica led the girls to the spartan, tired changing room.

The group's laughter and relief nurtured Ellie's soul. She'd expected the worst thing about the long injury layoff would be boredom—not being on the pitch, doing what she loved. Actually, loneliness had hit hardest. The months of one-to-one rehabilitation sessions didn't coincide with team training days. The girls were more than teammates; they were a huge part of Ellie's life. Being removed from that atmosphere had caused a lot of reflection about what the future held.

Cricket was all-consuming for Ellie, especially without someone special in her life. Still, it was essential to wind down when time allowed. Knitting and "Just A Minute" were a great tonic. She was also auditioning a variety of locally roasted beans for the perfect cup from her box-fresh, deluxe coffee machine.

After the cool-down stretches, the coach, Susie, held a brief team talk. 'Great win, girls. Our bowling unit was excellent, and the ground fielding was very solid.' She looked at Ellie.

Kat—Ellie's closest friend on the squad—pulled her into a shoulder hug. That catch had taken a dangerous player out of the game.

After the meeting, as Ellie stood, her thigh niggled in pain. She closed her eyes, hoping the rigours of the match—especially that dive—hadn't aggravated a vital muscle.

As a precaution, she collared the physio. 'Mads, can you give me a look over?'

'Sure.'

Ellie patted Kat on the back. 'See you outside.'

Mercifully, the physio found only a tightness in Ellie's quad, which she worked loose. Ellie made a mental note to focus on her thigh area during gym work and warmups.

She hustled down to the terrace. A weak late afternoon sun had lifted the greyness. Below her, the ground spread out in panorama. Beneath the towering floodlights, the stands were now empty, and along the boundary railing, the girls were working slowly down a line of fans whose excited body language verged on the right side of impatience.

However, before Ellie got there, she bumped into Grace and her mum, Diane. As usual, Grace sported the Scorpions cap and shirt. Her blonde hair was in a ponytail. Ellie had met Grace through the club's outreach programme two years ago. They'd bonded quickly and now the relationship transcended match day chats.

Grace waved her sign proudly. 'Did you see me?'

Ellie crouched down. 'Hard to miss *you*, Gracie.' She winked at Diane.

'That catch was *awe*some.'

'Thank you.'

'And you scored 28. That's the third time you've scored 28.' She was a forthright youngster—especially regarding Ellie's playing record.

'Is it really?'

'Yes.' Grace nodded firmly. 'The last one was in June 2022. You got three fours.'

'You could get a job as the statistician here, Gracie. I hope Richard won't mind you stealing his place.'

Confusion flickered in the girl's eyes. Ellie bit her tongue. Had she misstepped? Grace might take the joke the wrong way—her autism sometimes made it challenging to interpret things that weren't as straightforward as match statistics.

'I lost a tooth.' Grace pointed into her mouth.

'Ooh, that's a big one. Did the tooth fairy come?'

'I got *two* pounds. It only hurt for a little bit.'

'Well done. And thank you for making such a beautiful sign. I think you should fold it up so it doesn't get wrinkled on the way home.'

'I will.'

While the girl was dutifully folding the paper, Ellie leant in to Diane. 'I have something at home for her. I'll drop it in at work. Okay?'

The woman cupped Ellie's shoulder. 'You don't have to.'

'Anything for my number one fan.'

'Thanks, Ellie. It's so good to see you back. You had us all worried for a few weeks. Especially this one.' She pointed at Grace.

A memory flashed through Ellie's skull. Hobbling off the pitch, two teammates supporting her arms, tears streaming down her cheeks, her mind looping through the mantra, "This is it. You'll never play again".

Wrong. I did not go gentle into that good night.

'Thanks for sticking with me, Di. And all your support on socials.'

'You do so much for Grace, too.'

Ellie shrugged. 'We were all nine once. And someone has to discover the rising stars, right?'

'You really see a lot in her.'

'Honestly, you should keep pestering the school. Get her nominated for the county Under-11s.'

Grace went up on tiptoes. 'Ooh, can I, Mum? Can I play proper cricket? With a uniform and everything?'

Diane ruffled her daughter's hair. 'We'll see, Gracie. Come on. We need to get home for dinner.'

'*I* wanted fish and chips. From there.' Her finger arrowed to one of the concessions.

'Maybe next time.'

'Okay!' The girl fluttered her now-folded poster. 'Bye, Ellie!'

'See you at the next game.' Ellie waved at them. 'Toodles!'

She trotted down the stone terrace steps. Time for selfies and signatures. It had been nine months since she'd scribbled her name on a team sheet, glossy photo or match program.

Hopefully, *that* muscle was still in working order.

4th Over

A dam scanned the pavilion area, then the stadium. All the players had come out to engage with the supporters, but one was missing: 20 WAITES.

His heart sank. Then he realised this was silly. He supported the club, not merely one player. Yet, he felt a small kindred bond with Ellie. It was a topic he'd never raise because deep wounds take a long time to heal, and why would he, a random face in the crowd, pretend he *knew* her? He didn't. They lived in different worlds.

She had a long, illustrious Wikipedia entry. He had a webpage with an unfathomable HTML error on it. She was listed in Wisden's Almanack. He had a Google Business page. She had 174,000 Instagram followers. He had 1,000... to the nearest thousand... if rounding up. She was an elite professional athlete. He splurged paint on canvas and passed it off as art. She could hit a 6 over any part of the ground. He once got smacked in the face with a cricket ball. When bowling. While still holding the ball.

Nevertheless, hers was the one remaining space on his roll call of squad signatures for this new season. Whilst it was silly to act like a nerdy autograph hunter, he'd begun the ritual four years before, and now it was part of his match day visits.

He surveyed the area again.

No problem. She'll be here next time.

He hefted the rucksack onto his shoulder and headed for the concourse. Halfway there, he spotted two familiar figures and cut along the ninth row of seats to meet them.

'Hi, Lisa. Hey, Max.'

He high-fived the boy. Max was a Scorpions superfan and a promising cricketer. He'd been taken to the team's heart and was on first-name terms with the coach.

'Hello, Adam.' Lisa pointed. 'No camera today?'

'No. I leant it to a mate. Emergency. Shame. Wish I'd got a shot of that catch.'

'Did you arrive late?'

Adam grimaced. 'Yeah. Well, my fault for relying on the bloody rail network to run on time.'

'So you missed her innings.'

He frowned. 'I missed the whole team's.'

'There she is!' Max piped up. 'I'm going to tell her "Well done".'

'Okay,' Lisa replied. 'Say hi from me.'

Max adjusted his wraparound shades and Scorpions' baseball cap, and scuttled away. Below them, Ellie joined the line of players at the pitch-side hoardings.

'Don't miss her, now, Adam,' Lisa said.

'I'm here for the cricket, as well you know. And there are nineteen signatures on my squad list, okay?' Still, Ellie's arrival had buoyed him.

'The same as Max. Looks like he'll get the full set before you.'

Adam laughed. 'What, you expect me to push him out of the way, just for a squiggle of Sharpie?'

'"Just a squiggle"? Wait 'til she hears that.'

'Ellie? As if she'd care. Stop stirring.' He gave Lisa a playful jab on the shoulder. 'Everyone has a favourite player. Who's yours?'

Her eyes narrowed. 'What's this about?'

'Anyone *without* a favourite is weird if you ask me. Max's is Dani, right? Who's yours?' He eyed her with mischievous intensity. He'd give as good as he was getting.

Lisa gave a fake scowl. 'Alright, it's Bryony. She has all the shots. She's a great ambassador for the game, and a lovely girl. Happy now?'

'Delirious. So, I can sit where I want, cheer for who I want, chat with whoever. In any case, I think Jimmy Anderson is the greatest player of his generation, but that doesn't mean I want to sleep with him.' He lasered a gaze. 'Okay?'

'Sorry. I'll stop teasing.' She shrugged. 'Oh, I saw in the paper about your exhibition. Well done.'

'It doesn't start 'til Saturday. And, being honest, it'll probably bomb.'

She frowned. 'How can an exhibition "bomb"?'

'People could say I can't paint for toffee. Or nobody turns up. Or I don't sell anything. Or that godawful magazine does a scathing review.'

She wrinkled her nose. 'Oh, *ME & Tea*. I see what you mean.'

The glossy, gossip-obsessed local rag was the kind of publication Adam would refuse to use as toilet paper. Its best feature was the title—*ME & Tea* was a clever play on the Maidstone postcode whilst setting the expectation of juicy secrets within its pages. He'd idly thumbed through it once or twice, but finding scurrilous tittle-tattle about Ellie's personal life had put a rank taste in his mouth. Nobody deserved the rumour and slanging doled out to people in the public eye, and Ellie got enough vile creepiness and misplaced abuse on Instagram.

'Hopefully, I'll fly under their radar,' he said.

'Come on, Adam. There's no such thing as bad publicity.'

'Hmmm. Not sure about that. Anyway, I don't do this for fame. I just want to sell more art, more photographs.'

'Well, I promise not to ask for *your* autograph. But I'll come along to the gallery, have a peek. Although I'm sure your work is too rich for my blood.'

'That's sweet, thanks. Do feel free to bring any eccentric millionaire friends, though.' He nudged her.

'I'll hire a special minibus.' Lisa pointed. 'Go on. She'll be pleased to see you.'

'I doubt it. *Max* is the one the players really love.'

She winked. 'If only you were twelve, Adam.'

'And looked as cool as him in shades. Right. See you next time.' He clasped Lisa's shoulder in friendship—and forgiveness for winding him up—and scurried down to the side of the pitch. Sometimes, he felt like a kid inside, rather than a thirtysomething.

Last in the line, Ellie was finishing her fan hellos, so Adam joined the queue. Most other supporters were tweens, parents with kids, or guys twice Adam's age. Still, why feel guilty or self-conscious for pursuing something which gave such joy? He spent so many solitary hours in front of a canvas that fresh air and the excitement of team sport were an excellent tonic.

He pulled out the squad list and readied his pen, clicking it apprehensively. At his first autograph hunt, it was overawing to speak to people he'd seen on TV. Now, it was easier to be around the players, knowing they weren't unapproachable or grouchy.

He watched Ellie move, trying to spot whether she'd picked up a knock. She'd looked leaner and sharper than ever during the game, and now was moving fluidly, smiley and relaxed, hair loosely pinned up.

She stepped up to the digital advertising panels—the border between her world and his.

He proffered the pen and paper. 'Hi, Ellie. Great catch. Amazing catch.'

She met his eye, then focussed on her signature. 'Thanks.'

'Good to see you back.' He swallowed, throat dry.

'Good to *be* back.' She returned the pen and paper, smiling. 'Got your full card now.'

'Yeah. Saved the best 'til last.'

There was a sheepishness in her face. 'Not sure about that.'

'I am.'

She held his gaze, her lovely brown eyes full of so many emotions.

What are they? Determination, sorrow, gratitude, pride, awkwardness?

Probably relief to be playing again.

'Thanks,' she said. 'That... means a lot.'

'No problem.' He took an involuntary step back. 'See you next game.'

'Yeah. I hope so.'

'I'll... try not to be late.'

'I'll try not to lose my middle stump.' She raised her brow knowingly.

He hadn't seen the dismissal but got her drift. 'I'm sure it was an unplayable delivery.'

'Yeah. That was *my* argument.' She winked, then fluttered a hand in farewell as she walked away. 'Toodles,' she called, almost sing-song.

He sighed, expelling the remnants of nervous excitement.

It's so good to see you back, Ellie.

5th Over

Juggling the bouquet of flowers and her huge holdall, Ellie let herself into the house. She set the flowers by the kitchen sink, dumped her bag in the small laundry room, and flopped onto the sofa.

She released her hair from its tie, kicked off her trainers, and thumbed through notifications on her phone. The first was a reminder that an engineer was coming tomorrow to replace the broken washing machine. Next came a flurry of comments on her post-match Instagram story. As she scrolled these, she went to the kitchen and poured a glass of white wine.

Pricked by conscience, she called her parents to thank them for the surprise. Mum answered—Dad was out at a golf club *thing*—so they nattered about Ellie's first game back, Mum's bridge circle, and their decision to have a first-ever Christmas away from home.

It seemed very early to be making plans, despite Ellie's own calendar being set months in advance due to the match schedule. It meant she'd be spending Christmas alone for the first time in years.

Mum must have heard the disappointment in Ellie's voice and asked whether there were any *gentleman callers* on the horizon.

No, Mum. No "Mr Right" just yet.

Deflecting the conversation, Ellie promised to stop over after the match at Bristol in a few weeks.

When the call finished, she switched the TV on to a cricket channel, which was showing an India vs Australia match. After a few sips of wine, she retrieved the current knitting project from the sideboard, kicked her feet up onto the stool, and settled down. When teammate Gemma had told Ellie about the therapeutic properties of knitting, Ellie was sceptical. It seemed like something Mum would do. In fact, it was a brilliant way to relax, mentally and physically, freed from the rigours of the job.

Amidst the gentle click of needles, she voiced encouragement to the friendly faces on the TV. Yes, real family was only a few counties away, but cherished camaraderie existed around the globe.

The Mr Right thing, though? She was ready for that—someone who fitted with her, hand in glove.

Glove. Ho ho.

She had faith it would happen sooner or later.

Meantime, Ellie waits.

Two days later, as she arrived at the ground for training, teammates Jade and Lily crossed the road from the car park. Jade was easy to spot with her bouncy walk and spiked blonde hair.

Lily pulled Jade into a shoulder hug. Both heard Ellie's car approaching and waved. Ellie waved back.

They are such an adorable couple.

In the gravelled parking area, she hoisted her heavy kit bag from the boot and went to chat with the Strength & Conditioning coach. The niggle she'd picked up during Monday's match had spiked her nerves. It would be heartbreaking to let any muscle complaints go unchecked, in case they were an early warning sign that she wasn't back to full fitness.

After a helpful conversation and a full shakedown in the gym, she went to batting practice. As usual, the nets were occupied by batters practising against batting coaches and bowlers honing their techniques.

Ellie was surprised to see Sarah "Hawks" Hawksley working on her off-spin. The girl had been sidelined for well over a year with a serious back injury, which put Ellie's layoff into perspective. Sarah had kept in touch with the squad, but this was her first time back at cricket skills.

'Hi, Ells.' Sarah's hug was one of genuine companionship, as both had endured enforced absence from the game.

'Alright, Hawks. Didn't expect you back.' Ellie noted Sarah's earrings—teeny chocolate bars. The girl's passions for earrings and chocolate had found a perfect combination.

'I'm going gentle. But I've got the shed door at home painted up with stumps.'

'If you ever need a bat to beat...'

'You play spin too well, Ells, that's the trouble. My housemate's much better to bowl to. Can't hit a cow's arse with a banjo.' Sarah's brow arched. 'Odd, given she's a banjo player.'

Ellie nudged her. 'She is *not*.'

'Straight up. Plays in a local band. Cooks the best mac 'n cheese in town.' Sarah waved that away. 'Anyway, it's good to see you. Itching to get cracking again. You know what it's like. Being behind the mic is one thing, but it's not the same as pulling on the shirt.'

Ellie spluttered a laugh. 'Yeah, being behind the mic is a damn sight scarier.'

During Sarah's long rehab, she'd been asked to fill in for an absent local radio commentator, providing coverage of Scorpions' games.

This led to regular work. Then, early in Ellie's own injury layoff, Sarah asked if she wanted a shot at punditry, sitting alongside an experienced sports reporter.

Ellie had considered it a nice little earner on the side, and might open her eyes to a possible future direction. She had no clue what to do once she'd hung her bat up—and long days resting at home felt horribly like a window into retirement, something which didn't happen at a ripe old age. It would come soon, too soon.

Though Ellie was apprehensive, she'd agreed to give radio commentating a go. What was the worst that could happen?

Sarah eyed her with sympathy. 'Look, we all fluff up, okay?'

'But not like that! On day one.' Ellie shuddered, recalling her awful faux pas.

'I suppose it *was* a world-class fail.'

If *both* Hunt sisters in the Away squad hadn't played, she could have referred to Kerri Hunt as 'Hunt'. Sadly, they needed to be separately identified, and Ellie misspoke. A spoonerism. In front of hundreds of listeners. Which was absolutely the worst that could happen.

At least, because it was radio, the audience couldn't see the exact shade of beetroot she turned after swearing on air. Possibly with children listening.

Ellie rolled her eyes. 'When it comes to media and presenting, I always said I had a face for radio. Turns out I just don't have the talent for it.' She rapped the bat against the toe of her boot. 'Anyway, at least my year from hell is over.'

'Hey, you had *one* op. I had *three*.'

'And I lost two guys, remember?' Ellie shot a look. 'But I think I'd take another surgical repair instead of those four months with Harry. Without anaesthetic.'

'But now he's gone, and you're back. You were *always* going to come back. And, more than anything, everyone loves you.' Sarah looked around. 'Apart from Jonno, who wants you to stop gassing with me and practice your paddles and sweeps.'

Ellie glanced at the batting coach, hands on his hips: this wasn't a social occasion.

'Want to throw a few balls down?'

Sarah scoffed. 'No fear. You'll hit me round the park. I'll stick with banjo players.'

Ellie leant in. 'Hmm. "Stick with"? Anything I should know?'

Sarah nudged her. 'Stop fishing. She's not my type. Right. Gotta go.'

'Toodles!' Ellie called, waving as her teammate departed.

She strolled into the net.

Right.

Let's do this.

6th Over

Adam stepped back from the canvas, cocking his head as he examined the last hour's brushwork.

'Dunno,' he mumbled, a familiar reflection.

Sometimes, the self-criticism was a judgement of his painting. Here, it was caused by a lack of passion for the project. His best work materialised when he genuinely connected with the subject matter. This was merely a portrait that he'd taken on because there was nothing more pressing. As the picture was a surprise present for some rich guy's wife, Adam had to work from a photograph.

Tricky to extract personality from a stranger in an A4 image printed from a camera phone snap.

Adam simply needed to not screw it up. He hated being transactional, shallow, and in hock to a high street bank. But better than being a clichéd penniless artist.

His mobile rang.

'Tut.' He didn't enjoy being interrupted when in full creative flow.

He darted to the desk and scooped up the phone. 'Oh, hi, mate.'

The caller was Connor, a friend and fellow photographer. 'Hey, Ads. Look, sorry about this, but can I hang onto your gear for another week? There's been a delay on mine.'

Adam had loaned his primary camera while Connor's was in for repair.

He ran a finger down the wall calendar. 'I mean, it's not ideal, Con, but I can get by with my second camera bag.'

'Cheers. You're a legend. I picked up another job, which I'd have to turn down otherwise, so I'll bung you a few quid off that, okay?'

Adam sighed silently. It was hard to argue with the necessity to take every job that came along. They were both familiar with the hand-to-mouth nature of freelance work.

'Sure. Ten days tops, though, mate.'

'Oh, yeah, defo. Really appreciate it. Look, gotta go. Tons of editing to do.'

'Okay, no worries. Later.' He thumbed the red icon.

Typical Connor. Sometimes, I wonder why we're friends. Good thing I have a spare set of gear. Shame that Con doesn't. Irony, given that I'd rather be painting.

Talking of which...

He went to the easel and picked up the brush.

The doorbell rang.

'Unbelievable.'

Clearly, the universe didn't want him to finish the project.

If this is a salesman or a Jehovah's Witness...

He plucked a remote control from the paint-splattered trestle table beside the easel, aimed it at the camera hung from the ceiling, and clicked. With a beep, the red recording light vanished.

One of his sidelines was time-lapse videos of painting sessions. They were great fodder for Instagram, letting potential clients see the work that went into his creations. Whilst he wasn't a social media fanatic, his raw and honest content was necessary to achieve visibility and success.

He trotted down the uncarpeted wooden stairs to the front door. The unannounced arrival was his good friend Ben.

'Hey, Ads.' Ben spied the paintbrush in Adam's hand. 'Ah. Sorry—interrupting?'

Well, kind of.

'No, come on in, mate.'

They moved into the functional hallway, with its high ceiling and leaded paint.

Adam checked his watch: 15:33. 'Skiving again?'

Ben fiddled with his half-mast tie. 'No. Been meeting a developer. Thought I'd stop by and give you the good news.'

'You won the Lottery and decided to give a chunk to charitable causes?' He tapped his chest.

'Not far off, actually.' Ben leant in. 'Worth a cuppa.'

'Alright. I suppose it is tea-break time.'

Adam led Ben up the stairs. He smelled money in the air. Ben was an estate agent and occasionally secured Adam bits of work. Show-home photography, brochure images and 360-degree virtual tours weren't especially creative, but they helped pay the mortgage. At least he was *on* the property ladder, thanks partly to an inheritance from his grandparents.

The upper floor consisted of a bedroom with ensuite, study, kit store, and a spacious artist's studio, which had been created by knocking two bedrooms together. One wall was covered with prints of Adam's favourite landscape photos. Opposite this hung paintings he hadn't sold yet or wasn't brave enough to release into the world.

In one corner, where a bathroom used to be, stood a sink unit and a small worktop with a coffee machine. Adam basically ran on the stuff, so having a brew nearby minimised creative interruptions.

Adam boiled the kettle. 'So?'

Ben flicked aside his thick mop of hair. 'Yeah, this developer. Fifty homes, out Hythe way. We're handling the sales. Show Home will be ready in a couple of weeks, and they're interested in you for the photography. I talked you up, of course.'

'Legend. Thanks, mate.'

Ben shrugged. 'I know it's not your favourite gig, but I'd rather you were busy than bending my ears about the "impoverished artist" life.'

Adam thumped Ben's arm. 'I do not bend your bloody ears.'

'No. But you could get a round in occasionally.' He grinned deliberately.

'I'm getting a round in now, aren't I?'

'Hmm.' Ben pointed. 'How about a couple of those?'

Adam tossed him the chocolate digestives, then brewed the teas.

'Ta.' Ben tore open the packet and munched on a biscuit. He gestured to the work-in-progress. 'Who's she?'

'Nobody. Client. You think the nose is too much?'

Ben glanced between the source photo and the painting. 'Dunno. Did they want "accurate" or "flattering"?'

Adam handed over a mug. 'Didn't say. I mean, he wouldn't have married her if he didn't like her nose, right? And if I scale it back, he'll say it's not a true portrait. Besides, it's not about what hubby thinks, is it? So long as the missus likes her birthday present.'

Ben sipped pensively. 'Suppose so.' He looked around. 'Where's that... Instagram thing? The pouting girl?'

'At the gallery. Ready for the exhibition tomorrow.'

'Oh, yeah. I like that one. Social commentary. Clever. You should do prints. I bet it'd sell like hot cakes.'

'I am doing.' Adam went to a poster rack and pulled out an A3 sheet.

The pop art style picture was a lightly caricatured young woman taking a selfie. The phone image was overly flattering, and her expression was deliberately forced. He'd never painted anything similar and had debated whether it was too cutting in its take on modern life. Still, much worse existed in the world, and feedback had been positive, so he'd included it in the gallery collection. It was entitled "LIKE?".

'Does Pippa know you've done this?' Ben asked.

Adam frowned. 'Pip? Why would she give a toss? I'm dead to her, apparently.' He eye-rolled theatrically.

'Come on, this is based on her, right?'

That was arguable. The character was a brunette. Pippa was blonde, blue-eyed, popular, and, at 30, four years his junior.

I was a lucky sod, no doubt about it.

The first warning sign came when, in the first weeks of their relationship, he'd had a seizure. Despite giving her a rundown on what to expect of his epilepsy, she did a poor job of looking after him. That should have been a dealbreaker, but he took her plaintive apology and promises too readily. Probably because he was reluctant to give up such a stunner... and the sex.

Then, slowly, things unravelled. Pippa cultivated a huge social media following. Adam started being cropped out of pictures. She picked up sponsorship from a brand he'd never heard of. The ideal amount of makeup was just too much. She did things simply to be seen doing those things. She hung out with people so she could be photographed hanging out with those people.

Finally, one day, he was dumped. She never explicitly said, "You're not gorgeous or famous enough for me now", but Adam could read between the lines. Pippa was now a "celebrity", and Adam was merely a guy who took photographs of boring stuff like our magnificent world. And in this magnificent world, you could become a sensation by doing nothing of use to anyone... except perhaps yourself.

Adam laughed. 'I wouldn't give Pip the satisfaction. Like she needs any more exposure.'

Ben squinted. 'I mean, there is a likeness. Surely.'

'No. Loads of girls look like that, act like that. At a stretch, Pip might have been... inspiration... but not deliberately.'

Ben spread his hands out, like visualising a headline. 'Revenge porn as art. Money-making art.'

Adam thumped his friend's shoulder. 'Don't be a dick. Anyway, if either of us is the revenge type, it's that walking cosmetics advert.'

'Yeah. You should have stuck with Susannah.'

I love you, Ben, but sometimes...

'Remind me, how long were you living in that cave? I *would* have stuck with her, but she didn't have the same idea.'

Ben sucked in his teeth. 'Yeah. Sorry.'

'She was probably looking for a get-out anyway. I'm not sure "My husband is an artist" was in her vocabulary.'

Susannah had discovered her get-out during a three-month stint in Toronto. As a helpdesk manager for a global chain, she was often away on corporate jaunts and training missions, and whilst Adam was happy with his own company, her absences eroded their relationship. Returning from Canada, she was upfront that she'd found someone else.

Adam was crushed. They'd been dating for four years. The first year, replete with evenings snuggled in front of the TV, was the best. Of course, he'd never admit to friends that he wanted to settle down, and his libido clearly wasn't interested, as it catapulted him towards Pippa. Swapping the bright, safe, career woman for a hot blonde had seemed like a good idea at the time. In hindsight, it was amazing that he and Pippa lasted ten months.

He eyed the painting.

Even if this isn't you, Pip, and merely inspiration, then if it makes money perhaps that's just deserts.

And if it makes me famous, wow, how I'll laugh.

7th Over

Ellie was often an early riser, so she spent the first couple of hours on Saturday in the gym. Fitness work was usually done at the cricket ground, but she also used a facility near home, which saved driving to the Aurora Stadium.

Following that, the morning was spent washing and preparing kit for tomorrow's away game at Arundel. After lunch, she popped into town to pick up a new phone case and drop off Grace's surprise souvenir at the gallery where Diane worked. It wasn't a place Ellie would idly visit. Yes, she admired the odd famous painting, but art was for people richer or cleverer than her.

Ellie's nerved tingles as she entered the gallery. However good she was at her job, receiving adulation never came easy. She only wanted to repay Grace's loyalty and kindness, encouraging the girl to continue her fledgling cricketing career.

Diane hurried over. 'Hi, Ellie. Kind of you to come all this way.'

'No problem. I was in town. Grace at swimming?'

'Yes, with her dad. She'll be sad not to see you. And we can't make the game tomorrow.'

'Never mind.' Ellie smiled. 'Besides, there's next weekend's surprise, right?'

'Of course. How time flies! Everything okay with the cake?'

'Yes. I can't wait to see it... and her face.'

Diane squeezed Ellie's hand. 'You're too much, sometimes.'

'What are friends for?'

'Ooh, hold on, love.' Diane acknowledged a waiting customer and bustled away.

To pass the time, Ellie perused the variety of artwork prints, posters, greeting cards, and selected originals from local painters—none of which really appealed to her.

A wide doorway led to a rear annex, with a sign proclaiming "Exhibition - Adam Glenn - Maidstone Artist". Ellie nosed into the room. Only three people were inside, all nodding appreciatively beside a pop art-style painting of a woman taking a selfie.

We're now all masters of creating our own fame.

Another exhibit stopped Ellie in her tracks. Pride of place on the far wall was a brilliant and charismatic rendition of former England bowler James Anderson. The painting gushed with vigour and personality, movement and expression.

Wow.

It could have been five seconds or five minutes Ellie stood there, open-mouthed. Snapping out of the trance-like admiration, she turned to the room... and nearly clattered into someone holding a takeaway coffee.

'Shit. Sorry... I...' she offered, flustered.

Blimey. What are the chances? Swearing in an art gallery or bumping into...

'Oh.' Cricket Fan Guy broke into a warm yet mystified smile. 'Small world.'

'Yeah. I just popped in to see someone.'

'Right. Okay.'

'Are you... visiting? Work here?' she asked.

'Not as such. Art is my thing, though.'

'Have you seen the Jimmy one? It's amazing.' She frowned, self-conscious. 'Isn't it? I don't know. I'm no expert, but... do you like it? Jimmy—sorry, James Anderson.' She eye-rolled at her stupidity.

Of course he knows who Jimmy is! He's a cricket fan!

Breathe.

He was chuckling. She hoped it wasn't at her expense.

'Yes. That one's my favourite.' He looked away. 'Best thing I've done, probably.'

Her mind scurried like a batter who wished she hadn't called for a second run. 'Oh. Right. Ah. I get it now. Local artist. So... this is... you? Wow. It's amazing. Well done... er...'

Name? Name?

He held out a hand. 'Adam. I'm Adam. From before, and here, and all those other times.' His eyes twinkled.

She shook, a firm grip. 'I'm Ellie.'

His smile was broad. 'I know.'

Her cheeks coloured. 'Oh, yeah, of course.'

Over his shoulder, a young girl and a man were looking in their direction. Ellie moved so she wasn't blocking their view of the painting.

The girl, wide-eyed, tugged her father's shirt. He bent so she could whisper in his ear. He nodded, then winked at Ellie.

I'm not sure the painting is the attraction right now.

'Go on.' He encouraged his daughter forward with a gentle tap on her shoulder. 'It'll be okay.'

Biting her lip, the girl tentatively stepped up. 'Are... you... Ellie Waites?'

Ellie's insides softened. 'Yes.'

'Can... Would I please be able to get a selfie?'

'Of course.'

The girl skipped back to her father, who passed over his phone, mouthing at Ellie, 'Thank you.'

Someone coughed.

Cricket Fan Guy... no, Adam.

'Would you like me to take it?' he asked.

'No, it's fine,' she replied, at the same time the visitor said,

'Oh, cheers.'

Before Ellie could intervene, Adam had taken the phone and was looking for a place where the girl's memento wouldn't be spoiled by artwork in the background.

Ellie got down on one knee and rested a palm on the girl's shoulder.

'Say "Ellie",' Adam said.

Bemused, she complied, the "ee" sound pulling her mouth into a smile—like "cheese".

'Would you like one too, sir?' Adam asked the father.

'Sure, thanks, mate.'

Ellie posed while Adam did another sterling job. Things suddenly made sense—she'd often seen him with a camera around his neck. Perhaps he was as good at photography as he was at painting... plus being rather charming and easy on the eye.

'Hope to see you at a match soon,' Ellie said when the impromptu photo op was complete.

The girl grinned. 'Definitely.'

Then Dad shook Ellie's hand, offered thanks, and they ambled away.

Adam was looking at her as if he'd witnessed the birth of a lamb or a Rubik's Cube being solved blindfolded.

'What?' she said, amused. 'It's not like you haven't seen the drill before. Up close.'

'Oh no, not that. It's so cool how you inspire kids. What a role model you are. You're a natural.'

'Well... thanks. The community stuff is a big part of the Scorpions. I enjoy it.'

Diane entered. Hopefully, that would diffuse whatever was happening—chiefly a ridiculous feeling of being in the spotlight.

'Oh.' Bemused, Diane looked back and forth between Ellie and Adam. 'Do you two...?'

'No,' Ellie blustered. 'Not really.'

'On and off, Diane,' Adam said. 'A few years now. But as of today, we're officially on first-name terms. Right, Ellie? It *was* Ellie, wasn't it?' He grinned.

She coughed. 'Yes, it was, *Adam*. Do you know Adam, Diane? He's a local artist.' She flashed him a knowing look, gesturing around. 'This is his exhibition. He's *very* good.'

There was a moment when it appeared that Diane hadn't caught on to Ellie's dry wit.

Then, mercifully, she smiled. 'Adam and I go back a little way. But the lynchpin is probably you, Ellie. And the rest of the team.'

Oh, yeah. Reason I'm here.

Ellie swung the slim kit bag down from her shoulder, unzipped it, and pulled out the cricket bat.

Seeing the complete set of squad signatures on the blade, Diane's eyes misted over. 'Oh, you shouldn't have.'

'It's a pleasure. Just make sure that's not the willow Gracie brings when she starts at the Scorpions Academy in a few years.'

Adam was wide-eyed. 'What does a guy have to do to get one of those? Joking!'

'You wouldn't want the entry criteria,' Diane said. 'Ellie's friendship with Grace is no coincidence.'

Ellie's neck prickled. 'We don't need to talk about that.'

He touched her shoulder. 'It's okay. I know about your sister. And I'm sorry for your loss.'

Minutely, she arched back, like the dream in which you're naked at school. Then the penny dropped.

The internet.

It didn't hurt that he knew something of her life—she could have been much more guarded in interviews and articles, but Paige's death wasn't something to be ashamed of. Quite the opposite—it could be a source of strength... when the loss didn't feel burdensome.

If Adam knew Diane well, he'd surely have heard about Grace tragically losing her baby brother.

She sighed. 'Thanks. I guess I am an open book.'

A kind, sympathetic smile reached his eyes. 'Well, Wikipedia isn't one hundred percent, but it can help to understand someone a little, beyond career highlights and match stats.'

She pointed at his painting. 'Then maybe I should look *you* up.'

He laughed. 'Me? A Wikipedia page?'

'From little acorns...'

'I'm just a person, Ellie.'

'So am I. And not one who could produce art like this.'

He cocked his head. 'The way you *play* is art.'

She was sure she blushed. 'That's kind, but it's only technique and practice.'

'So's my painting style.'

'True. But I like it, I really do.'

'Then you're in good company,' Diane said. 'Customers are saying nice things.'

'Let's see if that lasts beyond the first morning, eh?' Adam winked.

Someone called Diane's name.

'Look, I should get back to work.' She clutched the bat to her chest and squeezed Ellie's shoulder. 'Thank you, love. Grace will be in floods.'

She pulled the woman into a hug. 'See you soon.'

Diane left.

Ellie took a deep breath and looked around, aware that Adam was watching her.

A mischievous idea formed, and he seemed like a guy who'd take it well. On a nearby pedestal lay a small pile of pamphlets—a low-rent programme for the exhibition. She lifted off the top copy, rummaged in her bag and found a pen.

She offered both to him. 'Excuse me. Are you the celebrated local artist Adam Glenn?'

A smile played on his lips. 'Yes, I am.'

'Could I get your autograph?' She couldn't help her impish grin.

'Sure. Who shall I sign it to?'

'Well, my name's Ellie, so—'

'That's a nice name. Here we go...'

He scribbled and signed, then gave back the pen and paper. It read, "To Ellie, Fondest wishes, Adam".

'Would you like a selfie?' he asked.

She was about to laugh it off—knowing he was half-joking—when she realised that, across the dozens of games he'd attended, he'd never asked for a photo. She'd penned plenty of signatures, and he'd offered many words of support, but never in return for something as... intimate?... as a selfie.

She wondered why. But at that moment she absolutely wanted one.

What if he's the rising star here now?

'Your phone or mine?' she asked.

8th Over

After the selfie, they chatted for a few minutes, then Ellie had to leave. The room suddenly felt emptier than the mere lack of people. Like a candle had gone out: He'd been unusually relaxed around her, the conversation easy and open. Why? Possibly because their meeting had been unexpected, he'd had no time to get anxious or feel he was entering her bubble of talent and fame.

He spent the rest of the afternoon at the gallery. Despite modest visitor numbers, there was definite interest in the pop art painting, so he posted about the exhibition on Instagram. He noticed that Ellie had posted a selfie taken in the room, complimenting him and the artwork. This was essentially free PR! Sweet, unrequested, and genuine. Just when he thought she couldn't be more warm, admirable and giving, she'd gone up another level.

Was it possible that she was an ordinary girl who did an extraordinary job?

Or even an extraordinary girl?

After cooking dinner, he settled down in front of the PC to plan the next few weeks.

He was reluctant to pursue another project like the James Anderson painting because it was an unusual style, a one-off. Unless that painting sold—ideally for five figures—there was no proof a market existed. Art is subjective. He loved the result, and Ellie seemed enamoured, but he needed the phone to ring.

That was out of his hands. The best course of action was to plan a few outings to capture stock images. The weather forecast looked good, so he decided to combine tomorrow's trip to the Scorpions' game with photography around Arundel. Some sunrise snaps, images of the castle, and photos at the match—long lens stuff, hoping for an eye-catching bat-on-ball action shot.

He went to the study, dug out his 'standby' camera, put the batteries on charge, and thoroughly cleaned the lenses. This second set of gear wasn't as new or adaptable as his primary camera, but it was fine for sports photography and an upcoming birthday party gig.

The Scorpions team sheet, now complete with signatures, lay on the desk. He found a cheap A4 frame in the corner cupboard, slotted the page behind the Perspex, then hung the memento on the wall alongside the previous four years' versions. In this small space dedicated to cricket was a signed headshot of Jimmy Anderson and a couple of England team sheets with various signatures, including Ellie's.

At around 10 p.m., the last task of the day was to open his post. It was always approached with some dread because snail mail seldom included anything of value and often contained bills.

Discarding the flyers from plumbers, pizza outlets and estate agents, he opened the first envelope. No bad news—merely confirmation of his council tax direct debit. The second envelope was from HMRC.

Deep breath.

But it was only a reminder to file a self-assessment tax return.

The third and last envelope was branded "Kent Business Forum".

Here we go. A survey? An invitation to join a useless paid-for directory service?

Neither.

'Whoah.'

He re-read the letter.

Nope. He wasn't imagining it: he'd been nominated for an award.

Who's done this? Secretly? And why? "Small Creative Business of the Year"? Me?

It would be preposterous if it wasn't for the evidence being there in black and white. His name and address were correct. They weren't asking for any money. He *was* a creative.

Was the award for business excellence or artistic prowess? Being self-employed hardly qualified him as a business. Whilst he had a "brand name", AG Images, his income wasn't on a meteoric upswing. He didn't make grand efforts to give back to the broader community or inspire the next generation—unlike Ellie and the Scorpions. Yet his work had earned a nomination... somehow.

He paced the room.

Am I really that good? Is this a black-tie affair? I don't own anything that smart.

Should I even go? How are the awards judged? Are my chances of winning non-zero? Should I publicise the nomination? It's certainly a coup—isn't it?

Who nominated me? Surely not Connor. Nor Ellie—she's barely discovered my name. A client? Diane? Perhaps Jez? Too late to text him now.

Feeling tired, he turned off the lights and climbed the stairs. The award nomination created a weight of expectation for the exhibition to be a success. For the Jimmy painting to attract comment, Press attention, even a moneyed buyer. For him to somehow repay Ellie's gesture of support.

As well as being perplexed, he felt emboldened.

Is this what it's like to walk out to bat for England?

He laughed that off. Chatting to Ellie today didn't mean they were any more similar than yesterday, when they'd been virtual strangers.

However, she didn't know they shared something in common.

9th Over

E llie's fingertip hovered over the photo of herself and Adam.

It was nice to discover his name. Another one to add to the list along with Lisa, Max, Diane and Grace... real people who pop out from the sea of faces in the stadium.

After posting the Insta update about Adam's art, she'd followed his account—one of only a few hundred she connected with. Scrolling through his feed, there was a sense of researching him, validating him as a person. Whilst there had been no warning signs that day—or over the past weeks, months and years of encountering Adam, she couldn't be too careful. It was always dangerous to scrutinise responses to her social media posts because, sooner or later, she'd find something lustful, creepy or abusive. Some blokes viewed professional female cricketers as objects, not athletes.

Adam wasn't like that. Nothing he'd ever posted or said in person gave cause for concern. His engagement was purely of appreciation and support. He didn't have a searching gaze, only blue-grey eyes, light stubble, toned arms and a playful demeanour.

But should she be worried that he'd pored over her Wikipedia page? No. The place was a public forum. It was a damn sight less invasive than googling disgusting crap like "Ellie Waites naked". Doubtless, a few "fans" out there had done precisely that.

She shivered, taking a calming sip of tea.

Don't fight the real world. If you were that opposed, you'd quit the game and live as a hermit.

And there was no way she was doing that. This year was the beginning of the final push.

You have to take the rough with the smooth. Like a golden duck in the game after hitting 50.

She followed a link to Adam's website and got carried away, browsing the imagery. He seemed to be as good at photography as he was at painting. Adam was chock full of talent. She felt oddly humbled, jealous. Her artistic talents peaked with decently framed selfies for the ever-hungry social media machine. His Insta feed had few. Did his brilliantly observed "LIKE?" artwork hide disdain for fake celebrity and shallow self-promotion, or was it merely designed to provoke comment and, naturally, sell?

Did it matter? So long as things worked out for him. He seemed like a bit of a catch.

Get real. He's bound to be dating. And it's a hell of a world he'd opt into. No nine-to-five. Lots of time away. It takes a special kind of person to make that work. Especially with me. I'm not the easiest ride.

Besides, she needed to knuckle down and focus on the job, not have flights of fancy about Mr Right, Mr Forever. History had shown she wasn't the best at juggling her work and personal life, emotional and professional multi-tasking.

So put the phone down and go to bed.

She'd set an alarm for 06:00 on Sunday. The players were making their own way to the game. There was usually a team bus when the Scorpions had a long trip, but today's match was under two hours from Maidstone, so she drove.

Arriving at the picturesque ground, set in the shadow of Arundel castle, she spied her opening partner, Bryony, and her stomach flipped.

'Shit.'

Today was Bryony's fiftieth game for the Scorpions... and Ellie was due to do the cap presentation. Her mind flitted back to her own first cap for the Scorpions. And her fiftieth. And hundredth.

And her first for England. Fiftieth. Hundredth.

One forty-seven caps so far. Will there be more...?

Arguably, Bryony's successes would easily outstrip Ellie's. She was a remarkable young talent and deserved a good speech.

Ellie rummaged in the glove compartment, found paper and pen, and corralled her thoughts.

Ten minutes later, she headed to the pavilion. Birds sang from the branches of giant oaks that ringed the ground, and the morning sun was evaporating dew on the well-kept field.

There were hugs and high-fives as she caught up with the girls.

Match number two of the Ellie Waites reboot, and it feels like I was never away.

'Didn't know you were into art,' said Tara, the diminutive wicketkeeper with the lightning-fast hands. Clearly, she'd seen Ellie's Instagram post.

'Well, you know what they say—I don't know art, but I know what I like.'

'That was mad good, that painting. You mates with this Adam guy?' Tara fussed with her ponytail.

'No. He comes to games, though. You might have seen him around. Sometimes has a camera. Tallish, dark hair, my age.' Ellie leant in. 'Why, problems with you and Finn?'

'No. We're good.' Tara glanced around. 'Did you see Harry is here?'

Ellie's stomach dropped. 'Shit. What the hell for?'

'Dunno. Come to beg forgiveness?'

'Fat chance,' she scoffed. 'His ego wouldn't let him stoop to begging. Or even asking nicely. Waste of time anyway. I wouldn't touch him with a bargepole.'

'Preach. Ignore Harry. Come on.' Tara encouraged them out into the weak sunshine.

Ellie surveyed the ground. She didn't want her diva of an ex-boyfriend making trouble. Why had she picked the worst person on the men's team to have a thing with? Hell, why had she picked a fellow athlete?

Because I rebounded. Desperate to rescue my year, my love life. Mistake.

Bad ball. Move on.

She focussed on the warmup. Stretches, resistance band work, keepy-uppy with a football, sprints. Chat and laughter rolled around as the squad went through its routines.

Then, it was time to pad up for batting practice. Next came ground fielding drills, then she walked to the wicket to assess the surface. Throughout, music pumped from an ever-present portable speaker.

Around the ground's gentle bowl, spectators were setting up chairs and picnic rugs. Mercifully, there was no sign of Harry, even when the team drifted back to the pavilion to change into playing kit.

As the clock ticked around to match time, captain Danica and coach Susie gathered the girls for the huddle. The opposition's team sheet wasn't too daunting—but games are won on grass, not paper. After the pep talk, Ellie was teed up. Crackling with nerves, she made her speech, presenting Bryony with her fiftieth cap. Their embrace was riven with emotion and mutual encouragement.

Applause rang around the group.

'Let's go, ladies,' Danica said.

Fifteen minutes later, Ellie and Bryony strolled out to bat. If the prospect of bumping into Harry had prickled her nerves, the sight of Adam patrolling the boundary, camera to his eye, calmed her immensely. It also, weirdly, gave a boost, as if she had a duty to perform well—which was silly because she always gave one hundred percent. It felt like having her sister there: a recognisable face, someone she had a bond with, someone to make proud. However, Paige was only a memory, simultaneously wonderful and heartbreaking. Adam was real and tangible.

Yet, even though he was merely another supporter, her habitual recon of the opposition's fielding positions lingered a fraction longer at Cow Corner.

The bowler marked out her stride.

Breathe. I've got this.

Ellie recalled the team briefing. The dissection of the opposition's strengths and weaknesses.

Maya. Right arm pace. In-swingers. Wants me to stay back.

In came the delivery.

Watch the ball.

On the stumps. Defended. Dot ball.

Ball two. Full. Marginal swing. Defended. Dot ball.

Third delivery. Short. Ellie took a stride forward and cracked the ball over Extra Cover. 4.

Walk up to Bryony. Exchange a few words and a fist bump. Take the crease.

Watch the ball.

Good length, Leg side. Ellie clipped the ball off her pads, deftly splitting Fine Leg and Square Leg. 4.

Applause from the crowd.

Tamp down the wicket. Fist-bump.

The opposition captain tweaked the field. Ellie surveyed again. Adam had moved... somewhere. It didn't matter. She wasn't playing for one person.

Play the match, the innings, the bowler, the ball.

Breathe.

Ball five. A real peach. A messy defence. Dot ball.

Last of the over. Full toss, unintended. Ellie took the invitation gratefully, punching it high and handsome, back over the bowler's head.

The umpire's arms raised aloft.

It seems like I do have this.

The end came too soon. She trudged back to the pavilion, shaking her head, seething.

Yes, she shouldn't have played across the line to that ball, but the LBW decision was marginal at best.

Breathe. I can't win back my wicket. Failure is part of the game.

As she passed the dugout, the faces of her three teammates said it all: You were robbed, Ells.

Still, 44 isn't too shabby.

Then she spied Harry at the coffee shack, which put her in an even fouler mood.

10th Over

A dam arrived at the Arundel ground in a rotten mood. This time, it wasn't the rail network that had riled him. It was bloody Pippa.

Everything had been peachy when he left home. The social media feedback on the exhibition had been positive. Ellie's post had received hundreds of views and comments—including the usual crap about how hot she looked, peppered with love hearts and offers of marriage.

Some people.

Yet, others were worse. One specific person had noted his early morning Instagram posts teasing a couple of his best sunrise shots, and used the opportunity to rain on his parade. Pippa had visited the exhibition, taken a photo of the Jimmy portrait, annotated a cowboy hat, googly eyes and a spangly bow tie, and posted it on her feed: "Look! I've improved this painting!"

Then she'd DM'd him, quoting the "LIKE?" picture: "Remove that shitty artwork of me from your gallery". Adam let out a *very* impressive string of expletives, then calmly took a screenshot of her message.

It's a good idea to compile evidence when your ex-girlfriend has gone Looney Tunes so that if or when she gets combative, you're the one with the facts, and she's the one with the conspiracy theory.

He hadn't replied. She wasn't worth the trouble. There were no grounds for her accusation, merely a shipping container of sour grapes. If Pippa genuinely believed the artwork was based on her, it implied she was a vacuous caricature—which would be a massive and hilarious self-own.

Despite trying to see the funny side of her ridiculous attempts at online revenge, Adam's hackles took a long time to calm. Ellie's blazing 6 in the first over helped. It was much healthier to move towards something joyful than to feel tied to something rank. Proof that real talent and celebrity trumped curated attention-seeking.

When Ellie's wicket was—debatably—lost, she remained in the pavilion for aeons.

Slowly, he grew worried. Had she suffered another injury, or had the dismissal cut her to the quick? That was unusual. She was such a mentally strong player.

He dismissed it. There could be a million reasons for her absence from the dugout—rudimentary physio work, chatting with a player, an early lunch. Perhaps she'd gone to the nets to work on something.

He continued photographing the game, periodically circling the pitch to find different angles. At the innings break, he grabbed lunch from the café hut and spoke to a couple of familiar supporters.

Happily, when the Scorpions went out to field, Ellie was there. He waved casually. She gave a thumbs up. All seemed well.

Sitting in his trusty camping chair, a few yards outside the boundary rope, it was an effort not to strike up a conversation with her, check that she was okay. Games at smaller grounds were always relaxed affairs. Often, he saw players' friends, family, and even longtime fans exchange words with girls fielding on the edge of the pitch. It was part of the atmosphere, a scene peppered with on-field chatter. That had been an eye-opener during Adam's first few match days—the camaraderie and constant mutual encouragement within the squad.

Ellie had her mates. She didn't need another, not if it risked causing a distraction and affecting her performance. What irony that would be—getting friendly with his favourite player, only to spoil her comeback? As things stood, there were maybe only three years left in which to see her play.

Despite being set a decent target, the opposition passed the Scorpions' score with 3 of the 50 overs to spare. As usual, Adam was disappointed by the loss. However, the girls didn't mope. They congratulated each other, both sides shook hands, then all moseyed back to the changing room.

The crowd thinned, dispersing into the mild evening. Cars lolled away from the grassy parking area. Adam gathered his things and wandered to the pavilion. He felt like a hanger-on, an outsider—which was ridiculous. One of the team was now an acquaintance.

Calling Ellie a "friend" would be pushing it, but checking up on her is okay, isn't it?

He was about to give up waiting—most of the squad had left—when she emerged from the building, vast kit bag on her shoulders.

'Oh, hi, Adam. Signature? Selfie?'

'No, thanks. I'm all caught up.'

She frowned. 'Everything okay? Is this about the gallery thing?'

'Your Insta post? No. Far from it. That was so generous. You didn't need to, really.'

She waved it away. 'Well, you've supported me for years. Least I could do. No promises it'll get you in the Tate, but the comments were decent.'

He snorted. 'Mostly.'

'Oh, that one, right? I saw it. What's *up* with some people?'

'Christ knows. *She's* the one that dumped me.' He winced. 'Sorry. Oversharing. Are *you* okay? That LBW decision?'

She mock bared her teeth. 'My stupid fault. Can't blame the umpire every time. Well, maybe only for an hour or so!'

'Understandable. Shame about the result, too.'

'Yeah. Not tight enough on our lines. Did you get any good photos?'

'A few. That slog-sweep over Square was my favourite. Shame I was on the wrong side.'

'Maybe I should give you signals, show you which way I'm going to hit.' She darted her eyebrows.

He laughed. 'And you expect me to run to the correct spot between the ball being bowled and you cracking it away? Remember which of us is the elite athlete.'

She shook her head, smiling. 'It's just a job, Adam. Same as you. Ups and downs. One day, that LBW decision goes my way, and I go on to fifty. Sixty. Whatever. One day, you get trolled by your ex. Another day, someone comes into the gallery and pays whatever that picture's worth. Which maybe puts you on the map. Or it's another normal day for Adam the artist. And photographer. And... person who hung around to make sure I was okay. Which is above and beyond.'

His head dipped, fearing he'd overstepped the care and concern. 'Sorry. Just worried you'd get some flak after yesterday. Or picked up another injury, which is stupid. Sorry. Again. You have a whole support network. Don't need me sticking my nose in.'

Another player approached, patting Ellie's shoulder as she passed. Katherine Davidson, Ellie's team bestie, offered a nod. Adam returned the gesture.

'See you at training,' she said to Ellie.

'Yeah. Good job today, Kat.'

'Same, babe. Crappy decision. Take it easy.'

'Later,' Ellie called.

Adam thumbed over his shoulder. 'Look, I should go. Don't want to keep you from a hot bath and a drink.'

She beamed. 'Yeah. Soak off that last bit of grouchy.' She glanced around. 'Look, thanks again. Tell the truth, I sort of had an "ex thing" going on today, which didn't help. So... sorry if I gave you a scare.'

He raised a hand. 'This is not about me. And yet, I'm still keeping you from that bath. All for saying thanks for your Insta post. Which I already did. And could have done on the app, right?' He smirked, and took a deliberate breath. 'Good knock, Ellie. See you next time.'

'Hope so.' She patted his shoulder. 'Take it easy, Adam. Good luck with the exhibition.' She pivoted sharply, waving in farewell. 'Toodles!'

As he ordered an Uber, his heartstrings vibrated gently. He put a fist to his chest, stilling it. His and Ellie's worlds had intersected again for a few moments, nothing more.

11th Over

I n the bath, with a sea of bubbles silently popping, and a bottle of lager perched on the tiled bath surround, Ellie scrolled through social media on her phone.

Distracted by the lavender-scented foam, her mind spooled back in time. She and baby sister Paige, maybe six and four years old, sharing a bath. Facing each other along the tub, giggling, scooping up handfuls of bubbles and blowing them at each other. Fashioning their lathered hair into spikes and Mohicans, giving themselves bubble beards.

Days when sisterhood was at its peak. Before boys drew Paige's eye more than cricket did Ellie's. When the sport, for women, was in its infancy. Before crowds. Before outreach. Before Ellie got the cricket bug so acutely that her perspective was tunnel vision.

Before Paige's twentieth birthday. That night. That drive. Her last.

Ellie set the phone on the floor. She threw hot water on her face, massaging, gritting her teeth against the tears which wanted to come.

Then she slouched under the surface, knees like icebergs above the bubbles, head tilted back, willing the water to draw the guilt from her. Guilt which was stupid and misplaced but which stubbornly remained.

She told herself to move on, knowing it was impossible. The hurt would lessen but never disappear. She would fail to get over it.

Failure is part of the game.

She toyed with the small feline pendant on her necklace. At age eighteen, Paige having just turned sixteen, they took a cheap flight to Malaga for a long weekend. Touring the market stalls, Paige spotted a silly piece of jewellery—the rear view of a cat with its tail aloft. They giggled like children. Ten euros later, Paige had something akin to a memento of Gizmo, the family cat which had not long died. Paige had always been a cat person.

They were the last to leave the hotel bar that night. Ellie sensed that Paige wanted to go with the swarthy young barman whose attention had certainly been on the prettier sister, but Ellie caught the guy's eye and warned him off with a gentle shake of her head. The weekend was about celebrating Paige's excellent GCSE haul, not getting laid. The next afternoon—a mercifully late tee-off—they played a round of golf. Paige shot six over. Ellie shot twenty over.

Same old, same old.

Ellie surfaced, determined not to wallow. She pulled her wet hair into a bun, covered it in bubbles, dried her hands on the towel beside the bath, took a slug of lager, then gathered up her phone.

She scrolled to Adam's Insta feed. That cruel comment, from user Pippa4GoodLife, had only one reply: "Ouch! Burn!". Ellie smiled. The shitposting wasn't getting Pippa her desired response, which presumably had been to stir up an army of naysayers against Adam's artwork.

What had he done to deserve such treatment? Something unpalatable? She doubted it. She was a decent judge of character—although she'd fallen for Harry based on his physical appeal and good humour, then discovered he was sexist, self-important, and standoffish with supporters.

So why am I comparing the two guys? I'm not attracted to Adam. Am I?

Monday brought a cricket skills session. These were distinct from fitness days. Ellie was keen to work on her batting to leg spinners, hoping to strengthen her defence to the type of delivery that had claimed her wicket at Arundel.

Fine weather meant practice took place on the Aurora Stadium's pitch, where the grass surface was familiar and the most representative of match conditions. Batting in the nets was good for technique, but it wasn't as faithful for playing spin.

Within a few balls, she was in the zone, shutting out the figures flitting around in her peripheral vision, the thwacks of other bats, the banter.

Over lunch in the team dining room, Ellie shot the breeze with her bestie.

Kat pulled up her cuff to show a successful tattoo removal. Getting her long-term girlfriend's—now ex-girlfriend's—name inked was the kind of mistake Ellie was pleased never to have made. Besides, she already had a tattoo, and her love for it was undying.

When the meal was done, and others on the table had drifted away, Kat leant in. 'So, who's the guy?'

Ellie frowned. 'What guy?'

'The one you were talking to after the game. And the time before. And, like, a million times.'

'Just a supporter.'

'You want to watch out.'

'Chill. It's fine.'

'He seems very... attentive. Maybe too much?' Kat said.

Now, Ellie laughed. 'No. He's cool.'

Kat's expression remained firm. 'You remember what happened, right?'

Ellie nodded. 'The guy who got... over-friendly in the car park.'

'Exactly.'

Kat had been the target of the rarest of unpalatable behaviours. This bloke—nothing like Adam—had been a regular in the selfie-and-autograph brigade, but there was something else about him. A creepiness which was proven when he followed Kat to her car and asked if she wanted to go for a drink. Her refusal was, fortunately, taken without malice, but coincidentally, the man hadn't been seen since. To call the fan a stalker might be pushing it, but the experience had made Kat wary.

Ellie knew Kat was only looking after her, proving that the Scorpions were like a family.

'Hon, it's fine. Thanks, but Adam and I are good.'

Adam spent Monday editing the Arundel photos. He uploaded a selection to his online stock media account and checked his royalty statement, which amounted to beer money at best.

A notification popped onto his laptop screen: "Callum Glenn: Rook to d4".

Finally, Dad had taken his turn. Adam went to the chess website, reviewed the board, and made his move. The game was five months old, but neither player was in any rush. An online game was no substitute for seeing his parents in person, but time and commitments pressed on them all. Besides, based on last week, if the rail network couldn't return him from fifty miles away within an hour of the advertised time, what were the chances of reaching Scotland in under a week?

He'd gladly travel for a week to turn up unannounced on their doorstep one day, brandishing the John Moores Painting Prize. All he'd achieved so far was one exhibition, one decent oil, and a thumbs up from a female cricketer his parents had probably never heard of.

Still, from little acorns...

On Tuesday, he visited the gallery to see if any acorns had seeded.

The place was quiet, but the news was good. They had sold out of "LIKE?" prints... although Adam had only made twenty. Diane showed him the local newspaper—something he never bought. It contained an upbeat article about the exhibition, so she was happy to extend his showcase for another week.

So much better than a write-up in the gossip mag.

'Have you had anything off social media?' Diane asked.

'Feedback? Yes. Sales? No.'

She shrugged gently, fine lines appearing on her kind face. 'One swallow doesn't make a summer. Nothing from Ellie Waites' post?'

He smiled. 'Seems like one celeb doesn't make a summer either.'

'"Celeb"? She is the most regular girl you'd ever meet. What am I talking about? You met her.' Diane glanced around—though the room was empty. 'More than met, by the looks of things.'

He sputtered a laugh. 'What's that supposed to mean? You're as bad as Lisa.'

'Oh, Max's mum? Why, what did she say?'

Adam's stomach knotted. 'That all my support for the Scorpions... for Ellie... is some thinly veiled... crush.' He frowned. 'Is that the right word? I mean, I'm thirty-four, not sixteen.'

She clasped his arm. 'Adam, love, I'm forty-seven, and I have a crush on Harry Styles. Crushes are not an age thing.'

'All the same, I appreciate Ellie as a *cricketer*. And a person. And now, I'm grateful to her.'

'Maybe for your next exhibition, you should ask her to do the grand opening.'

Adam snorted. '"Next exhibition"? "Grand opening"? I'm no David Hockney, just because of a few good comments online. Or are you waiting to drop the bomb? Someone offered six figures for that mess of oil and admiration?' He thumbed at the Jimmy artwork.

'Don't joke. People are asking if we sell prints. It will connect with someone, mark my words, so don't give up on your marketing. Do a post saying something like, "Lots of interest in this beauty already". Let's see... "Buy now before it's gone. Make me a sensible offer." Oh, and be sure to mention that the gallery's keeping it here for an extended period due to public demand.' She raised her eyebrows.

He swatted her shoulder. 'You're a stirrer, Di. Public demand, my arse.'

She raised a finger. 'I'm not saying *lie*. Promoting yourself, your art, your *talent* isn't shameless and tawdry... unlike *some* people's online mission.' A wicked smile played on her lips. 'Plus, I'm sure if Mr Fancy Pants Art Collector offered you fifty grand for this picture, and I gently suggested the gallery take, say, five percent commission, you'd be a fool to bite the hand that fed you.'

'And now you're a charlatan, too.' He sighed. 'Seven and a half percent. Final offer.'

'I only said five.'

'But I get a *free* extension on the exhibition, right?' He put his palms together in mock supplication. 'Struggling artist, milady.'

'You're a one, Adam Glenn. Go on, hop it. And get those prints done. Missed opportunity otherwise.' She ushered him to the door. 'I'll say hi to Ellie from you.'

He frowned. 'How? Is she a regular in here?'

'No. But she's at Grace's school this week for a team visit. She's a real star with kids.' Diane's expression became forlorn. 'I think it's a big sister thing, what with losing Paige. Ellie is the *most* caring, supportive person. On the field and off it.'

'It does seem that way.'

'And you're not too shabby either.' She winked. 'So, I'll send her your love.'

'You will do nothing of the sort. Love to Grace—fine. And if you want to indulge in your... middle-aged romantic fantasies or whatever you're trying to do, send Harry Styles your knickers. Okay?'

She fluttered a hand. 'Go on, struggling artist. Quit gabbing and paint another masterpiece.'

This was an excellent suggestion. But was there a market for his style? And who would make a suitable subject?

12th Over

Following Tuesday's gym session, Ellie met Bryony in town for an appointment. Rose should have been there too, but she'd had to see the physio after turning her ankle over.

Ellie and Bryony took adjacent seats in the familiar salon. Getting their nails done in matching colours and designs was a tradition. It happened in the England squad, too, often tailoring the varnish to whatever kit colour they were wearing.

She missed those days.

Still, it'll be nice when the day comes that I don't have to keep them this short.

The nail technician set to work on Ellie and Bryony's chosen design—spelling out S-C-O-R-P-I-O-N on the eight fingers, with scorpion motifs on the thumbs. The colours were black against red, naturally.

'That was sweet, what you said for my fiftieth cap,' Bryony remarked.

'Thanks. Don't tell, but I wrote it in the car park. Totally forgot.' Ellie pulled a face.

Bryony giggled. 'That's you—queen of the late cut!' One of Ellie's favourite strokes was to take a delivery right under her eyes, angle the bat and guide the ball down to Third.

Ellie held up her free hand. 'Not personal, okay? In fact, you're the one I should be making an extra effort for. Partner.'

They fist-bumped.

'You do already. You're a special person, Ells. Place was a lot quieter when you were out.'

'Get used to it. Nothing's forever. Anyway, Rojo's the life and soul, not me.'

The nail tech finished the background layer on the last of Ellie's fingers and shuffled across to start on Bryony.

'Did you Rojo know hid my batting gear? Last year, one game she was subbing, she sloped off before the break, the rat, and moved my stuff.' Bryony rolled her eyes. 'Give her credit, she didn't let me get too stressed. We had a laugh after. Still plotting my revenge, though.'

'Kat did that to me one time.' Ellie blew on her nails. 'Swapped my bat for an inflatable one. She has *no* poker face, though. As soon as I spotted it, she corpsed. She's such a wind-up merchant.'

'I wouldn't dare, Ells, not with you. Taught me everything I know.'

Ellie laughed. 'That's such bollocks. You've been playing for what, ten years? Since you were eleven? No way am I the one who's made a difference.'

'Yeah, but still. You know you're like my role model, right?'

'Well, if you want any more advice, don't tear your adductor tendon, and don't date Harry Owens. And maybe broaden your strokes. Paddle, sweep, reverse sweep. You are *so* good down the ground, but it's important to be a three-sixty player.'

Bryony pointed. 'This is why you should be a coach. The girls would love to play for you.'

Ellie swallowed. The prospect of managing, teaching, coaching felt like skipping from here and now into another life. And this life wasn't done.

'Thanks, Bry. But playing *with* them is good enough. Besides,' she joked, 'I've still got to kick you out of my England spot.'

'I'll take number two to your one. Deal?'

That sounded like a perfect plan. Walk out together, England colours on their nails this time, Test whites on their backs, and open the batting at Lord's.

Cresting the wave.

Believe.

On Wednesday afternoon, Ellie joined a group of Scorpions players and staff for a community outreach session. At Grace's co-ed school, the optional cricket tuition used to be solely populated by boys. Now, half the children at these sessions were girls.

At Ellie's first holiday cricket camp, she was the only girl. She grew up a lot that summer. Then, at school, she joined the boys team. At first, there was laughter, the Insta trolling of its day. Then she started batting them off the playing field. The laughter stopped. Nowadays, Ellie was the one smiling, in reminisces and perhaps well-founded smugness.

Initially, Diane had privately said Grace's enthusiasm might exceed her ability, as dexterity wasn't always a strength of those with autism, but the girl's hand-eye coordination had come a long way in two years.

Diane had later revealed that Grace lost her brother to a rare blood condition. As Ellie knew what it was like to lose a sibling, this cemented their bond. Still, she never mentioned Paige, wanting their relationship to be about cricket, and loved Grace's wide-eyed enthusiasm, directness, and enquiring mind. She'd even spent a few quid having "20 WAITES" printed onto the girl's shirt because replica player kits weren't sold.

When Grace caught sight of Ellie, she ran up and gave her a big hug. 'Thank you for my bat. It's the best thing ever. I managed to read all the signatures. Dani's is terrible. I had to work out who that was by a process of *elimination*.'

Ellie laughed. 'Yeah.' She shot her captain a wink. 'Good thing her bowling's better than her writing, eh?'

'Will *you* bowl to me? I'd love that.' Grace tugged Ellie's arm.

'Me? Don't you want a proper bowler?' Ellie crouched. 'Or is it because I'm out of practice and a bit rubbish, so you'll be able to hit me for 6?'

'You were out of practice with batting because of your injury, but on Sunday, you got 44, which is 16 more than in the last game. 44 has six factors. It's the first time you've scored 44. Mum said you posted on Instagram about practising your bowling. So, will you bowl to me?'

In the legion of requests that are impossible to deny, Grace's was right up there.

Heady days of youth. The long back garden. Bowling to Paige. Her missing almost every delivery, God bless her. She could hit a stationary golf ball but not a moving target.

'Okay. Come on then, get your pads on.'

Ellie warmed up and exchanged banter with teammates while the school PE staff and the club's helpers set up the environment. Inside, she glowed.

In her cricket whites, long fair hair plaited in a single braid, Grace really looked the part. It was a style she modelled on the team's blonde pace bowler, Rose "Rojo" Jones. Grace was tall for her age, like the towering Rose, so perhaps some hero worship was going on there, too.

Well, I don't want to be the only person she looks up to.

Still, a little pride was at stake as Ellie spun a few overs down to Grace, who handled the deliveries with aplomb.

'One more over. Pleeeease,' the girl asked when Ellie called time.

'Alright, Gracie.'

And with the third ball of the over, Ellie conjured a peach, which gripped and turned and beat Grace's bat, taking off the bails.

'Yes!' Ellie threw her arms aloft... then quickly realised that outfoxing a child on a school cricket pitch wasn't worthy of a victory dance. 'Er... I mean, howzat. Sorry, Gracie.' She patted the girl's helmet.

Grace cocked her head. 'Edwards, bowled Waites, for... fifty? Does that sound okay?'

'Yes, fifty is good.' Ellie winked.

Grace beamed knowingly. 'Fifty and out.' She chalked a finger in the air, mimicking Ellie's signature celebration.

Ellie laughed. 'Very good. Now, why don't you join Dani and do some ground fielding with your friends.'

'Okay!' Grace jogged away.

Soon, the bell rang for the end of the lesson and the school day. Ellie and the team cleared away the gear and headed for the gates. There, she spied a familiar face.

'Hi, Ellie,' Diane said. 'How did she do?'

'Same as ever, a superstar in the making. How's things with you?'

'Good. The gallery's keeping me busy. Funny that you know Adam.'

Ellie frowned. 'We've spoken at games. It's funnier that you already knew him.'

'Actually, I met Adam through hubby. He needed a photographer for one of his design projects. A brochure, you know?'

Ellie nodded. Diane's husband was an architect. 'I thought art was more Adam's thing?'

'He has to pay the bills. He's a good lad, Adam. Talented.'

'Yes, and the inner circle of my... "fan club".'

'Hmm. Well, you don't see many single, handsome thirtysomethings at the games.'

Ellie playfully swatted Diane's shoulder. 'He has much better things to do than hang out with me.'

Someone called, 'Oh, Mrs Edwards, can I have a word?'

Diane said goodbye to Ellie and hustled away.

That evening, Ellie had a shower, cooked a pasta dinner, then put on a bland TV programme and second-screened on her phone. After a few minutes, some US reality show came on, so she flicked through the channels. A striking portrait appeared. Her finger froze.

'Wow,' she breathed. Entrants were being introduced for a show called Portrait Artist Of The Year. She put down the remote.

Fifteen minutes passed. Then, during the ad break, as she scrolled social media, Facebook showed a "Memories" suggestion.

One year ago. What was I doing?

Remembering the emotional rollercoaster, she cringed, but tapped the post. Immediately, her spirits lifted. The photos were from an unofficial school reunion with her closest friends, Callie and Laura. The trio of high-flying athletic types all missed the official 15-year bash for various reasons, so had enjoyed a more intimate soiree a few weeks later.

So many mojitos.

She'd drifted off into recollection of that day, secondary school, and the gorgeous PE teacher, Mr Goodwin—when the phone rang.

After nearly tumbling from the sofa in alarm, she noted the caller and smiled.

I bet Facebook's hit us all with the same Memory.

'Hey, Lau,' she chirped.

'Ells, lovely! How're you doing?'

She muted the painting show. 'I have sofa and wine, so I am *all good*.'

Laura let out a typically tomboyish laugh. At school, everyone thought she'd come out as bisexual, but she seemed to be going steady with a stream of lower-league footballers. 'Me too, girl. And tonight, I come to you thanks to the all-seeing eye of Mr Zuckerberg.'

Ellie chuckled. 'Thought so. I was looking at the pics. I can't believe it's been a year.'

'Time flies when you're having fun.'

'Well, I'm glad *you* are.'

'Oh no, babe. What's up?'

'Hold on.' Ellie grabbed the wineglass and tucked her feet up on the sofa. Then she gave her physio friend the rundown.

Last Spring, things *had* been fine. She and long-term boyfriend, Jack, were good. Then, in June, he admitted to seeing someone else—another cricketer, of all people. Having a cosy home life unceremoniously ripped away played havoc with Ellie's mental health and her form. She started trying too hard, and had a rubbish stint in The Hundred competition. There, she stupidly ran into Harry's arms.

Attempting to regain her form, she was overstretching when she lunged for a ball in the outfield at Chelmsford and sustained that excruciating injury. The early weeks of recovery put the skids under her sex life, which showed up the cracks in her fledgling relationship with Harry, so she dumped him.

Then, in October, England didn't renew her contract. The injury layoff was days, weeks, and months without a love life or a work life. Alone in the house, reflecting on poor romantic choices and worrying where her life was heading. Financially, it had been tough, too—a winter without the bonus of playing in Australia, New Zealand or India. Fortunately, she always budgeted well, setting money aside, knowing it wouldn't be long before her playing days ended.

'Oh, babe,' Laura sympathised.

Ellie necked the remainder of the wine, shook off the blues, and insisted things were on the way up. She was back in the bosom of a fantastic group, ready to blaze a trail. There was no room on this call for "pity me". Especially when, a few minutes later, Laura dropped a bombshell.

'I bought a football club!'

'What the what? Hold on, lemme get more wine...'

And they were still talking at midnight.

People who genuinely care are everything.

13th Over

Thursday's weather didn't look promising, so Adam packed a waterproof and a book to read in case the game was delayed.

The term-time weekday meant crowd figures were low. With mizzle in the air, he headed for the covered stand area reserved for season ticket holders. He could have sat in the Members' bar inside, but the view was better here.

As he passed the stairs to the locker room, Ellie was jogging up, and waved. Preoccupied, he almost bumped into someone. First came recognition of England cricketer Harry Owens. Then recollection that he'd dated Ellie. Third came Harry's sneer.

Fourth came Adam's immediate dislike of the guy.

Harry looked Adam up and down, then glanced at where Ellie disappeared into the Players' Area on the first floor.

Harry's eyes narrowed. 'Hmm.'

'Sorry.' Adam stepped aside.

Harry visibly stood straighter, adding another inch to his 6'1". 'Just watch it, mate.'

'Sure.'

Harry left without another word.

Adam resumed his journey, picking up a coffee from the bar. He recalled an article in *ME & Tea* and a subsequent conversation with Lisa. Apparently, Ellie and Harry's relationship had ended because he was "difficult". Adam had interpreted that as "Harry was an arsehole". Then he'd berated himself for thinking poorly of a talented, famed, professional athlete.

Now, it seemed he was bang on the money.

Ellie deserves better. In fact, she deserves the best. Chris Hemsworth or some such. Someone in the bubble, but someone who treats her properly.

Adam meandered around the stand, sipping his coffee and chatting to a couple of familiar faces. Then he returned to the bar and read his book.

The drizzle faltered and then stopped. The sky brightened. The umpires strolled onto the pitch, and the covers were taken off the wicket. Adam went outside. A few Scorpions emerged, milling around and signing team sheets for a few hardy—and wet—supporters.

'Hi, Adam.' Ellie had appeared from behind him. She appeared tense, possibly because the delay was interrupting her match preparation ritual.

'Oh, hi. What do you reckon, reduced to forty overs?'

'Think so. Thanks for sticking with us. Sold the painting yet?'

'No. No news. But it only takes one phone call, right?'

'Yep.' She glanced over his shoulder and rolled her eyes.

He had a good idea what—or who—was there. 'Don't miss the warmup.' He fake nudged her. 'Can't have you stretchered off because I distracted you.'

She touched his arm. 'Thanks.'

He eyed her hand. 'Nice nails.'

'Yeah. Something different. Anyway, gotta go.'

'Have a good game.'

'Will do.' She trotted away, waving. 'Toodles!'

Twenty minutes later, Adam was in his regular spot, camera to his eye, tracking Ellie's walk onto the pitch. Her body language had a loose-limbed confidence.

Given the conditions, she played herself in gently, unable to trust how the pitch would behave. All the strokes were textbook. She barely put a foot wrong.

Is she being hyper-cautious or merely preparing for an assault?

Soon, his question was answered. Quickly, she was on 30. Then 40. Then, with a gorgeous slog sweep for 4, she passed 50. She took an embrace with Bryony, then pointed her bat to the pavilion, clasping her shirt logo. She surveyed the ground, then raised the bat towards Square Leg.

Where he was.

His index finger played rapid-fire on the shutter.

As she took guard for the next ball, his chest swelled with... what was it? Pride? Enthusiasm? Admiration? Hope? Without a doubt, the first 50 after her absence was a landmark. Did this mean she was back to full form? He hoped so. He wanted her to get noticed by the England scouts.

Come on, Ellie. You can do it.

Sadly, her masterclass ended on 67 when she didn't quite time a lofted drive and was caught at Mid-on. She abandoned the run, tilted her head back in frustration, then fist-bumped Bryony and trudged off, raising her bat to the crowd's applause.

Adam stood, adding his appreciation.

As the afternoon passed, he alternated between watching the game, moving to different photography positions, and fuelling up on coffee and snacks.

When the game concluded with a Scorpions win, he basked in the familiar and heartwarming atmosphere, then forewent the autograph signing session. He was keen to review his photos, killing time until the crowd had dispersed and there was less of a rugby scrum for the bus away from the stadium.

Time passed unnoticed as he scrutinised the images he'd transferred to his laptop, critiquing or revelling in what he'd captured. One image which brought a lump to his throat showed Ellie facing in his direction, eyes to the heavens. He knew what that signified, and it stoked a desire to capture aspects of Ellie's persona on canvas.

He became aware of someone standing over him. Looking up, his eyes met those of Harry Owens.

'Some people would call that stalking,' was the guy's opening put-down.

Adam closed the laptop lid. He rose. 'It's a free country.'

Harry put hands on hips, accentuating his toned arms. 'Stop bugging her. Okay?'

Don't you dare accuse me of that. I care about her like you never did. And she cares more about one single fan—Grace—than you do about an entire stadium.

Adam's lip curled. All the same, he wasn't about to start a fight. For one, he'd lose. For two, Ellie would think less of him. Thirdly, his hands were tools, his life support, and he couldn't afford to have them damaged.

'It's a free country for both of us. For you to *think* I'm hassling Ellie Waites. Which I'm not. And free for me to come to matches. To watch the team. To get autographs from whoever.'

'One person in particular, right?' Harry's dark eyes narrowed.

Adam glanced around. 'There are no rules against photography. Or speaking. In fact, the Scorpions actively *encourage* fan engagement. Whether a player, female or male, *wants* to is another matter.' He enjoyed that dig.

'I'm watching you. *Mate.*'

Ellie walked up, jaw set. 'Are you okay, Adam?'

'Peachy.'

'This guy bothering you, Waitesy?' Harry asked.

She sneered. 'Not for a second. This guy bothering *you*, Adam?'

Harry's eyes flared. 'What?'

She rounded on him. 'Stop being a dick. I don't need your help, your protection. Never did. Were you looking for me or just to cause trouble?'

'I don't like this guy getting cosy with you, that's all.'

She lifted her chin, shoulders back. 'You and I are over, Harry. Read the room. Adam's a club member. And a friend. You're neither.'

Adam's nerves crackled with the awkwardness of a former couple having a domestic... and him being the cause. He was emotionally stirred by her ballsiness. That steel which said, "I will not be cowed", as if facing an 80mph delivery from the world's best seamer.

And she'd hit her ex-boyfriend for 6. Glorious. Over the bowler's head. Over the rope. Out of the ground.

To Harry's credit, he didn't escalate. He knew he was beaten and had an audience. He merely cocked his nose at them and strode away.

'Prick,' she muttered, before turning to Adam. 'Sorry about that. You can see why I dumped him.'

'No. My fault. For having the nerve to venture onto what he clearly considers his "territory". Me speaking to her. Trying to get a freeze frame of her... prowess. I'm one of the great unwashed. The little people,' he mocked. 'Pay the ticket price, watch the game, cheer, go home.'

'That's Harry all over. Ignore him. I'm allowed to hang with who I want. So are you. And I'm glad you do. Fans aren't "little people". They're the wind in our sails. Besides, who's the one with a review in the paper this week?' She arched a brow.

'Yeah, that was a win.' Now wasn't the time to bother her about the portrait project. He was too discombobulated. 'Anyway, brilliant knock, Ellie.'

She frowned at his change of pace. 'I was really flying, right?'

'Like you were never away.'

'Thanks.' Another light touch on his arm.

Footsteps nearby announced the arrival of Dani and Jade, so Adam stepped back and allowed Ellie to join up with her teammates.

'Show me those pictures sometime?' she chirped.

'Sure.'

'Great. Toodles!' She threw an arm around Dani, and the trio pottered away, laughing.

He watched her go. If this rapport continued, he could get very fond of Ellie Waites.

14th Over

To celebrate the victory—and Jade's 25th birthday—a dozen of the girls went out for cocktails and karaoke. Letting off steam was easy when the day's result had put the Scorpions on top of the table, and Lily surprised Jade with the gift of a weekend away together in Madrid.

As Ellie stared at the bottom of an empty glass, her insides warmed by the second and last mojito, an arm was thrown around her shoulder.

'Wassup? Wishing someone would take *you* away for the weekend?' Kat winked.

'Always,' she joked.

'Is this about bloody Harry and that guy who keeps hanging around? Dani reckoned there might be a punch-up,' Kat said.

'Trying to forget it. Or at least learn the lesson.'

'What lesson?'

'That...' Ellie shook her head. 'I don't know. That cricket is a damn sight easier than men. That the person you think is the right fit might not be.' She swirled the few drops of cocktail and dripped them into her mouth. 'At least I figured Harry out after a few weeks rather than wasting three years like I did with Jack.'

'It's never *wasted*, Ells. You had fun, right?'

'I had more fun with you lot than I did at home, that's for certain.'

Kat laid her forehead against Ellie's. A sisterly gesture, something Ellie missed like crazy. 'Those guys should have known they'd always be second best to your true love.'

'That's fair. At least, for the time being.'

Kat pointed. Across the bar, Jade and Lily were laughing as they gyrated to the music. 'Those two have it figured out, right? I mean, they *get* it. The life. Give and take. Sure, it helps that they're on the journey *together*, but they danced around it for ages, the dating part.'

Ellie willed another drink to appear in her glass. She'd never danced around *the dating part*. Both Jack and Harry had been instant attraction. She hadn't... played herself in. She'd gone for a 6 off the first ball. Risky strategy.

A squeal of feedback from the speakers proclaimed that someone had picked up a microphone. Predictably, it was Rojo, the Scorpions' karaoke queen.

Ellie shook off the introspection. Tonight was about having a good time with her mates, her tribe. Not emotional wallowing, dwelling on mistakes.

She stood. 'Right, come on. I need a sing-song.'

At Friday's training session, a familiar but unexpected face was there. Jessica had retired at the end of the previous season, finishing a stellar career which included countless games for England and seven years captaining the Scorpions. It was odd to see an erstwhile teammate in a setting which was, for Jessica, neither match prep nor purely social.

They embraced.

'Hello, stranger,' she said.

'How are you doing? Good to see you back to match fit.' Jessica sipped coffee from a Scorpions branded thermal mug.

'Yeah, fit and flying. Working on playing spin. Screwed it up yesterday.'

Jessica laughed. 'Always the mistakes with you, Ells.'

'So we haven't lost you to the real world, Jess?'

'I can't completely escape. Hard to switch off, you know? Twenty years, then cold turkey.'

Ellie frowned. That didn't compute. 'What happened to coaching?'

Jess waggled her head. 'So much time commitment. Other people setting the agenda. All the work, none of the... excitement. Plus, hubby could use a break from my crazy diary.'

Everyone had assumed that Jess would be a coach, mentor... *Yoda* of some kind in women's cricket for years to come. To Ellie, it seemed like a huge loss. It also shone a megawatt spotlight on her own transition into post-playing life.

She gently probed Jess about "retirement". Jess was training as a mortgage advisor. Chalk and cheese. Control over your hours, a skill for life, weekends off.

Ellie kept chatting, kept smiling, but she was dying inside. It wasn't the prospect of leaving behind any semblance of fame or no longer being up close with fans and budding girl cricketers. Nor was it sad to be facing the end of something she'd always understood wasn't forever. The greatest disappointment came from not reaching as high as she wanted to. Knowing she was failing in her promise to Paige.

One day, I play. The next day, I never pick up a bat again?

It screwed with her mind. Yet, did she have any better ideas? No.

Soon, batting coach Jonno sidled over, and Ellie took the hint, giving Jess a goodbye hug.

It took a lot of effort to dismiss her ranging thoughts, take a firm grip on the bat, and focus on the next few minutes of her remaining cricketing life.

After training came the usual briefing for the next game. Player by player, the opposition's strengths and weaknesses were analysed, backed up with video evidence. Some analysis was aimed at the batters, assessing how to play the other team's bowlers; the Scorpions' bowlers focussed on the batters' vulnerabilities.

For Ellie, the headline was more about personalities than tactics. Well, one personality.

Mary Kallis. The girl who'd stolen Jack.

Stolen? Tempted away.

But if she'd been—was still being—too harsh on Mary, she'd also been blind to a particular aspect of Jack.

Blind?

No, she only saw it because it had been exposed by circumstance. Mary was much less of a globetrotter; she wasn't the in-demand talent that Ellie was... or had been until last year. Jack, clearly fed up with Ellie's absences, wanted someone more present in his life. In some ways, Ellie now understood his feelings. The injury layoff had revealed that she missed company, a body to snuggle up with. A long-distance relationship might be the only practical solution, but it had risks.

If Mary hadn't dangled the carrot of temptation, hadn't led Jack on, his weakness for infidelity might never have shown up... or, worst case, it might have shown up if Ellie married him. Which would have been a full toss straight to the face guard.

Yet, without that breakup, Ellie wouldn't have lost her form, been dropped by England, got injured, run into Harry's arms, had a miserable winter...

Mary was the butterfly who flapped her wings. A prettier, younger butterfly who played for the only side likely to beat the Scorpions to the competition trophy.

Why couldn't she have bloody well stayed in her native South Africa?

Ouch, catty.

But Mary hadn't. She was one of the Central Stars' imports. And in two days, she'd be steaming in to bowl to Ellie. Loved up. Possibly gloating.

Just don't get mad. Try to get even? Hmm.

Bottom line: play the conditions, the innings, the match position, the bowler, the ball.

15th Over

D uring Friday, Adam kept busy with something he'd stupidly left until the last minute—a cartoon drawing of Grace for her birthday. At least it took his mind off the previous day's events.

He didn't know what to make of the spat with Harry Owens. Disbelief that Ellie would date a guy like that? A sense of wanting to protect her? Why had she stood up for him, defended him against a guy she knew well? Was it her innate nurturing, inclusive, down-to-earth character?

Is it possible to be friends with people like Ellie? Surely, it must. Sure, she's known by millions and earns more in a week than I do in a month, but she doesn't act like that. She's the girl-next-door, like Diane said.

All the same, when he saw Ellie's latest Instagram posts—one bigging up a sponsor, another a "cocktails and karaoke with the girls" montage, it highlighted the gulf between their lives.

He fingered the medical wristband, wishing he could be as happy-go-lucky.

The letterbox's metallic twang shook away his reverie. He trotted downstairs and retrieved the three pieces of post.

One was a water bill. One was an anonymously addressed letter from an estate agent—which he immediately binned. The third was an emotional shot in the arm. The DVLA had given him the all-clear to drive again: the first anniversary of his last seizure had passed.

He punched the air, went to the kitchen and scoffed four chocolate biscuits. Then he texted mates Jez and Ben to arrange a celebratory pint at the pub.

Whilst he wasn't exactly itching to get behind the wheel—certainly not to drive to the pub—he needed to do the familiar admin of buying road tax and reinstating his insurance. There were pros and cons to owning a car. He could get by with cabs and short-term car hire, but as the seizures were infrequent, it was simplest to hang onto his trusty old estate car, which was ideal for transporting gear and art, and unlikely to be a target for theft.

However, Adam hated cleaning the car. Now, it was filthy with weeks of dirt accumulated as it sat, unloved and unused, by the kerb. Still, tedious though car washing was, he'd much prefer to do without epilepsy, even if it meant higher petrol bills and more soapy rigmarole.

He retrieved the trusty trickle charger from the boot and connected it to the battery, ready for the following day's photography job.

That evening, he met the boys at the Ship Inn. It was an old-school pub that had successfully resisted the march of big chain takeover, arty refurb, or wall-to-wall footy coverage.

The trio took a corner table and raised their pints in unison.

'Welcome back to the roads, Ads,' Jez said.

'I'll put out the hazard signs,' Ben added. Ironic, given he drove like his hair was on fire. Adam used to think it was designed to attract girls, but Ben still did it, despite having a long-term partner.

'Can't believe it's been a year, mate,' Jez said.

'Time flies when you're enjoying yourself.'

It seemed like only days since splitting with Pippa, perhaps because the spectre of her presence hadn't left his life. Conversely, Ellie's return skewed Adam's perception of time. A year ago, he'd been revelling in her play, and now he was doing so again. However, she'd certainly had a worse twelve months than him.

True, she didn't have epilepsy, but his episodes barely lasted a couple of minutes. She'd dealt with pain and discomfort, not to mention disappointment, for months. Temporarily losing his license was a mere inconvenience.

Imagine if I broke my right hand and couldn't paint? Life would feel pretty depressing.

Now Ellie was back, she'd be eager to make headway, and he wanted to be there every step of the way, cheering her on.

He couldn't say this to the lads. They didn't care about Ellie and cricket. One time, a few months back, they'd said she was "fit but only in a sporty way, and definitely not as hot as Pippa". They'd told him to stick to what he already had, oblivious that he wasn't interested in Ellie romantically.

Of course, they cared about his welfare. Six years ago, when Adam had a late-night episode, Jez had handled it brilliantly, like a true friend. All the same, Adam couldn't spend his life shacked up with the guy. The special person—The One—needed to be infinitely softer, more feminine, and blather much less about football and Bitcoin.

Critically, Adam mustn't repeat the mistake of dating a girl for her looks, merely to have someone constantly by his side. Most days, he barely thought about his epilepsy. He had meds and a wristband. He'd also sworn off aeroplanes.

The seizure he'd had three years ago, when unaccompanied on a flight, hadn't gone well. The fundamental lack of space, and an ill-prepared cabin crew member, left him with bruises for weeks. The acute embarrassment hurt, too. Whilst the shame of making a public spectacle was only in hindsight, it cut deeper because he was, at heart, an unassuming sod. It hadn't helped that, when Adam came to, one of the passengers was tutting and giving him the evil eye.

The seizure hadn't completely stopped him travelling—the Channel Tunnel opened up Europe—but globetrotting was off the agenda. Short haul might be okay, but holidays cost time and money, things in short supply when he was trying to carve out a career.

As the evening rolled on, he chatted about the Kent Business Awards nomination, and the lads encouraged him to attend the ceremony. He could publicise being shortlisted, network in the room and sniff out new clients. Although he wasn't thrilled about coughing up for a ticket, the price was reduced for nominees, covered a three-course dinner and a free drink, and included a plus-one guest.

He had to lean into this opportunity. Barely anyone knew about AG Images. To change that, he needed to embrace the "business" side of being an artist-photographer. The boys—and Ellie—believed in his talent.

Maybe things were looking up.

16th Over

E llie slotted her car into the last parking space outside the community hall and carefully lifted the cardboard box from the passenger footwell. Her stomach skipped: she enjoyed surprises—more so when she was the giver than the receiver.

A creaky front door led to a cool, stark interior enlivened by the joy of young voices. The noise came from the main room beyond the entrance vestibule. To her right, an open doorway led to the kitchen.

Diane noticed her and bustled out. 'Hello, Ellie, love. Let me take that.'

Ellie gingerly handed across the box and followed Diane to the long counter underneath a wide serving hatch. Beyond it, the wooden-floored hall opened out. Children scampered around, a few clutching balloons on a string, some chasing each other.

Paige's 10th was in a place like this. Happier days.

'Oh my.' Diane had opened the box.

The cake was a rectangular sponge with red icing, and the message piped in black read, "Happy 10th Birthday Grace". They hadn't asked the girl what design she wanted, but the Scorpions colours were a safe bet.

'If it tastes as good as it looks, then happy kids.' Diane said. 'And happy me.'

'I hope so, or you'll wish you'd picked something off the supermarket shelf.'

'I trust you. And Mrs Jones.'

Ellie hoped Rose's mum had come good; the cake she'd baked for her daughter's 23rd birthday had been brilliant and delicious. Mrs Jones ran a small home-based baking business, and when the topic of Grace's milestone birthday came up a few weeks ago, Ellie was keen to help out.

'Are you stopping for a few minutes? I can't imagine you'd leave without saying hello.'

Ellie wiped a tiny blob of icing from the box lid and licked it off her finger. 'No way.'

'Get yourself a cuppa. Urn's there.'

As Ellie made a brew in a polystyrene cup, someone caught her eye. 'Di? Is that...?'

Diane looked up from pressing black candles into the icing. 'Oh. Yes. Small world again.'

Ellie was about to take her tiny scorching cuppa into the hall when Grace pelted through the wide outside doors, bat in hand, zig-zagging around the photographer Diane had hired, asked or bullied. Grace spied Ellie and scampered over, fizzing. Her blonde hair was braided with ribbons.

'Ellie! Ellie! What are you doing here?'

She pointed. 'I brought your cake, Gracie.'

Grace's jaw dropped. 'Wow. It's amazing. Did you make it?'

Ellie laughed. 'I'm afraid not. My cakes always sink. Mrs Jones, that's Rose's mum, baked it.'

'It's brilliant. Thank you to Mrs Jones.' Her finger hovered over the inscription. 'I'm ten today. That's an even number, but it's the sum of the first three primes. And you came along, which is a *big* surprise.' Her eyes became saucers.

'I wouldn't miss it for the world.'

The girl pointed. 'Some of us are playing cricket.' Beyond the picture windows, a few children were knocking balls around a large grassy space.

'Want me to come and bowl to you?'

'Will you?' Grace asked.

'Definitely. Let me just finish my tea.'

'Thank you, Ellie. You're the *best*. But don't hit my wicket, okay? Because it's my birthday.'

You've seen my bowling, Gracie. Minimal chance of hitting your stumps—or whatever passes for stumps today.

'I promise.'

'Okay. Bye!' Pivoting, Grace broke into a run, almost clattering into Adam, who deftly fended her off. They exchanged a high-low five, Adam ruffled her hair, and she lolloped away.

Ellie went to meet him. She didn't know who was more amused, but his bashful smile alone was worth the trip.

'Yeah. This isn't quite how I want my fine art fans to see me, but still.' He extended his hand.

She shook. 'Not at all. And don't think for a second I baked that cake. But two fans at the same birthday party?' She cocked an eyebrow.

'Fans of who, that's the question.'

'Unless I'm mistaken, Adam, Grace's thing is maths, not art.'

'Plus cricket, of course.'

'Of course.' She gestured at the camera hanging over his shoulder. 'A master of many disciplines.'

'Hardly. Needs must and all that. Well, until my commissions rise above the level of nine... *ten*-year-olds.'

'You've done a painting of Grace? If it's anything like that one of Jimmy—'

He laughed. 'Diane's not *that* flush. No, only a little doodle. Her idea.'

He went to a cluster of plastic chairs scattered with coats and tweens' rucksacks, retrieved a sheet of paper, and brought it over.

Ellie inspected the cartoonish likeness of Grace, all flowing blonde locks and twinkling eyes, a cricketer with a princess vibe, as if Elsa from Frozen had picked up a bat.

'I'll bet Grace loves it,' she said. 'And now you're her official snapper. If you photograph as well as you draw and paint, they got a bargain.'

His lovely eyes creased in gratitude. 'Thanks, Ellie.'

She shrugged. 'I don't know art, but I know what I like.' She winked. 'That's what you're meant to say, right?'

Their conversation was interrupted a minute later when Grace joyfully bounded in and virtually hauled Ellie out to the makeshift cricket pitch. There, she became immersed in bowling and batting with a dozen youngsters. Inside, a voice suggested that coaching young players could be a future career. Someone like Grace made Ellie's heart swell with gratitude, pride, and a nurturing instinct.

Occasionally, her attention wandered to Adam as he captured the party vibe, moving contentedly around the kids, sharing jokes with Diane, and chatting with parents. A smile was never far from his face, and clearly he loved kids.

He was much more than a guy who had a favourite seat at the stadium, collected signatures and snapped photos. He was wasted in a studio; he was a natural with people. Perhaps that's why his portraiture was so engaging—an ability to connect with his subjects.

It wasn't so different from Ellie knowing her teammates inside and out, crucial in building a well-oiled machine. When she and Bry had clicked—on and off the field—it catalysed a friendship and batting partnership that was cherished and valuable.

One of the boys had stepped away from the cricket to kick a football around. When it rolled nearby, Ellie flicked it up with her toe, playing keepy-uppy for a few seconds.

Adam rattled off photos of her distinctly amateur skills, a cute, lopsided frown on his face. When the ball finally escaped her foot, she offered a little bow and got an appreciative nod in return.

An hour later, after the cricket, the craziness, the blowing out of candles, and the devouring of a most delicious cake, Diane and Grace departed with hugs. Adam had offered to stay behind and stack the chairs, so Ellie did likewise.

He seemed introspective, the good humour of the day now gone.

Ellie set down the bin she was using to collect rubbish. 'You okay?'

He rubbed his forehead. His sleeve rode up, revealing a wristband. *Don't pry.*

'Yeah. I'm fine. Just feel... old, you know?'

She smiled. 'Kids will do that, right? Especially ones like Grace.'

'She worships you.'

'I don't mind. We're all on this Earth for something. Maybe this is mine, being some kind of role model. For a while, anyway.'

'Well, coming here as a cake chauffeur, temporary coach, and janitor isn't the behaviour of your ordinary pro athlete.'

She waggled her head. 'Maybe. But I'd bet a tenner you're not charging Diane for this.'

His expression was sheepish. 'No, I'm not.' He frowned. 'Does that mean I owe *you* a tenner, or you owe *me*? I know which is easier on my bank manager's blood pressure.'

She laughed. 'I never pegged you as the penniless artist type, Adam. Please don't tell me you're on the bread line. It would break my heart.' She clutched her chest theatrically.

I love that he makes me laugh this much, without trying, without any side to him.

Some guys only use jokes as a way to unlock underwear.

If I hugged Adam now, I bet he'd turn to jelly.

'Penniless, no. And a tenner is fine. But if you want to lob me fifty grand for that Jimmy portrait, I'll shoot *your* birthday parties for free, too.' He nudged her playfully. 'You know, if Rankin's not available.'

'Do you do weddings?'

His eyes flared. 'Wow. That passed me by. Who's the lucky guy?'

She beamed. 'Fat chance! I meant, if I keep my ear to the ground, would you be interested? Bakes—sorry, Freya—is getting hitched this year. Hmm. But that's in Tuscany. And she's probably sorted it. But in principle?'

He bit his top lip. 'I try to steer clear, to be honest. Shooting weddings is a *real* stress. But thanks, Ellie. Really.' His eyes twinkled. 'Although if Freya's got a few grand to blow on a portrait of her and hubby afterwards, let me know!'

She touched his arm. 'Thanks. I'll keep that in mind. And if I see Jimmy Anderson again, I'll have a word. Unless the painting sells in the meantime, which I hope it will.' She checked her watch. 'Look, I should head off. Need to prep for tomorrow's game. Are you there?'

'Absolutely. The unpaid photographer's work is never done.'

'Like my laundry. And hoovering. And tax return.' She sighed. 'So I *definitely* should get going.'

He smirked. '"Lifestyles of the rich and famous".'

'Oh yeah, it's a real blast.' She eye-rolled.

'Go well tomorrow.'

'Thanks.' She considered offering a hug, but his body language said no, so she moseyed away, a spring in her step.

'Toodles,' she called breezily.

17th Over

The simple pleasure of a trip to the supermarket. In the car. No manhandling bags onto the bus, no need for a cab. No waiting in for a home delivery.

As Adam casually toured the aisles that evening, his thoughts were never far from the day's events. Not only the photography, the joyful kids, or the multiple helpings of tea and cake.

Ellie.

For years, they'd lived in the same town and never met outside her "work" environment. Now, after two hookups in as many weeks, he'd really warmed to her. Gone was the disbelief that they could be more than mere acquaintances. Yes, Ellie lived in the celebrity bubble, but she also stepped out of it to do "normal people" things like pop into town, connect with the man on the street, and help stack chairs after a birthday party. When that happened, his awe evaporated. He didn't need to stand on ceremony. He wasn't nervous or tongue-tied.

Why?

Because I'm not engaging with her as a pro athlete or trying to muscle into that world. I'm not trying to be somewhere I don't belong. Dating and getting dumped by a "celebrity" once is enough. And the lifestyle? I'm no globetrotter. No social butterfly.

If only things were different.

'Excuse me,' said a fellow shopper, bringing Adam down to Earth.

'Sorry.' He moved his trolley away from the own-brand pasta.

As he arrived home, another car was pulling up. In the darkness, he couldn't see who it was, so he took the shopping to the house and dumped it in the hall.

Connor walked up, a familiar bag across his shoulder. 'I came as soon as the courier dropped my camera back. Can't say fairer than that.'

Better late than never.

'Thanks, Con. We have to take those last-minute jobs, right?'

'Absolutely. Especially at five hundred quid.'

Adam thumbed at the hallway. 'Come in a sec. Lemme move this stuff.' He shuffled the carrier bags into the kitchen, then waved Connor upstairs.

Connor put the bag in the study then joined Adam in the studio. After surveying the artwork on display—the guy liked nosing at Adam's projects—he fumbled in a jeans pocket.

He held out five £20 notes. 'That gig? Client liked my work so much they've put me on a retainer. Regular work. So I said I'd see you right.'

Adam, with minimal reluctance, took the money. Perhaps Connor wasn't such a freeloading arsehole after all?

'Thanks, Con. Glad to hear it worked out. Anyway, you would have done the same.'

'Hundred percent.' Connor poked at a shrink-wrapped bundle of A1-size prints of the Jimmy Anderson oil painting. 'Any good news coming out of your little gallery thing?'

"Little"? Damned with faint praise—that's more like it, Con.

'It's... ticking along.'

'You reckon Jimmy will pop by, slip you six figures and take it home?'

Adam belly-laughed. 'No, mate. I don't think he'll schlep all the way down here to see a piece of art by some random artist he's never heard of, fall in love with it, and turn my career around at a stroke.'

'Fair enough. I'm not into painting, as a rule, but I like your style on that one.'

'You mean because it's something AI will never hold a candle to?'

'Different strokes, Ads. People like what I do. And you can't hold out forever. AI will get into your edit process sooner or later.' Connor took decent photos but overlaid them with machine-made improvements.

'Which is what I have a problem with.'

Connor held up a defensive hand. 'Don't shoot the messenger.'

'I'm not. Slippery slope, that's all. Soon, unmolested photographs will be rare, but people will always want paintings. It's a... purer art, so the exhibition is a big deal.'

'Purer?' Connor scoffed.

Adam held down ire. 'In five hundred years, the Mona Lisa will still be an attraction. Computer-generated landscapes with augmented *chef's kiss* lighting and expertly positioned sheep? Nah.'

Connor made a timeout signal. 'Whoa. I'm not dissing your work. I mean, I don't know Jimmy—who does—but there's so much *in* there. That's a gift, mate.'

'Cheers.'

Did Adam know how he succeeded in capturing a gamut of emotions in brush strokes? No. But apparently, he made a decent fist of it. The portrait had been a gamble. Painting it was cathartic after breaking up with Pippa. He'd become immersed in the project, lost down a rabbit hole of creativity, sentiment and connection. Feeling—maybe for the first time?—like a real artist.

'You want to drop Jimmy a DM, or his agent or whatever. Get him to come down and give you a photo op. A thumbs up on the painting or something.'

'And if he hates it? Files a… what is it… "cease and desist" letter? That's PR for all the *wrong* reasons.' Adam shook his head. 'And I already have Pippa for that.'

Connor snorted. 'No shit. I saw that Insta post. Mad bitch. How can she be so bitter when *she* dished out the dumping? You didn't do a thing wrong, mate. Better off single. Jealousy, that's what it is. Cos she knows that portrait's more beautiful and well-crafted than anything *she'll* ever create with a front-facing camera. Right?'

'Absolutely.'

Give Connor his due; sometimes, he has a good grasp of the world—and a decent word of praise.

'You can't please everyone, yeah? But you should definitely do another of those intense oils. When the Jimmy thing sells, someone's gonna ask what else you have.'

'I suppose.'

Imagine the possibilities if Adam found a *real* muse, not merely a sports star he looked up to? Someone whose essence he could attempt to put on canvas.

Connor spied something and walked to Adam's "ideas table", a paint-spattered, second-hand office desk strewn with sketches and prints. He held up one of the photographs from a Scorpions' game, a close-up of Ellie in full follow-through of the bat.

'What about doing this cricket bird you fancy?'

'I do not *fancy* her. I go to matches to watch the team.'

Connor scoffed. 'What? You go to see a bunch of women have a crack at a man's game, and it's not because you want to shag her? Or any of them?'

Adam cracked his knuckles. 'It's a sport. Anyone can play.'

'Bowl at ninety mile an hour? Hit it out of the ground? Nah. With Jimmy Anderson, you had it right, mate. Legend. These birds? Who's gonna remember them? I mean, barely anyone watches, right?'

Adam bit back a rejoinder. 'So why did you say I should paint one of these crappy nonentity "birds"?'

'Whoah! Only an idea. Might as well make use of all that time you're watching them flail around.'

'Flail? The women's game is about touch and technique, not just bludgeoning the ball. You should come along. It's bloody exciting.'

Connor sniffed. 'No chance. I'll save it for real games. But you go on, watch that Ellen girl. Dunno why, though. Sure she isn't gay? And hardly foxy. Not like Pippa was.'

You have no idea about her, you bellend.

Adam clenched a fist. '*Ellie* not being *at all* like Pippa is a major victory for Ellie. Trust me.'

'So why go?'

'Appreciating the finer things in life. Artistry. Talent. Heart. Dedication.'

'Women's cricket? Is it bollocks,' Connor snipped.

Adam pointedly checked his watch. 'Anyway,' he said with deliberate evenness, 'I need to prep for tomorrow. Thanks for stopping in.'

He led them down the stairs and saw Connor out. It took a lot of effort not to slam the door.

If we never speak again, that will be no loss.

As he assembled a bag ready to take the match, he reflected on the one sensible thing Connor had said during his misguided tirade.

Who better to paint next than Ellie? She'd surely approve, given they'd hit it off and she'd admired his artwork. Yes, it would be a speculative project—there was no guarantee she'd buy the finished piece—but having a passion project on the go was always worthwhile.

With women's cricket on the up, now was the perfect time.

18th Over

The following day, the Scorpions travelled to Chelmsford. It was Ellie's first time visiting the ground where she'd sustained the injury. She tried to put it out of her mind as she drove up, taking Kat with her.

As a distraction, they chatted about the evening's team BBQ—a superhero-themed bash at coach Susie's house in Maidstone. They joked about bowling out the Central Stars for a low score, so the match finished early and they could open the cold beers a couple of hours sooner.

Fielding first, the Scorpions had the Stars on the ropes at 88-5. Then Mary Kallis came in to bat. As well as being a class bowler, she was handy making runs, too... which she began demonstrating.

Soon, the Stars were 117-5. Then 129-5.

Ellie's stomach sank.

Someone, please take the damn girl's wicket. I will not have her steal this game like she stole my man.

On 47, Mary cracked a shot past Forward Square Leg. Ellie set off like a hare, aiming to intercept the ball before it crossed the rope. Ten yards away, her boot slid on the turf. Fear spiked through her. Last July, this slippery outfield and a gruelling chase caused her to do impromptu splits, wrenching her trailing leg and ripping her tendon.

Not again. Another long layoff and I'm done.

Instinctively, she slowed. The ball sailed past her outstretched hand and bumped over the boundary.

She slowed to a halt, panting hard, cursing silently, and scooped up the ball. Nearby, Adam rubbed his jaw and looked away.

Yeah. What I'm thinking, too, mate. Sodding injury. Sodding second-guessing myself.

She lobbed the ball back, hitting keeper Tara's gloves with pinpoint accuracy.

Mary's bat was aloft, taking in the applause for her half-century.

Sodding Mary.

Ninety minutes later, with a challenging target to chase, Ellie and Bryony walked out.

Over lunch, Ellie's red mist had largely cleared. She mustn't make the run chase personal. Trying too hard or losing focus were sure routes to failure. All the same, her eye did wander to the boundary, where a familiar lovely face brought a camera to his eyes.

Calmly and professionally, she and Bryony got into their groove, and the Scorpions reached 66-0. A good platform to build from.

Play the situation. The bowler. The ball.

Then Mary came on.

Her first ball was a loosener, short and wide. Ellie cut it through Cover Point for 4.

The next delivery was a cracker, straight and fast, so Ellie defended it with a straight bat.

The third, she padded away for a single, then took a breather at the non-striker's end.

As Mary returned to her mark, she shot Ellie a steely glare.

I get you. And I won't be beaten by you.

Facing Mary again, an over later, the first ball was a blistering Yorker, which Ellie barely kept out.

Very clever, Mazza. Try again.

The second was a slower delivery, which foxed Ellie, and she fended it off awkwardly. Mary ran through and scooped up the ball. Her expression said, "Lucky!"

Breathe.

Ball three was on Ellie's pads, so she clipped it away to Fine Leg for 4.

One-all, man-stealer.

She shot Mary a knowing look.

No, Ells. Focus.

'Come on, Mazza,' the captain called.

Delivery four was a zinger, and Ellie was beaten, the ball sailing through to the keeper.

'Bowled, Mazza!'

Now Mary shot the look. Ellie inspected the patches of rough grass in front of the stumps.

I was trying not to make this personal. But you are. And I will not be the victim of mind games. I'll just hit you round the park, Kallis.

The fifth ball was almost perfect, but wide enough that Ellie could slap it through Cover for 4, a rifle shot off her blade.

The game's afoot.

Mary had a face of thunder. She conferred with her captain. The field was tweaked, so Ellie checked the new positions.

Mary steamed in for the last delivery of the over. Ellie gripped the bat a little tighter.

The ball was short. Very short.

A bouncer. And you're bloody well going for 6, now, missy.

Adrenaline spiked through Ellie's arms, throwing the bat into a pull shot, aiming high over Backward Square Leg.

Except the timing was off. Sufficient for her to miss the ball entirely. In that tiniest fraction of a second after she realised she'd screwed it up, the outcome became clear. She snapped her head sideways, trying to duck for good measure.

Too late.

The ball slammed into the side of Ellie's helmet, knocking her down like a ninepin.

'Oof.' She hit the ground, head blazing with the shock and reverberation.

Clouds scudded across the sky. There were stars in her eyes.

No, that one's a bird. A real bird.

I'm on my back.

Get up. It's unseemly.

Using the bat for support, she levered herself upright. Someone was standing in front of her. A cricketer.

'Ells?' Bry looked worried.

'Yeah?' Ellie fought through the fog. Reality came into focus. She pulled off the helmet. Her temple burned with pain.

A second figure jogged up. It was the Scorpions' physio, Maddy.

Ellie dropped the bat and tugged off her gloves, blinking at the harsh overhead sun.

She's going to ask questions. I've taken a whack, Mads. I'll be fine.

'Hi, Ellie.' The physio picked up the helmet and examined it. It was dented.

'Hey, Mads.'

'How are you feeling?' Maddy smiled, but this was no casual enquiry.

'Like I took a hit.' Ellie shook her head. The pain didn't abate.

'Sure. So, what day is it today?'

'Um... Sunday.'

The physio nodded. 'Okay. And where are we playing?'

'At Chelmsford.'

'Okay, good. And do you know what the score is?'

'Seventy or so?' She sought out the scoreboard—which was cheating the concussion test—but only succeeded in picking out Adam, hands on his head.

Maddy asked more questions. And did a physical exam. And the Stars players used the opportunity to huddle and take drinks.

But Ellie's throbbing head didn't go away. Nor did the little voice which said,

Please don't take me off, Mads. I'm not losing to that cow.

19th Over

Adam's hands were held to his head for so long that if the wind changed, he'd be stuck like that forever.

When Ellie was escorted from the pitch, not even raising her bat to the supportive applause, his heart went out to her. She'd be furious, and disappointed, and regretful. But as long as she was physically okay and there were no ambulance sirens in the next five minutes, everything else would pass. Besides, Ellie had plenty of people to care for her.

Still, he checked his watch. And again a minute later. And paced.

No ambulance came.

Adam kept taking photos, but he must have checked his watch, and the pavilion, hundreds of times.

Two hours later, the Scorpions won the game, helped by a mature innings from Bryony. She played with guile and aplomb, reaching 76 not out, and was applauded off by her teammates.

Ellie emerged from the pavilion, apparently unharmed, to add her gratitude. Adam sighed with relief.

Ellie was fed up and cheesed off. Allowing a personal grudge to impact her game was a rookie mistake. Childish. Had she stymied her career so soon after reinvigorating it with three decent innings in a row?

Only time will tell.

The medical exam revealed no damage, but she scored below her baseline cognitive test result, a benchmark taken at the beginning of every season.

This was officially a concussion injury.

At least I'm not in hospital in a coma.

There was a time for being stubborn, and this wasn't it. She felt fine—under par, maybe—but head trauma wasn't to be taken lightly. The rules were clear: she couldn't drive home. She had to remain accompanied for the next 24 hours. She—or her babysitter—should call at the slightest sign of after-effects.

What a bloody ball-ache.

All because of some guy. You idiot, Ells. Wonder if that's in the coaching manual? When Bry said I was a role model, I bet she didn't mean behaving like this.

Breathe. Move on. Don't dig the hole even deeper.

After Susie had congratulated them on a good win, Ellie pulled up a seat outside. She wanted fresh air to clear her head, physically and mentally.

Adam was hovering nearby. She fluttered a hand in greeting.

He must think I'm an idiot.

Bryony came over and gently massaged Ellie's shoulders. 'Welcome to the concussion club, Ells.' Two years ago, she'd picked up a knock in the nets.

'Yeah. Great. Thanks,' she grouched.

'I'll run you back. Crash at your place. Okay?'

Ellie swivelled abruptly. 'What?'

'Partners, right?'

Ellie stood. 'You already bailed me out once, Bry, with that knock. I'll be fine. I'll get Ayla to come round.' Ayla was her neighbour, and they got on famously.

'You still have to get home. In your car?'

She groaned. 'Ah. Crap.'

'Then if I'm at yours, I'll hang.'

'No way. There's the barbie. At Susie's. And you need to get changed. And you live miles away.' She shook her head. 'You're not missing out on my account. Go on. Celebrate. You've earned it. I'll work something out.'

Ellie looked around as if willing an answer to appear from thin air. If she took the train or a taxi home, she'd have to return tomorrow for her car. Either way, she couldn't be alone on the journey.

Perhaps one of the support staff, someone who isn't going to the barbie?

Christ, my timing sucks. On that shot, for starters.

Adam was lingering closer, concern on his face.

'Hi,' she said, sheepish.

'Everything... okay? I mean, considering.'

Bryony looked back and forth between Ellie and Adam.

'Bry, this is Adam. He's a friend.'

Adam stuck out a hand. Bryony frowned at the courtesy, then shook. His reservation was understandable, Ellie considered. Fan engagement rarely went beyond a word, a selfie, or a Sharpie.

'Hey, Adam,' Bryony said.

'Hey. Great innings.'

'Thanks.'

Why do I feel awkward? Or is it Bryony who looks like a lemon?

'You go, Bry,' she said. 'Honestly. Have that drink. Who are you going as?'

'Wonder Woman.'

Ellie refrained from saying Bryony certainly had the chest for it. Not a comment for a public forum—although Adam had probably noticed Bryony's figure. Many times.

Wow, I must be concussed. Adam's about as likely to leer at any of us as... I am to be mistaken for Batgirl.

She couldn't believe that none of the girls had planned that outfit.

I mean, come on! Girl + bat? Slam dunk.

'Yeah. You'll rock that. Have a glass for me, too. I'm off the sauce tonight. And honestly, don't *worry*. It's only a headache.'

'I know you, Ells. It's a pain in the arse, not the head, right?'

'Hundred percent. Go on, shoo.'

'Okay,' Bryony conceded. She took Ellie in a hug, then nodded at Adam. 'Good to meet you.'

'You too,' he replied. 'Enjoy the barbie.'

'Thanks.'

Now, where were we?

Adam watched Bryony go. For a split-second, he pondered what she'd look like as Wonder Woman, then realised the images would appear on her Insta feed anyway. Susie's parties always looked like a riot. Last year's theme had been James Bond, to coincide with the release of a new film. Ellie had gone as a curiously appealing Oddjob.

He pinched his chin, watching Ellie's brow wrinkle and release. He was torn between chivalry and a crushing sense of intrusion. His idea was logical and practical but also incredibly presumptuous.

'Look, Ellie, you're in a spot, so if you need someone to drive you home, I'm here. I came on the train. We both have to get back to Maidstone.' He shrugged. 'Offer's there.'

Her face creased into surprise, then intrigue, then pensiveness.

He met her eye. 'I realise you have no reason to trust me. I might have a criminal record as long as your arm... or Rose's arms.' Ellie smiled. 'And I might drive like Lewis Hamilton or Stevie Wonder. Which would put us in hospital. Ironically, given your whack on the head.'

Stop digging. Let her say yes or no. So long as she gets home safe, is chaperoned, and returns fit and well for the next match.

Ellie took a long, slow look around the venue. Ground staff and a few players from each team milled around. The groundsman was inspecting the wicket. On the far side of the pitch, two children were playing with a tennis ball.

Adam was doing a poor job of not hanging on her reply.

Only one thing matters: do I trust him?

If I get a taxi, and work out the logistics later, I'm being driven home by someone with no providence. A person I don't know from Adam.

That made her chuckle. Either his offer was the culmination of years of brilliant manoeuvring and gaining her confidence, ready for some despicable act, or he was simply being a friend.

'You don't have to.'

He jammed his hands in his pockets. 'I know. And you don't have to accept. It's easier not to. Going home with a strange guy, right?'

'Strange? No. Supportive? Yes.'

Deep breath. We can do this.

She eyed him. 'One condition. I'll pay for your taxi home from my place. Oh, and I'll carry my gear. Appreciate the gesture, but I'm no invalid. Okay?'

'Deal.'

20th Over

Walking to Ellie's car, Adam's pulse pounded.

A stab of memory. His first driving lesson. Getting in a car with someone he didn't know but wanted to impress—or at least not disappoint. Now, the skittery fear was different. This drive was nothing like giving a mate a lift to the pub.

She had a nice car: an Audi S3 convertible. Feminine but not girly, classy, powerful, stylish and offering a sense of freedom.

Very Ellie.

She loaded her gear into the boot. He plopped his rucksack, camera and tripod in the rear footwell as if it were the most natural thing in the world. It absolutely wasn't. Logically, after following the Scorpions for so long and generating a rapport with Ellie, he should be at ease.

No. He was about to chauffeur a professional athlete. In her car. And his legs were like jelly.

Not ideal.

He slid behind the wheel, and she tendered the keys. He scrutinised the controls.

'You alright?' she asked.

'Me? Yeah. Fine. Are you? I mean, you're the one hit by a projectile today.'

She raised an amused eyebrow. 'Is this the point where you tell me you're still on a Provisional license?'

Best not to say I'm a bit rusty.

'Passed first time. No points. Never been stopped,' he replied.

'Good. Then let's get home. I may be sworn off drink tonight, but a hot bath is definitely in order.' She frowned, thinking. 'And there's nosecco in the fridge. Ayla and I'll get a takeout.'

'You earned it.' He inched the seat forwards, seeking the perfect driving position.

'I earned this bloody smack on the head, more like it. Trying to get one over on Mary.' She scoffed. 'Dick.'

He angled the rear-view mirror. 'We all have blind spots. Lapses. Don't beat yourself up.' He beamed. 'Or at least, not until I've dropped you off.'

'Bitch to Ayla about Kallis? And my... lapse? Yeah, good plan.' She looked him up and down. 'Ready yet?'

Now, it did feel like there was a judgemental instructor beside him. 'Sorry. Just don't want to roll your car. Being honest, this is all a bit odd.'

'You never gave someone a lift?'

'Well... yeah. Of course. But... you know?'

She nodded, a smirk playing on her lips. 'Ah. I'm this *celebrity*. Right. Better class of human being. And our cars work differently, too. This one has twenty-six reverse gears. And it flies.' She rolled her eyes. 'Honestly, I'll get an Uber.'

He raised a palm. 'I'd rather be bricking it for the next hour than have you cabbed home by someone who'll probably be texting or on the phone the whole time, and who doesn't appreciate your condition.'

She chuckled. 'I'm fine. A thick head and world-class guilt, but nothing ibuprofen and that bath won't fix. Plus the recrimination and bitching session.'

'Then let's go.'

For the next fifteen minutes, they didn't speak. He was too preoccupied with driving competently and following her unfamiliar satnav to muster anything resembling a conversation. Ellie was surely replaying the day's events, wondering what she'd got herself into, and hoping the ride passed safely.

Actually, he considered, she was probably thinking of how to repay his kindness—because that's the kind of person she was. This made him a lot more relaxed about the whole affair. About being *so* inside her world bubble that, if he stopped to consider it, he would have pinched himself. With hot tongs.

'Shit!' she exclaimed.

He gripped the wheel. 'What?' His attention darted between the mirrors.

'Sorry! Sorry, nothing.'

He exhaled hard, relieved not to have been alerted to an impending collision with an HGV. 'Right.'

'Sorry. No, I just remembered.' She tutted. 'Ayla—that's my neighbour—isn't there. They're away for a week.'

'Ah. Fly in the ointment.' He pondered. 'You must have a team WhatsApp group?'

'I can't ask them. They're at Susie's.'

'Every last one? Or do you have a neighbour on the other side?'

She shook her head. 'No. Landlord is refurbing it.'

'Parents?' He was about to add, "Siblings?" but luckily bit his tongue.

'They live in Bristol.'

'Ah.'

The car hummed along the M25. There was one obvious suggestion, but he didn't want to make it.

Silence fell.

'That was real class from Bryony, right?' he said.

'Yeah. She's... going to be a star. I'll miss her.'

He frowned. 'When? Why? Sorry. Team secrets. I won't pry.'

She laughed. 'No. England games, yeah? Home series against the Netherlands starts in a couple of weeks.'

'Of course. It must be tough to lose your best players for a while.' Then he realised what a clanger that was. 'Shit. Sorry. Didn't mean to—'

She touched his seat bolster. 'It's fine, Adam. Really. No offence taken.' She looked across, expression sober. 'I mean, you wouldn't follow me, do all... this... if you didn't think I was one of the best players. Would you?'

'People queue up to meet you because you're great at what you do, Ellie. Dedicated. Brilliant to watch. Inspiration to the kids. That's a hell of a combination.'

She blew out a breath. 'Thanks. Sometimes I'm not great with compliments.'

'You? That must be a big albatross. Would you rather be less good and have fewer admirers?'

She chuckled. 'Not really.'

'But I get it. And better to be humble than arrogant.' He indicated watchfully and took the slip road onto the M20.

'Right again.' Her smile was self-conscious.

'Sorry. I'll shut up.'

She shook her head. 'It's fine. We can't sit here in silence.'

'Well, I don't know, do I? You may be a nervous passenger normally. Or fancy a nap. I'm sure it's more fun with the girls in here.'

'Chalk and cheese. Yakking with Kat, Bry, or whoever isn't the same as a mercy dash.'

'Dash? Am I going too fast?' He lifted his right foot.

She laughed. 'You're fine. Being honest, you're a better driver than I am. I've got three points on my license.' She shot a mock glower. 'Which is need-to-know information, okay?'

'No online trolling, I promise.'

'Thanks. Talking of which, I should feed the machine.' She pulled out her phone. 'The thing about this *celebrity* lark is that the whole world will know I took a knock today. Better send out an update.'

So he left her alone and concentrated on piloting them home.

Driving Miss Ellie.

21st Over

When they pulled up outside her house, Ellie kept quiet about her plan to book Adam a taxi home and tell him at the last minute, when it was a fait accompli, and he couldn't refuse—which he wouldn't because he was a nice guy.

'I'll knock on Ayla's door anyway. She may have bailed on her trip. Hubby sometimes gets last-minute work stuff which screws up their plans.'

'Sure. I'll wait here.'

But there was nobody at home at number 92.

What are the alternatives? Come on, Ells.

Breathe. Knock it for a single, get down the non-striker's end, and regroup.

She opened the driver's door. 'No joy. Come in for a second. I can't make you wait here while I sort my life out.'

'Um... Okay.'

Poor sod. I'd better be quick. He's probably starving. We should have stopped. It's almost eight.

They grabbed their gear, and she led him up to the house. It felt strange, inviting a relatively unknown quantity inside.

He's a friend. I said so earlier. Wow, I must be concussed if I can't think straight.

As she opened the front door, her stomach sank. The place was a tip. 'Sorry about... this. I'm not normally a domestic disaster area.'

Chill. He won't care. I'm hardly trying to impress him. Worst case, he'll realise I'm not this slick, professional unit 24/7. This slick, professional "celebrity" who started a playground spat and got sent home by teacher.

'It's fine.' He prised off his shoes and left them by the door.

Immediately, she knew she was in good hands. She showed him into the living room. 'Find a seat. Want a cuppa or something?'

'Are you sure—?'

'Adam, I'm fine. All this is only a precaution. Believe me, I have no interest in collapsing unconscious onto a tiled kitchen floor. I'll put the kettle on. Just going to call Mads—I mean, the physio—and tell her I'm home safe.'

'Sure.' He eased tentatively onto the sofa as if afraid to dent it.

God, his deference is so sweet. And so bloody unnecessary. The things I've done on that sofa.

In the kitchen, she boiled the kettle and called Mads, checking in, as per the rules. Midway through, she peered out. Adam was on his phone.

Bragging? No. Taking pictures? No. Calling Diane?! A safe babysitter. There's an idea.

She took the teas into the living room. 'What about Diane?'

He laughed. 'Great minds think alike. No. Hubby's away on business. She can't leave Grace.'

'Oh. Well. But thanks for checking.'

He shrugged. 'I don't know your protocol, and I don't want to start any fights, but I'll feel pretty bad bailing on you until someone comes to take over.' He inspected his shoes. 'I know how important it is to have a friend by your side when you're not one hundred percent.'

His expression had an empathetic poignancy, which was all it took for her plan to crumble.

'Oh. I see. Well, thanks.'

'So...?' He picked up the mug.

Yeah. "So?" is right. Last ball. 6 to win. Get out of this, Ells.

He flinched, the tea hot on his lips.

Hotter was the question burning in his mind, the obvious solution to their situation. But how could he ask it? He was only drinking to delay making the suggestion he *had* to make, because if he left without speaking up, he'd regret it. Not because it would be a missed opportunity. There was nothing to miss.

He didn't want to leave her alone. True, her situation was nothing like his seizures—when company could mean the difference between life and death—but still. She should be mentioned in the sports pages for hitting a century or winning an International. Not in the obituaries because this idiot left her alone with a head injury, and she fell down in the bathroom and cracked her skull.

'Ellie?'

She broke off from whatever she was thinking. 'Yeah?'

He took a deep breath. 'Look, I have nowhere to be tonight. It seems like you're pretty short on options. And, being honest, I won't get a wink of sleep if I leave you alone here. You know, breaking the rules, not being... match fit.' He bounced deliberately. 'This sofa feels pretty comfy. But feel free to say no. Why have some random bloke crashing at your house? I mean, you haven't even checked my bag for axes.'

He flashed a crazy expression, trying to temper the seriousness of the offer. His legs were shaking. Actually shaking. She was within her rights to call the police.

She closed her eyes. 'Why didn't I duck that ball?' she murmured.

It seemed he'd overstepped. 'Sorry. I'm making this about me. Doesn't matter what I think. You're good at this... fitness thing. Discipline. Looking after mind and body. I didn't mean to offend. Sorry, Ellie. I should have just gone home.' He took a slug of tea, and rose. 'Thanks for the brew.'

She stood, grasping his upper arm. 'Wait. You're not some random bloke. I'd kind of thought we were... friends by now.' She bit her lip. 'Still, never would I *ask* you to stay. You already got me home, which is amazing and above and beyond. And I *do* want to stomp around, and break something, and tell myself I was an idiot, and curse this bloody "observation period". But it's for my own good. And, like you said, I've put *this*,' she gestured down her body, 'front and centre in everything I do. So it needs TLC.'

She pulled her shoulders back. 'Look, first, you don't mention this to anybody. What happens in Vegas stays in Vegas. Or, knowing my luck, some toerag will spill it to that gossip mag, and it'll be "Ellie Waites shacks up with random bloke".' She rolled her eyes, which glinted with amused irony.

'Understood.'

'Second, you stay downstairs at all times. Loo's there.'

'Absolutely,' he said.

'Third, even if you usually sleep naked, you're not doing it in my house.' He nodded hard. 'Fourth, in the morning, I get someone else here asap.'

'Sure.'

Her lips pursed. 'Fifth, I'm *really* grateful for your help, Adam.' She squeezed his arm.

He found a smile. 'No problem.'

'Sixth, I'm getting a takeaway. Right bloody now. Thai?'

'Perfect.'

She took a deep breath and let it out slowly. 'Good. What a day.'

He waggled his head. 'That On-drive in the fourth over was pretty special, though?'

She cracked a genuine grin. 'Yeah. Jonno liked that one, too. Real shot for the cameras. Did you catch it?'

'Think so.' He checked his watch. 'We'll have a look later?'

'Why not?'

22nd Over

As the takeout order was going to take twenty minutes, Ellie announced that she'd skip a luxurious bath and take a shower.

He watched her bound up the stairs. She'd come to peace with having him there. He absolutely hadn't. Especially when he heard the water running, and every brain cell screamed, "INTERNATIONALLY FAMOUS ELITE ATHLETE, ELLIE WAITES, IS TAKING A SHOWER NEARBY". He needed a beer, quick. But how could he casually march into her kitchen and snaffle a bottle from the fridge?

His skin prickled. Was the running water a ruse, a misdirect to cover the sound of her calling the police? And the sirens approaching. And him being handcuffed. For asking to kip over.

No, suggesting. For her own good. Possibly to save her life.

In that case, I should grab a packet of nachos with that beer.

He hustled into the kitchen, found a glass on the drainer, filled it with water, and necked it. One ear remained cocked for *nee-naw nee-naw.*

CHRISSIE HARRISON

Taking a few deep breaths, he looked around. It was a nice place to be, twice the size of his kitchen, with a coffee machine that probably needed a PhD to operate and a double fridge with an ice dispenser. On the fridge door, the month's calendar was held in place with a ball-and-bat magnet. The schedule was *chocka*.

It's a whirlwind lifestyle. So different to me.

He decided to skip the beer, and sank onto her huge, cosy sofa that certainly hadn't come from a DFS Sale. His gaze wandered around the spacious lounge. On the dining table was unopened post, a blown bulb, and an odd sock. She didn't live extravagantly, but he was still a little jealous of her modest yet newish detached house. Then again, true talent always pays.

Let's look at some photos of that talent.

He pulled out his laptop and perused the folder of today's images.

Ellie trotted down the stairs. She wore grey joggers and a burgundy T-shirt, and her hair was up in a damp ponytail. She looked fresh. Relaxed. Normal. Like a... person.

'Alright?' she asked cheerily.

'Yeah.'

'I'll bring a spare duvet down later. Beer?'

He frowned. 'I thought the rule was—'

She smiled. 'For you. Please don't stand on ceremony just cos I'm not drinking. Or we can split that nosecco?'

'Perfect. Fewer calories, no guilt.' He pointed. 'Everything okay upstairs? No dizziness?'

'I'm great.' She went into the kitchen. 'And thanks for asking.'

He watched, still feeling a little out-of-body, as she laid plates, glasses, and fizz on the table, then answered the doorbell, took possession of their dinner, and served it up.

They sat opposite each other, and he ate like he was with royalty. Focussed, measured. He sipped his fizz politely.

'Ellie?'

'Hmm?' She licked Pad Thai off her lips.

'Are you still sure about...' he waved his fork in the air '...this?'

She bit into a prawn cracker. 'Ah. Is this because of who I am?'

'A little.' By which he meant "A lot".

She thought for a moment. 'I met Jack, that's my ex from... before... when he helped me get the last jar of tomato sauce down from the top shelf in the supermarket.'

Adam inadvertently laughed. 'Sorry.'

'What? Because I'm this clichéd little old lady?' A smile reached her eyes. 'I'm not the tallest, true. But not that. I mean, God, if he'd known how I'm... my own person and *hate* asking for favours.'

He circled his eyes. 'Hence... this.'

'Exactly.'

'Hmm.' He sliced a piece of chicken. His finger slipped, and the knife clattered down. He jolted.

'Adam?'

'Yes?'

'Please chill. I'm just me. This tee is from Primark. The takeout was twenty-five quid. I sleep in a bed. I use a regular toilet. When I get hit by cricket balls, it bloody hurts. They don't bounce off. I'm not... Batgirl.'

'Well... kind of?' He raised his eyebrows, hoping she'd get the joke.

'Yeah, right? Which is who I'd be tonight, at Susie's party, if it wasn't for...' She shook her head and dug into the food with unnecessary vigour.

'You mistimed a shot, Ellie. That's not a first. Right? I think I can say that, now we're,' he made air quotes, still holding his cutlery, '"Friends".'

She didn't reply immediately but continued eating, nervously glancing at him. Then she drained her glass and pushed her plate aside. 'Between you and me, although I doubt it is, that mistimed shot was me trying to get one over on Mary Kallis. Which was very stupid. An iffy LBW decision? That's bad luck. Today was poor judgement. Emotional interference. I sowed the wind, I reaped the whirlwind.'

'Me crashing on your sofa,' he inferred.

'*Anybody* crashing on my sofa.' She poured more nosecco. 'Not that I'm averse to sleepovers. Though Fi snores like a foghorn. Watching Rojo trying to get comfy on that sofa is hilarious. And I've probably taken Tara for, like, two hundred quid in poker bets.'

He got a vision of poker nights *chez Ellie*. 'It could be worse. And you'll play Mary again sometime, when I'm sure you'll let your bat do the talking, not your emotions.'

She cupped a hand under her chin, gazing intently. 'You say all the right stuff.'

'That's the thing about us fans. It's belief. That the stars... players... people we like and admire can do anything. Can overcome. Can be... *Batgirl*.'

She glanced at the ceiling. 'Do you want to see the costume?'

'No. Because it'll remind you that you're not there. With the girls. I'm sure you look... the part.'

'Thanks. Who would you go as? To a superhero party.'

I'm sitting here, large as life, discussing fancy dress costumes with a trophy-winning sportswoman.

'Shazam, maybe. A character you can't take too seriously.' He raised the glass to his lips.

'Well, you do create magic from your fingers.'

He nearly spat out the drink. 'My work? Ellie, I'm one of a million wannabes. Art is subjective. Hitting a century isn't.'

'We were all wannabes once,' she said. 'It's just hard work and commitment. The county Under-18s saw potential in me... let's see... fifteen years ago. And women's cricket was nowhere. You'll fly, Adam. You only need a break.'

'As what, though? Haven't found my niche. Yeah, I like everything I do, but it's not with any real plan. I love that you've followed your dream, excelled at it.'

Her expression was earnest. 'Don't wish the time past. My dream ends pretty soon. Maybe I envy *you* a little. I don't mean I wish I could paint and draw, but you've got, what, another thirty years left... in whatever discipline the world calls you to. In three years' time, I'll be living vicariously through Grace... hopefully.' She shrugged. 'No shame in not finding your niche yet.'

He fiddled with a napkin. 'I suppose. It's a privilege to do what we love. So, enjoy the days. I do, and I'm only watching. And, for what it's worth, seeing you with the kids at Grace's party says a lot about what comes next.'

She frowned. 'In what way? Settle down, have a family?'

'No. Sorry, I wasn't pigeonholing you. I mean, you'll go into coaching, right? Somehow?'

She looked away. 'No idea. Figuring that out's not on my... priority list. You did say, "Enjoy the days".'

He exhaled hard. 'Sorry. Again. Your life, Ellie.' His fingers crackled with a weird electricity. 'But if I had a kid, and he or she was into cricket, I know who I'd love to have coaching them after school.'

Her jawline softened, a pinkness colouring her cheeks. 'That's... very sweet.'

'Day One will be "How to duck a bouncer", right?'

She laughed. 'Absolutely. Or have a Get Out Of Jail Free card in my fan club.'

'First Aid support. Another string to add to my bow. I'll have the widest niche in the *world*.' He beamed. 'Anyway, are you not texting anyone else? My sub?'

She waved it away. 'Too late now. Besides, you've not brutally murdered me yet, so I'm probably safe until the morning.' She pinched her forehead. 'When hopefully this will have gone.'

He stood sharply. 'Are you okay? Feel dizzy? Nauseous? How many fingers am I holding up?'

'Three. Or two, if you're one of those pedants who doesn't consider the thumb a finger.'

He shook his head in amusement at her very compos mentis, *witty* state. That easy-going persona, behind the professional steel and focus, beneath the toned yet feminine figure, had always been something he found attractive. The fact she didn't take herself too seriously. The gentlest West Country accent. Her ability to engage with the common man.

Specifically, right now, this man.

'Relax,' she said. 'I was briefed on what symptoms to watch for. If I get any, you'll be the first to know.'

His head fell. 'Sorry. Too much nursemaiding.'

'No, it's fine. Nice to be... watched over.' She stood. 'I'll get some painkillers.'

'I'll get the dishes?'

'Thanks.'

23rd Over

E llie tossed two ibuprofen down her throat and took a slug of water from a cupped hand.

She closed the bathroom cabinet door and looked in the mirror. She gently ran a finger across her forehead.

No sign of a war wound yet.

There came a clank of crockery.

And now he's loading the dishwasher. Careful, Adam, or I'll be putty in your hands.

She re-tied her hair and skipped down the stairs. Adam was at the table, arms folded like he was waiting for an interview.

'You have the sofa all night,' she said. 'You're allowed to start early.'

He jolted from his thoughts. Probably more nonsense about meeting celebrities, or what a failure his life was compared to hers. 'Thanks.'

'Cheesecake? I have some left over.'

His brow arched.

'Ah,' she said. 'You expected the "My body is a temple" mantra. Well, today, the temple is closed for maintenance. Pudding is medicinal. Or that's what I'm telling myself. And Mads. So?'

'Er, yeah. Great.'

In the kitchen, she assembled the dessert onto two plates with forks, then returned to the living room. He was eyeing the knitting pile on the sideboard.

'Yeah, I'm *that* cool,' she said.

'Oh. No.' He indicated the half-concealed Tom Daley book. 'I think you're right on trend, Ellie.'

She nudged him and passed over a plate. 'Maybe keep that between us, though?'

He beamed. 'Of course.' He plopped down on the sofa.

She considered the armchair opposite, then sat cross-legged beside him.

Silence descended. She darted glances, not eyeing him up but not *not* eyeing him up.

Where's the loose-limbed, chatty guy from Grace's party?

She finished the delicious treat and licked the fork. 'Please lighten up, Adam. The deference is sweet, but cricket is just a job. The fact it's on TV is a happy accident. It wasn't like this ten... even five years ago. I don't *care* that I have a hundred and fifty thousand followers... or whatever.' She pointed the fork at him. 'I'm sure you know the number, but that's because you're a fan. I'm no... Beyoncé, or Harrison Ford, or even Jimmy Anderson. I'm no global megastar.'

He sighed. 'You're right.'

'Do I know the leading names in the... art scene? No. Or table tennis. Or any YouTube creators?' She shot a knowing look. 'Yes, I'm grateful that people admire and support me, but I never chose this career for the *limelight*. It's a consequence of what I do, not a numbers game or a route to more sales like it would be for you. I am *so* lucky to do what I love, and the next generation will have even greater opportunities.'

'So, you're saying you want to use your power for good.'

'If I *am* Batgirl, then, yeah. Superheroes don't do it for fame, only to make the world better.'

'True.' He grimaced. 'Sorry for the fangirling.'

She cocked her head. 'Forgiven. Especially as you're here helping me out of a spot. Okay?'

He nodded. 'Okay. I've definitely had worse curries, worse beds, and worse company of an evening.'

She laughed. 'Snap.'

'Ah, this... Jack guy? The supermarket meet-cute. I'm guessing he *did* discover you are your own person.'

'He took me at face value. He had no idea who I was, which is good in terms of not having any baggage or... expectations. When he found out about my job, lifestyle, all that, he ran with it. He had a pretty dull job, not something I got excited about. Not saying that's critical in a relationship, but it's easier if you care. Like I do about your work. I definitely won't date another guy like Harry.' She held up both hands. 'Not that he's a yardstick. Jimmy Anderson? Now *that's* a yardstick. Man, if I was five years older. And attractive. And he wasn't married. And a million other things.'

Adam chuckled.

'What?' she asked.

'"If I was attractive"?' He cocked an eyebrow. 'You'll be saying next that you wish you were decent at cricket.'

Butterflies danced in her belly, bringing colour to her cheeks. She looked away.

'Sorry,' he said.

'It's fine. Nobody should have to apologise for compliments.'

'Okay. Well, if you wanted Jimmy, you could buy that painting and gaze at him every day.' He winked.

'Good sales pitch. Like it. Oh, how did the pictures come out?'

He pulled the laptop onto his knees. The screen showed an image of a shot she'd whipped off her pads.

She met his eye. 'Nice.'

'Thanks.' He tapped through the library. 'But this is my favourite so far.'

The photo showed her with a raised bat, acknowledging her fifty. It was head-on because she'd been facing him.

Deliberately. And not to line his shot up.

He pinched the touchpad, zooming into her expression.

She examined it, intrigued and reflective. 'A lot going on there,' she said softly.

The milestone. The past. Paige. Fighting back into contention. The uncertain future. Your support.

'Yeah. That's why I like it. It took a while to find something similar for the other painting. That's what I try to do. Not just the person's looks and what they do. Who they *are*.'

'And you succeed. It blew me away, the Jimmy portrait.'

'Thanks.' He slid the laptop onto the coffee table then eyed the ceiling. 'I wanted to ask you something.' He pinched his lip. 'I'd like to do the same... with you.' He raised a palm. 'You wouldn't have to do a sitting or anything. I'll raid my photo library and try to do a decent job. And if you don't like it, I won't display it. Or sell it. You have my word. Or say no. I understand.'

Unbidden, her hand came to her chest.

Ohmygod.

Adam was assessing her reaction. 'I don't want to turn you into something you're not, Ellie. But I think I know you a bit now and... I need a new passion project. It might even turn out better than

Jimmy. I never really met the guy, only to get his approval. And not everything you read or see is the truth, right?'

Her voice cracked. 'I'd be honoured.'

He chuckled. 'Honoured? Not sure about that. Who's the star here?'

Right now, me. But in three years? Probably you.

A silly idea hit her. 'Do one of those cartoons like you did for Gracie, okay? I loved that. Put me in that Batgirl outfit. Amp it up if you want. That could be bloody hilarious. Ellie the superhero. Batgirl in Scorpions colours.' Picturing it... or *something*, she chortled. 'I get a lot of fan art. Mixed quality, obviously.'

She patted the sofa, enthused, young again. 'Please. Do it. The girls will die laughing. Call it... Adam's fan project. Then do Adam's *professional* project.' She got lost in his eyes. 'Deal?' She offered her hand.

He shook, gentle, warm, and informal, unlike previous encounters. 'Deal. Wow. A commission from Ellie Waites. Maybe this is the beginning of something.'

'I hope so.'

Her phone chirped. In a Pavlovian response, she swept it up, located the notification, and opened WhatsApp. Immediately, he turned away, respecting her privacy. This wasn't fangirling, merely respect—a very attractive quality.

'It's okay.' She angled the screen. 'Look what I'm missing. God, they're all mad.'

She swiped through pictures from the ongoing BBQ. Kat as Spiderman—badly. Roddy as Deadpool. Bry rocking it as Wonder Woman. Fi hilarious as Christopher Reeve's Clarke Kent, complete with gelled side parting and thick glasses. All mugging shamelessly for the camera, drinks raised.

She sighed, a broad grin on her face.

My tribe. My family.

'It's like a sorority house, isn't it?' Adam said.

'It is *the* best life.' Deep breath, shoulders back. 'And I need to be fit for it.' She stood. 'I'll bring your bedding down, tell the physio I'm not dead, then try to sleep like I *am* dead.' She pointed. 'Loo's yours, kitchen's yours. Hope the sofa's alright. And... thanks. Again.'

'No worries. I'll do a bit of work, then crash. Just wake up *not* dead, please.' He glanced at the stairs. 'If you need me, shout.'

And he keeps turning up the dial of care.

'Sure. If you hear a thud or a scream, you have my permission to run up and investigate.' *That includes mouth-to-mouth.* 'And you're safe because *I* don't sleep naked.'

He laughed awkwardly. 'Um... okay.'

She patted his shoulder. 'I'll be fine. Honestly.'

'Good. Good.' His eyes were wandering, as if seeking something. 'What?' she asked.

'I think we've reached the acid test of this... relationship. Friendship. Firefighting episode.'

She put hands on hips, smiling, intrigued. 'What?'

'Can I have your Wi-Fi password?'

24th Over

In the darkness, Adam gazed at the living room ceiling. The fridge hummed. Light swept across the window—a passing car.

I'm staying over at Ellie Waites' house.

He pinched himself. He'd been wanting to do it all evening. It hurt, so this was real, raising the question of how he'd relax enough to fall asleep. It didn't help that he was simultaneously thrilled and apprehensive that she'd conceded to be his next art project.

Undoubtedly, the photograph of Ellie's half-century celebration was a great starting point. Her raised bat salute revealed so much of what he now knew was in her soul: pride, gratitude, relief, teamwork, grit... and loss.

If he could make this painting as magnetic as her real-life persona—on and off the field, he'd have a bloody masterpiece.

Ellie yawned, which was a signal to stop scrolling. She tapped out a couple of one-liners, reposting upbeat Insta posts from Jade and Rojo about their upcoming England series.

Go, girls. Do the Scorpions proud.

She put her phone on the bedside table and flicked off the light. The darkness had an unfamiliar quality. A sensation tickled her mind. Like... she'd packed for a trip but knew she'd forgotten something.

No. Not that.

A monster under the bed? No.

A weird sense that someone far away is thinking of you at the same time you're thinking of them? No.

You've left the outside light on, but it doesn't matter because it can't have any negative consequences, only positive ones.

Yes, maybe that's it.

Adam was downstairs. Voluntarily. Minding his own business. Making the end of a stupid day a little more bearable. Actually, much more bearable.

A warm friendship was developing, but even if she felt anything more, it wasn't reciprocated. Adam was almost... anti-flirting—if that was a thing. No problem. Dating now wasn't a great idea. Not at the start of a busy season, not with all the effort necessary to make the twilight of her career golden with success.

Anyway, there are two sides to every story. Why did Pippa really dump him? What don't I know about Adam? Plenty.

She rolled over, screwing up her eyes and cocooning in the duvet.

What's important right now? Practicalities. What to do in the morning?

She needed to check in with the club, work out her recuperation timeline, and get someone here until she was "allowed" to be alone. Ideally, she'd ask Kat, but the WhatsApp banter revealed that she'd be in no fit state. Roddy might be best, as she was teetotal.

What do I say when she gets here and sees Adam?

Chill. I'll say he's a friend. And she'll be sworn to secrecy. Because I don't want any insinuations. He's on the sofa. Like anyone would be. Any friend.

He's certainly not here.

She reached across the bed and stroked the sheet.

She woke around seven-thirty, then did the regular post-game recovery rolls and stretches on the bedroom carpet.

In the shower, she agonised about what time to venture into the living room. She didn't want any social faux pas.

What if Adam's asleep, and I wake him? That'll be poor payback for his help.

What if he's asleep and the duvet's fallen off? What might be on show? And what if he wakes up while I'm standing there?

What if he's gone home without a word? Is that good? Does it mean he cares enough not to cramp me any further, or is it a dereliction of duty?

What if he's up and has cooked me breakfast? With a single rose stem in a vase?

She massaged her face with water.

Where would he get flowers at this time in the morning? From the petrol station a mile away? And why would he think I wanted a rose?

She tapped her head against the shower cubicle.

Get real, Ells. Chill.

Just go down whenever. It's your bloody house.

So she dried, dressed, and crept downstairs. Entering the room quietly, she found the makeshift bed abandoned.

As there was no sign of Ellie by past eight o'clock, Adam extricated himself from the rumpled duvet and went to the downstairs loo. The unheated room brought goosebumps to his skin.

He took a leak, washed his hands, and eyed his reflection in the small oval mirror above the basin. His hair was askew, he needed a shave, and there was a line across his face, a pillow crease.

'You handsome devil,' he murmured.

His thoughts turned to Ellie. He'd heard nothing all night, which was a good sign—no frantic calling out, no thuds, no visits to the kitchen.

Then, a worry gripped him. *What if she's fainted in bed?*

One of his seizures had been at night. He'd fallen out of bed and cracked his head.

What if, right now—or hours ago—she'd developed a brain bleed?

A shiver racked his frame.

Ellie Waites critically ill—or worse—on my watch. All because I didn't check up on her!

Except... how would I have done that? Tiptoed up and peered into her room? Listened to her breathe? Sat on the hallway floor and conducted an all-night vigil?

He scoffed.

Idiot.

He had to trust her with self-care. She'd trusted him to spend the night.

So, ensuring his undercarriage was properly tucked into his boxers, Adam exited into the empty living room.

Which wasn't empty.

Ellie squeaked and dashed into the kitchen, cupping a palm across her face. 'Sorry!'

She leant on the worktop, her breath quick.

God, I'm glad I told him to sleep decent. That could have been a lot worse. Still...

She froze the picture in her mind's eye: his strong shoulders, toned arms—probably from endless hours of painting and hauling gear, decent backside...

'Sorry!' came his voice.

'My fault.' She hastily filled the kettle, making deliberate busyness noise.

'No, mine. Should have got dressed.'

She snickered. 'Going to the loo shouldn't be a formal occasion.'

'Still. Sorry,' he called.

'Forgiven and forgotten. Coffee or tea?'

'Oh. Um. Coffee? Look, you don't have to.'

'I'm making anyway,' she said. 'Don't worry, you'll be out of here soon. Roddy—sorry, Naira—is coming over, then you can head off.'

'Great, thanks. Right, all decent now.'

She peeked out. He was still a little dishevelled—in an adorable way, and they *were* yesterday's clothes.

'I would offer you a shower, but—' She was about to say, "Maybe next time", which was ridiculous. For starters, she didn't want to endure another whack on the head and a bout of enforced babysitting.

Although the babysitting part was fine. Fun, almost. Even better when the sitter is half-naked.

'It's okay. You're already the consummate host. Besides, I need to get home. Um... medication to take.'

'Ah. Right.'

Curious. Wonder what—

Stop. Don't be nosy.

He pointed at the framed effects on the far corner wall. 'You have a nice collection.'

'Thanks.'

A nook in the L-shaped room was filled with memorabilia: her first England cap, her first Scorpions cap, a bat signed by that first England squad, the shirt from her first overseas tour, and various photos. She called it The Temple. On good days, they were happy reminisces. Sometimes, recently, it felt like a memorial to a career that was already complete.

Today, it was neither. Pride, perhaps. And the sense of a new chapter opening. Her form was strong, and she had a new friend.

Coincidence? Surely yes.

25th Over

Adam watched Ellie dip in and out of the kitchen, bringing breakfast items. He dearly wanted to smell his breath and armpits. How could he look like a troglodyte in the company of someone so wonderful? However, it would have been tough to take that shower. He'd finally accepted the reality of everything, but going into Ellie's bathroom was a step too far.

'Assume you feel okay?' he asked.

'Yeah. When Roddy gets here, we're heading to the ground. I'll get a full workup.'

'And you can hear about last night's barbie shenanigans.'

'I think she'll be more interested in what went on here.' Ellie glanced away. 'I mean, concerned that I'm okay.'

He pulled up a chair and dug into the granola. It wasn't his breakfast of choice—he was a coffee and toast guy—but you don't ask elite athletes for cornflakes instead, having already cramped their style for over fifteen hours.

Ellie ate slowly, a glazed look in her lovely brown eyes.

He wanted to ask—again—if she was okay. 'Penny for them.'

'Sorry. Just wondering whether Susie will let me play on Wednesday. I doubt it. Safety first and all that. I'll go along, though. Can't beat five hours on the team bus with those maniacs.' A smile blossomed.

'I don't doubt it. Wish I could make it up there,' he said. The Scorpions' next match was away at Northern Storm in Leeds.

'At least you won't miss me playing.'

'True, but I come for the game. The squad. The atmosphere.'

She nodded. 'I know. And I reckon if you were the... babysitter of last resort for any of the girls, you'd offer a helping hand, too.'

'Of course. But I wouldn't wish a cricket ball to the face on anyone. Well, maybe Pippa. No, that's cruel.'

'Has she been up to any more tricks?' Ellie pointed at his phone.

He'd debated asking for a charger. There was only 14% juice left. Hopefully Roddy—no, Naira—would be here soon, and he could get home, charge up, and take his AED meds. They were vital in keeping seizures to an absolute minimum.

'No. Biding her time, probably. Working on some revenge ploy. Or busy putting on more foundation.'

She laughed. 'Don't let her get inside your head. Think of it as... a bad ball. Move on. Try not to make the same mistake again. I made two. It happens. Everyone wants the perfect shot every time, but it's unrealistic.'

And I won't make the same mistake either. Dating someone fake and shallow who puts themselves in a bubble and kicks out anyone who doesn't belong. No celebs for this guy.

'Yeah. And you mustn't let one split-second lapse define your season.' He stroked the table. 'You had me worried for a while.'

'Adam, I worried *me* for six bloody months. That tendon repair was a damn sight more painful than Mary's bouncer. Mentally *and* physically. I'll be fine. Honestly. Sad to miss the game? Of course. Susie might have dropped me anyway. Nobody's guaranteed a start.'

He frowned. 'Even with the England girls out? You're nailed on for Number 1 bat.'

'Well, moral support will have to do this week. Anyway, a chance for the juniors to step up. And don't apologise for not being there. Work on your art. *Sell* some.'

'I'll try. Believe me.'

The doorbell rang.

Ellie stood. 'Sounds like your relief is here.'

'That'll be a relief for both of us.'

She cocked her head. 'It's certainly been... interesting.'

'That's what they all say. "I'd rather be with Adam than in A&E.".'

She laughed, veritably skipping to the door. 'Tough call.'

Adam took the breakfast things into the kitchen. On the windowsill was a framed photo: a teen Ellie Waites, alongside someone bearing a strong resemblance.

He puffed out a sad sigh. His undeniable kinship with Ellie meant this fledgling friendship had changed things. He could never again see her in the same light. The light was warmer. Golden. More illuminating. It was the evening autumn sun streaming through his studio window, falling onto the canvas. The feeling through his brushstrokes as he painted her likeness would be richer, more insightful, more genuine.

'Adam?' she called.

He went to the living room.

'This is Naira,' she said.

Naira offered a hand. She was a slim girl with wide eyes, caramel skin, and best bowling figures of 6-21. He'd "met" her before, on the periphery of games, but asking for an autograph wasn't the same as this.

'Hi, Naira.'

They shook. Her grip was firm. 'Hi, Adam. I gather we were missing one superhero at Susie's last night.'

'Oh, I'm sure Batgirl will ride again.'

Naira smiled. 'I meant *you*, Superman.'

His cheeks warmed. He cleared his throat. 'Well, I'm sure Lois Lane will fill you in on the colour of my pants.'

Ellie's face lit with shock and amusement. 'Hey! Didn't I say what happens in Vegas stays in Vegas?'

Naira's eyes were wide. 'I think Tuesday's coach ride will be *very* enlightening.'

'Well,' he said, 'I hear that at least one pair of Ellie's have pizzas on them, so it's only fair I even the score about what underwear we like.'

Ellie covered her mouth. 'Oh, God. You say one innocent thing on player mic to thousands of TV viewers, and suddenly it's public knowledge.'

Adam cringed, worried he'd crossed a line, but she flashed a wink.

Naira howled with laughter. 'Oh, Ells! Your lucky pants!' She grabbed Ellie's arm. 'Please say you weren't wearing them yesterday. Otherwise, they're a bust. The magic's gone. They're for the bin!'

Ellie looked at a spot in space. 'You know what? I *wasn't* wearing them.'

'That explains it.'

She cringed. 'Getting pissy at Kallis had a *lot* to do with it.' She waved both arms as if warding off a ghost. 'Enough. Look, we have to let Adam go. You can push a favour too far. Get yourself a brew, Roddy. Green tea's in the usual place. I'll see... Superman here out.'

'Thanks, Ells. And thanks, Adam.'

He shrugged. 'What are fans for?'

Naira patted his shoulder. 'Fans are *everything*. Which you just showed. So I won't tell the girls about the pants, okay?'

'Thanks, Naira.'

She flapped a hand. 'Roddy's fine. Right. Tea.' She disappeared into the kitchen.

'You good to go?' Ellie asked.

Adam had already packed his rucksack. It contained the same as when this episode of madness had started yesterday afternoon.

He hoisted it onto his shoulder. 'Superman is leaving the building. On foot, though.'

She tittered. 'Yeah, don't try flying, or I'll be the one on *your* sofa. Or in A&E.'

'Clark Kent only. Promise.' He walked to the front door and pulled it open. 'Thanks for everything, Ellie.'

She frowned gently. 'Thank *me*?'

'I got to hang out with you. A lot of people would be jealous.'

'Not jealous of exactly this, I expect.'

He shrugged. 'You can only play the ball you're bowled, right?'

'Absolutely. And you played this one like a pro.' She chuckled. 'Better than I did.'

'All's well that ends well. So, hope to see you on Saturday at Newbury.'

She nodded. 'Definitely. Come and find me after the game.'

'Okay, sure. Have a good week.'

'I will,' she replied.

A pregnant pause, in which his body language mirrored her hesitancy.

She pulled him into a loose embrace. 'Thank you so much.'

Over the years, he'd noticed she was a tactile, open person. A hugger. He reckoned it stemmed from losing a sibling, the innate need for warmth and companionship now being satisfied by her peers.

'No problem. Lois.'

Her eyes glowed. 'I'll find some way to repay this. Better than a signed bat, for sure.'

He pouted deliberately. 'What, I'm twenty years too old?'

She laughed. 'Okay, okay, I'll get you a bat.'

'Great, thanks.' He took a gamble and turned away, saying, 'Toodles.'

She laughed. Again. 'Toodles!'

He managed five steps down the path.

'Adam?'

He stopped and turned. 'Yeah?'

She looked him up and down. 'Um... I've got things on all week, but how are you fixed for... next Friday night? Nothing fancy. Just a drink. As a thank you. Dani's mentioned this new rooftop bar. We could give it a try?'

His throat dried.

Wow. Friends have drinks, right? Even new ones. Attractive, single, athletic, awe-inspiring ones.

'Or, just the bat,' she added. 'Cheaper that way.' Her eyes smiled.

'I... think I'm free.' He was pretty sure he was. 'Talk about it on Saturday?'

'Great. See you then.'

He touched his hoodie. 'Right. Got to go and wash my cape.'

26th Over

As Ellie closed the door, she decided something.

Almost all of this is staying in Vegas.

As Adam was neither a boyfriend, ex-boyfriend, teammate, member of staff, or fellow professional, she wouldn't spill the beans. Firstly, nothing of note had happened. Secondly, if whispers started, and he found out, it might damage what they had.

Nobody needed to know what colour pants he had. *Navy. Unbranded.*

Nobody needed to know what the rest of him looked like. *Not too lean, no paunch, chest not too hairy. No six-pack—no problem.*

Or whether he'd left the toilet seat up. *No.*

Whether he'd made eyes at her. *Definitely not. Sadly.*

Roddy was on the sofa, sipping from a mug. 'We were worried about you, Ells.'

She sat. 'Which part? The ball strike or the "stalker" in my house?'

Roddy frowned. 'Adam? He's no stalker.' She leant in. 'Right?'

'Not in the slightest. He was the ideal... Get Out Of Jail Free card.'

'Good. I'm relieved. So, no symptoms?'

'Right as rain. But let's make sure the medical staff agree. And I want to hear *all* about the party.'

The ride up to the Leeds hotel on Tuesday was a riot.

Ellie had been told she wasn't playing. She sat next to Freya "Bakes" Baker, who, at 34, was the senior of the squad and also the most reserved. To avoid searching questions about the "Superfan sleepover"—as it was being called—Ellie spent most of the journey shooting the breeze and discussing tactics for the game, when Bakes would replace Ellie as opening bat.

However, this was curtailed when Rojo declared it was karaoke time. Bus karaoke, despite the lack of cocktails, was the equal of bar karaoke.

At breakfast in the hotel, Ellie was finishing her coffee when Hawks plopped down beside her. Hawks was now attending training days and matches, offering moral support, helping to carry gear, and doing guest commentary spots on local radio or the venue's livestream.

'Sleep alright, Ells?'

'Like a log. Anything happen with that waitress, the one who was giving you the eye last night?'

'Nah. Can't be doing with a long-distance relationship anyway. Anyway, girl, *you're* the one who took someone home the other night.'

Ellie gave her a firm shoulder nudge. 'It's not like that. He was a mate.'

'And he's an artist? Good with his hands, I bet.' She waggled her eyebrows.

'You're a bloody liability, Hawks.'

Not that I wouldn't mind finding out how good he is with his hands.

'He coming today?'

Ellie shook her head. 'Too busy. Says he'll watch online, though.'

'Ooh. Want me to give him a shout-out?' Hawks' bright blue eyes danced impishly.

'Hell to the no.'

'*You* want to?'

'Doubly so not.'

Hawks bit her lip. 'I was going to ask you anyway... I know this is a sore topic, but... how do you fancy doing, like, five minutes?'

A chill ran down Ellie's spine. 'Commentary? Thanks, no.'

'A guest spot. I'll be there. Like... a little interview thing. Just some perspective on the match. Easy. Honestly, Ells, it's not a bear trap. Nothing about Superfan man, honest. Just a... toe in the water for you.' She squeezed Ellie's wrist supportively. 'The Comments section will light up with well-wishers when they hear you're back and raring for Newbury. Come on. During our innings. Promise.'

Ellie eyed her friend. Hawks would never throw a curve ball; they were too close for that.

Breathe. I can do this.

It was a mixed day.

The Scorpions lost. The team was too depleted to compete with a strong Storm side. Guilt niggled at Ellie. Being dropped from the side was one thing; not playing due to a rash decision was another.

Move on.

The commentary spot had gone well. She'd done ten minutes behind the mic, and afterwards, Hawks and the in-house sports journo said Ellie came across as knowledgeable and relaxed.

Maybe there's hope for me in media after all.

Still, something niggled at her. Hawks had disparaged long-distance relationships, and Ellie's experience with Jack had borne that out. She'd been playing in New Zealand when his eye had wandered. Absence hadn't made his heart grow fonder; it had started the dominoes toppling.

Ellie didn't want long-distance again. She wanted something immeasurably better, deeper, cosier. She also wanted cricket. Any day, any town, any country.

I don't make it easy for myself, do I?

Thursday was a personal day. Nevertheless, after the usual recovery rolls and stretches, Ellie went to the local gym for an hour's fitness techniques—weights, thigh press, bicep curls, medicine ball.

At noon, news dropped from the England and Wales Cricket Board. As Ellie read the social media post, her mouth fell open, eyes glazing over. Finally, after too long waiting, the women's national team would be playing their first-ever Test match at Lord's, the home of cricket. The sport had truly arrived.

Ellie's heart rattled and skipped. She had less than a year to get her act together. Until now, the dream had been merely that. Now, it was attainable.

She played with the charm on her necklace.

I can do this.

27th Over

A dam had partially watched, partially listened to Wednesday's YouTube livestream while working in his studio. It had been a surprise to hear Ellie on the commentary, talking about returning from injury, her current batting form, and making light of her error in the previous game.

He decided to ask the club for permission to sell his photographs in online marketplaces. Over the years, the team had used a few pictures for social media, and once, he'd filled in for the official snapper, but Adam had never used any images for his own gain. Now, with Ellie, he had an "in".

On Friday, he finished off her Batgirl picture. Whilst the artwork was a caricature, it focused his mind on the upcoming portrait, so he made preliminary sketches of her face.

New facets swirled around his memory. Her appearance the morning after the "sleepover": T-shirt and joggers, hair roughly pinned up. No discernible makeup or perfume. Her gentle suntan:

Ellie liked a day at the beach, at home or abroad. Not hours on a sunbed... unlike *some* people.

Before turning out the light, curiosity had drawn him to investigate her living room nook, which contained something of a surprise. Ellie Waites collected superstar memorabilia. Some signatures had been captured on whatever she had to hand—a theatre programme, a napkin, a flyer. Daniel Craig, Robbie Williams, Usain Bolt. A headshot of James Anderson, another of Cate Blanchett.

And, on top of a low bookshelf, sat an exhibition programme. Signed by one Adam Glenn.

It would be funny if it weren't hilarious. Him, amongst these legends?

Still, if she hadn't asked for his autograph, shown her down-to-earth mischievous side, perhaps they'd never have hit it off.

On Saturday, he reached the Newbury ground in good time and bagged a spot near Square Leg. Unpacking the camera bag, he discovered a lens cap was missing.

How long has that been gone? Never mind. It's probably lying on the edge of a pitch somewhere.

He toured the boundary, watching the teams warm up. His instinct was to catch Ellie's eye, but he needed to let her get into "the zone". They'd chat after the game, as she'd suggested.

Unfortunately, it would be an awkward conversation.

"Opening the batting for the Scorpions, Ellie Waites and Gemma Enstone."

Ellie fist-bumped Gemma, then grabbed the toe of her bat and bent at the waist, stretching to touch the grass. Then she clasped the shirt logo, thumped her chest, and strode to the middle.

Let's go.

As it was a 50-over match, she could afford to play herself in. Naturally, the opposition, Western Fire, opened with their most potent bowlers, so she carefully weathered that storm. When Gemma was out for 29, before Bakes arrived at the crease, Ellie surveyed the ground. Adam was in his usual place, applauding Gemma off. It was good to see him again.

She and Bakes had a word about the wicket, then Bakes saw out the last three balls of the over. Scorpions were 66-1.

Ellie took strike. She needed to play deep into the innings. After Bakes and Dani, the batters were mainly juniors with low averages.

Breathe. One player can't win the match. But one can lose it.

Focus.

There was a bowling change. The Fire's squad had been depleted by injuries to two key players, so they relied on a relatively untested girl, Rhianna Lawler, to fulfil the quota of overs.

Ellie smelt blood. It's always helpful to have one person to target, a route to easy runs.

Because Ellie was a nice person and wanted to avoid any more silly mistakes, she gave the bowler three balls to find line and length.

Then, she began taking poor Rhianna apart. The next three balls all went to the boundary.

Soon, Ellie passed 50. She barely acknowledged it.

Just getting started.

The captain took Rhianna off, but she would be back. When Bakes was out, captain Dani came in to bat. Her only comment was, 'You take this, Ells. I've got you.'

So Dani played for Ellie, giving her the strike at every opportunity. On a score of 74, Rhianna returned. Within twenty minutes, Ellie was on 97.

Breathe. I've got this.

Rhianna conferred with her captain. The Off-side field was tweaked. Ellie noted everyone's positions. They wanted her to hit through her favoured and get out, caught on the boundary.

So, when Rhianna delivered the next ball on a hittable length outside Off stump, Ellie was ready to do the opposite of what they expected. She stepped right, dropped to one knee, and the bat connected like an absolute doozy.

Adam had put down the camera. Ellie's innings was too good to watch through a viewfinder. He wanted the full immersive experience. This athlete, this person, this... friend was taking his breath away.

Sod the naysayers. This is why I come. For this. For her, in this form.

And then, the click of ball on bat. The perfect noise. Right out of the screws, which was vital to clear the boundary. The boundary ten feet away.

He sprung to his feet, ready to applaud. Then he twigged the ball's trajectory. His eyes went out on stalks.

Run or stand your ground like a man? Avoid the incoming missile, or make a fool of yourself with an attempted catch?

Easy decision.

Heart racing, he stepped over his rucksack, zig-zagging. There was nothing in front of him; no crowd, no seats. It was Adam versus the ball. Crucially, he wanted the ball to cross the rope: Ellie deserved this shot, this 6, for her hundred.

Blocking out everything else, he watched the ball drop, drop. He adjusted his position, his stance, his hands.

The things I do for you, Ellie Waites.

Of course, he didn't have to. But he'd committed now.

The ball smacked into his fingers. It bobbled. He juggled. He gasped. He lunged. He gripped. The ball stuck.

The crowd whooped. Breath gushed from him. Pain radiated through his palms.

'Well held, mate,' called someone nearby.

He held the ball up like a trophy. Applause. The Square Leg fielder, who'd been beaten all ends up, trotted over. He tossed her the ball.

In the middle, the umpire's arms went up. Ellie broke her clasp with Dani, pulled off her helmet and held it aloft with her bat, turning a full circle, taking in the applause.

Adam's heart was in his throat. His eyes glistened.

Then Ellie arrowed the bat, absolutely unmistakably, at him.

28th Over

S he slipped the chin strap on, adjusted the helmet, and tapped her
bat on the ground.

Breathe. Move on now. He knows.

*This job's not finished. Still twenty-seven overs to go. But I really do
have this.*

By the end of the game, Ellie walked off, having scored 137. Her
heart was full.

*First ton in four years. If only the England selectors were watching.
Still.*

It would take a miracle to be called up for the national team.
Contracts were usually only awarded annually in October, leaving
months of waiting before she'd find out if there would be another
chance to pull on the England kit.

Two hours later, the Scorpions had won, undoubtedly thanks to
Ellie. It had been many moons since he'd seen her play with such
assuredness and quality.

Maybe if someone lobbed a ball at my head, it might make me a great painter?

Best not to find out.

The crowd drifted away. Across the pitch, with the sun low in the sky, Ellie was being interviewed by the Scorpions' media team, no doubt talking about today's career-best 137.

Adam packed up his things, found a vacant seat near the pavilion and waited. A few autograph hunters hovered in the vicinity. A small part of him said, "Yeah, guys, but I'm here to see Ellie. My *mate*." Then he realised that sounded like a crowing jerk. Especially as one of the people nearby was Fiona's dad. Through financial necessity, many of the younger players lived at home.

A few minutes later, Ellie and Gemma emerged from the pavilion, chatting merrily. He stood. Ellie spied him, paused, gave her batting partner a farewell clench, then Gemma offered Adam a cheery nod and went on her way.

Ellie tapped his shoulder. 'Nice catch.'

He gave a mock bow. 'Nice century.'

She did a little curtsey. 'Thanks. One-fifty would have been nice, but I shouldn't be greedy. Get any good pictures?'

'A few. But the important one's in here.' He unzipped the rucksack's study rear compartment and slid out a transparent folder containing a sheet of paper.

Her face broke into wry amusement, then wonder.

She laughed, hand on her chest. 'Christ, this is hilarious. Hilarious and brilliant.' A slight frown appeared. 'Wait, is this how you see me?'

'It's how you are. Or one version of it. I mean, *a lot* of liberties taken—'

'No shit. I'd kill for boobs like that. It looks like... if Elastigirl met, I don't know, Susie. One of the greats. Thanks, Adam.'

You're great, too, Ellie. Boobs? I wouldn't like to say.

'No problem. Hang it in the downstairs loo. Something to remember me by, pants and all.'

She nudged him. 'I'm trying to *forget* the pants thing.'

'Me too.' He glanced at his watch. 'So, I've got a train booked. Was there something you wanted me to hang around for?'

'Yes. Friday night. Remember? Drink?'

He kicked his feet. 'Look, sorry about this—and I know it's worse because you have a mad busy life—but Friday is no good. I forgot. I have a... thing to go to.'

Her face fell. She shifted the kitbag on her back. 'Oh. *Thing.*'

'Nothing, really. Some... awards event I'm invited to.'

Her eyes widened. 'Awards? Wow. Photography? Art?'

'No. That stuff is way above my level. It's only a local business thing. I'm...' he winced sheepishly '...nominated for something. So, kind of *have* to go. For appearance's sake.'

She searched his face. 'Really? You're up for an award?'

'Yeah. Point is, it clashes with our... your offer. Which is a pain in the arse because you don't *have* to buy me drinks or anything, but now I feel terrible, and—'

She touched his shoulder. 'Well... Do you need a plus-one?'

'Huh?'

'Do you need a plus-one? To the awards? You know, tag along, moral support.'

He smiled. 'I'm sure you have better things to do on a Friday night. Take Gemma to that bar. Or Kat.'

'No, but I asked *you*, Adam. You're the one who was my... First Aid kit last weekend.' She held up a palm. 'But no point in cramping your style.'

'You wouldn't, but,' he sighed, 'I can't ask you to come.'

'You didn't. I offered.' Her tone was quiet and measured, far from confrontational, yet he sensed she was losing patience. 'You've supported me for years, so this is *one* night of... payback. Plus, I missed Susie's barbie, thanks to getting poleaxed, so I'm owed a party.' She jabbed a finger at the deserted wicket. 'Especially after being... Batgirl today.' She waved her cartoon.

Wow. Um...

Amidst the opportunity to hang out, discover more about her as a person—things he could pour into the artwork, his brain clanged with warning bells. The risk of questions, gossip, insinuation. The media leapt on missteps by people like Ellie. Did he want to do anything which might cause that?

Aargh!

'I don't... Um...'

She took a step back. 'Never mind. Forget it.'

'Oh. Er... okay.'

'So, see you at the next game.' The smile didn't reach her eyes.

She strolled away, the picture wafting in her grasp.

'Shit,' he murmured, mind spooling.

A sound nearby startled him.

'Oh, sorry, Naira.' He stepped aside.

'Adam, isn't it? We met—'

When he'd kipped over at Ellie's. 'Yes.'

'Enjoy today? Have a good time?'

'Always.'

Naira nodded pensively, then pointed in the direction Ellie had gone. 'Maybe she needs someone to let *her* have a good time. You really cared about her welfare last week, didn't you?'

'More of a "needs must" thing, but yes.'

'We missed her at the barbie. We love Ells. She deserves nice things.' Naira glanced around. 'I think she just wants to repay the debt. And maybe a drink to celebrate that knock today.' She smiled. 'Not counting the one she'll have in the bath tonight. Loves a good bubble bath, does our Ells.'

'Hmm.'

'Anyway. Must fly. Thanks for coming down.' She patted his shoulder, then ambled away.

Adam looked at the gap where Ellie wasn't. Then he ran.

In the parking area, she was already behind the wheel, with familiar, blue-tinted mirror shades masking her eyes and, thus, her mood.

He went to the side window.

Her lips pursed, eyebrows tight. 'Yeah?'

'Ellie, I'm sorry. I just... couldn't imagine *you* being my plus-one. And you're bound to be papped by somebody—'

'Look, Adam, all I wanted was a night off and to say thanks for the concussion thing. Maybe hang out together.' She smiled sadly. 'But I don't want to muscle in on *your* gig.'

How could he turn her down? She'd clearly dedicated her century to him. He wasn't a fool. It was obvious that she cared.

Stop being so insensitive and fearful.

He squatted down. 'Ellie, I'd be honoured if you'd be my plus-one.'

She peered over the top of her shades, inspecting his face. She licked her lips. 'I'm pleased. So... I'll text you, okay? The number's on your website?'

His shoulders relaxed. He hadn't kiboshed their friendship. 'Oh, right. Of course.'

She thumbed at the passenger seat. 'You want a ride? Going the same way, yeah?'

He smiled. 'With you behind the wheel? No, thanks. A little bird tells me you have points on your license.'

She wrinkled her nose playfully. 'It's a good job I like you.'

'Sometimes I wonder why. Anyway, I don't want to miss out on another joyous public transport adventure. And I'm sure you've had enough of me for today. Maybe a lifetime.'

'Not yet.' She winked. 'But maybe after Friday, I will.' She started the car. 'Oh. Flats or heels?'

He shrugged. 'Flats. I can't wear heels. Too painful.'

She laughed. 'See you Friday.'

'See you. And... great knock today, Ellie. Superb.'

'Thanks, mate.' She pulled away, thrusting a hand through the window and waving. 'Toodles!'

29th Over

Ellie's Monday was spent at skills training. Rain meant the session was indoors, and the stark space rang with the hard cracks of leather on willow.

In breaks between the drills, Kat tried to wheedle out some gossip about Adam, but Ellie had none of it. She did mention the awards evening, and Kat jokingly suggested Ellie wear her lucky pants in case their oddly talismanic properties rubbed off on Adam's chances of taking home a prize.

Ellie said she had no plans to rub up against Adam.

What she meant was "No *immediate* plans". Especially as the attraction didn't seem mutual. That's why she'd given him a get-out about the awards, pounced on his indecision. If he wanted a relationship, he'd have bitten her hand off for a date. Still, his concern about media intrusion was touching, and it showed that maybe there was something brewing. She wouldn't give up; their innings was just getting started.

In the evening, she watched the England vs. Netherlands match, cheering on the squad—especially her Scorpions teammates—while her hands noodled with the knitting.

Her bat sponsor had invited her to the factory to see a new model being produced, so that took up Tuesday. She got the full tour, culminating in the chance to put the grip on her new stick.

Back home, she pulled on her gloves and spent a few minutes getting a feel for the bat. This would put a spring in her step: a new, perfectly weighted tool for her trade.

She rummaged around in the kit room and dug out her "knocking-in" equipment, which was nothing more than a cricket ball in an old sock. She sat on the sofa, TV murmuring away, with the bat across her lap, tap-tapping the ball against the blade. Hours of this would be needed.

Oh, the glamorous, "celebrity" life, eh, Adam?

Wednesday was a fitness day. In the afternoon, she and captain Danica took the train to London for a photo shoot commitment for the club's kit sponsor.

She'd known Dani for over a decade and, early in their Scorpions life, they'd shared a house for two years. Then Dani had started dating Laila, a beach volleyball player, and moved out. By then, Ellie had picked up her first England contract, which allowed her to cover the mortgage alone.

When the shoot wrapped, they sought out a tapas bar, ate their fill and shared a bottle of very decent red. Dani was great company, though the conversation never strayed too far from cricket. Dani breathed the sport and undertook her captaincy duties with deadly seriousness. It was one of the reasons the Scorpions had lifted five trophies in the last seven years.

Dani had never reached the national squad, which was widely considered a massive injustice. In truth, it was an accident of overlapping fortunes: when Dani was in her best touch, others were slightly better. When there might have been a spot for her, she'd had a dip in form.

Like Ellie, all Dani could do was work on her own game. And hope.

On Thursday afternoon, Ellie went to the nail bar. Wear and tear had taken its toll on the Scorpions motif, and it wasn't suitable for the awards bash anyway.

Later, while tidying the house, she found Adam's Batgirl caricature on the dining table. Something in it caught her eye, so she pulled up a chair and inspected his work.

Wow. This guy is a master of detail and insight.

Secreted within the locks of her ponytail, which flourished with imagined movement, was a number. Two delicate curls of brown scribed a loose "20". Naturally, he knew her shirt number. Doubtful, however, that he understood the significance.

She pulled out her phone. Their WhatsApp's to date had been brief and polite. Adam was keeping a respectful distance—his silly perception that their relationship was a blip, an accident. Yet, it wasn't right to belittle it before she understood why he felt like this.

We all have our demons, our crosses.

Apart from this reserve, he was so genuine, so likeable. Easy to fall for. And this detail in the drawing made him more endearing.

She took a closeup picture of her cartoon hair, added the comment, "Very clever. Very sweet. Thank you," and pinged off the message.

His reply was a wink emoji.

Good. We're into emojis now. I hope he's softening.

Friday night wouldn't be as much fun if he was on eggshells.

Ellie's message brightened Adam's Thursday, which had been aggravated by a LinkedIn message from Pippa. He'd—stupidly, in hindsight—connected with her when they were dating.

The one-line note said she was talking to a lawyer about the "LIKE?" picture.

He laughed. Either this was a lie, a bluff, or she had finally lost the plot. He didn't dignify her message with a reply. Instead, he removed their connection, but not before nosing at her profile. She had a new role in addition to her *highly skilled* position at "Influencer". She was now a columnist at, of course, *ME & Tea*. It was extremely Pippa to work at a digital publication that was like the bastard love child of Instagram and Hello magazine.

In the app's Suggested Connections widget was Dean Harcourt, the magazine's editor. He was 1st Connection with Pippa. Adam's first, cruel thought was that she'd got the job by sleeping with Dean. Then he tempered that. Perhaps they were dating.

You poor sod, Dean.

Adam wondered if Dean knew of Pippa's sad little crusade. She should be careful that these insane accusations weren't noticed at the office. One small slip online could ruin her reputation. He dearly hoped that didn't happen. Not.

His emotional palate was cleansed by a text from Jez, who wished Adam luck at the awards and invited him to the pub for Sunday lunch "to drown his sorrows". Adam was about to reply, "Thanks for the vote of confidence", then recognised Jez's excellent judgement about his chances of winning.

But first, he had to get through the awards evening itself. He wasn't *afraid*. That would be silly. Yet, there were many questions.

In a room of people who weren't his contemporaries in achievement or business type, should he be relaxed or businesslike?

How would it feel not to win? How much to drink—none, a little, or just enough to loosen up?

What about being with Ellie—should he act reserved or chummy? What to say when people asked who she was? What if people recognised her? How would they react to someone of her status accompanying little nobody, Adam Glenn?

What to wear? Jacket? Tie? Aftershave—or might she think that was a come-on?

A million things played on his mind, all more relatable than the mad scenario in which he won the award and had to stand up in public and speak coherently and not fall off the stage in shock. Plus, Ellie would be there, embarrassed by watching this bag of nerves make an idiot of himself.

Then she'd *definitely* wish she hadn't offered to be his plus-one.

30th Over

A ll of this meant that Adam slept appallingly.

By six p.m. on Friday, he would much rather have gone to bed than had a night out. Still, it was an opportunity not to be missed, in many ways.

He'd dressed appropriately for his profession—a casual jacket, smart trousers, no tie, and a dab of aftershave. He'd spent ten minutes on the perfect shave and five more on his hair. There would be an event photographer, not counting all the phone cameras, and he didn't want to look like he'd been dragged through a hedge backwards.

The sound of the doorbell buoyed him and got blood pumping into the bags under his eyes. Still, he pinched himself for good measure.

Opening the front door, he was grateful for the pinching, because the vision on the doorstep shook his sense of reality.

He wanted to look around and ask, 'Yes, but where's Ellie?'

Except this *was* Ellie. He *had* seen her like this before, but only in little rectangles on his phone. Now, he'd fallen into the world where she went to friends' far-flung weddings, drank at a swanky New York cocktail bar, or met a musician backstage at The Brits. Plainly, Ellie did things other than play cricket. She wore clothes other than those used whilst whacking balls into the crowd.

But to see it in 3-D. On his doorstep. Ready to step out for the evening with *him*?

Surreal. Odd. Crazy.

In the most delightful way.

Immediately, he felt under-dressed. Also, the luckiest man alive. If someone asked who she was, he could say, "This is Ellie, and she works in Hollywood", and they would believe him. She belonged at a red carpet premiere.

The calf-length blue dress covered both shoulders and was cut to show negligible cleavage. It wasn't skin-tight but showed off her figure. She wore heels, possibly to help bridge the gap between her 5'6" and his 5'11". Her hair was down—a rarity, and softened her features. Her jewellery and makeup were restrained and classy. A small bag was slung over one shoulder.

She was eyeing him expectantly.

Was I staring?

'Hi, Adam.'

He moistened his mouth. 'Hi.'

'Everything okay?'

'Sure. Yes.' He'd hold the compliments until later... when he'd worked out what to say.

'Ready? Limo's waiting.'

His mouth formed an O. 'What? Ellie, I—'

She cocked a thumb and finger. 'Had you there. It's an Uber. I'm not *royalty*.'

'Oh. No. Of course.' He grabbed the house key from the hallway table and pulled the door closed.

The taxi lolled through the streets.

His mind blazed. Whatever happened with the actual award, he felt like a competition winner. A raffle: An Evening Out With Leading Cricketer Ellie Waites. Or he was a footman, riding to the Ball in Cinderella's coach. Prince Charming he was not.

He tried to balance looking at her, not looking at her, and trying not to make it too apparent that he was avoiding looking at her. It was difficult. She looked *beautiful*.

And, unless he was mistaken, every time he *did* glance at her, she was looking at him.

I mean, I scrub up okay, but we're only friends, Ellie.

Their eyes met.

'Too much?' she asked.

He smiled self-consciously. 'No. No. It's... great. Lovely. Just... feels like I'm *your* plus-one.'

She touched his arm. 'I've never been nominated for anything. Ever. So I *am* your plus-one. Okay?'

'Okay.'

'And you didn't specify dress code, so I threw this together. I mean, it's hardly the Batgirl outfit I missed out on wearing, but I'm supposed to be flying under the radar tonight, right?'

Looking how she did, no radar was going to be flown under. 'It's great that you came, so at least I'll know *one* person there. I hope it won't be too tedious for you.'

'No. It'll be good. Better if you win.'

He laughed. 'There's no way I'll win, Ellie. I googled the nominees. They are businesses. I'm only me, scratching oil onto a board.'

'I've seen your "scratching", Adam. It was... effing amazing.' Her eyes were gorgeous pools of support.

You don't get that from an Insta story. How much warmth and empathy she radiates.

'Thanks. But I'm pretty sure the winning criteria aren't the artistic merits of one painting of a retired sporting legend.'

She frowned. 'So how did you get nominated?'

'Search me. Secret benefactor?' He waved it away.

'Got a speech ready?'

'Now you're *really* grasping.' He gave a cheeky elbow nudge, which didn't connect with any part of her.

'Adam,' she said, a serious brow above upturned and attractively glossed lips. 'Always have something to say. At the... PCA awards, Bry didn't have a speech prepared. When she won Young Player, she was so flustered at the podium. Admittedly, in a quite adorable way.' The memory made her chuckle softly.

'Then I'll go with that approach.'

She tapped his hand. 'I'm sure you'll smash it. And I'll pap you.'

'Me? If there's anyone in this cab, or at the event, likely to get papped, it's you.'

She laughed. 'After being out for eight months? No. People want pictures of the... star players or the ones who look best in a bikini. I'm neither. But if I get asked, fine. Part of the job. Anyway, the official photographer will want the nominees and winners, not friends and family.'

He reckoned most of that was way off the mark. 'Okay. But I'm not planning to tag you in any pictures. Nobody needs to know you've done this for me.'

'Oh, Adam. But do *take* pictures, okay?' She bit her lip. 'And I won't tag you either. I'll say I'm... with a friend, okay?'

'Sorry. It's... you know.'

Her eyes widened. 'You think people will get the wrong idea?'

He shook his head. 'When they see you and me, they'll never in a million years believe we're dating. Let alone if they recognise you.'

She sighed. 'Okay. Look. I understand this is your first rodeo, awards-wise, but don't get hung up on the plus-one thing. Whatever happens, happens. I know this isn't a *date*, but we can't stop people from making stupid assumptions. Believe me, that's my *life*. "She must be gay". "Waites' form is shot".' Her eyes sparkled impishly. '"She's arrived in a limo". I don't intend to get drunk, make a pass, or create a scene. *Not* good if I get papped like that, I agree. This isn't Susie's barbie, and a room full of two hundred middle-aged white blokes isn't the same as karaoke with the girls. But this is great PR for you. Even being nominated is good, right?'

There was a lot to unpack in what she'd said, but no time. They had arrived at the venue.

'Yeah, absolutely,' he agreed.

For now, the first order of business was whether to open the taxi door for her.

31st Over

S he watched Adam hurry out of his seat, round the car, and open her door. A drop of love entered her heart.

They walked up to the conference centre. She wanted to loop her arm into his. She had no problem being seen, being associated with him. He'd dressed sharp yet casual, and his tidier-than-usual looks were spiking her hormones. He ticked so many boxes.

Even though this isn't a date, it doesn't mean I wouldn't welcome one.

She followed at his shoulder as they entered the main "Banqueting Hall". Cannes, it wasn't.

There were maybe thirty tables of ten seats, a small stage, a corner DJ booth, and a ton of spotlights and black drapes. Upbeat music played, overlaid by chatter and the chink of glasses.

Adam pointed. 'Let's have a look where we are.'

They went to the table plan, located their spot, then weaved between tables to number 20.

'Coincidence or auspicious?' she asked, cocking an eyebrow.

'If *you* were up for the award, I'd say auspicious.'

The seats were unallocated, so they picked two facing the stage. Another was occupied by a balding guy with a bow tie.

He looked up from his phone, stood and shook their hands. 'Terry.'

'Adam, Ellie,' Adam said.

Sensing they'd be quizzed—and not for the last time that evening—on who they were, where they worked, etc, she opted for a sharp exit.

'I'll get us drinks?' she suggested to Adam.

'Yeah. I'll come along, see what they have.' He nodded to Terry. 'See you in a bit.'

They carved a path towards the long bar, whose ornate frontage was largely obscured by thirsty attendees. While they waited to be served, she surveyed the growing crowd. She wasn't overdressed. In fact, she'd nailed it. Adam, too, though his body language remained tense. She hoped a drink would loosen him up.

He handed over her glass. She tried the mojito.

The barman makes a decent cocktail. It's going to be a good night.

Adam took a long slug of beer, willing it to have an anaesthetic effect on his ridiculous nerves.

Ellie and I have hung out before. In public, too. Yes, the dress, and yes, the occasion, but still. Be nervous about winning... or rather, losing, but not about being with her.

However, as they drifted around the room, he overheard,

'Isn't that the cricketer? What's her name? Ella someone?'

His immediate instinct was to take Ellie's elbow and guide her away to "safety".

'Oh, yes,' the person's colleague said. 'I've seen her on the TV. That... Hundred... thing. What award do you think she's here for?'

171

'And who's that with her?'

Adam's heart sank. This was precisely what he'd feared.

Ellie touched his arm. 'What?'

He'd slowed to a crawl, as if examining wreckage on the opposite carriageway. 'It's started already.'

'Leave it, Adam. I'm a big girl.'

With a hand on her waist, he turned their backs on the oglers. 'But you don't need the gossip.'

'Look, I won't worry if you don't. The problem is that you're the important person tonight, not me.'

'Which is exactly why I was... apprehensive.' He flashed a plaintive smile.

She guided him away. 'Comes with the territory. It'll be fine.' She sipped her drink. 'You want to mingle?'

There was no point in being a wallflower or a grouch. She'd get pissed off, and he'd regret it. There was a memory to be created, and thousands of people around the UK, the world, would kill to spend an evening in Ellie's company. The award was incidental. The room was full of potential clients, and this beautiful athlete was offering to be his wingwoman.

Whatever else happened, he'd already won.

'Sure,' he replied.

Ellie saw gazes track their progress as they walked back to the table. The room was pretty crowded now. She hung her bag over the chair then glanced at her watch. 7:14. Showtime was half past.

We need something to break the ice. Where's the Adam who joked with me at the gallery, looked after me that night, or crafted that brilliant cartoon?

'Do me a favour tonight?' she said. 'Follow my lead, okay? And if you need rescuing from Mr Tedious Financial Advisor or something, hold your drink in your left hand. It's what I do.'

'Okay. And if you need rescuing?'

A wicked thought appeared. 'Same. Unless he and I are like... *getting on...* in which case it's safe to assume that I've found his white-collar job much less important than his piercing eyes and sparkling conversation.'

Adam shifted on his feet. 'Right. Sure.'

'Relax. The only person I'm planning to go home with is you.' Before any redness could colour her cheeks, she added, 'Our separate homes, I mean.'

Unless you want to make me a better offer...

A sharp-suited, grey-haired man scuttled over like he was on a mission.

A light went on in Adam's face. 'Paul, good to see you.' He introduced Ellie as a friend, provenance unspecified.

Good. The icebreaker.

It transpired that Paul was behind the award nomination. Adam had supplied commissioned photography prints for the company's office refurbishment. He showed her an example from his phone reel: an autumn sunrise in the New Forest, a pony's breath caught in the air.

Wow, Adam. You are such a talent.

It was Adam's customer engagement, as much as his work, which impressed Paul enough to make the nomination. Ellie got an odd stab of pride.

Paul wished Adam well, then excused himself.

A woman, who'd been hovering nearby, tentatively approached. 'Excuse me. Are you... Ellie Waites?'

'Yes,' she said.

173

'Oh, my daughter loves you.'

'Thank you. Would she like an autograph? I assume she's not here.'

'No, she's only seven. That would be lovely.' The woman rifled in her handbag then gave up and scanned the area.

Ellie grabbed her bag and extracted a pen. She pulled over a napkin—it was nicely sturdy—and signed with practised skill.

'There you go.'

'Oh, thank you so much, Ellie. We hope to see you playing for England again soon.'

Ellie smiled. 'Me too!'

The woman nodded, then beetled away.

Adam coughed.

Ellie turned. 'You okay?'

'You carry a Sharpie? Really?'

'Yes, in case I meet someone famous. And I used a napkin when I met Ryan Reynolds.' She shot a knowing look.

His mouth closed on a comeback. 'Okay. Sorry.'

Over the speakers, the MC asked everyone to take their places.

Adam pulled out her chair.

She'd fancied Harry, and he'd never done that.

She'd *loved* Jack, and neither had he.

Remember how you told Adam you wouldn't get drunk and/or make a pass at him?

That.

32nd Over

Adam found the next two hours challenging. It was a buttock-clenching wait until the twelfth award of the night—his category—was announced. Helpfully, the meal's three courses were interspersed with the awards, so nobody got hungry or bored rigid. Throughout, Ellie championed him to the other diners, as well as offering plenty of supportive, calming looks.

There was no need to worry. He would merely have to applaud for yet another winner he'd never met. He wanted it to be over so he could relax. The dessert was a mouthwatering cheesecake, but his roiling stomach couldn't face it. He debated a stiff whisky instead.

The award category was announced. Noting Ellie cross her fingers, he painted on a smile.

The nominees were listed. Their logos appeared on the large screen behind the stage. Underneath the table, Adam wiped sweaty palms on his trousers.

The next three minutes were a blur.

He remembered only three things. Firstly, he didn't trip up or down the stage steps. Secondly, he succeeded in saying a few sentences without fainting. Thirdly, there was some mad woman in a blue dress, bouncing on her feet, clapping, and yelling, 'Woo, Adam!'

Then, when he returned to the table, this excitable—and gorgeous—woman pulled him into a clench. The feel of Ellie's arms, her unbridled support and friendship, the hint of her perfume—they all cut through his disbelief.

'Effing brilliant, Adam.' She pressed a cheek to his. 'Well done. Didn't I say?'

'I... I...' He sat down hard, face tingling with the sudden, shocking intimacy.

'Well done, mate.' Their neighbour gave a thumbs up.

'Yeah... I... Thanks.'

Ellie squeezed his shoulder. 'Adam Glenn. Winner.'

He fingered the small, pyramidal glass trophy. 'Yeah.'

And doubly a winner because you're here. And you just... with your cheek...

'Drink?' she asked, eyes wide in excitement.

'Absolutely,' he enthused.

Half an hour later, the formalities wrapped up. With a meal and three beers inside him, Adam felt extremely settled. Gently oiled. Nothing bad had happened. He'd won. Two people at the table had asked for his business card. If that wasn't surprising enough, his foresight to bring some was a major victory.

As he and Ellie prepared to circulate, another familiar face approached. Tony Wyatt ran Adam's go-to local design firm and had produced the "LIKE?" prints.

'Well done, Adam.' They shook hands.

'Thanks, Tony.'

'You never said you knew... Sorry, this is Ellie, right? From the cricket?'

'Yes. Ellie from cricket.' She winked at Adam.

Hell, her wink is the cutest thing.

'Right, yes, thought so. Missus is a fan of the women's game. Seen your face on the telly.' Tony patted Adam's back. 'I wasn't aware you kept such hallowed company.'

'Well... er...'

'Yes,' Ellie said. 'Old school friends. Nursery, actually.'

Tony's eyes widened. Almost as much as Adam's. 'Really?'

'Yeees,' Adam replied, feigning nonchalance, masking amused disbelief at how Ellie had dropped them in it. 'Lost touch on and off,' he lied. 'Then we met up at a match, what, ten years ago, Ells?'

I called her Ells! I never do that. Except when shouting encouragement at the TV, of course.

'Wow, yes. Time flies.'

'Whizzes by.' He shifted on his feet. 'So, thanks, Tony. I'll be in touch about any new projects. Excuse us, will you? Need to... take a leak.'

Tony glanced between them. 'Oh, right, sure. Well done again, and nice to meet you, Ellie. Missus *will* be jealous.'

'Thanks, Tony. Send her my regards.'

Adam scooped up his award and led Ellie away.

She sputtered a laugh. 'Oh, Christ, I'm sorry.'

He beamed, shaking his head, utterly enamoured of her moxie. 'I remember when you were yay high.' He held a palm to his waist.

'And you were yay high too!'

'Oh, happy days. I'll miss that nursery.'

She patted his shoulder. 'Come on, Best Creative Business.'

'Small Category,' he added.

'Let's get a drink. Quick, before the autograph hunters catch you.'

While Adam went to the loo, Ellie found a space at the bar. A paunched guy of about fifty waved her ahead. Was it the dress, genuine kindness, or that he recognised her?

As she leant on the bar, awaiting service, he did too, mirroring her. It wasn't leering, so she exchanged half-smiles, the kind reserved for situations of mutual hardship or shared experience. Queuing, especially. That most British of hobbies.

'So, love, what do you do?'

Here we go. 'I play cricket.'

'Oh, really? Local side?'

'Yes, we're based in town,' she replied, poker-faced.

He nodded, jowly. 'I see, I see. Are you a batsman or bowler?'

Ellie let the gender-inappropriate term slide. To some, the movement towards "batter" was controversial anyway.

'Batter.'

Best not to bore him with the whole "lapsed bowler" history. Yet, would I be in a better position if I'd become more of an all-rounder? Was that ever on the cards? Pointless to speculate.

'Good, good. What's your best score? I managed twenty-nine back in the day. Charity match, you know?'

'One thirty-seven.'

His eyes bulged. 'Wow. Good stuff. Maybe you should... er... give England a call, eh?'

She smiled earnestly. 'That's a fine idea. I'll see whether they can fit me in.'

'Who's next?' the barman asked.

Walking away a minute later, clutching the two drinks, she spied her "date" being ushered into an ante-room. She followed at a distance, then hovered in the doorway. Adam was marshalled against a logoed backdrop, and the official snapper took shots of him holding the award aloft.

Then, when the poor soul thought the ordeal was over, another guy moved Adam to one side, flicked on a lamp, and grabbed a mic.

She watched, understanding Adam's pain, as he endured a brief video interview.

Roll with it, mate. You need the PR.

Quickly, he was done and, shellshocked, wandered to the door. Seeing her, he winced, eye-rolling. Then, with gratitude verging on desperation, he took the drink.

She gestured to the trophy and held out her bag. 'Pop it in here. I promise not to flog it on eBay.'

That cheered him. 'You're too much, Ellie.'

'Well, without that in your hand, you can go back to being plain old Adam Glenn. You won't get papped anymore. And who was joking about that, huh? *You'll* be the one in the paper tomorrow. At least I can say I knew you before you were famous.'

He nudged her. 'That's not the same, and you know it.'

She patted his shoulder. 'You did well.'

'I was crap.'

This is one of the many attractive things about you, Adam. The unassuming humility.

She guided him into the main room. 'Here's a secret. I get nervous every time I walk out to bat. And I've been doing it for twenty years. Even worse with interviews and speeches. You did great. Honestly. Believe in yourself a bit more.' She got lost in his eyes, which shimmered with reflections of the disco lights. 'This could be the start of something for you.'

He chinked his glass against hers. 'Stranger things have happened.'

The DJ had cranked the noise up a notch, and she found herself swaying to the beat. Luckily, there was no dance floor, or she would *so* have been there. The drink, and the good time she was having with Adam, put her in the mood.

CHRISSIE HARRISON

Someone was making a beeline for them.

'Ooh, more groupies,' she said. 'Who for though, eh?'

Adam poked his tongue out.

'Ah,' said the avuncular guy with a food stain on his tie. 'I heard we had a local icon in the room.' He glanced at her cleavage. 'Bill Clay, Geoghan Associates. Ellie Waites, yes?'

'The same. Hello, Bill. This is my good friend, Adam.'

Bill nodded. 'Ah, yes. Won that award, right? Missed out ourselves. Never mind, next year, eh? So, didn't expect to see a sports star here. Is this... er...?' He waggled a finger between her and Adam.

'Not as such. Moral support. Repaying a debt, you could say,' she replied.

'A debt. I see.'

Keep it together.

'Yes. A few years ago, Adam saved my life. He caught me when I fell out of a rollercoaster.'

Myriad expressions jostled for position on Bill's face.

Adam coughed. '"Caught" is overselling it a bit, Ellie. I helped out when she tripped while disembarking.'

She rubbed his arm. 'But I could have fallen between the cars. That would have been a hospital visit. Concussion isn't nice.'

This is FUN.

'Good thing I was in time, though. Right?' Adam put a hand to her waist, drawing her closer.

A breath caught in her throat. 'Absolutely. So, Bill, tonight is by way of thanks. Very belated thanks. And how great to be here, with Adam winning. Deservedly so. Have you seen his work?'

'Er... no.' Bill glanced back and forth. Possibly not knowing what to believe.

'Is art your thing?' she asked. 'I only ask because Adam is so versatile, and a large part of why he won is the corporate installation you saw a couple of slides of. What does Geoghan Associates do?'

33rd Over

F ive minutes later, Adam exchanged business cards with Bill and said he looked forward to arranging a meeting. The evening was getting ridiculous, not counting Ellie's propensity for leg-pulling.

'Okay?' she asked expectantly.

'You talked him into that.'

She fluttered a hand. 'You make it sound so devious. I pointed out your strengths. Which are real.' She tapped her bag. 'As evidenced here.'

He held her gaze. 'You went into bat for me.'

'Um... that's kind of my *job*.'

'Still. Thanks.'

'No problem. If you spot the England selectors, feel free to talk me up.' She grinned.

'Will do.' He pointed towards the bar. 'I'm getting some water. You want one? Still? Sparkling?'

'I insist on nothing less than the finest Andean mountain spring water, bottled by monks...'

He jabbed her side playfully. 'You're a liability, Ellie. Back in a sec.'

It wasn't a second. It was ten minutes. The barman seemed to have a blindness for award winners.

Maybe I should have sent a noted professional athlete in a striking blue dress.

Ellie had moved away and now seemed uncomfortably pressed against a wall. Not physically restrained, but the guy chatting to her certainly had a strategic advantage.

Adam hurried his step. As he approached, she flashed an uncomfortable smile. It wasn't exactly a cry for help, but she wasn't having a whale of a time.

He sneaked into the larger of the gaps beside her. 'Here's your water.'

The guy jolted, perturbed. His demeanour didn't seem aggressive or predatory, but you don't back a woman against a wall.

She took the glass. 'Thanks, Adam.'

Think of something. What would Ellie do?

'Sorry to interrupt,' he said to the suited and serious bloke. 'Remember the time... Zara. We'd better get going.' He flashed an apology at the guy. 'Do excuse us. She has a flight to San Fran in the morning.'

'Very nice. On business?'

'No. Crew.'

Ellie's waist creased with a held laugh.

The guy's expression implied Adam had suggested that Hitler was misunderstood. 'What? You're having me on. But... but she's drunk. And she'll still be over the limit tomorrow. She can't fly a *plane*. This is an outrage! I'll report—'

Adam patted the man's shoulder. 'It's okay, mate, she's only cabin crew. Most of them are functioning alcoholics anyway.'

'But—'

'Come on, honey.' He steered her away, not daring to glance back at the potential debris his hand grenade had caused.

When they were at a safe distance, he shook the tension from his shoulders.

She hooted. 'Oh, hell, Adam. *Now* who's the liability?'

'Sorry. I assume you weren't about to give him your number or call a cab?'

She necked half the water. 'He was fine. But... thanks. Anyway, I do need the loo. And he wouldn't stop *talking*.'

'Well, without a cricket bat or a glass trophy to clock him with, an intervention seemed the next best thing.'

'Thanks.' She leant very close, her perfume tickling his nostrils. 'And... Zara?'

He shrugged. 'Rolling with it, like you said. I could see you as a pilot, actually. Not in that dress, obviously.'

'Hmm. Look, loos, okay? I'm not getting papped with a wet crotch.' And she hastened away.

Despite the blanket of music and chatter, all went quiet in his world. Silent and empty. Dull. Like the end of a match, when he began counting the days until he could see the team walk out again. After tonight, those days would seem even longer.

He checked his watch. 10:42. It felt later, due to his poor sleep, stress, and the massive crash following the endorphin rush of collecting the award.

Better take a whiz while there's time.

There was a queue at the gents. He pulled out his phone, wondering whether to post something on Instagram. At the top of his feed was Ellie's latest Story, a mirror selfie of her in the dress, taken at home. She was making a peace sign, and the overlaid text read, "Glammed up for an awards night". The comments, full of heart and flame emojis, were predominantly from other Scorpions. She'd stepped out of that world and into his.

And she'd lit it up like a firework.

'Mate?'

Adam jolted. Someone behind indicated that the queue had cleared.

'Sorry.' He pocketed the phone, took a leak, washed his hands and threw water on his face.

Drying with a paper towel, he looked in the mirror.

What a lucky sod. A lucky, tired sod who should have got water instead of that fourth beer.

Re-entering the banqueting hall, he spied Ellie in conversation with a younger, bearded guy. She pulled the trophy from her handbag, showed him, then looked around. Adam's gaze met hers, and he hurried over.

'Well done,' the guy, one of the other Creative nominees, said flatly.

'Thanks,' Adam replied.

'Thought it was our year. But fourth time unlucky. Still, all subjective, isn't it?' the sore loser snipped.

Adam was about to point out that the category was judged on many merits, not all of which were aesthetic, when Ellie intervened.

She took his hand. 'Come on, Mr Glenn. Remember, you only paid for me until eleven o'clock.'

The guy looked at Adam with a new level of distaste.

Adam went rigid, partially to avoid corpsing. 'Of course... Cindy.'

There was a glint in her eye. 'Any more than five minutes over, and I have to tell the agency.' She leant in, brushing his ear with the faintest kiss. 'And I was hoping we could take the *long* route home,' she drawled with deliberate innuendo, loud enough for the guy to hear.

Goosepimples erupted over every inch of Adam's skin.

'Honestly,' the four-time loser harrumphed.

Adam clamped his jaw shut as Ellie towed him away, checking over his shoulder at the dumbfounded soul.

Jealousy's an ugly thing, mate.

A moment later, Adam stopped on his heels to avoid crashing into someone.

'Hold on.' The man raised a camera. He was older, fully dressed in black.

Adam didn't have time to object. All he could do was hold up the trophy and fashion something resembling a smile.

The flash went, a supernova to Adam's tired pupils. He blinked.

'Cheers!' The guy hustled away.

Ellie broke their pose and, still holding his hand, resumed their walk. This new level of intimacy, of verging-on-romantic entanglement, threatened to expel the booze from his bloodstream, replacing it with ambrosia. He suddenly felt utterly alive.

Bursting out of the main doors into a chill night, they descended into tucks of laughter.

'Oh God, I think that third mojito was a mistake.' A nearby streetlight threw glitters into Ellie's eyes and bounced beams off the glass award.

He wheedled out his phone. 'Come on, Cinderella. Let's get you home.'

The music playing on the radio was terrible. They were headed for Adam's house—the taxi would drop him first and then go on to hers. All she could think about was what to do or say when they parted. The warm sensation in her stomach threatened to head south.

Adam seemed to be studiously ignoring her—or perhaps he was merely tipsy and tired, overwhelmed by the occasion, the award, and the shenanigans they'd got up to.

Who needs a dozen teammates to provide a good time when I've got one stellar, adorable bloke?

She reflected on the decision to almost kiss him. He'd taken it well.

What if I'd kissed him properly? What if I try later? Should I? Or does it risk spoiling the evening?

She decided to see how things panned out.

The swaying of the car was playing murder with Adam's heavy eyelids and dull skull. Ellie occasionally broke into contained titters, probably recalling their immature hi-jinks. He'd had a brilliant, unforgettable time. Now, he truly understood why the Scorpions—and others—loved her. He'd always found her cricket play to be admirable and inspiring, and her presence made him happy. Tonight, the full Ellie experience had been intoxicating.

She *had* been quite touchy. How should he react to the merest hint of a pass? He'd have to find the words to say he couldn't be with her like that... which hurt. Her life was too busy, too alien.

This was merely one magical evening. He was Cinderella, not her. Still, it was going to be hard to say goodbye.

His head dipped.

'Shit,' he murmured, quickly zipping his fly.

She turned, so he covered his manoeuvre with a shuffle.

'Thanks for tonight, Ellie,' he said in case she made a remark. 'And you said Rojo was the joker of the pack.'

She nudged him. 'I have a good knock, now and again.'

The taxi slowed and stopped. He'd already opened her door before remembering she wasn't due to get out. 'Sorry. Force of habit.'

'It's okay. Actually, sorry, can I quickly grab the loo at your place? Not sure I can hold on for another twenty minutes.'

'Oh. Sure.' Adam went to the driver. 'We'll be a few minutes, mate, so you go on. I'll call my friend another ride from here. Cheers.'

The driver tutted, nodded curtly, then drove away.

He led Ellie up to the house. It felt like a furnace inside, but that was due to his off-kilter senses.

He pointed her to the downstairs loo. 'This is a cliché, but... coffee?'

'Oh, that would be great,' she replied, closing the front door.

He went into the kitchen and switched on the kettle. His head spiked with something. He blinked, then located two mugs, milk and instant coffee.

Too late to make proper coffee.

She came into the lounge. 'Thanks. Lifesaver.'

'No worries.' He tossed his jacket on the armchair. 'Sugar?'

It was all so easy, so natural. Hanging with Ellie, a brilliant evening with a friend.

Then, at that second, as Adam was realising things were *not* too good to be true but actually *good*, reality hit him with a sledgehammer.

34th Over

A dam's body went momentarily rigid, then he sloughed to the carpet, spasming.

A squeal of shock burst from her. Then came action. She'd never sobered up faster in her life. There was no time to process the revelation. Seconds counted.

Holy shit.

She shoved the sofa away from him. Now, his left arm whacked only the carpet. Near his twitching feet was a chair that she rudely flipped onto its back. With shaking hands, she scooped up a cushion, fell to her knees, lifted his poor head and thrust the cushion underneath.

'Hey, Siri. Start a stopwatch.' Her watch complied.

She looked around, panting in shock. Her brow furrowed.

What else?

She scrutinised Adam's rolling face, checking his tongue didn't choke him. All four limbs bumped a crazy and heartbreaking dissonance on the carpet.

Her mind raced.

Breathe. I can do this.

She needed to channel Ellie the cricketer, that calmness at the crease. Don't panic. Find a solution, or accept things and move on. Whilst she couldn't control Adam—not even he could do that—she could manage the situation.

She snapped up her wrist: twenty seconds had passed.

Add ten for the delay in starting. What to do?

Patience. Patience and hope.

Ellie had to follow the protocol she'd researched after Paige died. She'd spent days learning about epilepsy and postictal—post-seizure—recovery, determined to be ready to help someone if the need arose.

She had failed Paige. She absolutely would not fail Adam.

Sitting on her haunches, the high heels dug into her backside. She pulled them off, cast them aside, and wiped perspiration from her heaving breastbone.

The watch said 0:33.

'Come on, Adam,' she whispered, desperate to squeeze his hand and beg him to come round, but knowing it was foolish to get close to his jerking body.

Why now? Why, after such a fun time, do we—does he—get this punishment?

She wiped a nascent tear from her eye.

Come on, mate. Come back. Don't do this to me.

0:47.

This is going to be a long night.

But she *would* get through it. She would do everything in her power to help him. But first, the seizure had to stop. If it went on too long, an ambulance would be needed. She crossed her fingers and begged. As it was, his short-term memory would be frazzled, and his limbs feel like painful sacks of lead.

Her watch read 1:03.

Her chest hitched. She ached to hold him, to crush out the demons that jabbed at his every nerve. But it was too hard to even look at him in pain, so she scanned the room and tried to assess the layout of the house. A plan formed.

Hearing the thumping of his limbs quieten, she returned her attention to his face. The episode was abating. A tornado of relief left her lungs.

He fell still. She clenched a celebratory fist.

1:17.

It could have been worse. He'd unwittingly bowled her a Yorker, but she'd kept it out. Besides, she couldn't berate him. He needed a nurse. Florence Nightingale in a £500 evening dress.

If only you'd done this at my place, mate, I could get changed. If only I'd asked about your wristband. If only I'd cared a bit more.

Would it have helped? Right here, right now?

No. Not even Batgirl can stop seizures.

Breathe. I'll work it out. I've got you, partner.

His head lolled over, eyes lazy.

She stroked his forehead. 'Adam?' A nondescript noise came from his throat. 'Adam?'

He tried to focus, licked his lips. His eyes flared. 'Ellie?'

She scooped his clammy hand into her lap, speaking softly. 'Adam. It's Ellie. Ellie Waites. You've had a seizure. Everything's okay. I'm here.'

His fingers twitched against hers.

She clasped tighter. 'I've got you, Adam.'

His gaze haphazardly explored the room. 'Home?'

'Yes. We're at your place. Do you know what day it is?'

His brow furrowed. 'Friday. Night?'

'Yes. Can you sit up?'

Absent of an answer, she manoeuvred behind him and deftly pulled his shoulders up. He oofed in pain. She used her torso as a prop, his back against her shoulder blade. She craned round to examine his face. Perspiration decked his brow.

You're a beautiful patient, Adam. But God, I wish you weren't a patient. Paige didn't deserve this. Neither do you.

But we are where we are.

'We were out?' he asked.

'Yes.' She pointed at the trophy on the dining table. 'Remember that?'

He frowned. 'What did you win for?'

She chuckled. 'No. *You* won.'

'I won?'

'You won. Then we came home. Here. And you had an episode. Which was... a shock, I'll say.'

Pain swamped his face. 'Fuck, it hurts.'

'I bet it does.' She stroked his shoulder. 'It'll go away.'

'How long?'

'Episode? About ninety seconds.'

'Hmm.' He slowly brought a hand to his forehead, like lifting a barbell. 'What an idiot.'

'Why?'

'Tired. Too much drink.'

'Really? I mean, I don't know your history— Look, no inquest.'

'What's that?' He pointed, his expression suddenly blank.

She smoothed his messed-up hair. 'The trophy you won. Earlier this evening. You've had a seizure, Adam. You have epilepsy, don't you?'

'Yeah. I'm parched.' He tried to bring his legs up, preparing to stand. 'Aargh!'

'We'll not have any of that. Take it easy. It's the weekend. I mean, it's night. And I bet you'll sleep like a baby.'

'Always. So, I'm good. You go.'

'Fuck that,' she chided. 'Sorry, but I'm doing the thinking. You're in no fit state.' She took a long, deep breath.

Just get through the next ball. Then the next over. Stay on strike. Don't let him face any deliveries.

'We're going to the sofa. Then I'll get you water.'

And a skip full of coffee for me. I need my wits.

From behind, she tucked both arms under his armpits, hugged tight, and then, with a groan of effort, hauled him up like a sack of potatoes. Upright, she released her clench, tugged his right arm around her shoulder, and eased his jelly legs into motion. He grunted in labour and discomfort.

If he'd been much heavier, she might have struggled. As it was, despite his rubber chicken impression, her innate fitness won out. They collapsed heavily to the sofa. She untangled their limbs and made him safe and comfortable. His face swam with pain and incomprehension, which tugged at her heart.

She knelt, rubbing a thumb on his knee. 'Adam. You know me, right?'

'Ellie. Of course. Why are you here?'

She gritted her teeth, smiling to mask it. No time to get snippy about his discombobulated mind. It might be hours before he made reliable memories again. He couldn't be trusted or left alone for a minute.

I'll be watching you like a bloody hawk.

'We've been out to an... event. Hopefully, you'll remember that we had a lot of fun. Or if not, I'll tell you. Later. We were here for about... three minutes? Then you had a seizure.'

'Certainly feels like it.' He lifted a leaden arm onto his stomach. 'I like your dress.'

It's like an albatross around my neck right now.

'Thanks. So, I'm staying here for... a while. I'll get your water, okay?'

'Okay.'

In the kitchen, which luckily offered an uninterrupted view of Adam's prone frame, she boiled the kettle for coffee and ran a glass of water. She sat beside him as he drank. He looked all out.

'Sorry,' he said.

'No apologies.'

He looked her up and down. 'I like your dress.'

'Thanks. Want anything to eat?'

'I need to sleep.' His lids were heavy.

'No shit. Gimme a second.'

Keeping one eye on him, she made half a cup of instant coffee, added milk, topped it up with cold water, and drained the mug in four gulps.

Definitely a good job I stopped at three mojitos.

'Adam? I'm taking you to your room. Can't have you rolling off the sofa. Wait there.' She jogged up the stairs as best she could in a clingy dress, scouted the layout, and trotted down again.

He was looking at the trophy, head cocked.

'That's the award you won,' she said. 'Before your seizure. Which was about five minutes ago.'

He nodded lazily.

'Now we're going upstairs,' she stated.

'Okay. Then get a cab. It's late. Isn't it?' With effort, he raised his watch.

'Don't worry about me. Award winners get the red carpet treatment, which means it's you and me against epilepsy and stairs.'

Grabbing his wrists, she pulled him upright, and he clutched onto her waist with surprising willingness and strength. His face, however, betrayed the struggle against crushing aches. The violence of the episode had wilted his nerves and muscles.

With his arm over her shoulder and her hand gripping his wrist like a vice, they hobbled to the foot of the stairs.

'Ellie?'

'Shush, Adam. Please.'

Up they went.

35th Over

He had no sense of time. It could have taken a minute or an hour to make that climb. He only knew two things. It hurt like hell, which was to be expected. And Ellie Waites was a rock, physically and empathically. An iron fist inside the softest, nicest velvet glove.

He wouldn't fight this. Being temporarily invalided was painful, frustrating and a little emasculating. It also demanded assistance. Even with his mind working on only one cylinder, he knew he was safe—provided he respected his limits.

They were nearly at the top. The bedroom was in view. Fragments of the evening swirled, disjointed, in his head.

'I never made your coffee,' he said.

'It's fine. Come on. Last step.' She hauled up his deadweight frame.

They shuffled along the landing. His arm muscles screamed. He focussed on something else; the smell of her cologne. The curve of her neck. The sparkle of her diamond stud earrings.

Ellie laid him on the bed. The relief was immense. And then—

'Whoah. I'm in bed.'

How did that happen?

Ellie took his hand. Inside, she cried a single tear. 'You've had a seizure, Adam. It's Friday night. We're at your house. Your episode lasted about ninety seconds. I don't think you're hurt. But you need to mend.'

He pulled at his shirt. 'So hot.'

You and me both, after climbing Everest.

She pushed her now less-than-salon-fresh hair into something more presentable. Not that he'd care—or remember. She certainly wouldn't tell him that she'd had it styled that morning... and not entirely for the cameras.

He tried to shift his body, groaning in pain.

'Stay still,' she said. 'Do you have painkillers?'

His arm raised limply towards the ensuite. 'Cabinet.'

She went into the bathroom, quickly found ibuprofen and paracetamol, filled the small glass that was there, and returned to him. He took the tablets, handed back the glass, and flopped down. He shook, a full-body shiver, then wiped sweat from his forehead.

Okay. This was coming.

She leant over, cupping his face. 'It's nearly midnight, Cinderella. Time to lose the ball gown.'

He stared hard, then frowned. '*You're* Cinderella.'

'Neither of us is. *Buttons* are the order of the day... night.'

There are better circumstances in which to remove a guy's clothes. Even Adam's. Or especially his. But needs must.

She unbuttoned his shirt, helped him sit up, pulled off the garment, and tossed it in the nearby wash basket.

'Ellie?'

She sat at his waist. 'Yeah?'

'What happens in Vegas? Right?' There was fear in his eyes.

She stroked his forehead. 'Look. You know I'm a little... *qualified*... to help with this.' She batted away the memory. 'At the start of tonight, I said, "Go with the flow", "Follow my lead". And we did. I had a blast.' She cocked her head. 'You won, remember? Best Creative Business, Small category.'

His focus went briefly distant. 'Yeah. And you cheered.' A faint smile appeared.

That's it. You're still in there, endearing as ever. You'll come back, over time.

'That was your first rodeo.' She spoke levelly, earnestly, compassionately. 'This is mine. But I've read the manual. I'm opting *in* to being here. So, this *all* stays in Vegas. Especially the part when we basically implied I was a hooker. And the fact your fly was undone for most of the ride home.'

His face flushed. 'Shit. Look—'

She held up a hand. 'No apology necessary. Besides, you might never remember, right?' She patted his leg. 'Sorry, postictal joke there. Too cruel.'

'Don't worry. I might not remember it.' His wink was weak.

She laughed, welcome levity. 'Okay, there are two rules. That's a win, right? When you crashed at mine, I had *six*. So, rule one, you rest and get well. Two, you let *me* handle all this. Oh, and three, it all stays in Vegas. The fact you farted on the way up the stairs. The fact *I* farted in the kitchen while you were on the sofa. The fact I've now seen you topless for a *second* time.'

'You're amazing. Batgirl.' His eyelids slid closed.

'That cartoon will *not* stay in Vegas. I'm going public with it. Because *you're* amazing.'

He jolted, looking around. He clasped his bare chest.

'Okay, okay,' she said, as if calming a startled mare. 'Friday night. You've had an episode. I'm here. And you're hot and tired, so I'm putting you to bed. And when you wake up, I'll remind you I helped. Believe me, almost-comatose men are *not* my vibe.' She pulled the duvet over his lower half. 'Now, unhook your trousers, and I'll help them off. The modesty blanket is in place.'

His expression was forlorn, pained, and then resigned. He worked at his waistband, then she fumbled underneath the cover and tugged his trousers down by the ankles. She dumped them in the wash basket.

She hoisted up the shoulders of her dress, which had slipped forward. Adam had a decent view if he chose, but he hadn't.

'Now, rest. And remember—if you can—I'm here. Shout if you need *anything*.'

'Thanks.' He made himself comfortable.

She perched on the other side of the bed. Then, when his eyes closed, she gingerly sat up against the headboard.

Within two minutes, his body relaxed into sleep.

She puffed out huge relief. She put her watch on the small bedside table. There was no point in worrying about the time; events would dictate their sleep/wake cycle. Touring through different time zones, nights out with the girls, and early starts for match days meant a late night was fine. She was out like a light, regardless of the hour.

And tonight? Would she be too tense with worry? Not for fear Adam could fall out of bed, only that he might be forgetful and disoriented, and unwittingly do something foolish.

So, when's the best time to grab sleep? Now? He'll need the toilet before long. That will be an interesting adventure if he's only partially mobile.

She dismissed it, eased off the bed with cat-like stealth, and went to the ensuite.

Time to survey the pitch.

She assessed the room's geography, rinsed her hands and face, and looked in the mirror.

I've been better. And worse.

Deep breath.

Remember, she told her reflection, *don't do this for Paige, you, or your guilt. Do it for Adam. Play the ball that's been bowled.*

She dimmed the bedroom light, crept downstairs, reviewed the fridge contents, and confirmed that the sofa wasn't a sofa bed. She couldn't sleep down here anyway: Adam would wake to find the place ostensibly empty, and without full recall of his episode.

She went to the kitchen, ran two pints of water, and returned upstairs. At the bedroom doorway, she watched for a while. He dozed, spread-eagle. Superman without his cape.

She put one glass on his side and the other on "hers".

The bed was large. So what if he accidentally brushed her body? If he realised, or if she told him he'd done it in his sleep, he'd be mortified.

And anyway, if we demanded full disclosure, I might have to tell him I hope to return to this room under better circumstances.

36th Over

After perching on the bed for a few minutes, she retrieved her phone from downstairs, something to keep her occupied. There was a TV in the bedroom, but turning it on would wake him.

Curious, she peeked into the adjoining room, which was full of junk, equipment and painting supplies. There was a single bed, but it was inaccessible.

Her jaw tensed as she eased open the door to the next room. What if this was Adam's horrible secret? Walls plastered with pictures of her; a shrine, a stalker's den?

She closed one eye and stepped gingerly inside.

Moonlight through a large picture window illuminated his artist's studio. Her muscles relaxed.

See, idiot. Adam is just Adam. A cricket fan. An Ellie fan. An artist, fresh with an award. A photographer. A nice guy. Handsome. Dashing... in a laid-back way. Fun, considerate, talented, and respectful of me. A wonderful man.

A person with epilepsy.

And my charge for a while.

She browsed the artwork hung on the walls. There was also a diary planner, with certain, familiar dates marked with an "S" in red felt tip. Other one-word scribbles presumably indicated work engagements. August 19th was annotated with "35" and a sad face emoji.

Should I surprise him with a present? A cure for epilepsy would go down well.

The adjacent room was his study. Tentatively, she fingered the light switch.

Nothing to see. Except...

Modestly framed team sheets hung on the wall. As she ran a finger over the last five years of her playing history, a smile on her lips, her mind created false memories—all the times she'd scribbled yet another signature for this once-nameless fan.

Adam.

What memories we created tonight.

The smile vanished.

If he remembers them.

She returned to the bedroom, keen to ditch the dress. She didn't want to sleep in it. She'd have to borrow some of Adam's clothes. Trousers were no good; he was inches bigger in every direction. A T-shirt would do; nicely baggy.

She gingerly opened a chest drawer. Socks.

The next drawer held boxer shorts. She took a pair.

The third contained T-shirts. She pulled one out. Its colour didn't matter. This wasn't a fashion show.

'Wha!' came a shout.

Startled, she turned. Adam was awake, his eyes on stalks.

His breath was quick. 'Ellie. What are you doing here?'

She sat on the bed. 'It's okay, it's okay.' She methodically recounted the last hour, stroking his hand as she did so.

Suddenly, he yanked up the duvet. 'Holy shit!' His eyes circled frantically. 'Did we... have we...?'

A laugh burst from her. 'No, Adam. We haven't. With you like this? Come on, give me some credit.'

His lips pursed. 'Yeah. Sorry.'

'I know you probably feel stiff all over, but not—'

'Whoa. TMI.' His torso spasmed. 'Oh no.'

'What?'

Anxiety flooded his face. He met her eye, apology in his tone. 'Busting for a wee.'

'Amazed you lasted this long. Come on.' She stood.

'But—'

'Don't fight me. You're postictal. I'm in charge. No ambulances on my watch.' She grabbed his wrists and helped him sit. 'I'm not ruining a good night because you're precious about being in your underwear.' She winked knowingly. '*Again.*'

He processed that. And something else, apparently. 'How did I get up here? Did you *carry* me?'

'It was a team effort.' She pointed. 'Toilet. Now. I'm not sure our friendship stretches to mopping urine off your floor. Or scrubbing it out of your carpet. Okay?' She shot a matronly glower.

'Did I leave my award? Did it smash? Was I holding it when—?'

She cupped his face, rubbing her thumb across his cheek. Her tone was mollifying. 'Everything is peachy, Adam. We're safe. I don't have a game tomorrow. I know you hurt like hell and don't want to be nursemaided, but it's happening. Now, team effort to the loo, okay?'

Fight left him. 'Okay.'

She hauled him up, and they walked side-by-side for the few steps to the ensuite.

'You sit down when this happens, don't you?' She'd find out later how often this happened. There would be a *lot* of getting-to-know-you.

'Yeah.'

He groaned as she guided him to reverse onto the toilet.

'One of us needs to pull your boxers down.' She shifted the bra strap back onto her shoulder. 'I'm guessing you'd prefer to do it while I'm outside, and suffer the pain rather than embarrassment?'

He looked up, doggy-eyed. 'Yeah.'

'Right. Count aloud to one hundred. I'll be six feet away.'

She stood outside the door, feeling damn awkward, as he did nursery school maths over the sound of his weeing. A growl of pain and a flush later, he called, 'Ready.'

She escorted him back to bed and made him drink the pint of water.

He relaxed. 'Sorry about all this.'

'Please stop the apologies. I just...' She picked a stray feather from the duvet, 'wish you'd told me.'

His head dipped. 'I didn't think... I didn't want to worry you. It's pretty rare.'

She lifted his chin. 'All fine now. I'm here. And I won't leave until you're well. Sound familiar?'

'Sofa exchange programme.' A wry smile.

No point in saying I'll be right here on this bed. Don't want an argument.

'Something like that.'

Five minutes later, he was asleep.

She turned off the room light, leaving the ensuite door ajar for indirect illumination. Then she quietly arranged a pillow and laid down. How odd was it to be in—no, on—the bed of a guy she'd only known for a few weeks and wasn't dating? It was only the revelation of a shared demon, epilepsy, that had catapulted them together.

Would his seizure have happened anyway if I hadn't been at the awards? What if I caused his elevated levels of fun, stress, and drinking? Or would he have had the episode alone and been more at risk?

It was what it was, regardless of whether she was unwittingly responsible. She appreciated his situation. True, she didn't know what it was like to have your body wracked with uncontrollable violence for a minute and a half, though the first few weeks after her injury were a mess of pain, reduced mobility, enforced sofa surfing, indolence, regret and frustration. She had to move around *so* gingerly, listen to her body, and lean on other people—physically, mentally and emotionally.

For many reasons, she wanted to truly be there for Adam.

Ellie's eyelids fluttered open. Her watch read 06:44.

The heat had woken her: she hadn't intended to fall asleep, and the dishevelled dress had made her clammy. She'd also forgotten to remove her makeup. Panda eyes were a possibility.

Adam was dead to the world. She watched him sleep. It was hard to look away; a magnetism had developed. She wanted to know more about him. Everything. Why he painted, why he was a fan, his favourite meal, his taste in music, how long ago he'd removed the earring that created a tell-tale scar on his left ear, whether it meant he used to be a tearaway, whether he also liked deep, lazy bubble baths, whether he'd ever consider joining her for one...

Wake up, Ells. Play this innings, not a future one.

She rolled gently off the bed, entered the ensuite and closed the door. She tried the lock. It was faulty.

Shit.

She fingered her itchy scalp and inspected her face in the mirror.

I look like a bag lady. Probably smell like one, too.

If the lock got stuck while she was inside, he'd be marooned. If he cried out, forgetful and spooked, she wouldn't be able to get to him quickly.

The alternative was unfortunate but preferable. Besides, he was asleep, slow on his feet, and would hear the water anyway.

She glanced nervously at the door, then stripped.

37th Over

A dam woke with a start. His limbs were heavy against the damp mattress.

He raised a hand to his face. The aches were ebbing. He scoured his short-term memory for some highlights: the awards, the seizure, Ellie being there. The timeline was fractured, but glints of light through curtain gaps announced it was morning.

Thirsty, he necked the glass of water Ellie had presumably left.

She's probably kipping on the sofa. Or she went home?

He concentrated, willing frayed mental connections to deliver an answer. It wasn't there. So, corralling tired muscles into action, he hobbled to the ensuite. A revitalising bath always aided recovery.

He eased open the door.

'Fuck!' Quaking, he tugged it closed.

'Shit!' yelped the strange woman.

He reversed, chest pounding, and toppled onto the bed. 'Fuck. Fuck.'

The woman had been in the shower. Naked. And the woman was Ellie.

Panting, crucified by embarrassment and shame, he put his head between his knees.

Hearing the door, Ellie had half-turned. Her hand was on the tap, a moment away from welcome hot water.

She flattened herself against the wall, heart racing. Adam vanished.

'Shit, shit, shit,' she chastised.

Jittery, she stepped from the cubicle, grabbed his towelling robe from a hook on the back of the door, and pulled it on.

Breathe. It's not about me.

In the bedroom, she knelt at his feet. 'Adam. Adam.'

He was shaking his head, eyes closed, cheeks red as a beetroot.

She lifted his chin. 'Adam. Chill. It's okay. Easy mistake.'

He swallowed hard. 'But...' He turned away.

She sat on the bed. 'Look, mate, accidents happen. Like episodes. No harm done. I was in the shower. Fine. I'm the one who didn't lock the door.'

No point in explaining.

His voice wobbled. 'Oh, God. I'm sorry, Ellie. I thought you were downstairs, or gone, or—'

'Hey. I stayed, and I *will* stay.' Deep breath. 'So, you remember who I am and what happened?'

He grimaced. 'Yeah.'

'Good. How many fingers?' Her mouth creased into a smile.

'Three. Or two if you're one of those pedants about the thumb.'

She patted his bare shoulder. 'That's my guy. How do you feel?'

He frowned, as if doing a systems check. 'Less shit.'

'Good. So, did you want the loo? Breakfast?'

'Shower. But... you go ahead. Ladies first.'

She angled her head. 'Are you sure? You'll remember this time...
that I'm there?'

He looked away. 'Shit. Look, Ellie, I'm so sorry.'

'I already said no biggie.'

'But...' He put his head in his hands.

'Okay, now you're getting ridiculous.'

His eyes flared. 'Well, what do you want me to say? "Fine, Ellie,
please do it again"? Like all this has been some... grand plan, and I
spend hundreds of hours on the boundary visualising you naked.'
His lip curled in self-loathing.

*Well, I hope it's guilt and not revulsion. I'm no supermodel, but I've
never had any complaints.*

'Hell *no*, Adam, I do *not* think that about you. You are
unbelievably supportive and genuine. For Christ's sake, I invited you
into my house not two weeks ago! And I took a shower. And did I
stand there worrying you'd be trying to peer through the keyhole?
No. So this was an accident. An unfortunate side effect of another
accident, your seizure. Okay?' She put an arm around him, voice
falling soft. 'Please drop it. I don't want us to fall out.'

He nodded limply. 'Okay.'

'Good. So you stay here, lie down, and I'll try again.' She stood.
'For safety, I'll sing. A... permanent warning system. You know,
"Woman In Shower".'

'Um... Sure.' He moved under the covers.

'Any requests?'

He looked at her like she was one ball short of an over—which was
excusable.

Then he beamed. 'You know "Bat Out Of Hell"?'

'Oh yeah. Kat and I love that one.' She raised a finger. 'Rest up, and
I'll try to leave you some hot water.'

Ellie had a good voice. Not on a par with her cricketing talent or generosity of spirit, but it was no hardship to listen to her over the sound of the spray.

It was only soured by those few neurons in his brain, the primal instinct which kept sparking, trying to seed into memory, hoping to hold onto that split-second view of her.

He didn't want that memory. It would ruin what they had. Walking in on her naked was bad enough, especially after everything she had done and was doing for him. He clenched stiff fists, cursing his epilepsy for this. And drinking too much. And being stressed about the event and how her presence might backfire. And losing sleep worrying.

Why the hell couldn't he chill out? Things were great between them.

The bathroom door clicked open, startling him from the daydream of self-criticism. Dressed in his robe, towel over her hair, she tossed her old clothes into a corner of the room.

Her head cocked. 'Are you okay?'

'Yeah. And grateful. The awards, the helping me upstairs, the awful night you probably had on the sofa—'

'I didn't sleep on the sofa.'

His mouth hung open. He looked at the empty space beside him. 'Ah.'

She sat on the bed, drawing the robe across the V of her breastbone. 'You don't snore, which is a bonus. And you don't sleepwalk or sleep talk.' She looked him straight. 'And you didn't lay a finger on me. And I didn't lay a finger on you. Got that?'

He sighed. 'Yeah.'

'Do you remember the Vegas thing? Is that in there?' She tapped his forehead.

'It is.'

'Good. The shower... snafu... is peak Vegas. Especially as I looked shit and smelled worse. Now, your turn.' She thumbed at the ensuite. 'I'm guessing you'll take a bath. No need to stand up. Less risk.'

That was his postictal M.O. 'Yeah.'

'On a scale of one to ten, how's the pain?'

'Maybe five.'

'Fine. But don't take anything for granted. I'll run it and help you get in. Pants still on, please. I'm not sure we're at the *mutual* nudity part of our relationship yet.' She waggled her eyebrows. 'I'll stay out here and get dressed. We'll chat. *Constantly*. So I know you're okay. Then, somehow, you'll get out, dry off, and we'll rustle up breakfast? Plan?'

'Yeah.' He squeezed above her knee. 'You're a real diamond, Ellie.'

She winked. 'I know.'

Not feeling *too* undressed in his T-shirt and boxers, she sat outside the bathroom. The door was open a crack.

They chatted about how she'd got into cricket, how he'd become a fan. It took her back to England's 2017 World Cup Final win, the first women's match he'd seen, the day she—and the sport—really entered his consciousness. She revealed her dream to play a Test match at Lord's, and how circumstances now made that possible. His excitement, belief and support gave her warm flushes.

They discussed parents and how both sets worried about their kids' potentially hand-to-mouth careers. Adam was an only child, and his folks had moved to Ayr to look after his paternal grandparents; Dad's lineage was Scottish. They spoke occasionally: the trip north wasn't something to undertake lightly. It made Ellie self-conscious about her infrequent visits to Bristol.

They exchanged horror stories about exes; both had rebounded unwisely. The way Pippa dumped Adam was ridiculous, and undoubtedly, he was better off without the spiteful bimbo. Now Ellie understood his initial reservations about dating "a celebrity", but he seemed over the silly fangirling now. Much as she'd happily go out with Adam, a relationship would only work if he embraced their different circumstances.

However, it was tough seeing him like this. Would she be able to stop worrying he was okay, 24/7? She'd have to, in order to keep her game face on and perform well on the pitch.

Let it go, Ells. Focus on getting him through today.

Ages later, he hauled himself out of the bath and started to dry. She grabbed a pair of boxers from the drawer and went to the doorway.

'Incoming!' Gaze averted, she lobbed them blindly through the gap.

There was a gentle splash. He laughed. 'Bad shot.'

She sniggered. 'Spooned that to Short Mid-wicket. Hold on.'

She located another pair, which, interestingly, had a golf motif. This throw was less aggressive.

'Thanks,' he called.

She jogged downstairs, refilled the water glasses, and returned. He was perched on the bed, hair wet, fresher... and more of an Adonis than ever.

He indicated her discarded eveningwear. 'You wore your lucky pants. Lucky *game* pants.'

Her cheeks coloured. 'So?'

'A coincidence? Or you're as bad at laundry as me?' He pointed at the overflowing basket.

'No. I hoped it would bring you luck. And it did. You won.'

He flopped backwards. 'I don't feel very lucky. The seizure, I mean. Of course, I'm lucky to have someone here.' His brow furrowed. 'And you have much better things to do.'

'Right now, Adam, I *want* to be here. You chill. Mend yourself. I'll make some coffee and toast.'

Heading to the kitchen, she checked the time. 08:22. Ideally, she'd be home that afternoon, allowing time for fitness work ahead of tomorrow's game. But that wasn't the immediate priority.

She made the impromptu and none-too-healthy breakfast, located a tray, and returned upstairs. Taking one step into the bedroom, she froze. He was asleep, sprawled like a corpse.

Thank heavens I lobbed him those boxers. If he'd crashed out while towelling, it might have been one-all in the accidental nudity column.

Which would be fair. And not unpleasant.

She shook it off and went into his studio. She strolled the room, eating both their slices of toast, now able to admire the art and photos in daylight. The Jimmy portrait, sadly unsold, stood in one corner.

Despite being an enthusiastic social media user, seeing herself in pictures or TV interview playback triggered a self-consciousness about her appearance. Not her physique—it was fine, fitted the job, and she had control over it. Her face she was less comfortable with, so the prospect of Adam doing a three-foot-high painting was a little scary, notwithstanding his talent and how much the Batgirl cartoon had delighted her.

But then, every girl, every woman on the planet, wishes she was prettier, right?

Sipping coffee, she wandered to a desk scattered with photographs and preliminary pencil sketches of her. One sheet had a bulleted list: passion, drive, making a mark, teamwork, dedication, talent, overcoming injury, loss.

Her shoulders fell. Words like "beauty" or "femininity" were conspicuously absent.

That's why he hasn't made a pass. That's why the shower snafu put a sour taste in his mouth. I'm not his type.

She frowned.

Alternatively, because he talked about how shallow and fake Pippa is, he's over the whole "beauty" thing. Maybe, next time, he's more interested in character. So perhaps I have a chance.

She went to the bedroom, quietly put the empty toast plate on top of his mug to keep the coffee warm, and stood for a moment, watching him breathe, willing his pain to ebb.

An ache twinged in her shoulder—possibly from lugging a tall, dark, handsome guy up a flight of stairs—so she lay down on the carpet and did a few minutes of stretches and yoga poses.

Then, nicely loosened, she eased onto the bed and pulled a pillow up behind her. Soon, she was lost in her phone, reposting and commenting, supporting teammates and friends, trying to shut out the bubbling feelings about the man asleep beside her.

In bed with me.

Kind of.

38th Over

Adam's waking was gentle, normal... until he spotted the other person in the bed.

Shit. What the...?

Heart racing, his hand went to his groin, but the duvet concealed it.

Ellie raised a mollifying palm. 'I covered you up. I'm not into ogling bedridden men.' She eye-rolled. 'Oh, and morning. Again. You up to speed? Remember what happened? Who I am?'

He massaged his stubbled face. Things were freewheeling along nicely in his head, though his arms remained tender. 'Ellie Waites. Shirt 20. We went to the awards. I won.' He frowned. 'I told some guy you were an alcoholic stewardess.'

'You did. Bloody hilarious.'

He coughed. 'Right. Then I had an episode... and you stayed. And it's morning.'

'Tick, tick, tick. Seems like you're back in the game. Which is a massive relief.' She pointed at the side table. 'Have a coffee and take your tablet.'

'You brought my AED?'

She's done it again. Been even more amazing than before.

'One seizure on my watch is quite enough. Sorry for rifling through your cupboards. And do you take sugar?'

He didn't want her to run yet another errand. 'I'm fine.'

'And I borrowed your clothes.' She gestured down her body. 'Unless you want them back...'

A rabbit in the headlights, and with his underwear stirring, he poked her in the ribs. 'One flash is enough, thank you. The escort agency thing was a joke, remember?'

She laughed. 'You're *so* easy to tease.'

'Yeah, thanks, mock the chronically ill in their hour of need.'

She poked him back. 'Your hour of need is over, Cinderella. Fairy godmother here got you home safe. And I slept fine, thanks for asking.'

'Well, I tried extra hard not to snore or steal the covers.'

'Always the gent.'

He bowed in mock deference. 'Anything for you, godmother dear.'

She shook her head in amused disbelief. 'Then take your tablet.'

He did as told. The bedside clock said 10:19. The TV was on, its picture paused.

'And now you're sitting here, watching TV, like some... guardian angel?'

She shrugged. 'It's comfy, I don't need the sound on, and I didn't want you to wake up alone.'

His insides melted. 'You're the best, Ellie.'

'Yeah. I am. Oh, and I borrowed your phone charger. Hope that's okay.'

He grinned. 'It's all "take, take, take" with you cricketers, isn't it?'
She elbowed him.

He pointed at the TV. 'Don't mind me.' His stomach gurgled.

'Sorry, I ate your toast. Want some?'

'Please.'

'It's all "take, take, take" with you epileptics, isn't it?'

He elbowed her.

She disappeared, returning with the best toast he'd ever tasted.
Partly due to hunger. Partly due to its perfect buttery presentation.
Partly due to his mental and physical condition. Also, a little, because
it had been prepared by Ellie Waites.

My amazing friend. My plus-one. Guardian angel.

Angel, full stop.

The TV was playing highlights of yesterday's England game
against the Netherlands. Next came a tour of South Africa, then The
Hundred in August.

Ellie puffed a derisive breath. England had lost a cheap wicket.

He glanced over.

'What?' she asked.

'Rah-rah-rah for the home team?'

'Absolutely. But, come on.' She pointed. 'Torrers is a talent, sure,
but maybe not yet.'

Adam waggled his head. Beth "Torrers" Torrington was 18 and
making her England debut. 'It was a good delivery.'

'It was a rank ordinary delivery. Sorry, but they should have waited
a year.'

'The selectors?' He drained his coffee.

'Yeah. I mean, she's had a good domestic spell, but her play's too…
immature. Look, a half-decent off-break, and she's skittled.' Ellie
wrinkled her pretty nose.

'Harsh.'

'Nah. Certainly, she shouldn't be at three. I'd have her at... six or seven.'

'Hmm. Maybe. And put who at the top of the order instead?'

She did one of those mock frowns. 'Well, I'm biased... but... me.'

'Seconded.'

'Cheers.'

They watched the next batter walk in. Ellie rapped her thigh. 'Come on, Smithy!'

How ridiculous this all is.

Pippa had begged him to put a TV in the bedroom so they could snuggle while watching. Before long, she was making him sit through crap like Made In Chelsea and talk about which people had had Botox.

Now, I'm discussing cricket with one of the finest players of her generation. And all I had to do was lose control of my entire body for a couple of minutes. Win.

She brought both knees up, hugging them. The T-shirt, which was baggy to well below her waist, rode up, exposing a lot of *very* upper thigh.

Cripes, Ellie. You have great legs. Sun-kissed, toned, feminine.

Something caught his eye.

'Oh.' She chuckled. 'Yeah.'

'Sorry.'

'It's okay.' She pulled up the hem of his boxers... quite a long way. 'Only *special* friends get to see this. Like it?'

The tattoo, about an inch long, was of a scorpion. Naturally.

The whole vicinity is delightful.

He swallowed hard. 'Definitely. Did it... hurt?'

'What do you think?'

'Knowing you, not a flinch.'

'Mate, it hurt like a bastard.' She chuckled. 'Way to lose a fan, right? Ruin my reputation.'

Ellie Waites could never sully her character, especially after the last eighteen hours. 'Not at all. Is this a buddy thing, like the nails?'

'That's... need to know. A few of the girls have them, and no, I won't tell you who or where. They're like my family, and I don't talk behind their backs.'

'Vegas,' he inferred.

'Vegas.'

That was fine. He didn't care about the others. That they were great players and nice people was sufficient. Still, he'd discovered a little more about his favourite.

It made him sober. 'I'm sorry I didn't warn you about my condition.'

'I did wonder what the wristband was for. But I understand. You get on with your life. Better than living as a hermit. You... play forward.'

That amused him. She'd likened his approach to playing an attacking stroke, rather than being defensive, staying back in the crease. Yet, arguably, he was sometimes over-cautious. There *wasn't* anything preventing him from flying again—only the memory of a bad experience.

'I... try not to worry about it. My job is home-based, so I'm usually on safe ground. I needed a career that kept me out of danger as much as possible.'

'I think you chose well.'

'And I picked the right plus-one for the awards. Though I'm not sure I can ever repay this debt.'

She shifted to face him, sitting across one leg. 'You don't owe me anything. Actually, it's done me good.'

'Ah. You needed a bad night's sleep, a First Aid crash course, and the shower from hell?' He raised a palm. 'Sorry. Gallows humour.'

She shot him mock daggers, then gathered herself. 'Paige. You know it's about Paige.'

'I'm not prying, Ells. Reading a Wiki isn't the same—'

She took his hand. 'My sister died in a car crash, you know that. She had undiagnosed epilepsy, yeah? It was her first episode. Shittiest time for it to happen.' Ellie scrunched and released her hair. 'On her birthday. Twentieth birthday.' Her eyebrows pinched. 'So, that's why my shirt number.'

'Shit,' he breathed, squeezing her hand.

She interlaced their fingers, a friend needing support. 'I should have been in the car. I'd said I'd drive us to her party. But I was late home from practice.' She shook her head. 'Too busy yakking with the team.' Her lip trembled. 'By the time I got to the hospital, she was already...' Tears dripped down her cheeks.

Powerless to resist, Adam pulled her head onto his shoulder. His mind whorled. He brushed moisture from his eye. 'God, Ells.'

She sniffed. 'I never told anyone it was my fault.'

'It was *not* your fault,' he whispered. 'If that shot against Mary was misjudged, then believing you're responsible for your sister's accident is frankly idiotic.'

'So is crying. Strong women don't *cry*. Athletes aren't supposed to *cry*.' She sniffled. 'Here we are, trying to prove—proving—that women have as much right to play sport, play cricket, as men. At the highest level. That we're not weak, flighty little things. And now this.' She scrunched the duvet in frustration.

He wiped a tear from her cheek. 'For an amazing person, you talk such crap sometimes. It's silly to hold in all this ridiculous guilt. You *should* let it out. Maybe you can move on.' He gestured around. 'I get that all of this has touched a nerve. I can't imagine what it's like to lose a sibling.'

She met his gaze. 'I can't imagine what it's like to have a seizure.'

'It's not a lot of fun.' He forced a smile. 'But the aftercare makes up for it.'

She shook her head. 'I'm paying back, that's all. Selfishly trying to undo a mistake. All this time, I've been wishing it was *Paige* I was helping. That you were her, that I was there for *her* seizure, that it didn't happen in the car. I wished so hard I was here with her, not you.' She slapped her leg. 'And it's so cruel and wrong and disrespectful.'

She flounced off the bed and swept up her discarded clothes. 'I'm nothing to look up to, Adam. I'm a terrible friend to you. I should go.'

He scrambled up as fast as his limbs would allow and caught her before she'd moped to the door. From behind, he laid restraining hands on her toned shoulders.

'It's okay to feel like that, Ells. You being here is... immense.'

Her head fell. 'And now I was about to walk out on you.'

'Then, okay. I'm fine.'

She put a hand on his. 'No. I can't take the chance. It would kill me if you had a... blip. If you fell down the stairs.'

'Then, okay, stay.'

She pulled his arms across her chest, a big spoon to her little spoon. The outline of her breasts pressed against his forearms. His heart thumped.

'Be what you want and need,' he said. 'Safe space. Ignore the cricket, the spectacle, the joy I get from it. Ignore your talent, your three hundred and seventeen innings, and your crazy lucky pants. I have this... burden, and when I discovered you shared it too, in some way, I felt a connection.' He shook his head vehemently. 'Sorry. That sounds like I follow you because your sister died, which would make *me* this terrible person—'

'Whoah, whoah. Time out. I believe you do everything for the right reason.' She lifted his hands and faced him. 'Spending a small fortune coming to games. Cheering us on. Sticking with me while I was laid up injured. Let alone the concussion thing and letting me gatecrash your awards. If there were more people like you, Adam, the world would be a better place.'

Electricity surged through him. 'Thanks.'

Their eyes locked.

Don't kiss me, Ells, and I won't kiss you.

39th Over

She decided not to kiss him. Looking into his eyes, full of empathy and appreciation, and having felt his arms around her, it was so tempting.

Like trying to hit Mary Kallis' bouncer for 6.

And look how that turned out.

This wasn't the time or place. Plus, he plainly didn't fancy her, despite how she looked in his clothes.

I mean, he can see my legs to waaay up, and they're my best feature. Well, and my late cut through Gully for 4.

She paused for one more second, moistening her lips, waiting for his.

They didn't arrive. And the moment passed.

'Right,' she announced. 'Coffee and toast may be a "Cures all ills" thing, but it's no breakfast. Especially for a woman who's allegedly an elite physical specimen. So, get dressed, and we'll eat.'

While he forced tired muscles into clothes, she jogged downstairs, found an empty plastic bag under the sink, stuffed her dirties inside and left it by the front door. Then, she escorted him from the bedroom to the sofa. As he sunk into it, her phone rang.

It was Kat, with two pieces of news, neither of which was palatable. Fortunately, it meant no searching questions about what had happened overnight.

She hung up and slapped the phone on the table.

'What?' Adam asked.

To catch her temper before it exploded, she gave him a timeout signal, went to the kitchen and devoured a banana.

Unbelievable. Un-be-lievable.

Simmering, she sat beside him and swept up her phone. She clicked on the link Kat had sent, then showed him the screen.

The article in *ME & Tea*, written overnight, was about the awards... kind of. Underneath a photo of them, Adam holding his award aloft, was the headline, "Who's The Winner Here?".

As she read aloud the lazy, sensationalist "journalism", bile tickled her windpipe.

"Former England cricketer Ellie Waites attended the Kent Business Awards last night with a new partner. Mystery man Adam is the first to be seen on Ellie's arm since her high-profile split with fellow pro Harry Owens. Looking stunning in a risqué blue dress, Waites seemed to enjoy the evening and definitely had the attention of her beau."

She sprung up, throwing her hands in the air. 'Aargh! Where to start?'

'Ellie—' Adam said, aiming to placate her.

Read the room, mate.

She paced. 'First, what's this bullshit about a "risqué" dress? Jesus, the barmaid's skirt was shorter. My "split" with Harry wasn't "high profile"! It was a relationship between two people, which stopped because he was a cock. It's only high profile when the gutter press bang on about it because they think it counts as "news".'

She puffed out anger, shaking her head.

Un-be-fucking-lievable.

'Film me playing, fine. Interview me about the game, my career. Hell, you can even ask about Paige. But love is private. Stop bloody muck-raking.'

'Amen,' Adam said.

'And what's worse? This whole article is about *me*. I'm the *plus-one*! I'm not the *story*. The awards are about you... and the other winners. Why can't people stop gossiping, assuming? They basically said you're my new bloke.' She whacked the dining table. 'Fucking presumptuous, inflammatory bullshit.'

Not that I don't wish we were together, but that's not the point.

'This is what I was worried about,' he muttered.

She thumped down beside him. He wasn't helping, the poor sod. 'But you can't protect me from that. Nobody can, friend, relative, boyfriend, whatever. I don't like some of it, but it's part of life. If I hated the limelight, I'd quit cricket. But I can't. Cricket is who I am.'

'All the same, millions of people know you.'

'Millions? Thousands of people know *of* me. Come on, they don't *know* me. Not like you do. I'm a face, a player, a shirt number. I have a job. We're *regular* people who breathe and eat and shit. So we get mentioned online? That doesn't make us better, cleverer, more successful, or... less attainable.' She took a deep breath. 'The problem here is not that I went out, or went with you. It's that I was probably the least bloody important person there, but some bottom feeder wants to fill his column inches with low-hanging fruit.'

She slumped back on the chair.

And... hang on...

She snatched up the phone. Teeth clenched, she held the screen to Adam's face. 'And read this, mate. "Former England cricketer". "Former"? "Former"!' She snarled. 'I'll fucking show them.'

Adam didn't reply. He went to the kitchen and loaded the dishwasher. He had to give her space, behave as if she'd lost her wicket to an appalling LBW decision.

The disaster, like his seizure, couldn't be undone. They could only move on and hope there was no lasting damage, especially to her reputation. He could spend hours feeling guilty for taking her to the awards, but one stupid article didn't negate the fact that they'd had a bloody good time. Hell, even the night here had been fun... in a shredded nerves, faulty memory, sore muscles kind of way.

Ellie Waites *was* a regular person. A startlingly giving, open and delightful one. Yet the world focused on the image, the headline fodder.

Unbelievable.

If she wasn't who she was, and they were dating, there would be no story. As it was, they were only friends, and anything more was ridiculous speculation.

While he was pouring out the cereal, she came in, offered a reflective smile, then grabbed a bowl and served herself.

They ate silently at the dining table.

'Sorry,' she said. 'Went off on one, didn't I?'

'Understandable. Let it lie, is my advice. Our non-story will be forgotten tomorrow.'

She puffed out her cheeks. 'Hopefully.'

'Well, when weeks go by without us being photographed together, they'll drop it for some other tittle-tattle.'

'Hmm.' She made a pantomime of chasing the last nub of granola around the bowl.

'Something I should know?'

She gave up the chase and eyed him pensively. 'How's your golf game?'

He frowned. 'Random. Really?'

'Yeah. I mean, I'm imagining you're not the... Ellie Waites of the golf world,' she nudged him playfully, 'but I saw your souvenirs. Do you play?'

How to say "Not really"? She's clearly going somewhere with this.

'On and off. I got a hole in one, last time out.'

She leant forward. 'Wow, that's amazing.'

'Yep. Straight between the windmill sails, past the gnome, in the hole.'

'Now I *know* you're medically out of the woods.' Shaking her head, displaying that infectious, gorgeous smile, she took their crockery into the kitchen.

'I'm serious,' he called. 'And the windmill sails move, too. You have to time it juuust right.'

She stood in the doorway, hands on hips, an impish—if under-dressed—matriarch. 'Ever play with *grown-ups*?'

'That *was* with grown-ups. Ben and Jez. Last summer.'

'Fair enough. Look, you said you'd do anything to thank me for all this... Nurse Batgirl stuff. So, fancy filling in on a golf day?'

'Me? A *proper* course? If it's a charity thing where I have to pay a fiver a stroke, that's pretty much bankruptcy.'

She fell serious. 'No. No charity. A... tradition. I play with three of the girls. But that call just now? Kat's pulled her shoulder. Out of tomorrow's match. Can't play our foursome on Tuesday either.'

He went to her. 'And of all the people in the world, you want *me*?'

'As a favour, at short notice, absolutely. Nobody I'd rather spend time with.'

That could have been bluster, but her eyes said otherwise. He certainly couldn't think of anyone better to be with—especially if he was sober, awake, and not a forgetful, tender mess.

'Is it a keeping score, bragging rights thing?'

She bit her lip. 'No,' she said softly. 'It's a bit of fun. With my mates. Okay?'

At least there won't be any effing photographers out on the fairways.

'On the understanding that whoever gets lumbered playing with me will lose *catastrophically*, then I'd love to.'

She pulled him into a hug. 'Thank you.'

He held on, hands in the small of her back. There was no way back now. This woman was in his life.

40th Over

Adam's mobile vibrated. He hadn't checked it since the seizure. Unsurprisingly, there had been more important things to do, like regaining full use of his limbs and faculties. Notifications of a social media comment, an emoji-heavy text from Mum, or a phishing scam from a "delivery company" could wait.

He scooped the phone from the table and answered. 'Hey, mate.'

'Ads, what's going on? Have you seen Instagram?' Jez asked.

'Why? Pippa again?'

Jez whistled softly. 'Tip of the iceberg. Where've you been? And what's this about you and the cricketer?'

Shit. That bloody mag is stirring things up on every platform.

'It's all rubbish. I went to the awards. Ellie was there. End of.'

'Hmm. Not sure about that. But you should look, honestly. It's blowing up. I'll come round, okay. I wanna hear the story. The real story. Unless this *is* the real story.'

Adam sighed. Then he realised Ellie now had a sub, a relief batter. He glanced over.

'What?' she mouthed.

'Okay,' he told Jez.

'Cool. Give me half an hour or so.'

He hung up and feverishly opened Instagram. He'd been tagged in so many comments he didn't know where to start, so he scrolled to the original post.

Shit. Shit.

He collapsed into the dining chair so hard it could have broken.

Ellie was immediately beside him. 'What?'

Shaking, he showed her the screen.

Someone—not the official photographer—had snapped them on their way out. *No problem.*

It was in focus, and both were smiling. *No problem.*

A chink of white shirt showed that his fly was open. *Problem.*

Someone had highlighted the area with a box and zoomed it out. *Bigger problem.*

They'd added an arrow. *Huge problem.*

They'd put a caption, "Wonder what they were up to before this pic was taken!?"

The *ME & Tea* story was nothing compared to this. No wonder his feed was besieged by comments. He rose and paced, trembling.

Apocalypse. Doomsday. Potential career-ending problem... for either or both of us.

'Oh, crap,' Ellie said.

He crumpled to the sofa. 'Oh, shit.'

'Yeah. Um... Adam?'

'Mmm?'

'Sorry, but...' She perched beside him, angling her own phone.

He looked. After all, how could it get worse?

This was how. Pippa had just commented. "Typical Adam, taking advantage of another woman in the public eye. But I suppose the bathroom's ideal for his despicable behaviour because he only needs a couple of minutes!"

He pushed the phone away. He wanted to die. He wanted to seize. Or wake up from last night's seizure and find this was all a dream. He'd accepted Ellie into his world, and now this.

He hugged his knees. 'Please go,' he muttered.

'What?'

He forced down the lump in his throat. 'Please leave, Ellie. I need to go apeshit, and you shouldn't be here.'

She took his shoulders. 'Adam! Get a grip. I'm not *leaving*. And you are *not* going apeshit. What happened to letting go, moving on, rising above? Huh?'

'But look at it all! The implications. What will it do to your career?' He screwed up his eyes.

She laughed. 'Not a bloody thing. Susie won't drop me because I stood beside an award-winning creative who forgot to zip his zip. You know what *will* get me in trouble? Going off on one at these people. Getting into an online spat and saying something offensive. Being, basically, as combative and bitchy as you-know-who.' She shot him a glare.

His mind, which had barely returned to normal, spun and crackled with regret and frustration, impotence and indecision.

She put her phone on the coffee table. 'And anyone who knows you, truly cares, will see it's all lies. Right?'

He focussed on her plaintive, pretty eyes and mollifying expression.

It was ridiculous, wasn't it? Nobody who meant something to him, to her, would believe it was anything other than a wind-up, a bottom-scraping cry for attention. The evening hadn't been a *date*. They weren't *dating*. He'd never shag *anyone* in a public toilet—certainly not Ellie. He'd treat her like a Fabergé egg. Let alone the suggestion *she'd* risk public humiliation by having a quickie in a conference centre cubicle.

It was laughable.

A chuckle burst from him. Then, a laugh. And she smiled, then snickered. And she clasped his hands, and they bellowed with mockery and disbelief.

'Oh, Christ.' She wiped a happy tear from her eye. 'They have *no* clue. I've seen some pretty left-field stuff about me, but this takes the prize. What a bunch of losers. Build us up so they can knock us down. Wow. Jealousy 101.'

Are "they" jealous of me or her? Probably me, allegedly having sex with Ellie Waites. Her notoriety. Her talent. That dress.

'But my favourite,' Ellie continued, 'is your delightful ex. I *love* the "another" in "another woman in the public eye". If *she's* in the public eye, it's because she's a cataract.'

He howled with laughter, tears streaming down his face, until his belly hurt.

This was Pippa vomiting out all the frustration she'd bottled up while they were dating. Despite, like many couples, pursuing separate interests, her apathy for cricket was tinged with poorly concealed suspicion. She allowed him to attend matches—he wouldn't have dated her otherwise—but the green-eyed monster was lurking. It was ridiculous to believe he was cheating or had designs on someone else, especially someone in the celebrity bubble. Clearly, Pippa didn't know him that well. Ironically, she'd spent increasing amounts of time out with her mates, including blokes, when her "stardom" took off. Did he resent her? No.

Face it, Ads. It was ten months of mutual tolerance and sex.

Having regained perspective, he grabbed his phone and, with a flourish, hit Block on Pippa's account. He exhaled hard. Finally, she'd given him reason to kick her out of his digital life.

'Adam?' Ellie was biting her cheek. 'You don't regret it, do you? Us going together?'

'Not for a second. You?'

'No. The photograph? Could have done without you flying low, but ashamed to be with you? Not a bit of it. I wasn't too full-on, was I?'

His palms moistened. 'The... kiss was... unexpected.'

She frowned, amused. 'That was *barely* a kiss. And anyway, it was method acting.'

'Ah.' He narrowed his eyes in mock disbelief. 'Channelling your misspent youth as a pay-to-play lady of the night.'

'You've got an odd understanding of escorts. It's not all back alleys and one-hour hotel stays.'

'You have *really* done your research.'

She shoved him. 'You're a snake, Adam Glenn. And don't get off topic. What I meant was that however good the evening was—'

'And it was bloody wonderful.'

'—you wound up having an episode... and all that entailed. Not specifically the shedding of clothes and listening to me caterwauling in the shower, but, you know?'

He was hit by an image of her beside him in bed. Her utterly selfless, down-to-earth care. Pouring her heart out.

And don't forget how fine she looked. Still does.

'I wouldn't change a thing,' he said. 'Sounds odd, right? Ask me yesterday whether I'd like to have an episode, and the answer is always a hard no. But we'd still have had a good time. And you did look stunning.'

She met his eye, and then glanced away. 'Thanks. But... the articles?' Her grimace was gentle, apprehensive.

'You can't help getting papped for being who you are. You do *get* that's why I was worried?'

'Adam, your concern for me and my reputation is *the* sweetest, most thoughtful thing. Yes, I'm used to media exposure, and abuse, and bullshit, and I *can* handle it myself, but your support is the *most* marvellous bonus.' She looked down, stroking his fingers. 'And, for the record, if people want to say we're dating, whilst it's rash, ill-informed gossip, it's not *embarrassing*. It's not like they said I was sleeping with Quasimodo, and he was about my level.'

He stilled her fingers. 'He'd be lucky to have you. Anyone would. You're incredible.' His pulse raced.

'You too.'

'Thanks. Sometimes my wiring's faulty, but I have my moments.' A penny dropped. 'Shit. Only just got my driving license back, and now bang goes another twelve months.'

'Ah. I didn't... Sorry. I expect that changes your perspective on all this.'

He shrugged. 'Pointless to wish it was different. I'm used to it. Perils of being me. Burden of whoever's sitting where you're sitting. My life is a lot to opt into, Ells. The unpredictable income. I don't fly. One seizure on a plane is plenty for this lifetime.' He held up his right hand. 'Bruised for weeks. Luckily not broken. This is my livelihood. I can't lose it.'

She gently rubbed his forearm. 'I've been there. I know what it's like.' Ellie had broken her wrist when she was young, necessitating an unorthodox grip on the bat.

'Hmm. Didn't stop you being a hell of a player,' he noted.

'And this didn't stop you being a hell of a painter.' Their eyes met. 'She'd understand, the right person. She'd have to, right?'

'I don't live like a hermit, and I don't plan to. I do want to see the world... but I *am* a big fan of nights in.' He chuckled sadly. 'Commitment isn't something to be afraid of. Marriage, kids. Or maybe I'm five years too young to be thinking like that.'

She shook her head. 'No. We all want happiness. But being in *my* life is a big ask, too. Especially at the moment. You only see the upsides, especially if you judge me based on Insta—'

'Which I don't. Not anymore.'

She laid a hand on his leg. 'Finding people... someone who understands, who rolls with the punches, who is there for me, that's everything.'

'Same here. My problem is the inertia. To keep dating someone as a safety net. That's a recipe for disaster. So, for me, *friends* are gold. The ones who have my back. Like you. It's corny, but last night is something I'll remember forever... At least, the bits I *can* remember.' He beamed.

'I'm glad I was here.'

He lifted her hand away. Not because he didn't enjoy it, but pretty soon he might reciprocate. He wanted to. And much more. Things would escalate. Quickly. A *romantic* episode. With fallout. Not only aches and pains, but in his heart and maybe his life.

'You coped better than anyone who's been my life support. And we're not even going out.'

'Maybe... Maybe think of it as a dry run for if we did,' she murmured.

His scalp prickled. 'Hmm.'

She laid her head into the crook of his neck. 'I'm very fond of you, Adam.'

He moistened his dry throat. 'Likewise.'

Silence, apart from blood roaring in his ears. He felt her take a deep breath.

'You know how I said I let things get to me? How I make rash decisions. Sometimes, my wiring's as faulty as yours.' She tutted. 'Sorry, that's insensitive.'

'No, it isn't.'

'I hold onto people in my head, in my heart. I care too much. I cry about them. Ignore the cricket. I can move past a bad shot, bad game, no problem. I can't get over an *emotional* hurdle.'

He stroked her hair, inhaling her scent. 'That only makes you human, Ells.'

'Thanks.' She patted his thigh. 'But luckily, I have all my marbles this morning.' She tittered. 'One of us has to, right?'

'Yeah.'

'So this isn't the time to explore how fond I am of you. If your mate's coming round, we don't want to be discovered... *up to* anything.'

Suddenly, it was hot in the room. He eased her away. 'I... Yeah.'

She winced. 'Sorry. Too much? Don't want to lose my wicket early to a rash stroke.'

'No. You read the ball well. Which is very you. Batgirl.'

'Thanks. So... we're still on for golf?'

He was momentarily thrown by the change of pace.

That's Ellie. Move on to the next delivery.

'Definitely.'

'Good,' she said purposefully, standing. 'I'll get ready to head off.' She looked around. 'If I wear that manky dress, the cabbie will think I'm a stinky stop-out. And if he recognises me, we don't need more bloody rumours. Do you have a big coat?'

41st Over

While she went upstairs to make herself as presentable as possible, he stayed on the sofa, letting everything sink in. Despite not being in tip-top physical and mental condition, it was clear that he and Ellie had something.

The doorbell rang.

'Huh?' Jez could never have got here that quickly.

Praying it wasn't a reporter, Adam went to the door.

Ben's goofy face was almost a relief.

'Alright. Something up?' Adam asked.

'I was going to ask you the same question. You win the award, or what?' Ben didn't really do social media, certainly not trash like *Me & Tea*.

Adam frowned. 'You came over to ask? You *can* text.'

'I'm on the way to the big Asda. So, what's the story? And why didn't *you* text? Thought you'd dropped off the planet.'

'Sorry, mate. Look, come in a sec.'

Ben stepped into the hall.

Footsteps sounded behind.

'Right, Adam, I'll head off.' Ellie was sporting his long coat. Underneath was a double layer of boxers and T-shirts. High heels completed a decidedly *individual* look. She picked up the plastic bag of last night's clothes.

'Okay.' His soul deflated a little. He didn't want her to leave. Still, she had to get back into her routine.

She inspected his face. 'Do me a favour? Rest. Hydrate. And please don't bust a gut to come tomorrow. I'll be... disappointed if you're there. Take a day, okay? Find a good place for your trophy.' She winked.

'I will. Thanks again for everything. And, see you... Tuesday.'

She embraced him. 'Stay in touch. And don't worry about the trolls. Shout if you need any pointers.' She pecked his cheek.

His skin tingled. 'Okay.'

She nodded to Ben, whose face was a picture, then fluttered her fingers. 'Toodles.'

The door closed behind her.

Ben returned from some kind of stupor. 'Who's she?'

'Ellie.'

'Hmm. Looks a bit like that cricketer you watch... Wassaname?'

'Ellie.'

Ben eye-rolled. 'No, the cricketer.'

'Ellie.'

Cogs moved inside Ben's head. A light went on. Probably a gas-powered one. 'You mean...? Fuck, man. Was that...? Did I just...?'

'What?'

Ben pointed at the door. 'Meet Ellie... wassaname?'

'Ellie Waites.'

'Yeah. Did I meet her?'

Adam shrugged. 'On some level, I suppose.'

Ben's eyes widened. 'Wow.'

Adam waved him through. 'Relax. It's only Ellie. Cuppa?'

A grand's worth of pennies dropped through his skull.

It is only Ellie. A regular woman. One who, in different circumstances, I might... could... would...

He shook that off.

'Yeah,' Ben replied. 'What's this about having a rest tomorrow? You have a skinful last night?'

Adam debated.

Best to recap the essentials. Ben will never go to the papers. He's a good mate... in a gormless way.

'No, I had an episode.'

'Oh. Shit. One of your fits? Shit.' Ben held up both hands. 'Whoah. Should you be walking around?'

'You know what?' Adam flopped deliberately onto the sofa, groaning for effect. 'No.'

'Stay there, Ads. I've got you. Milk, one sugar, right?'

'Cheers.' He reached plaintively for his mobile, which was two feet away on the coffee table.

'Whoah. I've got it.' Ben passed him the phone. 'Tea coming right up.'

Adam had a fun half hour, glossing over Ellie's presence, talking about the awards, catching up with Ben and his girlfriend's cosy life, and shamelessly letting the guy butler to him.

Then Ben left, keen to get early-season BBQ ingredients. The temperature was above 20 degrees, so the supermarkets were shamelessly cashing in on the June heatwave.

When Jez arrived a few minutes later, the tone changed. Jez knew the ins and outs of Adam's condition and was relieved to hear that support had been readily available. However, he'd seen the

"ZipperGate" Instagram post, so wasn't easily dissuaded that Ellie's sleepover had been purely selfless ministrations.

'You are *in* there, mate.'

'It's not like that,' Adam protested.

'It must be. She stayed. So, did anything happen?'

Adam was open-mouthed. 'No!'

Jez eyed him obliquely. 'How do you know? Have you suddenly had a "perfect short-term memory" type of seizure?'

'No. Anyway, she would have said if anything happened.'

'But she must have seen you... *tackle out*, if it was like last time when you needed help getting to the loo.'

'I'm pretty sure I coped. She certainly didn't mention it. Look—'

'Maybe she found the sight too ghastly.' Jez's nose wrinkled. 'Maybe you're not actually *in there*.'

A freeze-frame, until now lost in Adam's memory, leapt forward. He grimaced.

'What?' Jez asked hurriedly.

'I...' He sighed. 'I walked in on her having a shower.'

Jez sprung up. 'Wow! And what did she look like?'

'Err... no idea. Hello! Epileptic here!'

Jez whipped out his phone. 'Right, let's find an image on Google, maybe a bikini one, and extrapolate from there. Next time, take a phone into the bathroom, okay?'

Adam wrestled his friend's mobile away and put it face down. 'I am *not* mentally undressing her, you dick. She deserves better than that.'

'You're an idiot, Ads. I saw the award pics. She is fit, pretty, and talented. Seems like she's pretty caring, too. Not to mention well famous.'

'Exactly, famous. Busy. Not what I want.'

Yet she *was* also caring, fit, talented, and pretty. And easy to talk to. And funny. And had great legs. And a smile he'd never tire of seeing.

'Fair enough, your choice. Wouldn't bother me, though. Maybe... if I pretend to have an episode, she'll look after me.' A light went on in Jez's face.

Adam was nonplussed. 'That is probably the most politically incorrect thing you have ever said. Which is a hell of an achievement. But if getting Ellie into bed is *that* important, I tell you what, let's switch bodies, and you can have epilepsy for real, and I'll have a regular life.'

'Why? What's so good about a regular life? I'm not the one who's had a smoking hot athlete buck naked in my house.'

'Look, I love you, mate, but it's not like she was parading around starkers, saying, "Come and get it, big boy".'

'Or "medium-sized boy", being honest.' Jez grinned.

Adam clubbed him round the head with a cushion.

42nd Over

When Ellie got home, she had an early lunch and took stock of things: the awards fun and games, his bolt from the blue, the shower snafu, her emotional wobble, his compassion. Their hugs, their chats. And the stupid assertions that they'd gone on a date and shagged in the loos.

Unbelievable. A lot of it.

But lovely. A lot of it.

I reckon I could tell him anything. We were just being... us.

A seed had germinated in her heart.

But do I water it?

She went for a run, using the clear air to figure out how to respond online if the gossip went viral.

In the late afternoon, she took the blue dress to the dry cleaners, prepped kit for tomorrow's match, then indulged in a long bubble bath.

By nine p.m., after a crazy 24 hours, she was fast asleep.

She was at the Aurora Stadium by eight thirty, ready for a ten thirty start time. The match was a welcome diversion from recent events.

The buzz in the changing room certainly focussed her mind on cricket. England's veteran captain, Anna Ritchie, had announced her retirement from the sport. She'd won the World Cup and won at least one series against every national team. The last piece in the puzzle had been beating the Netherlands. There were no more worlds to conquer... plus, she was 36, and it was time to pass the baton to someone younger.

What did it mean for the upcoming tour to South Africa? The room bubbled with rumour and speculation. If England dropped the young Beth Torrington, as seemed likely, the squad would be two players short.

As the team warmed up on the pitch, Ellie's eye kept wandering to Dani. Would the captain finally get a deserved England call-up?

Thirty minutes later, she was pitchside, raring to go.

"Opening the batting for the Scorpions, Ellie Waites and Fiona Plummer."

Ellie fist-bumped her current partner, clasped her badge, swung the bat in wide circles, and strode out.

Time to go to work.

After playing herself in nicely, she was on 32 when she clipped a beautiful delivery off her legs, hoisting it over the fielder for 4. That completed the over, so while the bowler got ready to run in to Fiona, Ellie surveyed the ground.

Adam wasn't there.

Good. But I should call him.

A siren lit the air. She glanced towards the main road.

Police? Ambulance? Ambulance for Adam?! Oh God, no.
I'll call him. Soon as.

'Yes!' Fiona shouted.

Shaken back to reality, Ellie pushed off into the run. The Cover fielder dashed in, scooped up the ball, and arrowed it to the keeper.

Shiiiit.

Ellie dived.

The keeper swept off the bails. Ellie thudded to the floor, her bat crossing the crease.

Fuck.

Chest aching, she picked herself up, eyed the umpire's raised finger, punched the bat with her left glove, shook her head to Fiona in apology, and trudged off.

In the changing room, Ellie gave herself a long talking to.

During the second innings, she fielded with determination and intensity, chasing down everything around Deep Square Leg, including preventing three boundaries.

Nevertheless, with 49 of the 50 overs gone, their opponents, The Tornado, were six runs from winning the game, with one wicket remaining. Their number 7 batter had played a blinder, and no bowler could unstick her.

On delivery three, she tickled the ball to the vacant Backward Square Leg area.

Ellie left the blocks like an antelope, tracking the ball's dribble. The batters turned for a second run. Ellie collected the ball, slowed, planted her feet, took aim and launched it for the stumps.

Half an hour later, after the autographs-and-selfies line had been duly serviced, Ellie spotted two familiar faces and stepped over the advertising hoarding.

Grace was bouncing like Tigger. 'Ellie! Ellie! You won the game.'

Diane winked.

'The team won the game,' Ellie said.

'Yes, but *you* got the last batter out. With a direct hit. And you scored 36. You've never scored 36 before. 36 has 9 factors, and one of them is 9. Which is a little bit funny, but only in a maths way.'

'Last time, I scored 137, and that's a prime number, isn't it?'

I looked that up especially for you.

'Yes. And it's also a *very* good score.' Grace's attention was caught by something. 'Ooh, I want to go and get Jade's autograph. Okay, Mum?'

'Go on then,' Diane replied.

The girl bounded away.

'How've you been?' Diane asked.

Where to start? 'You know, this and that.'

'Oh, I wrote to the school again, like you suggested. You really think Grace can get into the county Under 11s?'

'It doesn't hurt to try. But, yes, I see a lot of promise.'

Diane pursed her lips. 'It would seal the deal if you were her coach.'

Ellie's stomach butterflied. 'Maybe one day. If she makes the Under *13s*... never say never.'

'I know, I know. Bigger priorities for you right now. Like winning your *own* award.' Her eyes were mischievous.

Ellie checked that nobody was within earshot. 'Did you see Adam's Insta post? My posts?'

'I saw your beautiful dress. And that garbage about his fly being open.' She shook her head. 'Lowlifes.'

'Thanks. So, no point in asking if *you* think anything happened. Besides his seizure.'

Diane's hand came to her mouth. 'He had a seizure? When? At the awards?'

'Just after. Did you know he was at risk? That he has epilepsy? I didn't.'

'Yes, he did confide last year. So that's why he's not here. Gosh, is he okay?' Diane nibbled her lip.

'Pretty much right as rain when I left him.'

So why was I worried about the ambulance? Because I'm an idiot.

'Left him where? At the hospital?'

'No. At his place. I had to... stay for a bit... make sure he was okay. I mean, it wasn't pleasant seeing him like that, but... needs must.'

Diane clasped Ellie's arm. 'And after Paige and everything? Gosh, what a trauma for you.'

'Honestly, it was fine. He's a trooper. And... kind of easy to spend time with.'

Understatement of the year.

'Who is?' Grace asked, trotting up.

'Oh, er. Adam.' Ellie said.

The girl looked around. 'He's not here, is he?'

'No, he was... poorly. But he's okay now.' She checked her watch. 'I should go. I want to give him a bell.'

'Is he your boyfriend?' Grace asked, wide-eyed in matter-of-fact innocence.

Ellie chuckled. 'No, Gracie. He's my friend.'

Diane shot a knowing look. Ellie replied with "Don't you start too" daggers.

'Well, send him our best. Come on, Grace.' Diane took her daughter's hand. 'And well done for winning us the game, Ellie.'

I suppose I did.

Got myself out of jail with that one.

Adam was under her skin, but he mustn't live in her mind, too. Distraction had caused failures before, not to mention today's. Her career couldn't stand another wobble.

43rd Over

A dam didn't own any golf shoes. Or gloves. Or plus-fours, peaked cap, or trolley. His clubs had been bought off eBay ten years ago. He and Jez had played six games before Jez got a long-term girlfriend—who was no longer on the scene—and lost interest in getting out of bed, let alone chasing a small white ball through the countryside.

Adam had chosen an ensemble that was the least likely to get him laughed at. Still, if Ellie did laugh, it would only be leg-pulling. He was preoccupied by her last text message, which arrived at 7 a.m.

"See you at the clubhouse. x"

That final letter simultaneously worried and excited him. Her almost-kiss at the awards wasn't entirely for show. Saying she was "very fond" of him was a euphemism.

Two years ago, on player mic, Ellie had confessed that she'd wanted to be a window cleaner when she grew up. If she *was* a window cleaner, he'd have asked her out in a heartbeat. It was a no-brainer.

Except that wouldn't be the Ellie Waites he was drawn to in so many ways.

The battle between his head and heart raged.

The taxi dropped him at the golf club in good time for a nine o'clock tee-off. A familiar car, in pristine condition, caught his attention.

Ellie was taking her bag from the boot. 'Hey, Adam.' She came in for a hug.

The squeeze was tight, and he gave as good as he got. 'Hi, Ells.' He patted the car's roof. 'Do you wash this *every* day?'

'No. Every week, though. You know me, mate, I love cleaning.'

'You're welcome to come over and do mine,' he joked.

'Sure. Fifty pee, okay?'

'Deal. Any time in the next twelve months. Oh, great throw for the last wicket, by the way.'

She cringed. 'Ah. You watched the livestream.'

'Every ball. I stayed away like you asked. But... is it my imagination, or were you looking for me in the crowd?'

Her head drew back, lips a thin line. 'No.'

'Not even before getting run out?'

She folded her arms. 'You're a bit full of yourself.'

That indicated he was right. 'You weren't backing up, Ells. That's unlike you. Oh, and the other time, was that century salute for me?'

She took a step back. 'No. For everyone.'

'Yet the photo shows you pointing the bat right down the lens.'

'I did it for your photograph. You *are* looking for material for the portrait, right?' Her eyes were wide.

He took a breath. No point in creating an atmosphere. They had 18 holes to spend together. 'Okay. Sorry. But if you're ever tempted to look for me, don't. It's a distraction. To cause a... loss of concentration would be disappointing. No, worse. I'd be gutted.'

She eyed him for an age, then her sternness broke. 'Yeah. Okay. Sorry.'

'Stop playing for other people. *Please*. Play for *yourself*. If you want to reach that Lord's Test, channel your quality and determination to do it, not to impress others, dead or alive. I *know* doing it for Paige means a lot, but doing it for me is silly.' He stepped closer. 'Don't let other things get in your head. Just be as brilliant as you are.'

He stood back. 'Sorry. Soapbox done.' He watched for warning signs of a knee in the groin, a smack in the mouth, or his marching orders.

She pulled him into another bear hug, pressing her cheek to his. 'I don't deserve you, Adam Glenn. On many levels.'

His body jittered. 'Hmm. Let's see if you think that when we've finished the round.'

They wandered to the clubhouse to await the other two Scorpions.

On the sun-dappled terrace, they discussed ZipperGate. Ellie had posted a bland but firm denial. Adam had done similar. She said something wise: treat Pippa like a child with a tantrum, and eventually, she'll calm down and STFU.

She complimented his updated website, Facebook and Insta profiles, which now used the official photo of the award presentation. He'd also revised the bios: there was good PR in his win... providing he could ward off the gossip. He said he'd made good progress on ideas and sketches for her portrait. She was excited to see it finished.

'Hey, Batgirl!' Naira and Fiona walked up, golf clubs rattling in their bags.

Clearly, they had seen the cartoon.

The girls exchanged hugs, and Ellie introduced Adam to Fiona.

Naira rubbed Ellie's shoulder. 'Thinking of you, Ells.'

Ellie nodded, her smile thin. Adam wondered what he'd missed. He doubted they meant the awards fallout. Was Ellie's uncharacteristic dismissal on Sunday caused by something deeper? Surely, the teammates wouldn't be so sombre over a stupid run out. His stomach knotted.

As they headed for the first tee, the Scorpions exchanging private jokes, he felt like a spectator. Yet Ellie hadn't sidelined him; she was simply with people she'd known for much longer. It wasn't a fame thing; it was a mates thing.

They were playing a foursome: each team of two taking alternate shots with the same ball.

Ellie lined up on the tee. In a tight jumper and trousers, golf shoes and a Scorpions cap, she looked the part, and Adam knew she had a decent handicap.

With a graceful, powerful swing, she cracked the ball down the fairway. It was different and similar to watching her nail a cricket ball down the ground for 6. Adam's heart pattered.

Naira went next. Her ball didn't travel as far.

The quartet set off down the fairway, Adam subtly lagging a yard behind.

Naira slowed. 'Loved your cartoon of Ells, Adam.'

'Oh, cheers.'

'How much would you charge?'

His mind backflipped. 'Charge?'

'For one of me.'

'And me,' Fiona piped up.

'Seriously?'

'Absolutely. Can't have Ells be the only one with a commission from an award-winning artist.'

He didn't say that Ellie's had been a jokey request rather than a paid gig. 'Um... I don't know. A hundred quid?'

'Deal,' Naira said.

'Me too,' Fiona added.

Unseen by the others, Ellie shot him a raised eyebrow.

They came to stand beside Naira's ball. Adam set his bag down.

Fiona fingered the clubs in her bag. 'What bat d'you reckon?'

'Five bat,' Naira replied.

Adam frowned, amused.

Fiona pulled out the 5-iron and played her shot. They walked to his and Ellie's ball. Could he hit a decent iron shot towards the green? Ideally, the green on *this* hole? It was more nerve-racking than walking up the award podium steps.

He tried to ignore the three watching professional athletes, took a couple of practice swings, then, mercifully, connected with the ball and sent it, roughly straight, down the fairway. With a shaking hand, he slid the club back into the bag.

'Nice shot, partner,' Ellie said.

Well, nobody laughed, which is a win.

Ellie took the next shot, landing them on the green, about ten feet from the hole. Naira hit her ball to within six feet.

With a deep breath, Adam pulled out the putter. This was *his* domain: putting. And today, there were no windmills.

Notwithstanding the flat and easy green, he was stunned to sink the putt. Ellie high-fived him. Then, when Fiona missed her putt, handing Adam and Ellie victory on the hole, Ellie high-tenned him.

'Brought a ringer, have you, Waitesy?' Naira asked.

'Oh yeah,' she replied, deadpan. 'He's a jack-of-all-trades, is our Adam.'

'Master of none,' he added.

Ellie looked at her colleagues. 'Hands up all award winners.'

The girls eyed him.

'Careful,' he said. 'Or I'll draw a picture of you three round a cauldron.'

44th Over

B y the 4th hole, he started feeling like part of the group.

By the 9th hole, Ellie was calling him "Ads", and the other girls insisted he use their nicknames too. He'd stopped caring about being the worst player. The banter and cricket chat was natural and infectious.

On the 12th hole, after Ellie's excellent tee-off, he joined in with Naira and Fiona's jokey terminology.

He lined up the fairway shot. '7 bat?'

Ellie smirked. 'I'd go 6.'

He selected the 6-iron but shanked the shot badly, and the ball rolled into bushes. 'Sorry.'

She clamped her mouth over a titter. They trudged over, set their bags down, and entered the bushes.

'No nonsense, you two,' Naira called, snickering.

Ellie shook her head, tutting. 'Sorry about them.'

He shrugged. 'I whip it out once at an awards ceremony, and suddenly I'm Don Juan.'

She laughed, kicking branches aside until they located the ball. Taking a drop shot in the rough, she addressed the ball.

'Breeze off the left,' he said.

She tutted. 'I know.'

Then, she promptly hooked the shot into bushes sixty yards across the fairway. He coughed deliberately and strode away. She caught up and jabbed him in the ribs.

Fiona hit a glorious 7-iron onto the green. She and Naira waited while, again, Adam and Ellie set their bags down, he grabbed a club to use as a poking stick, and they disappeared into the bushes.

As soon as they were out of sight, mischief broke on Ellie's face.

'Here, Adam,' she called, 'Pull these down, and you'll get a better look.'

He clamped his lips over a snigger. His cheeks reddened, and his skin prickled. 'Whoah! That's not my club!' he shouted.

'Stick it in here. Oh, yes!' Her pupils danced.

'Deeper?'

Why was he upping the stakes? Blood was already funnelling to his lower body.

She stepped close, licking her lips. 'Hold on. Don't get it caught in the undergrowth.'

'I can't see properly. Open your legs a bit more.'

Heaven knows why, but she actually did. 'That better?' she called.

Please, Ellie, you are just too much. In the best possible way.

'Lemme try this.' He let out a grunt of effort.

Air snorted from her nose. He was about to laugh, but she clapped a hand over his mouth.

'Come on, Ads. Wiggle it around a bit.' She scooped up the ball. 'That's the spot. I think you've got it! Yes!'

He wagged a finger, shooting a devilish grin.

They rustled the bushes for good measure, tittering like children, then took many, *many* seconds to put on serious faces, and headed to the fairway.

Ellie stretched. 'Ooh, that's cleared the cobwebs away.'

Naira and Fiona were in tucks, aghast. 'Wow, that was even quicker than at the awards.'

Adam, straining every muscle to keep a straight face, said, 'Yeah, but we did it *twice* in the bathroom.'

'He's *very* efficient,' Ellie said, dropping their ball in a convenient spot.

Fiona eyed Naira. 'Methinks they do protest too much.'

Adam folded his arms. 'Do you want superhero costumes with the cauldron or just regular cowls and hats?'

They were on the 14th green when Ellie's pocket trilled.

'Shit,' she said. 'Sorry.'

She pulled out her mobile and answered, strolling away to get some privacy.

'It's the stewards,' Fiona called. 'Sex in the rough is against club rules.'

Naira fake kicked her partner in the shins.

Adam leant on his putter.

Is this the magazine, calling to issue a retraction? That would be a win.

He could barely hear Ellie, but things sounded businesslike. When she ambled back, trance-like, her eyes were wide.

'What?' he asked, worried.

'I've... been called up to the England A squad.'

'Woo-hoo!' Naira screeched, pulling Ellie into a hug.

Fiona was next. 'Yas queen!'

Adam beamed. The news, the reaction, the luck to be there when it happened. Ellie grabbed him, so he lifted her off the ground and spun around joyously.

You did it, Ells, you absolute legend, you beauty.

She let go, arched back, and punched the air with both hands. 'Yes!'

In a gap between the trees, four other golfers in flat caps and tweeds shook their heads and muttered.

Ellie eye-rolled theatrically, but her grin was uncontained.

'I'm assuming Adam knows what England A is,' Fiona said.

'Is it one above England B?' he joked, knowing it was like a subs bench for the main squad, sometimes even a team in itself.

Naira did a little dance. 'You're going to South Africa, Ells!'

'Chill, Roddy. They're only bolstering the squad. Squad and playing are not the same. Come on, let's finish this hole before we get tutted off the course by the *men*.'

Adam was preparing to tee off on the 16th when *his* pocket buzzed. The adrenaline rush of Ellie's call-up had barely dissipated.

'God, it's like Piccadilly Circus round here,' Fiona muttered.

'Sorry, sorry.' He fished out his phone. 'Adam Glenn.'

'Probably a call-up for England B,' Naira joked.

'Nah. Ryder Cup,' Ellie added.

He poked out his tongue and wandered away.

Half an hour later, the four were sat around a table in the clubhouse, guzzling much-needed coffees. The game's result was, by all accounts, unimportant, as every year.

Still, at least I only helped us lose by 2 holes.

Being clichéd, the journey was more important. This was another scrapbook memory. Spending time with three delightful people was one thing, and their status elevated the experience. The mischief in the bushes was a highlight, but Ellie's call-up was the icing on the cake. His own phone call had been a great bonus.

The caller was Bill Clay from Geoghan Associates, who Ellie had smooched at the awards. He'd received two endorsements of Adam's skills and wanted a quote for a series of bespoke photo prints for their new office. It wouldn't exactly put Adam on the gravy train, but it might let him through the barriers onto the platform.

Having an unfastened fly and a loopy ex-girlfriend felt like a small price to pay.

The trio raised their cups.

'To Paige,' Naira said.

'To Paige,' Adam chorused, a half-second late.

Suddenly, things made sense. Yet, why did he feel aggrieved, shut out?

'You're the best. All of you,' Ellie said, sombre. 'But we did her proud today.'

'Amen,' Adam added, for something to say.

Ellie excused herself to the loo. Possibly to dry a tear.

Adam leant into Naira. 'So... this is an anniversary thing?'

'Yeah. Paige's birthday.'

'Shit,' he breathed, looking away, remorseful. He was disappointed in Ellie.

'They used to play. Paige was better. This is to stop Ells from wallowing around at home. We aim for as close to the exact day as possible. It has to be a rest day for the Scorpions *and* England.' Naira brightened. 'Which may be useful for her next year.'

'Let's hope,' was all he could say.

He held in the frustration until he and Ellie were alone at her car. She passed over his borrowed coat and—washed and ironed—his T-shirts and boxers. He dismissed the peculiarity of having an England cricketer do his laundry.

'What's up, Adam? You've been like a bear with a sore head since we finished.'

'It's... I've been laughing and joking with you when we're meant to be remembering your sister. I feel awful. Why the cloak and dagger, huh?'

'*This* is exactly why.' She cupped his arm. 'Because you are the most caring, understanding guy, I had a feeling you'd go all serious. Maudlin. Trying to empathise. Especially because you live with epilepsy.' She looked deep into his eyes. 'I didn't want to feel self-conscious. The idea is to have *fun*. To celebrate Paige's life. We had such a blast on the course, her and me. So doing the same with other girls, with people I love, is the next best thing.'

'I suppose. But... Christ, pretending to have a quickie in the bushes?' He sighed. 'I wish you'd told me, that's all. I felt like... an outsider.'

'You're not,' she snipped. 'And will you please stop this? A year ago, fine. But not now. Not after all we've been through.' She took a deliberate breath. 'Look, they like you, Roddy and Fi. They think you're good for me. As a friend, I mean.' She folded her arms. 'And enough of the holier-than-thou crap. You kept your epilepsy secret, and that's life or death.' She shot a pointed look.

He lolled against the car. 'Yeah.'

She took his hand and wiggled it. 'Sorry for not being clear about today. I... wafted at a wide one, nearly edged it.'

Guilt gnawed at him. She was too wonderful to be cross at. 'Okay. Forgiven. I don't want to fight. Not today.'

'It's tomorrow, actually. The anniversary. But, thanks.'

He had a vision of her crying in the bath. 'Do you want me to come over? Distract you? I play a mean game of Scrabble.'

'No. Emotional situations can make people do silly things.' She met his eye, then inspected her feet.

That sunk in with lightning speed. His scalp prickled. The vision he'd had of her in the bath morphed, the bubbles evaporating. He shut that down. 'Yeah.'

She patted his back, moving the topic on. 'Well played, partner. I had a blast. I hope you did, too. Thanks for filling in. And well done on that new commission.'

'Plus two cartoons for the girls,' he reminded her.

'There you go. I might make a decent PA, right?' She grinned.

'You? PA to me? Says no-longer-former England player Ellie Waites.'

'Woo hoo!' She held up a fist to be bumped.

He tapped. 'I never doubted you.'

'I know. You're a star.' She opened her arms. 'Still friends, number one fan?'

He took the hug. 'Of course. And it's "number one fan over the age of ten".'

She laughed, her breath tickling his neck. 'So, see you soon?'

'Definitely.'

Her smile faded. 'Or as soon as I have a spare minute, right?'

He shrugged. 'Ride the wave, Ells.'

'Believe me, I will.' She pecked his cheek. 'Toodles, Ads.'

45th Over

When Ellie got home, she went to the living room nook, The Temple. On the sideboard opposite the wall of memorabilia stood a picture of her and Paige. It was positioned there to let her sister gaze at the achievements.

She held the photo to her chest, breathing deeply, fingering her necklace.

'I did it, P. Nearly there now.'

She made a cuppa and rang her parents to give the good news. They seemed genuinely happy.

That evening, she invited neighbour Ayla round for a takeaway and a bottle of wine: a *proper* toast to success. She didn't mention the Adam situation; that was her private circle to square. Anyway, it would have to wait; life was about to get crazy.

The following morning, she went to the gym, did chores and worked on prep for joining the England squad.

Around lunchtime, a text arrived from Adam: "Thinking of you". He was concerned for her welfare on this, the anniversary of Paige's death. She wished he was merely thinking about her, because she was thinking about him.

In the evening, she called Laura and had a good natter about the call-up, Laura's new bloke Tom, and how the England women's football squad, the Lionesses, were progressing.

It was a lovely catch-up, and the topic of Paige didn't arise.

Nevertheless, as Ellie laid down to sleep, she allowed herself a bit of a cry.

Thursday was a training day. Her head was clear, and she felt pumped and ready.

Pulling into the car park, she noticed Abi "Mills" Miller, the young spin bowler, sitting in her car, head bowed. She'd changed her hair colour, opting for a vibrant purple on her pixie cut.

Ellie parked nearby, pulled out her kit bag, and walked over. Abi nodded a greeting but didn't move.

Ellie debated briefly, then climbed into the passenger seat.

'Hey, Ells. Well done on the call-up. Such good news.'

'Thanks, Mills. Everything okay?'

'Yeah. Just... having a moment. You know?' Abi's freckled face was pained.

Ellie didn't need it spelling out. The self-doubt, the continual ebb and flow of the starting XI, questioning when you'd get a game, knowing it wasn't only about your form but others' too. It was doubly hard for Abi, a junior in the team at 19. This was her debut season in the squad, having come up from the Academy over the winter. She was still waiting for her first game, and with the England girls back for a while, her chances of selection were even less.

Sometimes, the mental challenges of the job outweighed the physical ones.

'Look, Mills, last July, I thought I was done. Bry had such a great year, and Kat is in the form of her life. Fi, too. I worked bloody hard all winter, but there are no guarantees. Susie's not *obliged* to pick me. Doesn't matter that I've been around the block. I used to bowl—you know that, right?'

Abi nodded.

'Didn't take much for me to lose that spot. Pound to a penny, there's always someone better, but that's not the same as "I'm no good, not worthy of the contract, the shirt".' Ellie fixed the girl with a sober smile. 'I cried so much in the last nine months, Mills. I was lonely as *hell*. Sitting in the dugout, not training with everyone, seeing Bry taking my England spot.' She shook her head, the memories hurting. 'But nothing is forever, the good or the bad. Last year, you took 6 for 19 in that Academy game at Beckenham, right?'

Abi nodded again.

'Dani never had figures like that, at your age or since. And she's skip. And she's won The Hundred. Finished as leading wicket-taker in the comp. Ten years ago, she *lived* on the bench. Me too. And we realised the same thing. I can only play *my* game and be the best I can. You believe *you're* good enough, right?'

Another nod.

'Good. Because you are. Nobody is here to make up numbers. Everyone is here because of talent. Potential. Value to the team. In my first season, I got three games. Three. I wondered what I'd done wrong.' She shook her head. 'Nothing. It just wasn't my time. Until it was. It'll be yours, Mills. Promise.'

Best not to lay it on too thick. About the nights she'd lain awake, questioning if Dad had been right. Whether a 9-5 job would have been safer, less stressful. Made them prouder.

But she wouldn't quit. Not after all the investment of time and energy. She wouldn't give her parents the satisfaction of caving in. And she couldn't let Paige down. She had to live, and succeed, for them both.

Abi smiled weakly. 'Yeah.'

'I know it sounds trite, Mills, but there's opportunity in every setback. Getting injured, or not being selected, is a gift of *time*. Time you can use to improve something, somehow. To be even fitter and more ready for when the chance comes. Honestly, I'm a yard faster than last year. So, find the wins, okay?'

'Hmm.'

'Look, have a drink with Dani. She's missed out on an England call-up for her entire career. That hurts. Yet she perseveres. She's an amazing character. Have a chat. It'll be good for you. Please?'

A nod. 'Okay.'

Ellie leant across and pulled the girl into a hug. 'And I'm here. Anytime you want.'

Abi wiped her eyes. 'Thanks, Ells.'

Ellie patted the seat bolster. 'Come on. Do some netting with me.'

The training area rang with noise. There was a buzz whenever the England girls returned from a series—and Ellie had seen it from both sides of the fence. Now, she felt like a taxi driver in Arrivals, ready to greet those who'd been on less humdrum adventures than she'd had over the last few weeks.

The thing was, hers hadn't been humdrum. If she'd been in the England camp, she would have missed the time with Adam. On the flip side, she was sober about her upcoming absence from the UK.

No, not the UK. Him.

Bryony pulled her into a hug. 'Ells!'

Ellie held tight. There was so much to discuss... but lots to keep under wraps. 'Missed you, Bry.'

Bryony laughed. 'That 137 says otherwise.'

'Well, I had to give the selectors something to think about, didn't I?'

Bryony bounced on her toes. '*So* good to hear you're coming on tour.'

'Roomies?'

'Definitely.' She spied Dani, patted Ellie's arm, and dashed away.

Ellie chatted with Rojo and Jade "Jet" Black, the other two England players, then padded up and went to the nets. After a few minutes with batting coach Jonno, Abi came over, looking much happier. Today's focus was spin, and Jonno agreed to let the two work together.

Abi bowled Ellie a few overs, then they swapped positions, and Abi worked on her batting while Ellie practiced her spin bowling.

They spent twenty minutes trading tips, Abi called time, thanked Ellie, and went to do ground fielding drills.

Susie wandered over. 'This is why I said you should apply for the coaching badge.'

Ellie chuckled. 'Me?'

Jonno, nearby, nodded enthusiastically.

'Absolutely,' Susie said. 'The game's crying out for female coaches. What have you got to lose?'

I could fail the course.

'I'll think about it,' she said, keen to change the topic.

There was too much going on at the moment to worry about this. Besides, didn't the future, the cliff edge, seem a little further away, a bit less scary? It was wrong to consider a post-playing future at the exact point she was honing her fitness and her game, keen to stake a claim in the starting XI in South Africa.

After practice came prep for the upcoming game. When the team talk was done, the girls drifted away.

Sandy walked up. 'Ellie, can we grab you for an interview? Ask about the call-up, that kind of thing?'

'Sure. Give me five minutes.'

'Thanks.' Sandy returned to her myriad duties.

Naira plopped down in the adjacent seat. 'If I was being cruel, I'd say you were avoiding me.'

Ah. Kind of.

'No. Why?' Ellie couldn't spend the time chatting to all fifteen players.

'The bushes.'

Ellie laughed. 'You *know* we were pulling your leg.'

'It sounded very convincing. You certainly got into character.'

'What character?'

'A girl with real hots for Adam.'

This laugh was nervous. 'It sounds like *you're* the one with the hots.'

Naira glanced around. 'I mean, sure, he ticks a lot of boxes, but I'm talking about chemistry, Ells. And boy, do you two have it.'

Damn. She's nailed it.

Ellie gave her friend the full SP. How things with Adam had developed. The undeniable connection. How he was the "Goldilocks" man—neither safe and steady Jack nor possessive hotshot Harry.

'He's a regular guy, Roddy. He does his laundry but doesn't fold his pants and arrange them by colour or days of the week. The toilet's clean. He's no health freak, but his cupboard isn't full of junk food. He's not got posters of me on the bedroom ceiling. He's a bloody good artist but doesn't take himself seriously. And he doesn't wear Lynx Africa.'

'So where's the fire? Why not ask him out?'

She shook her head, remembering Adam's criteria for her portrait and the times he could have taken the opportunity to make a move.

She sighed. 'I'm not sure the ball is there to hit.'

Naira squeezed Ellie's hand. 'Just do you, Ells. We're *all* our best when we're playing *our* game, not trying to force a shot. If he *truly* understands you, it'll work out.'

'Yeah.' She tutted. 'Anyway, I can't get distracted. He already balled me out for that.'

'The run out?'

Ellie nodded, grimacing.

Naira bit her lip. 'Yeah, best you don't do that in Cape Town.'

'He won't be there.'

'Then, good. And who knows, maybe absence will make the heart grow fonder.'

Ellie wondered whose heart she meant. 'Hmm.'

'When do you fly?'

'Er... twelve days.'

'So we have you for two more matches.'

'You'll get by without me,' Ellie said. 'Or you better bloody well do.'

46th Over

F or hours, the house felt oddly empty. Yet nothing had changed.
Nobody had moved out.

Adam put his finger on it. Life had returned to normal. The
madness was over: the concussion sleepover, the awards, the seizure,
the golf game. Artificial, enforced proximity.

*You get immersed in a painting—in a passionate and rewarding
way, and then the portrait is done, and whilst there's a sense of
achievement and contentment, there's also a hole in your life.*

His life had an Ellie-shaped hole, and it had only been one day
without her.

Still, it was ridiculous to expect things to continue as they had
been. She had a life and friendship circle. She was an elite athlete with
heavy demands on her time, and the England call-up meant a hectic
timetable of preparation followed by a long time away. It didn't mean
they were no longer friends—of course not. Only that they'd see each
other less frequently.

The best medicine was to embrace the other part of his life which gave joy: work.

The first job was Fi and Roddy's superhero caricatures. These cartoons might be a new string to his already well-furnished bow. They were fun and quick to create, and, with a player's blessing, could be sold as digital art.

He set up the time-lapse camera over his desk and got to work.

While digging out his toothbrush charger the following morning, he stumbled on a pair of earrings. Ellie's. She'd left them somewhere safe before showering.

He put the earrings on the dining table, planning to take them to Saturday's match, and grabbed his mobile, ready to text her.

At that second, the phone rang.

'Shit,' he exclaimed, alarmed.

The incoming caller was his business landline, a dummy number permanently forwarded to his mobile. It helped to separate legitimate business calls from the numbers of mates, clients and scammers.

'Adam Glenn.'

'Ah, yes, hello,' said a well-to-do man. 'I picked up your number from the website. My name's Charles Lyle. I wanted to speak to you about that portrait of James Anderson, the cricketer. A chum of mine from The Garrick spotted you in some publication or other, and I'm something of a... collector of cricket memorabilia, do you see, and, so, I saw your painting. I was taken by it, I must say. Is it available for sale, by any chance?'

Adam nearly leapt onto the table to do a jig. He put on his business voice. 'Thank you for calling. Yes, the painting is still available.'

'Right, well, excellent. Bit tied up for the next few days, but I assume I'd be able to see it?'

'Absolutely. Just let me know when.'

'Super, super. I'll look at the old diary, and we'll work something out. Down in Maidstone, aren't you, Adam?'

'That's right, Mr Lyle.'

'Oh, do call me Charles. So, I'll give you a ring soon. You will hold the painting for me, won't you?'

'Of course.'

'Good, good. And do Google me or whatever you want. Assure yourself I'm not some timewaster.'

'Oh, yes. But no problem to keep the artwork aside for you.'

'Good, good. And on price? What sort of money are we looking at? Ten? Is that the sort of ballpark?'

Adam sat down hard. 'I... yes, that would be... fair.'

'Excellent. Well, subject to viewing, let's have a gentleman's agreement at a nice round ten thousand.'

'I think that's doable, Charles. So... I'll... wait for your call.'

'Indeed. Right, must rush. Good to talk. Speak anon. Bye.'

Adam thumbed the red icon and shakily laid the phone on the table.

Then he punched the air. 'Yes!'

If only Ellie was there to share a celebratory hug.

Half an hour later, with a nice cup of tea and four chocolate biscuits inside him, Adam regained composure.

Seized by self-belief, emboldened by an unequivocal appreciation of his work, he went to the easel where the beginnings of Ellie's portrait awaited his brush strokes.

His gaze rested on the loose depiction of her face.

Had this sudden upswing in fortunes really been triggered by those hours spent with her? The meeting at the gallery which led to her glowing Insta recommendation? The coverage of the awards, which had generated both great local press coverage and mudslinging cheap shots? As many people had probably laughed at him as had been impressed by the award win.

Was there such a thing as bad publicity? Leaving his fly undone might be the best PR stunt he'd ever do... even if it was accidental. And inviting Ellie to be his plus-one? It hadn't hurt her career one iota. She'd been selected for England, for heaven's sake.

And now a random art buyer wanted to pay him ten *thousand* pounds.

Sure, he'd never be as famous or talented as Ellie Waites, but she'd thrown a pebble into his pond, and the ripples were lapping against his online following and, soon, his bank account.

Making a good job of her portrait was the least he could do to repay her.

He went to the wall, switched on the time-lapse camera, and began to paint.

"Opening the batting for the Scorpions, Ellie Waites and Bryony Taylor."

Music pumped from the Aurora Stadium's speakers, and the crowd applauded.

'Dream team.' Bryony fist-bumped Ellie, and they walked out to the middle.

Ellie had looked towards the Square Leg boundary more than once. It was instinctive now, and she believed it was merely a habit devoid of emotion. After all, if she *felt* anything, it meant she was ignoring Adam's cautions. She was there to play cricket, not to prove anything to anyone. Not, in some lame, girlish way, to use flair and talent as a come-on.

Besides, today, it was useless. He wasn't there.

She scoffed.

I don't need him here. I can't treat him as a... University Challenge mascot. He'd hate that. We'd fall out. And I don't want that. In fact, I want more.

Shaking off the distraction, she took up stance at the crease, surveyed the field, and awaited the first ball.

Still, where is he...?

Ten minutes later, she was sitting in the dugout, seething. The ball from the visitors' front-line seamer had been decent, but Ellie should never have lost her wicket to it. 8 was an embarrassing score.

I have to stop this.

Adam's right. No sense in playing for him or Paige. No point in looking for him, expecting him to always be there.

As the nearby chatter flitted between the game, tales from Bry and Rojo about high-jinks on the last England tour, and personal miscellany, Ellie managed to dispel the anger and disappointment.

Kat leant in. 'Want to get lunch?'

Ellie knew that was code for "Want to chat?".

Do I? Will it solve anything?

'I know you don't,' Kat added. 'But I won't see you for weeks, and you'll give yourself a hernia stewing on whatever it is. Stuck out there in the sunshine, with only the good times to keep you company. Plus, I did see that Insta post, you know. C'mon, spill the tea!'

Ellie's resolve crumbled. Her bestie needed to hear the full story because Ellie couldn't do this alone.

They sat at the far end of the room, away from the others.

Kat dug into her chicken and pasta lunch. 'I'm guessing this isn't about your innings. Or your selection. Or the prick on social who said you looked like a whore in that dress. Please say you didn't do it in the loos.'

'Babe, you have him so wrong it's untrue. You and the magazine.'

'So there's nothing in it? Nothing happened?' Kat sipped her water, a knowing look in her eye.

'Define "nothing". We went to the awards, had a *bloody* good time, came home, and he had a seizure.'

Kat's hand came to her chest. 'The fuck?'

I'm sorry, Adam. I know what we said about Vegas, but...

Ellie looked around, then angled her head towards the door. Kat grabbed her plate, and they went to the deserted changing room.

Kat grabbed Ellie's arm. 'Shit, Ells. What?'

She held up a finger. 'I trust you to the end of the Earth, yeah?'

Kat zipped fingers across her mouth.

Ellie took the deepest breath and gave a summary of the unplanned sleepover at Adam's. She left out the accidental nudity, the waterworks, and the burning desire to kiss him. She recounted the laughter, him rescuing her from oglers at the awards, and plenty of detail on what he said, how he acted, and what he looked like in his underwear. Then she gave chapter and verse about the golf day. They were on the same page... and Adam damn well knew it.

Kat fluttered her hand like a fan. 'Ells, this sounds *serious*.'

Something exploded in Ellie's chest. A cannonball of glitter and feathers. 'I think...' She closed her eyes against the moisture which wanted to form.

Holy crap. This is it. The perfect shot. That sound. That feeling. No need to run. Simply stand and watch. The glorious arc of the ball, high and handsome.

She perched on the edge of the stark wooden seat. 'I think... he may be my person.' She clenched a fist. 'And I don't know whether to love or hate it.'

Kat frowned, clasping Ellie's thigh. 'What's to hate, girl? He sounds ideal for you.'

'Not him. It. The situation.'

'What situation?'

'Big Bash, IPL, you name it. Away from home for months is hardly the recipe for the right stuff.'

'Other girls manage it. Hell, *you* managed it,' Kat pointed out.

Oh, yeah.

Ellie hadn't spent the last decade avoiding dating, unconvinced she could make time for it. Hell, she'd still be with Jack if his eyes hadn't wandered, or even Harry if he hadn't been so flawed. Her *career* hadn't kiboshed those love stories.

Now, the stakes felt higher. She *really* wanted this to work—but Adam had to want it too.

'Those were separate lives. That's not what I want. Hell, I'm sitting here and *already* I want to see Adam again.'

Kat whistled. 'Wow. He must have been *great* in bed.'

Ellie fake-slapped her. 'We did *not* sleep together. And, frankly, he'd have to be a bloody car crash to ruin all the rest of it. But it's not about that.'

'What is it about? You playing over the winter isn't news to him, right? He can't have his cake and eat it.'

Ellie picked at a nail. 'I'm not sure he even wants his cake.'

Kat pulled her into a clench. 'Then don't lose sleep over this, hon. Not now. You have the tour to think about.'

'Yeah.'

It was a welcome diversion—from Adam *and* making a decision.

47th Over

It was churlish for Adam to resent a client for making him miss a cricket game, but it didn't stop the split loyalty niggling away. It was a little harder to see perspective now he'd been accepted into the Scorpions "family", as if he was letting the team down by not being there. Plus, exchanging texts with Ellie was a poor substitute for seeing her.

However, business came first. How could he tell Bill Clay that a lunchtime meeting was inconvenient? The universe was ushering his fortunes onwards and upwards, and the universe isn't something to be messed with.

First had come the successful gallery exhibition, then the trophy, and an excellent opportunity to sell the Jimmy portrait. His online stock photo account was flourishing, his Insta following had tripled, and he was considering approaching the Stadium shop about stocking prints of his player cartoons.

The meeting with Bill at Geoghan Associates' offices was productive, and Adam was asked to submit a quote for the brief—a five-figure job. If this and the sale to Charles Lyle went ahead, he'd have funds for a new camera, with some left over for a decent holiday. If Ellie was still in the England squad in a year's time, he might even consider taking a trip abroad...

He couldn't wait to tune into her first game in South Africa. With all his soul, he wished success because she'd undeniably been a catalyst for *his* upturn in fortunes.

The following day, he resumed work on Ellie's portrait. The basics were done—the rough outline of her body, the beginnings of the background scene, and much of the focal point—her face.

After an hour, he stood back from the canvas, cocking his head. 'Yeah. Pretty damn fine.'

The sticking point was whether to paint her in England kit or Scorpions' attire. Who *was* she? She'd never played for any regional team other than the Scorpions, and to many fans, that defined her. Yet playing for England was a more significant achievement. Which shirt better depicted her career? Which colours looked best on the canvas—the Scorpions' red or England's blue? Ultimately, which would generate more sales?

He was debating this when the doorbell rang. Setting down his brush, he went to answer.

It was the one person guaranteed to set his day back by a few weeks.

'Hi, Ads,' Pippa said with undeserved and brazen good humour. She even had the temerity to use his nickname.

Smile to my face while you stab me in the back.

'Pippa,' he replied cordially.

'Can I come in?'

He laughed. 'You're kidding, right?'

'No. I hoped we could... smooth things over.'

Like soil on the professional grave you've been digging for me. 'What things?'

'That comment I said online.'

'Oh, the zip thing.' Amongst many others.

If I don't mention the "LIKE?" artwork, will she? Hard to say. Frankly, it's hard to figure out what the hell she's doing here.

'Yeah. Just... the green-eyed monster, I think.'

That was ripe for comment, but he avoided it. 'Fine. Bygones. Back to our lives. Thanks for popping by.' He stepped back, easing the door closed.

She tried to peer inside. 'What's the big secret, Ads? Is *she* in there?'

It seemed the green-eyed monster wasn't a temporary affliction for poor, mad Pippa.

'She who?' he asked innocently.

'Her. The cricketer.' Pippa's nose wrinkled.

He smiled sweetly. 'No. Ellie's not here. We're only friends. Cohabiting is a *little* further down the line.'

'But going to fancy award nights is okay?' She folded her arms. 'I knew there was something all along. I let you go to all those games, and, what, you were cheating on me the whole time? The bloody nerve—'

He leant in, eyes wide, hackles standing to attention. 'You are so far off the mark it's untrue. I go to cricket matches. End of. And if I want to be friends with Ellie, or even more, that's my sodding decision.'

Pippa scoffed. 'God, I dare you. Why? She's *so* beneath you.'

Adam was proud of his record of never hitting a woman, but that record was being sorely tested.

'Ellie is twice the woman you are or will ever be, Pip. You and I are done. Now, go away.'

She stepped forward, like a small child trying to pet a horse. Her hand landed on his chest. He decided to be the better person and not rip it away.

'Ads, look, things got out of control, and I wanted to say sorry, and I'm not really that person, and I did always love you.' She sighed pathetically. 'But the magazine needs stories, and—'

'Horseshit.'

A hundred-watt bulb went on above his head. Not an LED; one of the good, old-fashioned globes that could illuminate and heat a tiny student flat.

She wants me back. She's gone fruit loops.

She put on puppy dog eyes. 'The thing is... Mark and I broke up, and I suppose I realised that you and I had a good thing, and—'

'You were shagging your boss.' No surprise there.

She moved on, but a facial tic gave the game away. 'So it's not been an easy week, and you seem to be doing *very* well lately—'

Ah. Now I've had fifteen minutes of low-grade fame, that's apparently sufficient entry criteria for the Pippa bubble. I'm "acceptable" now.

Unbelievable.

He retreated further inside the hall. 'Thanks for the apology—if that *was* one. Sorry about the breakup with Mark. Have a good life.' He pushed the door.

She pushed back, exhaling like one of her £300 hairdryers on full power. 'Fine. Okay. I *get* that I'm not your favourite person. I was only trying to be civil. *Alright?*'

"Civil"? Accusing me of cheating on a girlfriend? Belittling Ellie's talent? I think the word you were looking for, Pip, is "desperate".

His nerves crackled. 'Pip, *please*. I'm working. There is no *us*. Not anymore. Go home. Before one of us says or does something silly.'

She eyed him for an age, thick lashes fluttering. 'Fine. Be like that. You know what you're missing out on.'

He did. Most of it was on show. The memories of Pippa in the shower were undeniably more embedded than the one-second flash of Ellie, yet he knew which woman he'd rather spend a pub lunch with. Or a weekend with. Or longer. Much longer.

'Certainly do,' he said lightly. 'Bye.'

She puffed a sigh of resignation, then frowned, biting her lip. Something was up. Something other than seduction, misdirection, or insult.

'Ads, be a love. Can I use the loo?' She eye-rolled theatrically. 'Bus was like ten minutes late, and it's an hour home.'

He wanted to point out that there was a café half a mile down the road, but the role of bitch point-scorer in this duel had already been taken, so he opened the door. 'You're impossible.'

'Yeah.'

She took the opportunity to squeeze past, face to face, puffing out her chest and flashing the glint in her eye.

'Unbelievable,' he breathed as her stacked heels clopped up the wooden stairs. 'There's a downstairs—'

She disappeared onto the landing. This was the problem with her knowing his house. A box-like loo was very un-Pippa. She wanted space, comfort... and probably to check whether Ellie's bra was lying on the floor.

If only you'd been here a week ago.

The memory resurfaced: Ellie beside him on the bed. The tattoo. The shapely legs. The upper thigh. Her hands on his. The bear hugs. Being utterly comfortable in her presence.

He shook that off, went into the kitchen, thumbed the kettle switch, then flicked it off. Whilst it was cuppa time, circumstances called for beer. He pulled a bottle from the fridge.

A minute later, Pippa locomoted down the stairs, mini-skirt barely covering the essentials. There was something almost supercilious about her air.

'Thanks, Adam.'

He led her to the door, only *slightly* concerned she'd decorated his ensuite and bedroom with her wee. 'We all have our little emergencies.'

'Yes,' she said sweetly. 'And I realise, now, that sometimes we can get obsessed about the wrong person, and we should let them go.'

'Absolutely.'

'Byesie bye.' She trotted away, making a meal of flouncing her hair as she went.

He closed the door. Hopefully that was the last chapter in whatever their relationship was or had been. It was ridiculous to believe that Pip would do something as disgusting and pointless as soiling his room. Wasn't it?

Still, he climbed the stairs, shaking more with each step, his body pre-empting the horror he expected to discover. He entered the bedroom with his eyes half-closed.

It seemed fine. No awful smell or stains, although the duvet looked somewhat rumpled.

The bathroom had been left pristine.

He poured cool lager down his throat, carrying away the relief that there was no nutty, despicable revenge.

His mobile pinged: an Instagram notification. He opened Ellie's post and watched the short interview. She answered questions about the match and her recent form, finishing with excitement about the upcoming England series.

He clicked his fingers, now knowing which colours to paint her in, and excited to resume the afternoon's work.

The studio was exactly as he'd left it. With two exceptions.

His brush had been moved.

And there was a six-inch wide cross, in glistening black paint, across Ellie's face.

48th Over

The three-day gap until the next match—Ellie's last before the South Africa trip—passed in a flash. There was a training day, extra gym sessions, promo work, arranging for Ayla to pop into the house a few times to collect mail, chats with her agent, a celebratory night out with a few Scorpions, and a spot of retail therapy.

She'd needed the retail therapy to lift her spirits after an interview spot that felt poorly timed. It focussed less on the future and more on the past, like a career retrospective. She couldn't help feeling aggrieved. Her career wasn't *over*. You don't print an obituary while someone's alive and kicking.

There had been no time to see Adam. Yes, they texted, but it was a poor substitute for hanging out. Would she miss him while she was away? Deeply. Could she afford to let that affect her game? No. If she performed well, England might give her a central contract in October. Then she'd be in prime position for that Test match at Lord's. The dream was within her grasp.

But first, there was today's innings to play. Still, she couldn't avoid glances towards the Square Leg boundary. Especially as someone was missing.

Never mind. Play the game. Play for the team. For me.

Adam looked through the viewfinder. From his position at Long On, he had a great shot of Ellie, almost straight ahead. He could zoom in with a long telephoto lens, capturing half-body or full-length poses as she played. Sometimes, there was enough joy and admiration to be gained by merely watching, as if through binoculars, as she plied her powerful yet graceful trade.

Sadly, it didn't last as long as he would wish—Ellie couldn't be expected to hit 137 *every* game—and she was caught behind on 23, wafting at a shot she should have left alone. Hardly an ideal launch pad for her England restart, and she did seem below par. Distracted, perhaps?

Stay in your lane, he told himself. *She already balled you out about picking holes in her form.*

When the match ended with a narrow defeat, he went to the Members' Bar for a coffee and waited for the players to emerge from the debrief. Around him, a few staff and fans came and went. He wondered why the players had been held up.

Roddy and Mads trotted down the stairs, the physio carrying a cake. Perhaps this was the explanation?

Roddy came over. 'Hi, Adam. How's things?'

Best not to burden her with the Pippa episode and its fallout.

'All good, thanks. Shame about the result today.'

'Can't win them all. Ells will be down in a sec.'

'Actually, it was you and Fi I was after.' He pulled Naira's cartoon from his rucksack.

Her face lit. 'Wow! This is brilliant. Look, Mads. Hilarious, right?'

Mads looked up from carving the cake. 'Oh, that's so you, Roddy. Adam, right?' He nodded. 'Have you done one for all the team?'

'No, just Roddy and Fi.'

'Oh, yeah. Fi said you were doing a drawing. Superheroes. Brilliant.'

More players took their seats, nattering and sharing jokes. Adam backed away, picking up his rucksack. 'I'll wait over there.'

Roddy tapped his arm. 'It's fine. Mads' birthday, that's all.'

'Don't ask how old,' she interjected.

'Have a slice of cake, Adam,' Roddy said. 'Friends and family, all welcome.' She inspected the cartoon. 'Is it alright if I post about this on social?'

His eyes widened. 'Umm... be my guest.'

Fiona appeared, and soon they were sitting at a table, discussing the picture. Roddy brought him a slice of cake on a paper plate. Then pizzas appeared. And a boom box. Soon, a chorus of Happy Birthday, a cooler of drinks, and more players complimenting his artistic skill.

When Ellie finally appeared, she didn't make a beeline for him, which was pleasing because this wasn't the environment in which to stoke malicious rumours. Roddy and Fi had surely recounted the tale of the fake flirting on the 14th hole.

Eventually, Ellie patted his shoulder and pulled up a seat. 'Hi.'

'Hi.'

'Missed you last time out. Not like... I mean...' She winced.

He'd seen her low score. Was she hiding something?

'I had a work thing,' he said, sparing her blushes. 'Potential client. That Bill guy, actually.'

'Oh, great. Nice problem to have, the day job giving you leads.' She pointed. 'The girls love their cartoons. I think there'll be more requests coming your way.'

'Today, Kent. Tomorrow, the world.'

She shrugged. 'Well, I'll be spreading the word around the England camp. If that's okay.'

'You've done enough, Ellie. A lot of what's happened over the last few weeks is because of you.'

She put a hand on his, her voice low. 'It's my pleasure. Besides, I need to save some of my *celebrity influence* for when my portrait is done.' Her wink was small and self-mocking.

He gritted his teeth. 'Yeah. About that.'

'What? Problem?'

There was no point hiding the Pippa catastrophe—especially as he wanted Ellie's advice. They'd smoothed over ZipperGate, thanks to bland yet firmly worded responses, followed by radio silence and not engaging with anyone who tried to stir up rumour.

He summarised Pippa's visit and showed a video on his phone.

Ellie sipped on a juice, her expression veering between disbelief and amusement. 'I mean, this would be hilarious if it wasn't so bloody awful. Christ, if this happened to me, I'd be tempted to hire a security detail. But the video? That's gold.'

'Yeah. But if I post it online, she will go apeshit. Or *more* apeshit. You're used to this kind of abuse, so I wanted you to tell me to hold off, be the bigger person.'

She shuffled her chair closer. It felt like a war room. 'I say keep your powder dry. You have evidence of criminal damage. If she thinks she's got away with it, maybe she'll leave you alone.'

'And you,' he pointed out.

The portrait had been a red rag to a bull, and the vandalism was Pippa's way of warning Adam not to "cheat" on her. This was impossible for two reasons, at least one of which she knew: they were no longer dating, and Ellie was merely a friend. Shame that Pippa hadn't spotted the time-lapse camera. It had provided a few minutes of much-needed laughter when he discovered the accidental recording of her act.

'I don't care,' Ellie said. 'I'll kick the shit out of her if she tries anything.'

'Should I at least *tell* her I can prove what she did? Send her a... screenshot of her painting technique?'

Ellie drummed her fingers on the table. 'Yeah, why not? A warning shot. Just don't go public. Be the better man. She can't *do* anything. She has no ammunition. Look, I'm out of the country for a bit, aren't I? If her visit was about trying to win you back, then even the maddest bunny boiler will recognise nothing is going on when I'm halfway around the world. Let it blow over. Maybe she's pissed off because your stock is rising, and hers is falling.'

Ellie was right: Pippa's Insta following had declined recently. Being derogatory about an ex wasn't as popular as cosmetics reviews, sunset selfies, and glimpses of her arse crack. What crushing irony that she resented Adam for hanging out with someone *more* famous. Pure insecurity. Jealousy.

'Thanks, Ells. You're a star.'

'You too.'

He stood. 'Feels like this is the point where I wish you good luck in the series.'

Her smile faded. 'Yeah. Odd to be stepping out of all this,' she gestured around, 'So soon after coming back. Odd in an exciting way, obviously.'

'Definitely. So... go well, Ellie. I'll be tuning in.' Inside, his soul was withering.

How can I handle weeks without her?

She hesitated, then angled her head to the door. 'Come outside for a second?'

'Sure.'

He grabbed his rucksack and followed her to the stands, where they took two of the thousands of empty seats. Below them, the groundsman was rolling the wicket. The silence, the emptiness, was unfamiliar. Portentous.

'Sorry I've not been around much,' she said.

'You don't have to apologise. I'm thrilled that you're busy. It means you're on the up.'

She gazed into his eyes. 'There's two sides to everything, Ads. Don't think I don't miss your company. Just because you don't hear from me for a few days doesn't mean I've filed those things in my memory bank, and now it's... back to reality. My friends understand that some days, some weeks, hanging out is a tough ask. But we hook up, and things are as good as always.'

He squeezed her hand. 'I understand. Same here.' There had been a time when he didn't see Jez for a year.

'So, text me, okay? Ideally, not during games.' She winked.

'Deal.'

'Good work on the portrait, by the way. Looks fab. Before the arrival of the nutjob with the black paint, obviously.'

'Thanks. I was hoping for a big reveal, but...' He shrugged.

She stroked his knee. 'Don't worry. I'll try to act surprised.' Her eyes twinkled. 'But you definitely have the boobs more accurate this time.'

'I worked *extra* hard on that part.' He nudged her.

'Well, if you need any detailed research later...'

He looked down, his neck burning. 'I know who to ask.'

She pecked his temple. 'I will love that picture, no matter what. Because you painted it.'

He met her eye. 'Thanks, Ells.'

She stood. 'I need to go.'

'Yeah.'

All it took was one look from her, a familiar one, and he pulled her into a hug. She laid her head on his chest. She fitted perfectly with him, hand in glove.

'I'll have everything crossed for you. Batgirl,' he murmured.

'Me too, Superman.' She broke off. 'See you... whenever.'

He brushed hair from her temple. 'Go well, Ellie Waites.'

'I hope so.'

He hefted up his rucksack. 'Toodles.'

She laughed, but her smile was laboured. 'Toodles.'

49th Over

The days before Ellie's departure were an emotional and logistical rollercoaster.

She was mainly occupied with logistics and prep, media spots, gym, and batting practice. There was a three-day training camp in London, so she stayed in a hotel and took the opportunity to catch up with friends there. A handful of the squad met up for the traditional pre-tour visit to a nail bar, followed by cocktails and tapas.

Her mobile pinged with a message from Diane—a photo of Grace holding up a drawing of Ellie with "GOOD LUCK IN SOUTH AFRICA" emblazoned across it.

'I'll do my best, Gracie,' she murmured.

Over two evenings, she finished the knitting project—a scarf in Scorpions colours. It had been an idle project with no recipient in mind: Grace had plenty of gifts lately, red wasn't Mum's colour, and she didn't think Adam would wear it. No matter; she'd find a home for it in due course.

She tried on the newly minted England shirt and examined how well the nail varnish toned. She took a selfie and sent it to her parents, Ayla, Laura, Diane, and Adam.

He replied, "The uniform of a future legend. Go well, Batgirl."

He hadn't ended it with an "x". She wished he had.

Move on, Ells. You have a friend, a dear one. Make that enough.

Adam worked hard to fill his hours.

He messaged Pippa, saying he was aggravated by her silly antics and she should tread very carefully, or he would go public. She didn't reply.

He found a home for the award trophy, setting it on his study desk. He wrote to the DVLA, informing them of the seizure, thereby cementing another 12 months without the ability to drive.

He restarted Ellie's picture from scratch. It wasn't a chore to pore over pictures of her and become immersed in brush strokes. The painting was different this time. Better. Sometimes, he caught himself looking at a photo, staring.

The official snap from the awards showed her in a different light, a different mood. He sat at his studio desk, examining an A4 print, running a fingertip over her face, lost in the memory of their crazy, life-affirming adventure. Something became clear: yes, she'd looked stunning that night, but in truth, her beauty had always been there. He'd just been an idiot not to realise.

Social media, sponsorship ads in cricket gear, and quick howdies in the autograph line didn't do her justice. It barely scratched the surface. He'd had the works, full-colour, HDR. Some painters in history had used drugs. Adam was high on Ellie Waites. Nothing else was necessary.

He painted at a glacial pace. Plenty of time to finish the portrait before she returned from the tour. It would be a nice coming-home gift... although he didn't plan to hand it over for free. She might mean the world to him, but he had to eat...

Charles Lyle proposed a date for the visit to scrutinise the Jimmy portrait. Bill Clay accepted the quote, securing Adam's work pipeline for the summer. He spent long hours planning the project.

Dad finally made his counter-move. Adam tapped his fingers, pondering whether to go in for the kill. If he won this game, it would be 3-3. Would the old man notice if Adam didn't seize the opportunity? Did it matter? The joy was in playing, not the victory. He moved a pawn.

At the next Scorpions' game, there was a warm welcome from Roddy, Fi and a couple of other players who now knew him. After the match, keeper Tara commissioned a cartoon.

In the evenings, he researched ways to spend this upturn in revenue, watched promotional material from the England Women's squad, and pinged the odd message to Ellie. She said that, at a farewell dinner for outgoing captain Anna Ritchie, she'd had a *very* promising conversation about a potential portrait of the England legend.

Unarguably, Adam's life had changed.

Ellie's last day before the flight to South Africa was an odd one.

After her early run and a gym session, Mum and Dad rang—on the landline, of course—to wish her luck. Perhaps they'd realised she was right to stick to her guns.

She packed the kit bag and cases. Her passport sat on the dining table, a gateway to another country and, perhaps, a new chapter. Its photo, conversely, was old. A more naïve Ellie looked out from the page. A junior professional with so many adventures to come. A woman who had recently lost a sister but found a family of girls. Someone who had committed her life to cricket and all it brought.

Now, it had returned her to the national team. That was no longer an unmet goal.

But there were others.

At a loose end and in danger of letting matters of the heart weigh, she tried to keep busy. Dusting, she stumbled upon the Batgirl picture, still unframed.

She hated the inertia of the Adam situation. It was like being stuck on a score of 99, the milestone so near yet so far. She remembered her first 100. She'd reached 99 just before the tea break. She couldn't stomach food or drink. She wanted to press on, get it done, pass the silly mental "Will I, won't I?" barrier. The nerves were ridiculous because accomplishing the feat was well within her.

Now, the challenge seemed impossible. Her mind darted between two realities: spending every day with a bat in her hand or spending every day with Adam. Waking up with him, holding him, talking, laughing. Kissing. And more. Yet, she couldn't imagine removing cricket from her mind, from her DNA. All the same, right now, cricket wasn't uppermost in her thoughts... which was invigorating, unhelpful, and worried her sick.

In a last-ditch effort to eliminate those feelings, she donned a pair of old joggers and a sweatshirt and started cleaning her car inside and out. For an hour, it was a brilliant diversion. Then, something plasticky clattered against the vacuum cleaner's nozzle.

Adam pushed the earrings around his palm. He'd been so focused on work that he'd forgotten to reunite Ellie with her jewellery.

Now, he was at an impasse. He was wary of a second goodbye and an awkward conversation. Whilst she hadn't kissed him at the stadium, her texts still had that signoff. If he popped over now, and she decided a kiss *was* appropriate, it would be hard for him not to kiss back... which might light a firework. A firework he was still holding, which would take their faces off.

Bad idea. Ellie was already being affected by having him in her life. Her last two terrible batting performances showed that, much as she might deny it.

Much as he wanted one, a relationship wasn't feasible. Not when she stood on the cusp of greatness. The past fortnight had been a window into that life: sometimes, it took hours for her to reply to messages. It couldn't have been through lack of motivation—clearly, she cared for him—so it was purely logistics. He remembered her words from a few days ago: "...nothing is going on when I'm halfway around the world...".

See. She knows it would be tough.

And things would only get tougher. She was off to play for her country. She'd be with her mates, her colleagues. The agenda was non-stop. And, if she took his words to heart, she wouldn't risk her mental focus by thinking about him. She'd spent years blazing a trail, all without him close by, so if his friendship now caused the wheels to fall off, it would be like summoning the courage to touch an endangered butterfly, only to inadvertently squash it. He would be distraught.

He toyed with her diamond studs. This wasn't about *him*. It was foolish to debate the merits of popping over to return her earrings. What if she'd been frantically searching, hoping to wear them to some swanky official shindig? She *should* look her best.

He showered, scrubbing flecks of paint from his hands and arms, pulled on something less slovenly, popped the earrings in a small envelope—not knowing if they were *real* diamonds—and took an Uber to her place.

Before he reached the door, it opened.

Startled, he stopped dead. Ellie also froze.

After a moment in which they were surely both thinking, "WTF?", she laughed.

'I mean... what?' she said.

He held up the envelope, which didn't clarify anything. She pulled something from her back jeans pocket. His lens cap.

'I wondered where that had gone.' He shook the earrings into his palm.

'I wondered where those had gone,' she parroted cheekily.

'Just in case you wanted something to go with a blue dress and a quickie in a Cape Town bog.'

She shot fake daggers and handed him the lens cap. 'Just in case you wanted to photograph someone else *for a change*.'

'Oh no. I only work with *England* cricketers now, don't ya know?' He slid the earrings back into the envelope and passed it over.

'Good. We top-tier *celebrities* demand a more dedicated level of fan, *don't ya know*?'

He held up the plastic disc. 'You've been vacuuming the car, right?'

She held up the envelope. 'You've been cleaning the bathroom, right?'

'Well, until I become a top-tier *celebrity* artist who can afford a cleaner, yeah.'

'You'll get there, Adam. I'm convinced.'

'Thanks.' He took a step back. 'I'll let you go. But... you were going to drive all the way over with a cheap bit of plastic?'

'Yeah. No big deal. Clearly, if I was a *proper* celebrity, I'd have a Jeeves to chauffeur it to you, but until then...'

'I should drop the whole "celebrity" thing, shouldn't I?'

Her expression was plaintive. 'Sometimes, it's endearing. But mostly, it's *really* bloody annoying.'

'I know. Sorry. So, anyway, go well. Again.' He backed off.

She stepped close. 'Look, I was hoping we could... chat. Come in? I could ask Jeeves to rustle up a cuppa.'

He rubbed his chin. 'Last night before the tour? Better not.'

She checked her watch. 'Adam, it's five-thirty. I'm already packed. The alarm's not until seven a.m. And I'm so bored shitless I topped up the washer fluid *and* used a pin to clean the wiper jets. Jeeves is *such* a slacker with those nozzles.' She winked, then explored his eyes. 'I'll sleep a lot better if we can... figure some things out. Please?'

Her self-deprecating good humour was as infectious as ever. He'd never had a mate he missed like this. Only girlfriends. Which said a lot.

He waved her inside.

50th Over

M ilk, one sugar, right?' she asked.

'Good memory. Nice nails, by the way.'

She wriggled her fingers. 'Cheers. And thanks for dropping the earrings over. You didn't have to. But I'm glad you did.'

'No problem. Didn't want you scrabbling around tonight. But please tell me they're not five-quid fakes from Argos. The taxi cost more than that,' he joked.

She brewed the teas. 'Not sure what they're worth. Gift from Mum on my England call-up. First one, I mean.'

He leant on the kitchen worktop. 'Nothing this time around? "Been there, done that"?'

'Other than having them chauffeured here by an award-winning artist? No.'

He grinned. 'This "award-winning artist" thing. Sometimes, it's endearing. But mostly, it's *really* bloody annoying.'

She passed him a mug. 'I'm glad we're over that.'

They sat on the sofa. Her heart pattered, seeing the tension on his face. But she *had* to know.

She squeezed his hand. 'Look, I have to tell you something. When you were postictal, and I was... bored... I went into your studio. I saw your notes about me.'

He shrugged. 'Okay, so I'm not a perfect study of character. Or a perfect artist. You know those portraits are more than painting a pretty face or slapping on an Insta filter. What did I miss?'

'Maybe nothing. But you didn't mention... looks.'

He frowned gently. 'No need. Your external beauty is there for all to see. It's the *internal* battles, the fires, the *soul* that I need to convey.'

Her chest filled.

Oh gosh. This is going to be even tougher now.

She smiled. 'And you're a beautiful soul, too. I meant what I said before, on the golf course. I don't deserve you. As a friend. Much less as my... batting partner.'

He eased back a few inches. It said plenty.

She shuffled closer so their hips touched. 'We *are* on the same page, aren't we?'

He licked his lips, eyes sad. 'Yeah.'

She caressed his fingers one by one. 'When we lost Paige, my game suffered so badly. Yes, I took time away, but even when I came back, my mind kept drifting. It has... drifted to you a *lot* lately. You saw the run out. And the last game. You were right. I *was* thinking of you.' She clenched her jaw. 'It's so *fucking* annoying and unprofessional, and I *wish* I was more of this... woman of steel, this cold-hearted automaton. That I could dial in to my game one hundred percent, every single second. Shut out the world and my heart and my feelings and *everyone* who meant and means something to me. If I'm this... superhero you drew, *that's* my kryptonite.'

His face creased into empathy, and his palm came to her cheek. She pressed into it, wanting the touch to never end.

He spoke gently. 'Ellie, I'm not sure I would care about you more, or less, if you were this... ice queen. It would make you a better player but less of a person. We all have our weak spots, errors in judgement, frailties. From the outside, everyone watching only sees your... mistake. A batting error. Only *you* have the guilt, and I'm so lucky you've told me, and hopefully, we can stop another bad spell.'

She kissed his knuckles. 'And that's why I adore you, Adam. You want the best for me.'

'Always.' His smile was weak, pained.

'Fuck,' she breathed, pulling him into a hug. He squeezed back so hard that she thought it would be the final straw, wringing out her soul until tears came.

She spoke into his neck. 'I've faced the top bowlers in the women's game, and *this* is the hardest match of my fucking life.'

'I'm so sorry, Ells.'

'Don't be. Just...' She let her body fall limp, relaxing onto him.

He stroked the back of her head. She ached for an impossible togetherness.

'Hmm?' he murmured, gently prompting her.

Reluctantly—against better judgement—she eased away.

Damn this.

'I know love and cricket aren't the same. Even though I want both. Maybe I'm crazy to want both *now*. To not have to wait until the career is gone and I have time for the "normal people" hubby-and-two-kids life. Which is bollocks because I'm *already* normal. I want the person who is right for me. Whenever they turn up. Is that selfish? Is that too much to ask?'

He brushed her hair. 'No. No, it isn't.'

That was enough. That and the sadness in his eyes. The forlorn hope. The understanding. The affection.

She took his face in her hands and kissed him.

His skin prickled, the hairs on his neck leaping to attention. Her kiss was firm and brief, a statement rather than a question. A coda, not an overture. No come-on. No lust. Only "This is how I feel".

And yet.

He already knew her feelings. He didn't need the kiss. But he was elated to receive it. And when she broke off, examining his face for a reaction, a comeback, he saw a tic of nerves, worry that she'd crossed a line.

Misplaced, Ellie.

So, with two fingers, he gently cupped her jaw and kissed her. Softly, affectionately. The way you do when you've met the woman of your dreams: "You're magnificent".

Five seconds of that heady experience was fifty years too short. But it was done. He'd scratched the itch. An itch in the middle of your back that's difficult to reach, so you have to contort your arm. And you risk pulling a muscle, causing an ache which lasts longer than the itch would have, if only you'd been sensible enough to let it go away.

Had they both pulled a muscle?

An awkward silence fell. He manoeuvred her to his side, put an arm around her waist, and pulled her in. This would avoid more kissing. He didn't need more. He'd had enough to make a decision. To know that things were precisely as exasperating as he'd realised over recent days.

One ball left. 7 runs to win.

Not even Don Bradman could manage that. Or Eleanor Amanda Waites.

She laid her head on his shoulder.

He squeezed her thigh. 'I want more time with you than I can have. You won't be here for days. Weeks. Months, soon. And I can't be at every game. And when I'm not, but I'm on your mind, it affects your game. And I *will not* do anything to spoil your comeback.'

She trailed fingers up and down his leg, then over his hip and stroked his chest. His skin crackled with her touch. Hercules never mustered restraint like this.

Then she sat up, crossed one leg over the other, and faced him. 'I know. And I wouldn't only *think* about you when you weren't there. I'd worry.'

He shook his head. 'It's not your job to worry. You've got more important things on your plate. Like being Batgirl. *I* don't worry, and I'm the one who could die.'

She closed her eyes against those words. 'Yes. Die if I'm not there.'

He caressed her cheek. 'I've had this for years, Ells. I'm still here. You cannot sacrifice your job, your passion, your *life* to be my bloody... carer. Then *I* would be the guilty one.'

She pressed a fist against her leg. 'I know. I *know*. This whole thing has been living in my head for days. And it's shown me two things. You have a life, and you don't fly. I have a life, and it takes me where it takes me. It's full-on. And those things don't go well together.'

'Not really, no.'

'Something else I've realised, and, sorry, I hate comparisons, but will you indulge me?'

'Anything. You know that.'

'I never thought too much about Jack when I was playing. He didn't come to a single game. He was like... a comfort blanket I came home to. After the first date—'

'"Eyes met across an empty soup shelf".'

She laughed. The levity was welcome. A release valve on a bulging gas tank.

'God, I adore you, Adam.' She stroked his nose, then painted on a serious face. 'With Jack, there wasn't much debate about how it would work. The pitfalls. The distance. We simply... got on with it, felt our way. I was going hell for leather on my career, and he let me.'

'Fair enough. Decent guy.'

'Until the end, yeah.' She grimaced. 'So I've been thinking, "Why the big inquiry now?"'

'And...?'

'No soup aisle this time. I already care more about you than I ever did for Jack. My last two relationships, especially the breakups, buggered up my game for months. You know that. And I'm already having blips, wondering if you felt the same. Missing you.' A sombre smile appeared.

'Understandable. I'm quite the catch.' Gallows humour.

She bopped his chest. 'I can't risk falling even harder than I have. Failure is part of the game, remember? The game of love, I mean. And a breakup isn't what I need right now. I need something that sticks. Long term.'

'Which is not with me?' he inferred, the flame in his heart cooling.

'I don't think it's with anyone. It's asking too much to keep hold of my coattails.'

'It... isn't forever, though, right?' He winced, afraid she wouldn't take kindly to being reminded about her very finite career.

'No. But what do you want me to say? "Wait for me"?'

He waggled his head. 'I mean—'

'No. That's madness. Ask you to fend off the perfect woman for the next three years while you wait for me to hang up my bat? No way.'

'So...?'

'This gig of mine is all about timing. And ours is... off. Right?' she asked expectantly.

He slumped against the backrest. 'Yeah.'

They wanted the same thing: entwined lives. Closeness. Mutual care and support. They also wanted her to go out in a blaze of glory. A blaze which would last as long as it did, hopefully longer. And then she would find her second calling, somehow.

She pulled her legs across his. 'This is why it hurts so much. You get it, like I knew you would. Because you're my perfect batting partner. It's why we can't risk anything which kills this.' She pointed at them both. 'I'm pretty damn sure I can get through a game without thinking about a *friend*. But not someone I'm dating. Especially if that someone is you. In fact, *only* if it's you. I don't *want* to get you out of my mind, Ads. Not for a second. But I *need* to. Either that or I have to become a robot ice queen by next week.'

He pointed a finger at her forehead and pressed gently. 'For-get A-dam. For-get A-dam,' he intoned mechanically.

She kissed his hand. 'It's still going to be... difficult.'

'But you can do anything, Batgirl.'

Her smile was thin. 'It's the shot I'm playing. The choice was to come forward or stay back. I reckon stay back.'

He gave a resigned nod. 'I reckon too. Defensive. Safest.'

'But you bowled a hell of a delivery, Adam Glenn.' She stroked his cheek. 'Best I ever faced.'

'I had to be good to stand a chance of... getting your wicket. Missed out on the maiden, too.'

'Maid. I've played *quite* a few overs.' A faint but impish smile appeared.

He patted her knee. 'I hope we'll have a lot more. As friends. Good friends.'

'I guarantee it.'

In that silence, she licked her lips, but a kiss didn't come. He was pleased. No point in muddying the waters.

'Stay for dinner?' she suggested. 'Last supper before the convicted woman ships out?'

'I think... thanks, but no thanks. I'm all out of conversation.' He drained his mug. The tea was cold. 'I'll go. Dinner *would* be lovely, but... how about a welcome home meal for the conquering heroine? Next month, venue of your choice.'

Hopefully if his finances continued to improve, he could wine and dine her—as a friend—in a manner to which she was accustomed. Then again, knowing Ellie, she'd be happy with a curry.

'It's a date. I mean, not a *date*, but... you know.' She cocked her head.

'Good.' He rubbed her shoulder, then stood.

On the table sat a woollen coil, striped in red and black.

'Want me to run this over to Grace while you're away?' he asked.

She fingered the scarf. 'It wasn't for her. Wasn't for anyone, really.'

'Okay.'

'Fancy a leaving present?'

He frowned. 'You're the one who's leaving.'

'But it's hot enough in Cape Town.' She shook out the scarf and affectionately hung it around his neck.

He didn't care what it looked like, if it suited him. 'Thanks, Ellie.'

Her smile was laboured. 'S'okay.'

She showed him to the door. Every step was leaden. The silence was horrendous.

'Thanks for... coming over,' she said, flat, small.

'Thanks for... everything.'

The most uncomfortable standoff.

He pulled her into an embrace. She clung on like a limpet.

'Go well, Ellie Waites,' he whispered, pecking her cheek, moisture in his eyes.

'Go well, Adam Glenn,' she replied in kind.

51st Over

The plane climbed into the sky.

Ellie watched the ground recede, willing herself to leave worries behind in England. She was trapped in a metal tube for twelve hours and mustn't stew about their relationship. It wouldn't solve anything, and there were more important matters.

The job. Ellie 2.0.

Don't let the girls down. Don't let the country down. Paige. Yourself.

She bit her lip.

Adam.

Adam had a troubled night, endlessly replaying the heart-to-heart, knowing the decision was for the best, but hating it. It felt like a breakup, which was ridiculous. Had they dated, a breakup might have happened anyway, and realistically, he was as likely as Ellie to be the cause. As she'd said, relationships, like innings, end. It's simple statistics.

He sipped his breakfast coffee, hoping it would perk his spirits.

The cloud lifted when he saw the upbeat Instagram posts from @EllieWaites20 and a few other England players. She was where she belonged. She'd be back next month, and unless either of them did something dumb to kill the friendship, they'd have that meal, chat about the series, he'd show her the finished portrait—maybe they'd work out a payment plan. She might recommend him to more people, the business would flourish, and he'd always have the memories.

So long as she was *happy*. He wanted to be happy, too. Ideally, with her. But 7 to win? Was that possible? How could they be apart and not miss each other, not worry? Was it as easy as turning off a light, extinguishing the embers that glowed in their hearts? Or, was there a way to be together every day... or more often than they were now?

The lens cap sat nearby on the table. He ran a finger around its circumference. It had been lost on the day he drove her home. The day things really started. He wondered whether she'd taken those earrings to South Africa. Whether she'd wear them. Whether she'd think of him. He hoped not.

He chuckled sadly, realising how lucky he was in comparison. There was no harm in thinking about her.... except a sense of wasted thought, of banging his head against a brick wall.

He was entitled to remain in love with her.

After all, it *was* possible to score 7 runs off one ball. Rare, but with hard running—and a slice of luck—it could be done.

Over the next couple of days, he finished two more player caricatures and spent many diligent hours on Ellie's portrait, her scarf across around his shoulders. Roddy and Fi had permitted him to put the cartoon time-lapses online, and the videos quickly gained a slew of positive comments.

Then, a spanner was thrown in the works. Pippa replied to his DM, saying she had no idea what he was talking about. "Vandalism? You're mad."

So he sent her the freeze-frame, along with the comment, "Red-handed."

Nothing happened for a day. Then she put out another Insta post. It was a rehash of the ZipperGate photo, but this time, she'd drawn an arrow to his groin, overlaid a picture of a worm, and added the comment, "Guess what's in here?"

How could he remain the better person? He wanted to break something. She deserved to be taken down a peg or two, but in public? That was stooping to her level. She wasn't trying to destroy his career, only to inflict emotional hurt. Yet the laughter at his expense had to stop unless it somehow *did* impact his standing. Things were going too well to be ruined now.

His WhatsApp pinged. It was a picture from Ellie. They'd been messaging intermittently—open, not regretful, wishful or flirty. She was standing under a sign for "Adam's Bar"—a random joint in Cape Town—and pointing, grinning inanely but adorably. That relaxed him. Calmly, he thanked her for the message and asked her to look at Pippa's feed.

There was no reply for ages.

Then she said, "You're a risk-averse person. Not sure I can advise. But I'd give the bitch both barrels."

"Thanks. Good luck tomorrow."

"Thanks. You too."

Adam chose something tedious to do while watching the game so he could give the TV due attention. He worked on website revisions on his laptop at the dining table.

Seeing Ellie in an England shirt again filled him with joy. But how would she perform? Had the plan worked? Could she focus? Would sidelining love allow her to be as brilliant as she empirically was?

His fingers drummed on the table.

The match was an IT20, the first of five, after which came a 3-match ODI series. On paper, England should win both series, but nothing was certain, especially with a new captain, Olivia, in place. It might be more challenging today because South Africa had batted first and posted an excellent score of 176.

"Please welcome to the field your England opening batters, number 14, Bryony Taylor and number 29, Jess Norcroft."

Whoops and hollers rang around the balmy Cape Town stadium.

Sitting in the dugout, Ellie's foot jiggled impatiently. After the sightseeing, the nights out, the training days and the media spots, zero hour was a massive relief. It wasn't ideal to bat at 3 rather than 1, but she was lucky to be in the squad. The mentally toughest time in any game was the countdown to batting. It was easier for an opener than for a lower-order batter, as there was certainty about timings.

Here and now, Ellie had no idea whether she'd be needed in one minute, ten minutes, or an hour. It frazzled her nerves. At least she wasn't thinking about Adam.

She had a new bat in her hand. New opportunities at her fingertips. She was exactly where she'd wanted and worked hard to be.

Chill. I can do this.

Bryony and Jess accelerated to 82-0 after 10 overs, the halfway mark. Then Jess was out for 35.

Ellie strode purposefully to the middle.

Adam stopped working. He clenched a fist. 'Come on, Ells.'

Things didn't start well. She wafted at a couple of deliveries, then narrowly escaped being caught at Gully when on a score of 8.

He closed his laptop.

This is too stressful. Imagine if we were dating—I'd have to watch her innings through my fingers or from behind the sofa, like it was Dr Who.

By the 13th over, she'd found her groove but was playing second fiddle to Bryony, who'd swept past 50.

With four overs to go, England were in sight of victory at 167. Ellie, on 42, was carving out a measured and mature innings. She knew, as did Adam, that Bryony was the in-form batter that day.

Adam moved to the sofa, elbows on his knees, rapt.

In the next over, Bryony moved to 96, England to 173.

4 to win. 4 for Bryony to hit her maiden professional century. All Ellie had to do was *not* score. In the next over, she was on strike and could have won the game at least twice, but she defended every delivery for a dot ball.

Penultimate over. Bryony at the crease. Perched on the edge of his seat, Adam saw the knowing glances between the women, a sense of excitement and yet apprehension.

Bryony hit the first delivery for 2. The next three balls were dots.

Had Ellie gambled the game away on a sentimental milestone? If the team lost now, the coach would be fuming.

Eight balls. 2 to win. 2 for Bryony's century.

Adam would have poured a steadying whisky if there had been time.

There wasn't. Bryony launched the next ball over Mid-wicket for 4.

Adam leapt up, punching the air. 'Come on!'

On the TV screen, the girls exchanged a hug, then Bryony raised her bat to the crowd. Ellie patted her partner on the back. She hadn't played for Paige, or Adam, or even, really, for herself. She'd played for the team and shown utter class and generosity by handing Bryony her hundred.

A tear formed in Adam's eye. 'God, you are an amazing woman.'

Ellie had said that if someone else came into his life, someone better, more suitable, he should take the opportunity, and she would acccpt it.

That could never happen. There was nobody better than Ellie. She was everything. She was who he wanted.

52nd Over

I t was a night for celebration, but Ellie took it easy. It was Bryony's party.

There was another reason she left after two cocktails, returning to the hotel room, which she'd taken sole occupancy of.

Although she'd done well not to pointlessly scour the crowd for Adam's face or Paige's soul, she hadn't reckoned on spotting Jack. Sure, girlfriend Mary was playing for the home team, so why shouldn't he fly out to be with her?

Because it's bloody hard, that's why.

I already have to share the stadium with Mary, but this, too? Not fair. I suppose it shows we weren't meant to be. He never gave a shit about cricket. Now he's flown intercontinental to stick by his new love?

Wow. I really wasted those years. And the real kick in the teeth? It was while I was away in New Zealand, and Mary was still in the UK, that his eyes wandered.

Breathe.

I did damn well to play Mary's bowling carefully today, so I will not rise to revenge on either her or Jack. That's Pippa territory.

Instead, Ellie could only see the void in her love life and the desire to fill it with someone more suitable. Someone who wouldn't cheat while she was abroad. She wanted to show Mary and Jack that she was alright now, thank you very much.

She wasn't alright.

She moved the earrings around her palm. Recalling the awards night. Taking the earrings off in Adam's bathroom. Not missing them but being delighted when he returned them. Loving that he cared that much.

And then, the kiss. Not hers, which was merely caving under pressure. His kiss, which had been the most tender, well-judged, spine-tingling thing.

Unfortunately, it had effectively been a kiss goodbye. Goodbye to love.

So, move on, Ells. Like you promised him.

Adam felt odd going to the Scorpions game without Ellie there, but it didn't affect how he was received. Roddy and Fi greeted him with hugs, and he thanked them for their Insta posts. They'd shared pictures of their cartoons and namechecked him. In the last week, his follower count had risen by almost a thousand.

He caught up with Lisa and Max, giving her a potted history of the awards and the aftermath. He didn't go into detail about the almost-but-no situation with Ellie, although Lisa's eyes betrayed that she knew—and had probably seen for some time—a spark between Adam and the plus-one he wanted by his side every day.

Wicket-keeper Tara stayed to chat after he delivered her cartoon in exchange for five crisp twenties. Her new sausage dog, Flo, scampered around their feet until she scooped it up. Adam smoothed its small, soft ears.

He was undeniably inside the bubble now. Dating Ellie would absolutely not be as carefree as this, although he'd be able to smooth *her* ears... and other parts.

Moot. Move on. Like we agreed.

Charles Lyle came to view the James Anderson portrait. He was precisely as Adam had pictured; silvery hair, cravat and pocket square.

The painting stood on the easel in the studio, centre stage. Despite being apparently short of time, Charles spent an eternity scrutinising it from different distances and directions, firing off questions, not all on-topic.

Adam's nerves were shredded.

Is this what the "real" art world is like? Perhaps I should stick to cartoons and photography.

Charles pulled his chequebook from a jacket pocket and leant on the side table as he wrote a cheque for the agreed £10,000. Adam remembered cheques from his youth.

'What's all this?' Charles asked absentmindedly, pocketing his gold pen. He flitted a finger at the photos and preliminary sketches of Ellie.

'My current project, Mr Lyle.'

'Ah.' He peered at the almost-complete portrait which leant against the wall. 'Seems a bit odd.'

'In what way?' Adam knew he'd done a sterling job.

'This a... sportswoman of some kind?'

Adam's palms moistened. 'Yes. Another cricketer, actually.'

The best one. The loveliest one. In other circumstances, my dream future.

'What?' Charles' bushy eyebrows furrowed. 'A *woman* cricketer?'

'Absolutely.'

Lyle scoffed. 'What rot. Not in my day. Cricket's a man's game.'

Adam's neck prickled. 'Well, things change.'

'Why on earth would you waste time on *girls'* sport, Mr Glenn?' He pointed at the artwork he was about to own. 'There's your heroes. There's your athletes.' He tendered the cheque. 'Anyway...'

Adam unclenched a fist, gently took the career-altering piece of paper, and tore it in half.

He gave the pieces to an astonished arsehole. 'Your money's no good here, Mr Lyle.' He grabbed the man's hand and pumped it once. 'Thanks for coming down. I'll see you out.'

Things went from bad to worse that evening.

Pippa posted a doctored picture of him holding the award, except the inscription on the trophy read "Biggest Loser Ever". Now he *really* wanted to pop to the big Asda, buy a baseball bat, drive to her flat and smash all her car windows.

However, that was the behaviour of a moron. Instead, he tracked down the email address of Dean, Pippa's boss and most recent ex/victim, and sent him the time-lapse video, along with a factual and non-inflammatory covering note. Adam justified it on the basis of warning Dean to be mindful of having his brake lines cut or waking up next to a horse's head.

Fame can do strange things to people. It hadn't harmed Ellie—in fact, it barely seemed to change her.

Pippa, it had ruined.

Me?

He was more visible, but there was no *fame*. And, despite the setbacks, he was flying high.

Shame about that ten grand, though.

The following day, it was the second IT20 match. Unsurprisingly, after a good knock last time out, Ellie was named in the team.

He pinged her a good luck message. Best not to bother her with the Charles and Pippa fiascos. He wanted her mind to be on the game.

She replied a while later: "Thanks! BTW, I may have someone interested in your Jimmy painting."

This was getting a bit silly. She'd done enough for him already.

"Who?" he replied.

"Someone on the commentary team out here."

Blimey. Not a snotty-nosed art collector. Someone who cares about cricket.

He typed, "Wow, that's great. No problem sending pic to SA for the right price!"

Sod the shipping cost. More important to rescue victory from the jaws of self-inflicted but feel-good defeat.

"Oh, he is from the UK," she replied.

Even better.

"OK, cool. What's his name?"

She didn't reply.

Bugger. What a way to keep a guy on tenterhooks!

Then his phone pinged. The message was a selfie of Ellie, grinning wildly—as usual—and pointing to the person beside her.

James Anderson.

53rd Over

An hour later, Ellie sloped off the pitch, bat across her shoulders, shaking her head.

Idiot. Failure WILL happen when you don't focus.

In the changing room, she ripped off her pads and whacked them repeatedly against the locker.

Jade wordlessly left the room.

Ellie roared primevally.

Out for 5. Christ.

To a good ball, fine. To that ball? No. Stupid cow.

Luckily, it hadn't been a delivery from Mary Kallis. The source of her dismissal had been the other demon inside her skull. The one who wasn't a demon but who she couldn't exorcise.

The plan wasn't working. Talking to Jimmy about the artwork had put Adam in her mind.

She paced the changing room, trying to expel him from her thoughts. It was tough. She could really use one of his hugs.

During South Africa's innings, she fielded like a bag of wet cement. She dropped two catches; absolute sitters. She was absolutely furious. Guilty. Ashamed.

Back home, Adam would be watching, shaking his head, knowing she was better than this. Which she was.

Just not today.

Adam wondered what had happened to Ellie. For sure, England lost the match.

It's probably the Mary thing. It better not be because I'm still rattling around her skull. Anyway, what can I do from 8000 miles away? If I call her, it'll make things worse.

He could only play his own game, so he doubled down on work, finishing Ellie's portrait and planning the shoot locations for the Geoghan Associates project.

Dean from *ME & Tea* emailed, thanking Adam for the heads-up. Pippa's employment was being terminated, but Adam wasn't implicated. While Dean was happy to run a gossip magazine, he drew the line at employees being vindictive graffiti artists. Plus, if her online behaviour spiralled further downwards, she was a PR liability.

Adam hoped that was the end of the Pippa debacle... but doubted it.

After a troubled night, Ellie had an early breakfast in the hotel.

James Anderson was at a table, so she pulled up a chair and soon they were chatting. It was getting easier to be around a sporting icon. He'd complimented her media spots and said if ever she wanted to do a few minutes on Test Match Special, he'd put in a good word.

She reached under the table and pinched herself.

It was a rest day. Three of the girls had planned a round of golf, so she tagged along—something to lift her from an introspective gloom.

The golf course, in the shadow of Table Mountain, was stunning. The weather and company were perfect. Ellie's body was loose, and her shots were generally excellent. The camaraderie was doing a fine job of sealing her tight inside the England bubble, shutting out home and what she'd left behind, physically and emotionally.

Then she shanked a drive into the bushes lining the fairway. As she poked through the undergrowth with her rented 3-iron, she fell still, reminisces tapping at her skull. A smile spread across her face... then faded.

I can move past a bad shot, but I can't get over a person. Over him.

What kind of player can't do this? What chance do I have of making a decent fist of this second chance?

Ball in hand, she trudged onto the fairway and took the shot. Watching the ball sail onto the green, her eye was drawn by a vapour trail in the sky. She traced its course, imbibing the scenery below the canopy of blue.

Adam would love it here. I bet his landscape photos would be gorgeous.

Her shoulders fell.

She played the last five holes lazily, as if doing well didn't matter. She was consumed by the fear that by turning her back on romance—for the greater good—she was missing out on the Goldilocks Guy. It was a player mentality: one ball at a time. Live in the now.

That's me. Don't look to the future. Put off the decisions. Sort out my new career later. Find a bloke when it's convenient.

Cricket. Cricket. Cricket.

And I thought Dani was the single-minded ice queen.

Yet it wasn't selfishness. She was saving Adam from a difficult choice; face his travel fears and compromise his work by shadowing every step of her journey, or have a long-distance relationship, ships

315

that pass in the night. Either way, the challenge would get greater in the short term. To squeeze the pips on her career—and build a financial nest egg—she'd be throwing her hat in the ring for all the far-flung winter tournaments.

Adam knew all this.

It didn't stop her wondering whether Mum and Dad would approve of him. Not that she needed their blessing; it was *her* life. She hadn't stayed with Jack simply because her parents thought he was the right guy, a safe pair of hands with a good job, a man who could carry her through a post-cricket life. Perhaps if they couldn't have a daughter with a traditional career, a son-in-law with a 9-to-5 was the next best thing. Dad was old-fashioned like that, borne of a life in professional services, Mum the dutiful housewife.

Similarly, Ellie hadn't stuck with cricket out of spite. She'd been driven by passion and talent, although there was always a sense of Paige on her shoulder, an angel you need to do right by. As well as being the tearaway, Paige was the smarter daughter and had been studying bioscience. Her loss was life-shattering, but Ellie didn't have to take her sister's place to make Mum and Dad proud, certainly not at the expense of her happiness.

Years of intense dedication and focus had brought Ellie to this point. Still, it was hard to maintain that single-topic attention when something else lived in her heart now, too. Someone who set her world on fire.

And I think Paige would have liked him.

Three days later, Adam tuned into the next England game, the third IT20. So far, each side had won a match. It was important for England to get their noses in front.

He sank deeper into the sofa. It had been a productive week, and he deserved a break, watching his friend represent her country.

Again, his chest swelled with love and pride as Ellie walked out to bat. Yet she seemed unusually listless, head bowed.

'Come on, Ells,' he willed, clenching a fist.

She was out for a duck.

Her walk off was trance-like. She couldn't even be bothered to be angry. Still, he noticed a tell-tale glance to the Square Leg boundary.

He put his head in his hands. 'Oh, shit.'

She hadn't scored 0 in three years. He didn't need Grace to tell him that.

"New batter for England, number 52, Talia Kemp."

He muted the TV and trudged up to his studio. Arms folded, he faced the portrait.

'What is it, Ells?'

A little voice in his head had the answer... or *an* answer.

She'd been in sparkling form, had trained like a machine, and was arguably at the peak of her career. Everything was in her favour. She should be on an emotional mountaintop. And, on the 99% chance that he *wasn't* responsible for her recent failures, he simply wanted her to be as adorably brilliant as she fundamentally was.

He stepped closer to her likeness, her dynamism and larger-than-life persona captured in a hundred colours. He'd never been prouder of, or more satisfied by, any of his work. Still, it gnawed at his bones.

He ran a gentle fingertip over the brushstrokes that formed her lips. His eyes misted over. 'Please, Ells. Let me go.'

317

Arm in arm with Bry and Rojo, Ellie moseyed down the urban Cape Town street to their destination. The place was alive with noise, heat and light.

She'd dressed in a favourite trousers and blouse combo and, on a whim, added the earrings Adam had rescued. It wasn't done in honour of him. That would be silly. She was trying to do what they'd agreed, to focus on the job. Ignore ridiculous notions of dating the man of her dreams. Obviously, that mantra needed work.

Don't panic. I've had dips in form before.

Except this one was on the world stage.

She felt hollow, sapped of confidence.

Still, nothing a karaoke bar won't fix. Hopefully.

Rojo had the honour of choosing the venue, as her wickets—a maiden International five-fer—had helped England to a narrow win. Ellie's first-ball capitulation hadn't cost the team dearly, so she was going to let her hair down. She was with her mates. England led the series. Her mojo *would* return.

It better do. Or I've lost both my form and my man.

Overnight, Adam wrestled with his conscience. Was there any way to shake Ellie from whatever mental or emotional slump she was in?

But what to say? "I still believe in you"? "Buck your ideas up"? "Thinking of you"?

All three were valid.

After breakfast and a strong coffee, he cleared his unread email. Then, as a reward, he checked Insta. The England coach was upbeat. Bryony had posted a picture of herself, Rose and Ellie dressed up for a night out. Rose had been interviewed about her five-wicket haul. Ellie hadn't posted anything.

Refreshing the feed, a new post appeared.

His stomach began to eat itself.

Pippa's visit hadn't only been about jealousy-fuelled graffiti. She'd kept one more arrow in her quiver.

It explained the ruffled duvet he'd noticed that day. She'd slipped off her blouse and bra straps to give the impression of being partially or fully naked. The shoulder-length selfie showed her with the bed, wardrobe, and ensuite door behind. With a rank taste in his mouth, Adam had to concede that the vile witch composed a decent photo.

The text read, "So pleased to be back in this room again! Lotta memories [wink emoji]"

Fighting for breath, chest tight, he gripped the sofa arm, trying to calm the zinging paths of his mind.

He should have nipped this in the bud earlier. He'd been too meek, letting Pippa tilt at windmills, believing she couldn't do any real harm.

This, however, wasn't just an arrow she'd fired. It was a missile.

54th Over

Ellie woke late. She didn't have a hangover; gallons of booze weren't necessary when you had teammates and friends like this. When Rojo was belting out songs, getting up to mischief. When the music in the club was perfect for cutting loose after a hard day of disappointing people.

People.

Under the sheets, she pulled her knees up to her chest. The hotel bed felt enormous. What she'd give to be the little spoon, a big spoon behind her, his lips on her neck, hands on her hips, backside, thighs...

She screwed up her eyes.

You will not go, will you, Adam?

Her mobile pinged. She uncurled and took the phone from the nightstand.

Diane's text read, "Thinking of you. Love from Grace too.".

Ellie sighed hard, shaking her head. 'You need to be better at this than me, Gracie. Maybe you ought to start looking up to someone else.'

She replied, "Thanks."

Then, she made the mistake of looking at Instagram. Quickly, a theme developed: the world was not happy with the performance of Ellie Waites.

Her throat constricted, yet she stupidly doom-scrolled the comments.

"What were the selectors thinking?" "Useless bitch." "Overpaid underperformer." "Step aside, Ellie." "You suck, Waites." "Not worthy of the shirt." "My 6yo could play better." "Past it. Retire NOW!!!" "Can't bat for shit."

Chest thundering, she frantically swiped away the vitriol. She needed an emotional pick-me-up. Now.

Wonder if Adam's painting has sold?

She froze mid-scroll, staring, heart turning to stone.

Shit. He can't... he wouldn't...

Hand shaking, she quit Instagram, held down the icon and deleted the app. Tossing the phone aside, she flopped backwards, staring at the ceiling. The smoke detector's light glowed.

Desolation gripped her.

Surely he couldn't have rushed back into the arms of a woman who had been trying to make his—and Ellie's—life miserable? Yet, the evidence was there: Pippa, naked, on what Ellie knew was Adam's bed because she'd lain there too. Caring for the man she'd fallen in love with.

And now he was gone.

She grabbed a fistful of hair, lolled over and curled up foetal.

Tears dripped on the duvet.

An hour later, after a long cry and a longer shower, she was, more or less, ready to face the world.

As it was a post-game day, no training was scheduled, but she couldn't face sightseeing. So, despite the heat, she went for a run, hoping to expel from her pores the crushing disappointment at what Adam had—apparently—done.

As her feet pounded the paths of Tokai Park, perspiration trickling from her brow, Ellie realised she was culpable too. If she'd had the balls to opt for a relationship, she was certain his eyes would never wander. Neither would hers. Adam had everything—looks, talent, humour, generosity of spirit... and he *got* her. He *got* the job, the lifestyle. He understood what made her tick, her sorrows and her passion.

She hadn't asked him to wait for her, to put his love life on hold. How could she? Yet, what if she changed her mind in six months—or less? Realised she *could* date him, wanted it more than anything... and then discovered he'd found someone else?

Retracing her steps to the hotel, she cursed silently. Over and over.

She'd screwed it up. Coming away to forget Adam hadn't worked. It had made things worse. And, if he *had* stabbed her in the back by returning to Pippa—won over by despicable behaviour, all for a perfect body and vacuous personality—she'd never speak to him again.

In the hotel, she showered and went for lunch. A few of the girls were in the air-conditioned restaurant.

Bry patted the table. 'Ells! We missed you at breakfast.' She didn't seem the worse for wear, other than a croaky throat.

'Yeah,' Ellie said noncommittally. 'Rojo okay?'

'Rojo is bulletproof. She's in the sauna. Oh, and she's found a nail bar. Come for a refresh later?'

'Maybe.'

Bry threw an arm around Ellie's shoulder. 'What's up with you?'

'Nothing,' she snapped.

'Hey, Ells, chill. Is this about your duck? What happened to "Move on", "Failure is part of the game"?'

She scoffed. 'It's not about that.'

Time out. Before I torpedo this friendship like I torpedoed a chance with Adam.

'I'm getting some food.'

She went to the buffet, served something for her body rather than her mood, and sat.

'Is this about that Adam guy?' Bry asked.

Ellie set down her cutlery. 'No,' she lied. 'This is about I screwed up, two games now, and I let you all down, and I want my bloody mojo back.'

Bryony took her friend's hand. 'There's always a seed. I went off the boil when my nan died.'

Ellie laughed, hollow. She knew exactly what her seed was.

After lunch, she went to see the coach and was candid about her state of mind, though without specifying the cause. The coach suggested a conversation with the team psychologist. Ellie agreed, but it was hard to see a recovery happening in the two days before the next match.

He said she was a vital component of the squad but hadn't covered herself in glory in the last two matches. She sensed her selection was under review—and rightly so.

I don't deserve a place. In fact, I'd rather not play. They need someone who's in the zone, pumped, and able to contribute. Right now, that's not me.

Throughout the afternoon, she tried everything to square the circle.

Already, her confidence was shot. Her so-called fanbase had turned on her. The media were ready to stick the knife in. One of the South African commentators had already called her mistakes "unacceptable at this level".

If things with Adam weren't straightened out, she might never regain her focus and form. She'd lose her place in the squad. Then lose her contract. Her chance would be over before it had really begun.

She had to fix this.

Adam sorely needed the evening of "pie and a pint" with Jez and Ben. He gave them chapter and verse on Pippa's latest escapade. He'd already posted a steadfast denial that they were sleeping together. Now, egged on by his mates, he messaged Pippa to say that if she didn't delete the post within 24 hours, he would speak to the police, presenting video evidence of her vandalising the portrait.

He didn't discuss the Ellie situation. The lads wouldn't have the magic bullet to fix whatever was happening. They didn't know Ellie, the challenges of her job, or her as a person. They couldn't stop the hateful mud-slinging he'd seen online.

How can people treat such a wonderful, talented person so awfully? We all have bad days.

Yet, over the third pint, when she wouldn't leave his thoughts, he excused himself and stood outside the pub door, watching dusk fall. Sucking in fresh air, he gazed at the palette of colours overhead, trying to get perspective. It was impossible to stand by and watch Ellie fail. He needed to help.

But how?

You can't tell an elite athlete to "try harder". Even one you're in love with.

In the shower the following morning, he pondered what to do. The evening hadn't solved anything. It only temporarily dulled the pain of being apart from her.

He found himself glancing at the ajar bathroom door, as if willing a presence there. Snatches of conversation resurfaced; Ellie's voice through the gap as they'd chatted that morning. The morning after the night before. When he'd climbed out of the bath, achy but with his head and heart full of her, the water was cold.

Over breakfast, he researched flights to Cape Town. It was ludicrous to consider jetting off, hoping his presence would magically turn around Ellie's fortunes. But how could it hurt? Her form was already in the toilet, and unquestionably, he was the cause.

It would certainly hurt his wallet. He didn't have three grand to gamble on a whim. What if the problem *wasn't* him?

He decided to give Ellie one more game—today's match—to turn things around.

Outside, rain drenched the town.

He spent the morning tidying the studio, updating his website, and organising for the Jimmy portrait to be digitally scanned, ready for prints to be made. Just because he'd lost—rejected—the sale of the original didn't mean he shouldn't try to monetise the project.

When the TV coverage started, he envied the South African sunshine. Here, the rain hadn't let up for six hours. So much for flaming June.

Pitchside, the commentators previewed the match. The team sheet graphics came onscreen.

'What?' He thumped the sofa arm. 'Unbelievable.'

The England captain, Olivia, joined the duo.

'It was a blip!' he shouted at the screen. 'Give Ells a break!'

The pundit asked Olivia to explain the squad changes. One of the bowlers had been switched out due to an injury niggle, and apparently Ellie was "Stepping back for this game".

'I have to ask whether this has anything to do with what you might call... a couple of disappointments recently,' the pundit asked.

'Yes, there is that,' Olivia replied. 'Also a few issues on her mind away from the game, so we like to give our players the space they need. I'm sure Ellie will come back stronger next time. She's a vital part of our setup.'

Adam shook his head.

She's hit rock bottom.

Did it mean he wasn't going to watch the match? No. He grabbed a 0% beer and a packet of nachos, then settled down to see whether England, even without Ellie, could take an unassailable 3-1 series lead.

His phone was on silent. No disturbances. Time to be in his happy place—although he'd rather have been happier.

England's opening batters walked out.

He clapped. 'Come on, girls.'

The doorbell rang.

'Oh, for fuck's sake.'

Unwilling to be sold a new driveway, handmade jewellery, or religion, he ignored it.

Ten seconds later, it rang again.

'Great. Thanks a million.'

He muted the TV and grouched to the door.

55th Over

H e turned the latch.

If this is bloody Pippa, I will not be responsible for my—

'Fuck.'

His heart skipped at least one beat, then went ballistic. His mouth opened and closed like a fish.

'What?' he breathed, rigid with incomprehension.

Water dripped from her eyelashes. Hair was matted to her scalp and cheeks. She gripped the handle of a carry-on wheelie case. In the distance, thunder cracked. Rain hissed on the path.

'I should have played forward.'

His mind spun, powered by a hamster on acid. 'Huh?'

She looked over his shoulder into the house, where a faint female voice issued from the TV.

He frowned. 'What?'

Her jaw wobbled. 'Is... *she* here?'

'Who?'

'Pippa.'

'Why the fuck would she—?' A penny dropped. 'Oh, that. You saw it. Shit.'

She tugged her sodden coat further over a drenched sweatshirt. 'I thought... I worried...'

The knife tickled his back. 'You expected I'd find another woman as soon as you were out of the country?'

'I did say not to wait for me.' Her voice was small, mousy.

'But a worse, *awful* person? Really, Ells? Come on, you must have known that was bollocks. Another crazy stunt.'

She half reached towards him. 'I don't know, Ads.' Her voice cracked. 'My game was messed up. You saw, right? You were on my mind. A *lot*. And then I thought, and yes, it's crazy, that I'd lost you. I screwed up. I should have played *forwards*.' She flicked rain from her eyelashes.

'But you... came back from South Africa to tell me?' His jaw hung slack. 'Why not text?'

'Because you'd tell me to stay put.' She stepped close. 'Right?'

'Well... yeah.'

'Look, I had to *try*. My job is on the line. But things only work if my batting partner is on the same wavelength. So, if you're not, I'll go.' She thumbed over her shoulder, where the unmistakable shape of a Prius waited.

The grey light on her pale face couldn't hide a familiar expression, one of determination and passion, a fire inside that raged with a desire for success.

He took her suitcase. 'Come in.'

In the hallway, drips decorated the carpet. Unbidden, Ellie removed her shoes. She'd have done better to shake like a dog.

She didn't care about being wet. It came with the territory—though this drenching was pretty extreme. She didn't care about the last-minute ticket price, but the long, lonely hours on the plane were more nerve-wracking than many things she'd experienced. The only saving grace had been the words of support ringing in her ears, the England teammates rallying around, the Scorpions texting to offer sympathy for the online abuse.

She would get over the trolling. It had happened before. Part of the job, the life. What she cared most about, what she hoped with all her heart, was that Adam would see the solution to their conundrum... and not the answer they'd previously settled on, the answer that started the downward spiral.

He looked her up and down. 'It's crazy that you're here.'

She shook her head. 'No. I thought I could move on. I *really* tried, Ads. I'm sorry. To coin a phrase, I let myself down, I let you down, I let the whole school down. I played the *worst* innings.'

A drop of water trickled down her cheek. He brushed it away. 'And it was killing me that things weren't working out. What people were saying.'

She pressed his palm to her cold, damp skin. Her very soul warmed.

'My own stupid fault, getting all emotional and... girly. I *have* to fix that. It's my *life*.' She shook her head. 'Sorry, that's so selfish.'

'No. We tried to do what was right.' He wiped his hand on his T-shirt. 'You're freezing.'

'Well, you might have answered the door earlier.' She raised one eyebrow.

Finally, a smile broke on his lovely lips. 'You want a cuppa?'

'Fuck, yes.'

She squelched into the living room, peeled off her waterlogged coat and hung it over the back of a dining chair. It dripped steadily onto the carpet.

'Milk, no sugar, right?' he called from the kitchen.

'Yeah. Not too strong.' She'd been awake for twenty hours and didn't want the caffeine to impede sleep.

The TV was showing the England game.

She grinned, suddenly infused with joy and camaraderie, and clenched a fist. 'Let's go, girls.'

Adam came in, still nonplussed. 'You flew eight *thousand* miles, Ells.'

'Eight thousand, two hundred and ninety-one, actually. Which is a prime number, as Grace will tell you. I had a *lot* of time on the flight without the girls for company.'

He gently pushed rat tails of hair from her forehead. 'But... I can't believe you left the tour for me.'

'Only temporarily. I *have* to work this out.'

His smile was sad. 'Yeah. In a funny way, it's lucky you were dropped.'

'Being dropped is *never* lucky. And I wasn't. I *asked* not to play.'

His eyes flared. 'What?'

'I asked for personal time. I can chat to the girls, I can speak to the psychologist, but they're not miracle workers.' She tapped his chest, then her head. 'They can't get you out of here.'

He kissed her hand. 'You've been in here too, Ells.' He moved her fingers to his temple.

She stroked his ear. 'Look. Saying no to us was... a wasted over. There is only one alternative... right?'

'Seems so.' Hope entered his lovely eyes.

Her shrug was small. 'I can't be *worse* off than I am now. But that's only for *me*. *My* life. You and I might not... carry our bat, but I reckon it's worth a shot. That's why I came back. I can't text you from another continent and say, "Actually, how about it, mate?"'

'But the *airfare*.' He whistled softly.

She shook her head. 'Fuck the cost. Fuck waiting 'til I'm retired. Clearly, my stupid brain wants you *and* cricket to live in here.' She tapped her skull. 'But it's your life too. Don't do it for *me*. It's not *your* responsibility to fix this.'

There was supplication in her face. Was it only a 6, not a 7, they needed to win the game of love? She was right: if they were together, it *might* fix things. *If* dating helped Ellie focus on her game. *If* they could live with the logistics, the absences. If he simply grew the balls to get on a plane.

That's easy, right?

After all, she'd made a crazy intercontinental dash. She'd believed in his award chances and been right. She'd believed in his talent, and his career was blossoming. Now, she believed he could live in her life. If he *didn't* give this a go, he would certainly regret it forever. If he *did* give it a go, failure might still be *possible,* but not *certain.*

He put his arms around her waist. Holding her again was manna, but now, this was more than a friendly hug. It was a loving one, and it felt so *right...* if rather damp.

'We can do this, Ells.'

Her face lit up. 'Yeah?'

He ran a thumb over her lips. 'It's what I want most in the world.'

She touched her nose to his, gazing so deeply into his eyes that she could probably see his whirring, joyful mind. 'I'm completely in love with you, Adam.'

He held the back of her neck, sodden hair against his palm. 'I'm in love with you, too, Ellie.'

How good does it feel to say that out loud?

She pressed her lips to his, firm and brief, more like relief than desire. 'I'll try *so* hard. At my game. At ours.'

'That's all anyone can do.'

She eased away, then brushed at the wetness she'd deposited on his shirt. 'Yeah.'

'But hypothermia is *so* not a celeb thing.' He winked, then glanced at the ceiling. 'Definitely not on my watch. Get out of these wet clothes. Please. Have a shower... without rude interruptions this time. I'll make that cuppa. Hungry?'

'Famished.'

'I'll dig out some dinner. Nothing fancy. I'll bring your case up. Hope it's waterproof, or it'll be Adam's pants a-go-go again.' He cocked his head. 'Unless you have a fetish you'd like to declare?'

She poked his belly. 'Yeah, I flew all this way to steal your wardrobe.'

'Go on, Batgirl.' He thumbed at the stairs. 'You're up.'

56th Over

S he disappeared from view. Contentment flooded his body.

He went to the kitchen. There was a pizza in the freezer. Was Ellie a pizza kind of person? Possibly, given her pants.

He turned the oven on, then set two teas brewing. A gentle whirring indicated the shower pump had started. He took Ellie's coat upstairs to the airing cupboard. Gentle singing wafted out from the ensuite. A memory tickled the back of his eyeballs. That freeze-frame. That barely formed image, that clanging social faux pas.

Except this time, he didn't hate himself. Actually, he was pretty curious about what she looked like in the shower. No, very curious.

He trotted downstairs, retrieved her case, and laid it on the bed. It wasn't locked, so he checked for water damage. Patting the top layer of clothes, he confirmed everything was dry.

The singing and shower noise stopped. He went to the kitchen, grabbed the mugs of tea, and sat on the bed. How was it that this felt so real yet so fantastical?

She emerged, *rocking* his towels. One tied at her chest, one draped over her shoulders.

His ardour deepened.

'Hey,' she said, loosely drying her hair.

'Hey.' He tendered a mug. 'Your suitcase is fine, and the oven's on.'

'Thanks.' She sipped, then regarded him with the warmest, most intense expression. 'So, to confirm, you are, in fact, still single.'

He stepped close. 'As are you.'

'Yeah. But not for much longer, right?'

He put his mouth to her ear. 'No.'

Her lips brushed his cheek. 'Good.' She handed back the mug. 'Hold this a second?' She went into the ensuite. 'Great shower, by the way. And you actually *fold* your towels on the rack. I should have you stuffed and mounted.'

'Is this because you want a trophy, too?'

Her laughter echoed around the tiled room. 'Well, I play to win.'

She padded into the room. She'd ditched the towels. She hadn't put a robe on.

He almost dropped the mug. 'Fuck,' he breathed.

'So, this is my opening shot.'

His mouth dried. Goosebumps swarmed down his arms. Ellie Waites had cleared the boundary rope. She'd cleared the stadium roof. She'd cleared the Customs border.

'And it's a... *great* shot, Ellie. Very... pleasing to the eye.'

She slowly turned on the spot. He regarded her figure, a heady mix of tightness and curves.

Then she winked, offering the widest smile he'd ever seen. 'So I think we *are* at the mutual nudity part of our relationship now.'

'Sounds good.'

She laid a gentle, tantalising kiss on his lips, then slowly unbuttoned his shirt and eased it off. 'Hmm.'

Her hands moved lightly over his chest, the careworn light blue nail polish dancing in his vision.

He kissed her temple. She stroked his neck, then, impossibly slowly, her fingertips explored every inch of his face. Endorphins rampaged.

She unbuttoned his trousers and slid them down, kneeling to ease off his socks. His pulse hammered with pent-up desire.

'Drinks break.' She grabbed the mug and drained it. Slowly, her attention never leaving his physique.

His eye was drawn to the piercing in her belly button—a surprise, but perhaps not unexpected—then to an uninterrupted view of the Scorpion tattoo and everything in the neighbourhood.

She glanced at the quartet of articles on the floor and then at his boxer shorts. 'Four down. Two balls to go.' An eyebrow arched.

It took Herculean effort not to smother her in deep, urgent kisses.

She put down the mug. It wasn't caffeine supercharging her veins. It was desire.

This innings feels fantastic. Its construction is perfect. The pitch... Wow.

And he hadn't eyed her like a slobbering dog. He'd contemplated her appreciatively. He wasn't the type who'd bed her for bragging rights down the pub: "Alright, lads. Get this. I shagged that famous cricketer, Ellie Waites. Beers on me!" His restraint was almost a turn-on, especially given his visible arousal.

She caressed his shoulders and chest, wishing he'd reciprocate, but he only stroked the curve of her waist. That was enough to deliver hot flushes inside her. She slid his boxers to the floor, kneeling and helping him out of them. Then she stood, acquainting herself with his body.

'Phew,' she breathed.

He slowly turned on the spot, finishing with a wink. She let out a giggle.

'Don't hold your stomach in,' she said softly. 'It's not a competition. I'm not after six-packs and Armani suits.'

His belly sagged a little. After all, it was unfair to expect him to match her toned abdomen. So what if he couldn't bench press 130lbs? He was built for art, support, and care.

She put her arms around his waist, rubbed her nose to his and kissed him lightly on the lips. 'Only *one* rule tonight, Adam.'

'Only one? I *am* in luck.'

She nipped his backside. 'You're impossible.'

'You're perfect,' he retorted.

She traced his lips with a finger. 'Let's wait until tomorrow before you give the final verdict.'

'Okay.' He kissed her fingertip. 'What's that rule?'

'I only sleep with men I'm dating.'

His gaze explored every millimetre of her face. 'Will you go out with me, Ellie?'

Her knees were weak, like a month on the treadmill. 'Hell, yes.'

'Good.'

She laid her head on his shoulder, and he pulled her tight.

'Play,' she murmured.

He lifted her chin and kissed her gently.

Their lips moved tenderly together. It was a kiss of love, not lust. One which made others pale. She savoured every second, like an ice cream you want to eat by the molecule, not the spoonful. Time vanished.

If he makes love like he kisses, I should have flown back First Class.

A gurgle emerged from her midriff. She gave a gentle grimace. 'Ah.'

'Oh, yeah. Forgot. Want to eat?'

'Hell to the no.'

'As your boyfriend and number one fan, I insist you keep your body in good shape.' He stroked her breast. 'Because it is in *excellent* shape.'

She licked her lips. 'Here's the deal. Sex first, then eat, then bed.'

'Good idea. You must be knackered.'

'I meant bed for more sex. Assuming you have a good first innings.'

'Well, I'm trying to play with a straight bat.' His brow arched.

She looked down. 'Yeah. Good job with that.'

Now, he kissed her with less reticence, and she responded in kind.

As their hands began to explore, her only hunger was for him. Sooner or later, they'd make it to the bed. For now, she didn't want *this* over to be over.

57th Over

The note on the bedside table read, "Going for a run. E." The E was inside a heart.

On one level, Adam wished he'd woken up beside her... and been able to indulge in spooning. Conversely, he didn't want her to deviate from routines and obligations. He was unequivocally buying into her life and lifestyle. Asking her not to be a professional cricketer was like asking him not to be an artist.

For sure, life now would be an education and a rollercoaster, certainly a challenge, but the prize was fabulous.

The shower hissed. "E" had evidently already returned from her run.

He glanced towards the bathroom. This time, there was no need for reservation. Last night's lingering intimacy, twice over—when it could have been a frantic release of pent-up energy and desire—said so much.

He eased open the door. She stopped shampooing and beckoned him in. The warm spray and her embrace were nourishing.

'I have one rule in showers.'

'You do like your rules, Ells.'

She poked out her tongue, then showed him the old scar on her left elbow. He'd spotted it during an earlier *extensive* survey of the pitch. 'No sex on slippery surfaces. I don't want to have to explain another season-ruining injury to Mads. Or anyone.' She soaped his chest. 'Okay?'

He traced the rivulets running over the curve of her breasts. 'Agreed.'

She embraced him. 'Short of that, good morning.'

Their lips met.

After getting clean—without getting dirty in the process—she dried while he dressed and gathered up yesterday's discarded clothes.

'The lucky pants again?' He held up her underwear. 'I thought these were for games, not long-haul flights.'

She tossed wet towels into the laundry basket he was holding. 'I needed to win *you*, Ads. I reckoned having luck on my side couldn't hurt.'

He eyed her figure. 'The nudity didn't do your chances any harm.'

She waggled her lithe hips. 'I know you're not dating me for that. Which is one of the many reasons this will work.'

She took the basket, put it on the bed, and pulled him close. 'There are two kinds of relationship. A fast innings. 26 off 15 balls. Entertain the crowd. Then get cocky and cloth an easy catch to Cover. Or... play yourself in, set up a great partnership with the other end. Talk. Run smart. Only hit the bad balls. Bat the end. Maybe make a ton. But walk in after the last ball.'

He nibbled her soft, perfect ear. 'Okay.'

'I've had my tens and twenties. Now, I'm after the kind of game you never want to end. Where you're seeing the ball like a watermelon. Where you always find the gaps in the field.' She pressed her cheek to his. 'This time, I want to carry my bat.'

'Same at this end. Partner.'

'So, although my cricket shoe is on the gas pedal, I want us to have as much time as humanly possible.'

He nodded. 'I never doubted it. Nobody goes into a relationship wanting *less* time together. But being unable to spend all the time you want isn't a reason not to date.'

She pecked his cheek. 'No. And, all things being equal, life will get easier.'

He stroked her wonderful backside. 'Any minute with you is a good minute.'

'Ditto.' She bit her lip. 'So... I won't put in for the drafts this winter.'

He shook his head firmly. 'No. Sorry, Ells. That's not how this works. You don't compromise your career for me. Not now. I said yes to everything. If that means a lot of texts—'

'And phone sex.' She jiggled her eyebrows.

'—and phone *calls*, then fine. But I will fly as much as I can. Because real sex knocks phone sex for 6. Especially when it's with celebrity athletes.'

She slapped his arm. 'You're impossible.'

'And you're perfect.'

'Yeah. I probably am.' She pressed her lips to his. Time stood still.

When time resumed, they went to the stairs, ready to head down for breakfast. The studio door stood ajar.

She pointed. 'Is it... done?'

'Yeah. Well, unless you can spot any mistakes. Or you hate it.'

Girlish excitement took her. 'Can I?'

He waved her on. She skipped down the landing and peered in the room, as if afraid to accidentally catch the King taking a dump.

Her hand came to her mouth. She walked, rapt and shaking, to the portrait. Moisture pooled in her eyes.

Nobody in the world has ever known me like this. Like he does.

The floorboard creaked. 'Well?'

'I'm...' Her voice cracked. 'Holy crap, babe.'

He cupped her waist. 'The subject approves.'

'The subject more than approves.'

Quivering, she inspected every inch of the portrait. Something near the lower corner caught her attention, and she cried proper tears.

Partially and deliberately obscured by her left pad, the small but visible letters on the pitchside advertising hoarding spelt PAI--GE. She ran the gentlest fingertip over the brush strokes.

Breathe.

She pivoted, drooping into Adam's arms and pulling him impossibly tight. 'Name your price, my love.'

For the next hour, they snuggled on the sofa. Highlights of yesterday's game were playing—although the result was all over the socials, and Ellie's teammates had told her the story. South Africa had levelled the series at 2-2 with one game left.

A smile broke on her lips. Desire to play coursed through her. She ached to pull on the shirt and walk out to bat.

I'm ready.

And the beautiful irony? Whilst she'd already considered flying back to win Adam's heart, Pippa's Insta post had been the clincher. The lying, vindictive cow had shot herself in the foot with a Gatling gun. Even if Ellie only had a sliver of suspicion that Adam would toss her aside to date Pip, if she'd been an idiot to even consider it a possibility, it had put her on that plane home.

Thanks, Pipsqueak. You might just have saved my career. Effing hilarious.

'Ells?'

She jolted from her thoughts. 'Hmm.'

'Next time you go for a run, mind if I tag along? I mean, for the first hundred yards before I pass out.'

'Tag along anytime. Gym, wherever.' She stroked his thigh. 'And no mickey-taking. Ever. I promise.'

'But mouth-to-mouth is available if I need it?' He nuzzled her neck.

'Always. Because *that* workout routine you have *nailed*.'

'You're not so bad yourself.'

She elbowed him. He ran a palm *way* up her inner thigh.

She trailed a finger along his jawline. 'Talking of your *wide* skillset, Mr Glenn, d'you ever watch that Portrait Artist show?'

He gave her a suspicious side-eye. 'I know where this is going.'

'Never say never.'

'I can't paint anything in four hours. That's the brief, right?'

She touched her nose to his. 'Jack-of-all-trades? You can accomplish anything. Hell, you tell *me* often enough.'

He gazed at her. 'Okay, Ells. Never say never.'

She kissed him. 'No catch I took, or will ever take, beats this one.'

When he kissed back, her spirits soared as much as during that first real kiss yesterday. It was still shot through with tenderness, adoration and unfettered longing.

She stroked his face. 'Promise me one thing? Never grow a beard. Don't spoil... this.'

'Deal. Providing you don't grow a moustache...'

She slapped his arm, then piled in for a snog which lasted until her phone chimed. She moved him away and read the message.

'What?' he asked.

'Coach wants to know if I'm okay.'

'Tell him, "Yes, thanks. Nothing like a twelve-inch dong to really press my reset button".'

She grabbed his chin *fairly* gently. 'I have to go. Amy's had to step back. Her parents came out to watch, but now her Dad's in A&E with a heart thing.'

'Shit.'

She stroked his cheek. 'Sometimes the ones we love need a bit of TLC.'

'True. So go. You can't stay here for compliments on my artistic skills, armchair viewing and quite superb sex. After all, if you get sacked for going AWOL, how will you afford the half-million quid for that painting?'

She elbowed him in the ribs.

'Go, babe. I'll cheer you all the way... and keep this bed warm. I can even knock up a cardboard cutout of me for you to put at Square Leg.' He winked.

She ran her fingers through his hair. 'Or... you can come for real?'

'To South Africa? But...' His eyes circled.

Her spirits dived. 'The work. Yeah. Sorry. I can't stand in the way of *your* career. Not now. Not when you're hitting the big time. Much as I'd like you there. Day *and* night.'

'No... I mean... the work can keep. Have camera, will travel, you know? Just... I can't ask you to pay for my ticket. Or my hotel room, or—'

'It's a double.'

'Stay in the team hotel?' He rubbed his forehead. 'Wow.'

'Partners do. You're my partner.' She looked deep into his eyes. 'Come back with me.'

58th Over

He secured one of the last three seats on her flight and thanked whoever invented credit cards. They rustled up lunch, then she borrowed his car to collect a few things from home and throw a hundredweight of junk mail in the recycling.

When he opened the front door, she dumped the shopping bag and squeezed into his arms.

He kissed her. 'So, what next?'

'I can think of something involving hot water and lots of bubbles.'

He began to salivate. 'Sounds good.'

'I promise you won't be disappointed.'

Half an hour later, he examined the result of her physical exertions. 'Beautiful. Looks like you missed your calling. Or you know what to do when you hang up your bat.'

She poked him. 'Don't joke.'

He pulled her close. Holding this amazing, adorable, beautiful woman would never get old. 'You can do anything, be anything you want. And you damn well know it, Ells.'

'Maybe.' She stroked his face. 'For ages, the most important thing in life was cricket. Lately, I've been wondering what would come afterwards. Now I know. It's you.'

'That's very sweet, but where's the half-million for my painting going to come from if you're on the dole?'

She nipped his backside. Hard. 'You're a snake, Adam Glenn. Anyway, talking of money...' She held out a palm.

He fished a quid from his pocket and slapped it down. 'Done. Fifty pee for the car, fifty for the wheels.'

'Pleasure doing business with you, sir.' She handed back the pound coin. 'There. Now, I only owe you four hundred and ninety-nine thousand, nine hundred and ninety-nine.'

After lunch, he tied up work-related loose ends, preparing for a three-week absence.

Being a jack-of-all-trades was no longer aimless or embarrassing. It was a blessing. He wouldn't be chained to an easel, surviving on high-price but infrequent commissions. He could do landscape photography and digital art anywhere in the world... especially if the love of his life was in that exact location. The alternative was a tug of war between Ellie and art, and he would never rely on her to be the breadwinner. Their relationship was built on each carving their own path.

She came into the studio and showed him her phone. She'd created Adam Glenn a Wikipedia page.

'See—you're in the bubble now.'

'You're a devil, Ellie Waites.'

He smothered her with kisses until she writhed from his grasp.

'What's for dinner?' she asked.

He tutted. 'It's all the same with you celebrity athletes, isn't it? Take, take, take. "Paint my picture". "Carry my luggage". "Cook my meals".'

She curled a fist and laid it under his chin. 'I meant, *darling*, we have weeks of hotel and bar meals ahead of us, so how about you do something romantic and cook a candlelight dinner? And I *don't* mean pizza.'

'Hmm. Date night? Woo you, all that crap?'

She pressed close. 'Well, I'm a sure thing. Plus, it may be the last quality time you get from me for a while.'

Fair point.

A fulsome snog would have been on the cards... if the doorbell hadn't sounded. He didn't berate it. The last time he'd railed against an interruption, a beautiful woman was about to change his life.

He trotted downstairs and opened the door.

It was a less beautiful woman. In many ways. His hackles leapt to attention.

With a scowl, Pippa thrust an envelope at him.

Clearly, he was expected to open it immediately. So he did.

What fresh hell is this? What scheme so Machiavellian it would make Dick Dastardly look like Mary Berry?

The typed letter, on headed notepaper, was entitled "Notice To Cease And Desist".

He read. The paper shook.

She was formally claiming that he'd violated her image and IP when creating "LIKE?". He was ordered to cease selling the prints and destroy the original.

He read the letter twice more. He inspected the company logo. Then he relaxed. In fact, he struggled to keep the grin off his face.

'Thanks for this, Pip. It's made my day.'

'You what?' she snarled.

He tapped the page. 'I count at least four typos. I recognise the logo from my stock image website. And I'm *pretty* sure that Donnelly & McPartlin isn't a real law firm.'

'It bloody is. And this letter—'

'Is a fake. Like you, Pip.' He pushed the paper into her hands.

She fumbled and dropped it. As she bent to retrieve her scam prop, Ellie appeared at Adam's shoulder.

'Look, Ads—' Pippa began, visibly trying to soften. Then she spied Ellie, and her nose wrinkled.

He pointed at the road. 'Fuck off. Or I'll get a very real and legally enforceable restraining order if you ever come near me again.'

Ellie cracked her knuckles. 'And I'll punch your lights out. *Pipsqueak.*'

Harsh but fair.

Adam saw something unfamiliar in Pippa's eyes. Fear. Resignation.

Finally, it was over.

She shot them daggers... or tried to. Then she fucked off.

The plane taxied away from the stand.

Adam had packed a compact but flexible set of camera gear. He'd barely begun to conceive the opportunities for landscape photography but wasn't expecting a week-long jaunt into a nature reserve.

All Ellie had brought was the same roller case. The rest was still in Cape Town. Except...

'Shit.'

She touched his leg. 'What?'

'I never got your lucky pizza pants out of the dryer.' He looked at her with apology and anguish. Had he kiboshed England's chances of winning the series?

She ran her fingers through his hair. 'It's okay. I have another lucky charm that's stuck with me much longer than those stupid pants.'

The engines' whine increased in pitch. His heartbeat raced.

She entwined their fingers. 'I'm here, Adam. Nothing bad can happen.'

She hadn't told him to grow up or stop worrying about the minuscule chance of a seizure. She had simply offered love and support. He reckoned she could handle anything that was thrown at her.

The question was whether this trip threw any bouncers at *him*—and could he play them well enough? If not, their partnership would be over very quickly.

The next morning, at the team hotel, Adam slept in. Ellie didn't have that luxury. There was a training and prep session for the upcoming game.

Adam reminded himself this wasn't a holiday. Ellie was on a business trip abroad; except she was in the business of hitting cricket balls, sometimes carefully, sometimes violently, but always with poise and eye-catching talent.

He spent the day getting used to the climate, the city, and the crazy fact of being there. The flight had passed in no time. They'd only stopped talking—and kissing—to watch the movie.

They had dinner in the hotel. A few of the England squad were there, and Ellie introduced Adam as her boyfriend. As the sun set, she took him outside for a selfie, which they shared on both Insta accounts. This time, it wasn't gossip. It was glorious reality.

They hit the sack early.

After Ellie's early morning run the following day, she suggested a game of golf. He asked which of the England stars he'd be playing against this time, but it was only a twosome.

They went to a course in the shadow of Table Mountain and shot 9 holes. Naturally, she thrashed him. He didn't care.

That evening, they went into town for dinner.

As they were entering the restaurant, Ellie froze.

I mean, how many people live in this city? And how many visitors and tourists?

Unbelievable.

'Follow my lead, Ads,' she murmured, recalling how good he was at that.

He frowned, then blanched as he spied the imminent car crash.

She was already steering onto the opposite carriageway and painted on a smile. 'Mary. Jack.'

'Hey, Ells,' Mary said flatly.

Jack's face was pure embarrassment. 'Oh, hi, Ellie.'

She wondered whether to introduce Adam, but the fact that they were holding hands said everything.

'Good spell for you last time out,' Ellie said sweetly. Mary had taken three wickets, helping to trigger England's defeat.

Ellie hoped her nemesis' race was run. Surely, Mary wouldn't make things personal. If anything, Ellie was the one with a score to settle. She'd love to do that, provided the red mist didn't descend.

'Thanks,' Mary replied. 'Everything alright at home?'

'Peachy.'

Meaning, I have the best guy in the world, and my mojo, and we will whip your team's ass tomorrow.

'Good.'

Jack didn't offer a word. He was too busy sizing up Adam.

Ellie nodded tersely. 'Have a good night.'

'You too,' Mary said.

Ellie tugged Adam's hand. 'Come on, hon.'

They'd barely taken their seats when Jack walked over. Alone.

Adam cracked his knuckles.

Please don't make a scene, guys.

Jack's gaze darted between her and Adam. 'I wanted to say sorry, Ellie. I shouldn't have treated you like that.' He coughed. 'Hope you have a good tour.'

Knock me down with a feather. Seems like there's competition for who can be the most civil. Perhaps it's the African air.

'Um... thanks.'

He turned to Adam. 'Ellie's a good person, mate. I ballsed up. Hope you have better luck.'

Adam's shoulders relaxed. 'Yeah. Right. Cheers.'

Jack smiled thinly. 'Have a nice evening.' Then he walked away.

Ellie blinked away her wide eyes. 'Did that just happen?'

'Seems like it.'

'He didn't have to do that. And now I feel bad, but the apology I *really* want is from Mazza. You know, to clear the air properly. She started all this.' Her palm shot up defensively. 'Not that I want him back. God, no. I've got *you.*'

'So promise me that tomorrow you'll let things be. Or at least don't get mad, get even.'

'Yeah. Last time I got mad, I nearly ended up in hospital.'

'Instead, I wound up on your sofa. Which was a hell of a result, in hindsight.'

She laid a palm on his cheek. 'So, now I've got my man, I'm not planning any more knocks to the head.'

59th Over

E llie was number 3 on the team sheet. She would have loved to open the batting but had to take what she was given. Getting back into the side was never guaranteed—not only because of the loss of form but also due to her unscheduled absence.

On the plus side, because Mary usually bowled the opening overs, Ellie would miss out on that fusillade.

Remember, it won't be personal. Mazza just wants to take wickets. To help win the match. The same as I want runs. To help win the match. And the series.

Play the game, the situation, the ball.

At 47-1, Adam watched Ellie clasp the three lions on her chest, whirl her bat and jog onto the pitch. His feelings vaulted between those of a fan and those of a boyfriend. Would this be an even harder watch than last time?

He adjusted the earpiece, which was tuned into the TV commentary. He hadn't brought his camera; he wanted to lap this up. The atmosphere was unfamiliar, so partisan to the opposition. Plenty of Union Flags flew, but the stadium was primarily decorated in the Proteas' green and yellow.

As Ellie faced her first ball, Adam's heart was full of love... and lodged in his throat. Could she cast off recent challenges and failures, not to mention the physical demands of a splash-and-dash trip home?

After forty minutes, she'd reached 48 off 33 balls, which was a cracking pace. Adam crossed his fingers. They stayed crossed for five tense deliveries. Then she latched onto a poor ball and short-arm pulled it high over the Square Leg boundary and into the stands.

He punched the air. 'Come on!'

The commentators enjoyed it, too.

"Oh, what a shot! What a shot to go to fifty. The very best of Ellie Waites. Bowl it short on this pitch, and she will smash you for six."

"Absolutely sensational from Waites. She's a devastating player in just about any format. She has been brilliant today."

On any day, this was a great sight. Today, however, Adam wouldn't simply nod and smile and say, 'Great knock, Ellie.' He'd close the bedroom door, hold her tight, and whisper in her ear that she was effing incredible. In so many ways.

Ten minutes later, Ellie was at the non-striker's end when her partner cracked the ball towards Long On.

'Yes,' Bry called.

Ellie was already backing up, ready to run, three yards out of her crease. She winced as the ball arrowed towards her midriff and whacked into her glove. She spun under the shock and impact. The ball dropped at the bowler's feet. Disoriented, Ellie lunged for the crease. The South African seamer whipped off the bails.

'Fuck,' she spat in disbelief, picking herself up off the turf.

She tossed the bat across her shoulder and trudged off. Her thumb throbbed.

Unbelievable. The ton was there for the taking.

She shook her head. That run-out, almost comedic in its impossible ballet, was one for the archives.

Move on. 59 is a good knock. 59 more than last time.

The England supporters were applauding. She raised her bat, offered a sober shrug to the girls in the dugout, and headed for the pavilion to see the physio.

South Africa's reply to England's 218-6 ebbed and flowed. Standing, as usual, at Mid-wicket, Ellie was vocal in urging her teammates on. Other than fielding with sharpness and focus, there was nothing more she could do. No point in raking over old mistakes.

Like, for instance, if I'd batted decently in the previous games, maybe the series wouldn't be on a knife edge.

Chill. It's a team game.

With three quick wickets, the game swung in their favour at 152-8. Then Mary Kallis came in to bat.

Four overs later, things were looking grim. The Proteas were on 198-8. Mary had raced to a score of 41 and risked winning the game single-handedly.

England captain Olivia had tried everything to unstick the stubborn all-rounder. She'd used all her bowlers, including Rose and Jade, but Mary had the measure of them all. If England could get her out, they'd be one wicket from victory—and the Proteas last batter should be an easy scalp.

Ellie looked at the scoreboard.

This isn't personal, Mazza, but you need to get back in the hutch.

202-8. Three overs to go.

Sod it.

She jogged to Olivia and had a word. Last throw of the dice. Rose joined the discussion, as did the wicketkeeper.

'Why not?' Rose said. 'Mary's never faced you, right, Ells?'

Ellie shook her head. 'Years ago.'

Olivia pursed her lips, then tossed Ellie the ball. 'What field do you want?'

Adam strained to see.

Is this really happening?

Sure, it made sense to give Mary something unfamiliar to deal with, but Ellie hadn't bowled in anger for years. This was a huge gamble, potentially setting herself up for failure... and more online trolling. He crossed his fingers, willing her not to get belted around the ground.

Is the muscle memory still there? Has she even practised recently? Not counting at Grace's party...

Ellie spun a couple of practice balls to Rose and whirled her right arm to warm it up. She marked out her stride.

'Come on, darling,' he murmured.

Mary defended the first two balls for dots. The third was hit back over Ellie's head for 4.

Adam eyed the scoreboard. The hosts were within striking distance of the win.

Ellie conferred with Olivia, then walked back to her mark. Her pulse thundered. The ball was feeling less alien in her grip. She concentrated on the match prep, on Mary's preferred hitting areas.

How can I outfox her?

'Come on, Ells,' called Rose from Cover.

'Let's go, Waitesy,' said Jade.

The keeper clapped her gloves. 'Bring it down, Ells.'

Breathe.

I probably can't do this, but never say never.

Ellie surveyed the field, beckoning in the Square Leg fielder. Mary responded as planned, sending the next ball over that fielder's head for an easy 2. The crowd whooped and cheered, sensing victory.

Don't listen. Don't look at the scoreboard.

Ellie stroked the ball's stitching.

Focus.

She danced down to the crease, giving the ball a little more air, more speed, and as much spin as her rusty fingers could conjure. Mary went to hoik the delivery over Square Leg again.

The ball landed. And gripped. And turned. And passed Mary's flashing blade.

And snicked off the bails, which lit and tumbled.

Ellie leapt high, punching the air.

You fucking beauty!

The England supporters roared. She faced them and chalked a finger in the air. The lofty Rose lifted her up and twirled her around. Ellie felt like a kid again. Teammates piled in. The biggest family hug ever.

Mary trudged past. Their eyes met.

Ellie was a split-second away from giving the hard stare, a knowing, wide-eyed "Gotcha". She didn't. They were even now. A stare might restart the battle.

Ellie let the team return to their fielding positions and jogged to catch up with Mary.

She patted the girl's shoulder. 'Good knock, Mazza.'

After a flicker of disbelief, Mary gave a rueful smile. 'Great delivery, Ells.'

Both nodded. Mary left the field.

Adam continued clapping. At first it had been for Ellie, then briefly for Mary. Now, masked by the Home fans' appreciation for their batter, he applauded more loudly for the bowler.

Slowly, the stadium fell silent. Adam couldn't relax. They hadn't won yet.

Thankfully, the last two balls of Ellie's over were dots.

208-9. 11 runs to win.

Rose bowled the next over, with the hosts' last batter on strike. Somehow, the first ball was gloved past Fine Leg for 4.

Adam wrung his hands. 7 for South Africa to win, and 11 balls—plenty—to do it in.

'Come on, Rojo,' he beseeched.

Rose walked back to her mark, playing with the beaded bracelet on her left wrist. Then she hurtled in and delivered the next ball like a missile, full and straight, knocking the tail-ender's middle stump two yards down the strip.

Adam, already feeling somewhat weightless, leapt to his feet, cheering with uncontained joy. England—*a little bit* thanks to his girlfriend—had won the series. Moisture welled in his eyes. He wiped it away. It was unseemly for a grown man to cry at a bloody cricket match.

After the celebrations had died down, the crowd began to disperse.

Adam collected his belongings and went to the pavilion steps to wait. A couple of England players nodded as they passed. Rose stopped to chat. A few minutes later, one of the match commentators happened along, slowing as he did.

'Adam, right? Adam Glenn?'

Adam swallowed the lump in his throat. 'Yes. Hi, James.'

'Didn't expect to see you out here. Ellie said you couldn't make it.'

'Well... I changed my mind.'

'Great.' James pointed at the pitch. 'You came on the right day. She played a blinder. Look, I have to run, but the painting's still available, right?'

Adam's breath caught. 'Yes.'

'Good. It's been crazy busy but I'll email you, okay? Can you, like, put it on reserve or something?'

'Definitely.'

'Great. Cheers. Look forward to seeing it when the tour's over.' James Anderson patted Adam on the shoulder and wandered off.

Adam had barely regained his composure before another commentator approached. England's recently retired and legendary captain, Anna Ritchie. His mind whirled.

Wouldn't it be funny if she also wanted to commission a portrait? Wouldn't that be the peak of utter craziness, personally, professionally and financially?

He scoffed.

Why would she even know who I am?

'Hi,' she said, lifting sunglasses off her nose. 'Are you Ellie's friend? The painter?'

Final Over

B *reathe. I've earned this.*

It was hard not to be overawed. Despite the legion of matches she'd played, the huge number of venues she'd walked out in, the mental and physical preparation, the support, the love, this was something different. Something hard to beat. The pinnacle.

"Please welcome to the field your England opening batters, number 14, Bryony Taylor and number 20, Ellie Waites."

Ellie took in the thunderous applause of the capacity Lord's crowd and walked out to face the Australian attack.

Focus. No rush. Play yourself in. Test Match mentality.

She checked the fielding positions. There was no point in scouring the crowd at Square Leg. Adam wasn't there.

She took guard.

The bowler ran in.

From the VIP box, Adam watched on.

It had been a long nine months. The South Africa tour, The Hundred, the end of the domestic season—with the Scorpions winning a trophy double. He'd become immersed in her professional bubble, learning not to be clingy and to coexist effortlessly with other players.

At the end-of-season regional awards, Ellie won MVP, so they were finally equal on trophies. Next, Ellie was awarded a full England contract. Then came a tour to New Zealand, which he didn't attend due to work pressure. The winter stints in Australia and Pakistan. Ellie's first steps towards her youth coaching badge. A couple of slots commentating on Test Match Special. Countless sponsor promos, hundreds of miles jogged, thousands of reps in the gym.

Meeting friends. Meeting her family. Meeting his. Nights out. Endless laughter. Kissing. Learning.

Falling further and further in love.

They spoke every day, regardless of circumstances. She called him her rock, someone she could, physically or metaphorically, come home to. After a lengthy debate, they'd decided they couldn't fit into one house, so they would keep both homes but buy a new place soon.

He'd completed portraits for Anna Ritchie and current captain Olivia. All the Scorpions and England players had requested superhero cartoons, and the time-lapse videos went down a storm online, increasing his follower count and volume of work enquiries. Then, a researcher at the BBC got in touch. The corporation wanted graphics and idents for use during coverage of the upcoming Women's Cricket World Cup. At that point, Adam stopped believing the craziness was over.

Ellie still hadn't paid him half a million quid for her portrait. She was washing his car for free, though.

Adam focused on the game. His girlfriend, in Test whites. She was playing calmly, building a foundation. At the other end, she lost one batting partner, then two.

Lunch came.

He chatted with Ellie's parents, then strolled down to the stands to see Diane and Grace. The girl had painted a new sign; "WE LOVE YOU, ELLIE", in England colours. Her grin was wider than ever, thanks to her recent selection for the Kent Under 11s.

After lunch, the match resumed. Ellie eased past 50. She briefly tipped her bat to the pavilion. Adam sensed her mindset: "Just getting started".

On 63, trying to sweep, she skied a delivery to Short Fine leg. Adam froze, eyes half-closed. The fielder dropped the catch. The crowd ooh-ed and cheered.

On 88, the bowler hollered for an LBW. The umpire declined. The Aussies asked for a TV review. Adam gritted his teeth and cracked his knuckles.

This fandom lark is bloody stressful.

"Pitching in line. Hitting... in line. Wickets... missing," came the playout from the third umpire.

He exhaled a tornado. The crowd applauded.

With every ball, he felt less and less like watching.

How the hell is she keeping it together? Because she's brilliant, that's how.

The tea break came. Ellie was on 96.

This was torture. Adam didn't want a cup of tea. He needed a double whisky.

The game resumed. Australia tried a different bowler. Perhaps they'd noticed Ellie's cunning plan against Mary Kallis?

The young spinner's first ball was a Wide. The second was a dot.

The third... Ellie launched over Long On... into the crowd.

A few litres of dopamine flushed into Adam's skull. He leapt up and down like a lunatic.

Ellie pulled off her helmet, kissed the England crest, then looked directly upwards and raised her bat to heaven.

Adam scuttled to the Gents to dry his eyes.

From a score of 102, she had a choice: either play with freedom, now the milestone was breached, or remain cautious and try to see out the innings.

Sadly, five overs later, Ellie's indecision cost her.

Shit. I was hoping failure wasn't on the cards. Not today.

Still. 114. We did it, Paige.

She strolled off, refusing to be maudlin. The crowd stood as one. She saw the MCC ties, the England flags, thousands of hands raised in applause. The homemade poster held aloft by a familiar young girl. Mum and Dad. A wonderful, understanding, brilliant and gorgeous man in the VIP area.

Ellie raised her bat again, turned full circle, and then pointed the blade at him. He blew kisses.

She fixed on a smile and took deep, calming breaths.

Don't cry.

She fist-bumped incoming batter Dani, who'd secured her first England call-up. When Ellie crossed the boundary sponge, teammates rose from the dugout to pat her on the back.

Ellie climbed the pavilion steps of Lord's Cricket Ground, fans shouting her name, phone cameras tracking her.

She passed into the iconic Long Room. People stood, clapping. Her heart was full.

Don't cry.

She glanced at the Honours Board, soon to bear her name, and weaved between the tables.

At the far end of the room, someone came through the doorway. She smiled. Much as she wanted to, it would be unseemly to hug him in front of this auspicious crowd.

Her boots clacked on the wooden floor. The applause faded.

The man reached into his jacket pocket.

Then he took a step forward and went down on one knee.

Her heart overflowed.

Okay, time to cry.

The Scorpions squad

NAME	NICKNAME	AGE	ROLE
Ellie Waites	"Ells"	32	Top order batter
Bryony Taylor	"Bry"	21	Top order batter
Fiona Plummer	"Fi"	25	Top order batter
Katherine Davidson	"Kat"	30	Batter
Freya Baker	"Bakes"	34	Batter
Lily Butcher	"Butch"	22	Batter
Danica Pritchard (C)	"Dani"	32	Batter, spin bowler
Gemma Enstone	"Gemstone"	29	Batter, seam bowler
Jade Black	"Jet"	25	Seam bowler
Rose Jones	"Rojo"	23	Seam bowler
Naira Rodrigues	"Roddy"	26	Leg spin bowler
Abi Miller	"Mills"	19	Leg spin bowler
Sarah Hawksley	"Hawks"	27	Off spin bowler
Tara MacGregor	"Mac"	24	Wicket Keeper

The Scorpions squad

Fielding Positions

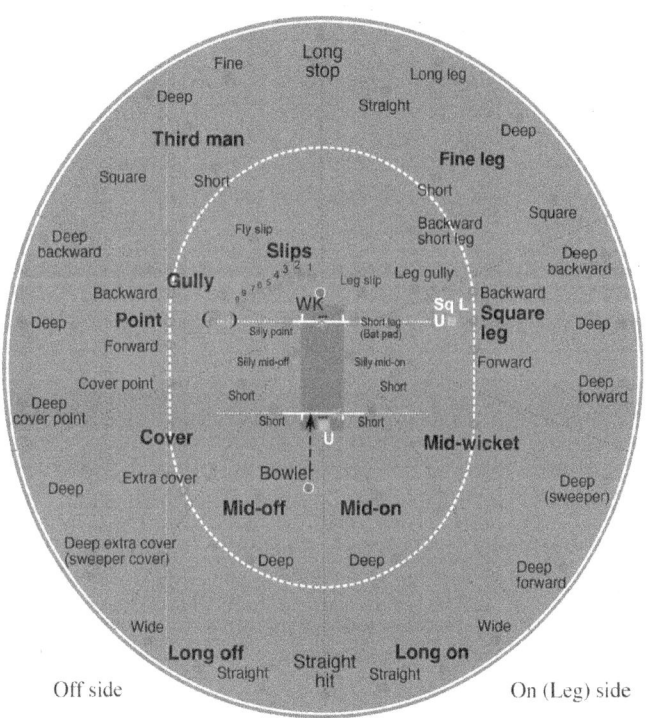

Off side

On (Leg) side

Easter Eggs

Some of the cricketing events in this book are inspired by real things. Congratulations if you spotted any!

Chapter 1
Ellie's first score of 28 is Danni Wyatt-Hodge's shirt number.

Chapter 3
Ellie's diving catch was inspired by Maia Bouchier's against the Northern Superchargers in the 2023 Hundred final.

Chapter 9
Ellie's dismissal was inspired by Maia Bouchier's at Wormsley in 2024.

Chapter 14
Ellie's score of 67 is the same as Danni Wyatt-Hodge's against the Welsh Fire in the 2023 Hundred, and she also holed out to Mid-on.

Chapter 27

Ellie's 6 for her century was inspired by Danni Wyatt-Hodge's match-winning shot against the Oval Invincibles in the 2024 Hundred.

This ECB announcement was actually announced while the book was being written. It meant a quick rewrite, but also allowed Ellie to achieve her dream IRL (if that isn't a contradiction!).

Chapter 43

Ellie's direct hit for a run out was inspired by Maia Bouchier's throw against the Welsh Fire in the 2023 Hundred.

Chapter 54

Ellie helping Bryony to her maiden IT20 century was inspired by Natalie Sciver-Brunt's brilliant and selfless support for Maia Bouchier against New Zealand at Worcester in 2024.

Chapter 63

Ellie's shot for 6, to reach her 50, was inspired by Danni Wyatt-Hodge's against the Welsh Fire in the 2023 Hundred.

Ellie's crazy dismissal was inspired by Danni Wyatt-Hodge's against the Northern Superchargers in the 2023 Hundred final.

Acknowledgements

This book would not have been possible without the unstinting assistance of a Tier 1 professional women's county team. It was a privilege to gain insight from a number of players, and this shaped not only the cricketing elements to the book, but offered nuances to the story itself. Never has research been so humbling and enjoyable. Thank you – you know who you are.

There was also a research contribution from, randomly, Lauren Bell's mum! Also a special mention for fans Elisa and Billy.

I'm indebted to Emily Inkpen, Sarah Haynes & Aimee Johnson for their insight into living with epilepsy. Thanks to my advance readers Susannah Hockham, Sarah Saya, Stuart Moore, Yuki Dennis, Wendy Barker, Roy Towndrow, and Ingrid Weel. It continues to be a pleasure to work with my editors, Becca Errington & Ellie Hawkes. A special mention for my valued author buddy Elizabeth Holland. Thanks to all three for your input and wisdom.

Last but by no means least, huge thanks to Alex Allden for another amazing cover design.

About the Author

Writing romcoms is my happy place. After working in other genres for many years, I couldn't resist the pull towards comedy and romance. I have a soft spot for stories with strong women, nice guys, and a touch of the bittersweet. I like the connection between my protagonists to be more than physical – a bond that helps solve their problems. Often I shine a light on mental health issues, especially neurodiversity, which is close to my heart.

Fundamentally, I try to write the books I like to read – those with wit, heart and intelligence.

Away from the writing desk, I enjoy great scenery, a relaxing train ride, delicious coffee and cake, and catching up with friends and fellow authors.

Chrissie Harrison is a pen name.

To get early notice of future releases, free excerpts and more, join my Readers' Circle at https://www.chrissieharrison.co.uk/newsletter/

Find me on social media @AuthorChrissieHarrison

Also by the Author

The Cathedral City Comedies – a romantic comedy series

"Floored"
Book 2 – Coming October 2025
Book 3 – TBC

Touchline Girls – a sports rom-com series

"Match Daze"
Book 2 – TBC
Book 3 – TBC

Pavilion Girls – a women's cricket rom-com series

"Wicket Maiden" – May 2025
Book 2 – 2026
Book 3 – 2027